Doughnuts for Amy

John Malik

For my Amy

The following is a work of fiction.
Any character that has any resemblance to any person,
living or deceased is purely coincidental.

At the time of publication there were an estimated 1,900 Continuing Care Retirement Communities, over 16,500 nursing homes and approximately 28,000 assisted living facilities licensed in the United States. Currently the average entrance fee of a CCRC in the United States is $248,000.

1

If I had to name the most infuriating part of being this old, I would have to say that first and foremost, it's the crumbs. I cannot seem to control the food crumbs. They pile up on the edges of my mouth, the tip of my chin, and are scattered from the top of my shirt to the edges of my lap, often giving me the appearance of a wheelchair-bound Santa at the bottom of a snow globe before he gets shaken up. I would wipe them away, but in order to do that one needs to be able to control their own hands, and on some days my hands shake so bad I can't even hold a napkin. Today the service staff at this over-priced retirement community has more pressing business than to bother with the crumbs on an old man's shirt. I'm rolling down the hallway after a messy breakfast so I can continue shaking behind closed doors, when the prettiest woman I have seen in years comes into focus. She is maybe five feet, eight inches tall with shoulder length brown hair, high cheeks and green eyes behind thin eyeglasses. She smiles at me. It is an absolutely gorgeous smile, and I am covered in flecks of grits and toast, sausage grease and a smear of grape jelly, a rolling menu that my fellow residents can practically place their own orders from. If she stops to talk to me, there will be no limit to my humiliation.

I'm a retired fire fighter. In my day, I stood six feet, four inches tall and my chest and biceps crowded the fullest shirts. Even the most sophisticated women – such as this young lady in front of me – would routinely be reduced to smiles, incomplete sentences and nervous giggles when I showed up at their minor kitchen fires, usually created by their fumbling children or inept husband's attempt at a Mother's Day breakfast. My guys at the station house called my ability to render women incapable of uttering a coherent sentence the "Bannon Effect." The reports filed after minor fires often read something like: The homeowner attempted to provide a statement at the scene. However, the trauma associated with the incident coupled with the Bannon Effect provided by the Station Captain prevented the homeowner from offering a reasonable statement regarding said incident. And now, old age has reduced me to a 225-pound crumb-covered and palsied burden that even I cannot be bothered to care for. Please God, let this woman walk past me.

Amy Sommers was horrified. Who would let this man out of the dining room looking like this? She opened up her pocketbook and fished around for some tissues, then knelt down in front of him as he rolled up to her feet. "Good morning. My name's Amy, and your name is?" She smiled and carefully wiped the crumbs from his silvery, bearded chin and the corners of his mouth.

"I'm Chet. Chet Bannon. I live here, room 202, been here for nine months." Chet tried to offer Amy his right hand, palm down, but it shook so hard he was afraid he would shake this woman right out of her shoes. Amy placed her left hand on his and brought it down to the armrest of the wheel chair and held it there. Chet blushed; her skin was so young.

"What brings you here to Woodmont, Amy?" Chet was from Memphis and his words had all the hurry of a cold jar of honey tipped at a ninety degree angle.

"I work for a tissue company. We're test marketing a new line of tissues that even the toughest of gentlemen will not be afraid to use. This one is scented with motor oil, others smell like freshly chopped wood, stainless steel and – my personal favorite – this one smells like a leather football." Chet giggled.

"You're making that up. Let me guess. You're too pretty to work for any state agency; I'll bet you're another consultant, I've met plenty of them."

"Well you're close Mister Chet Bannon. I'm Amy Sommers, the new Director of Woodmont and your new best friend."

"That right? Well then Missus Amy Sommers, mighty pleased to meet you."

"You can call me Amy. No need for any formalities."

"Oh, single huh? Well then, that's even better news because I just so happen to be the newly elected chairman of the Amy Sommers Fan Club."

Amy smiled and stood up. "Mister Chet Bannon, I do believe that you and I will get along just fine. However, if you will excuse me, I have a staff to meet and I'm sure they have a two-hour long Power Point presentation ready for me."

"Don't bother listening to them, just start over. Oh, but you can keep that fella Nick, your Chef. He's worth whatever you all are paying him."

"I'll take that into consideration, Chet, have a lovely day."

Amy continued down the hallway of Woodmont Retirement Community. It was her first day on the job as Director of a community that embodied everything that she had lived for in her last 10 years. When Woodmont was announced five years earlier, the developer promised to redefine the type of care that came with retirement. Woodmont, a continuing care retirement community (CCRC), would not only offer traditional amenities for well-off retirees, but also ease the later stages of life with an assisted living community, care for those with Alzheimer's in its memory care unit, and provide a skilled nursing facility for those that needed assisted living combined with constant medical attention. It was the Memory Care unit that had the most promise. Alzheimer's had taken Amy's mother just when she had needed her the most, and Amy was determined to play a vital part in the innovative care and research of Alzheimer's disease. Of course, there would not be any clinical research at Woodmont, but plenty of therapy. Her new employer, Creek Side Management, was the leader in memory care programs and its findings and evidence had appeared in all of the dementia journals.

Eight weeks ago, Creek Side had approached Amy in confidence and presented her with the opportunity to run a flagship retirement community, one with an innovative memory care unit where she could personally create and implement therapeutic programs for dementia and Alzheimer's patients. Amy was all for it, but was certain she would be asked to move at least 400 miles away and uproot her girls. The girls were young but eventually, they would understand. Amy thought about it for two days then met with Rivers Williams, the chief operating officer, and gave him a yes. She was dumbfounded when Rivers told her it was Woodmont, on the northeastern side of the county just past Paris Mountain, maybe a 20-minute drive from her home. Creek Side would take over management from The Magnolia Company on April first, and they wanted her there that morning. Magnolia's break-even projections for Woodmont were off course and if they continued on their present path the investor would not see a positive return for perhaps four years, double what they had counted on. When your investor is a publicly held company with responsibility to its shareholders well, this path just could not continue. The investment firm had sought out a new management company and Creek Side was the logical choice. They were notoriously tight with money and held their people to rigorous financial standards. Amy was told Creek Side's CEO even flew coach. It would be a big change from her previous employer, Piedmont Hospital System, which never had a problem spending money. Amy had taken a ten percent pay cut, but if it meant being a leader in Alzheimer's care, it was worth it. She now had her toughest few days in front of her. Creek Side was planning layoffs and reductions in overhead. Over the next 48 hours, perhaps fifteen percent of the staff would be laid off, and her face would be the one everyone associated with this. It was unfortunate but necessary. In order for Woodmont to thrive, it had to be fiscally responsible. Rivers Williams the Chief Operating Officer, Gerald Durkins, the head of Human Resources, and Harriett Baltz, the vice president, would all help with this ugly task.

Amy had said a heartfelt prayer that morning asking for forgiveness and understanding, strength and guidance.

Nick sat down and opened his Outlook calendar, April 1st. "Happy April Fool's Day, Chef," he said to his reflection on the window of his office. Some days – such as today – the work piles up like dry leaves in October and it's best to start the morning with a list that would get you through five o'clock and dinner, but Nick was certain he had 12 hours of work ahead of him and it was already eight thirty.

"Focus."

He could not put off the private dinner for 16 and the two cakes for Mrs. Jensen, the cakes had to get done early so they could chill before being frosted. The dessert for the private party used the same chocolate cake batter, only baked in a muffin tin. It made sense to do that first. The vegetables for the private dinner were already on the dinner menu, so his dinner crew could do that. The ducks had to be cleaned, duck stock started, he would do the sweet potato hash after putting the cakes in the oven then he would have to go to the April events meeting with Melissa. He also had a meeting with the dining committee and lunch was going to be busy, so he would probably spend an hour helping out on the line. That would bring him to one thirty and if he did not have those cakes ready to be frosted then, he would fall desperately behind on everything else. If that wasn't enough, Nick had already heard the new Director would be at the nine a.m. staff meeting. Woodmont was changing hands and as of today, The Magnolia Company was out and Creek Side Management was in. Creek Side would probably lay off some of Woodmont's staff in the next week. With any luck, he would be the first to go. The night before, his dining room manager, Tony, told him that the new boss was Amy Sommers, a nurse with no hospitality experience.

"Of course! Why would you want someone with hospitality experience to run a gigantic country club that also has a very small nursing home attached to it? I mean, come

13

on Tony, what are you thinking? A 240-room, four-star private hotel with four dining venues and, oh yeah, an 88-room nursing home attached to it, wouldn't you want a fat, old stubborn nurse to run the whole campus, right? I mean really, what were you thinking?"

"Sorry babe, promise to stop thinking first thing in the morning," Tony smiled.

So here Nick was, a monster day staring him in the face and he was about to go into a staff meeting and have to sit down with his new boss, someone that probably had no clue as to what she was doing much less what he did every day. He would have to smile, tell her how wonderful life is and how she can help him be successful, and so on and so forth. Please lay me off first, he thought. It would be a blessing. His son was finishing his junior year at Greenville High and was already being recruited by basketball programs at several top-tier universities. The money he had set aside for his son's education was suddenly a fat savings account. He could go to work for any number of southern restaurants in the area. He wouldn't make much money, but he didn't need much. He could cook like he used to. God how he missed working with his beloved southern staples such as stone-ground grits, okra, country ham, cheese from South Georgia, yams and field peas. Getting fired from Woodmont would be the best thing that could happen to him.

"Focus!" He stood up, rolled his office chair out of the way and dropped to the ground to do a couple of dozen pushups, exert some energy and move some adrenaline around.

"One, two, three."

Nick found that counting out loud made the task a bit harder and when he exercised, he never tried to short change himself.

"Seven, eight, nine."

He heard the elevator door ding, then the staccato click of a pair of ladies' high heels approaching. The heels stopped in front of his office. The toenails were bright red and neatly trimmed from a recent pedicure, the ankles were smooth and creamy. This was a very pretty pair of feet.

"Are you Nicholas?"

"Yes." He brought his knees to his chest, then stood straight up and exhaled.

"Nicholas St. Germaine. May I help you?"

"I'm Amy Sommers, your new Director."

"Oh, uh, Mrs. Sommers. I'm sorry, but uh, my apologies. Please forgive me."

"Forgive you for what?" He tried to compose himself, but Amy was sumptuous. She was a trim five feet and maybe eight inches tall, with flowing milk chocolate brown hair that curled just past her shoulders, blushing high cheeks and sparkling green eyes behind thin Italian glasses. Her smile gleamed from teeth that must have cost her father a fortune. Dressed in a knee-length black skirt and matching black wing collar jacket, with gleaming silver buttons, a white linen blouse, and shimmering silver earrings that looked like little clock faces, Amy Sommers hardly matched his picture of a fat old nurse.

"Uh, forgive me for being on the floor when you walked in."

"OK, I forgive you, Nicholas. I suppose this isn't the first time you've been interrupted in such a manner. I've heard a lot about our Chef, and I just wanted to say hello."

"Well don't believe everything you hear about me. Maybe half of it has a glimmer of truth and furthermore, just because I ran a small restaurant doesn't mean I am qualified to run this place. Every day here is a monumental challenge that taxes my meager capabilities well beyond their limits."

Amy hesitated and furrowed her brow.

"But I understand that your meager capabilities are very much appreciated by the residents. I'll see you downstairs at the nine a.m. staff meeting, Mr. St. Germaine." She turned back to the elevator. Was this guy serious, she thought? Did he really just tell her, his new boss, that he was not qualified to run this place?

"Mrs. Sommers?" Amy stopped and turned to face him.

"*Miss* Sommers, and yes, Mr. St. Germaine?"

"The stairs are to your right."

"Um, thank you Mr. St. Germaine, but I'll take the elevator."

Now she was mad as she hit the elevator call button repeatedly. Was this guy calling her fat? Was he trying to tell her she needed to exercise? The elevator opened, she walked in, turned around and folded her arms across her chest, and caught Nick looking at her so she hit the down button again and the doors closed. Surely he knew budget cuts and layoffs were coming in the next 48 hours and nothing would be sacred and here he was, Woodmont's highest paid staff member telling her he was not qualified and she needed to lose weight. Did he just ask to be laid off? He must be nuts! Well, he was doing pushups on the floor of his office. Who does that? She hoped to develop a new management team with his help because on paper, she believed he was worth keeping. She knew he and his wife had owned a restaurant on Stone Avenue for years, his wife had passed away a few years ago, and he had been the Chef of Woodmont for the last six months. She also heard he was a workaholic and the residents loved him. Before accepting the Director's job, she had read resident satisfaction surveys that ranked the food's quality very high. The survey contained many personal remarks made about Nicholas, such as, "Best thing about living here," "Chef Nick is the best part of Woodmont," and "He better stay here for a while." Then there was her personal favorite: "Looks great in swim trunks," although it puzzled her why he would be seen in swim trunks at work. Yet here he was telling the woman that held the fate of his immediate employment at Woodmont that he was not qualified and she was fat. By the time the elevator opened she decided the residents would miss him but a month down the road, their anger would have subsided and everyone would move on. Fat, indeed!

As Amy turned and walked towards the elevator, Nick tried not to watch, but he couldn't help himself. Damn, she had pretty teeth, and did she ever look good in black. He considered doing another set of pushups, but instead sat down at his desk to finish his daily schedule. He glanced at the photo of Robin, his wife of almost 14 years gone now 18 months. He picked up the photo and sighed. Everything he loved about Robin was summed up in this one photograph: her determination, her athleticism, her smile, her sense of adventure and her love for him were all here. She was from North Carolina, but people that met her for the first time assumed she was from southern California. She was tall and fit with long, straight, sunflower blonde hair, gleaming white teeth and shimmering blue eyes. When she was on her bike, she twisted her hair into a ponytail that dangled out of her helmet. He picked up the portrait and looked into her eyes. They had been on a long bike ride in May and Robin was sitting up, hands off the handle bars, and she turned around for Nick's camera. She was smiling even though she had her sunglasses clenched between her teeth and a water bottle in her right hand. The Carolina Mountains and the grueling climb up Caesar's Head loomed in the distance, and Robin could not have been happier. They were a third of the way into a 60-plus mile ride and, she was smiling as if she had just won the lottery. She loved being outside and if the two of them were together, then life was pretty near perfect. He felt the tears coming. He put the photo face down, bit his bottom lip and forced himself to finish writing his schedule. "Please let me go, Miss Sommers," he whispered to himself.

A few minutes later, he made his way down to the conference room for the staff meeting only to find Daniel Stern, the head of engineering, standing outside the room.

"The big shots are in there so don't bother going in Chef."

Stern was from Anderson, S.C., and words such as "there" came out as "th-arr." Daniel was short and heavy, overweight by 60 pounds and wore a thick goatee. He was known to rub his belly and refer to it as "good groceries and great barbecue."

"So are we supposed to just stand out here and look stupid, or should I go back to work?"

Stern just shrugged his shoulders. Nick looked around then looked at his phone. It was exactly nine. He opened the door and walked in and saw Amy Sommers, three frowning faces definitely from Creek Side corporate, a woman whom he recognized as someone he had previously seen in the dining room, and two men. All three were cutting their eyes at him. Melissa Montague, the head of special events at Woodmont, or, as the recently deposed general manager preferred, Director of Divertissement was also there. Melissa looked like she was about to cry. Amy Sommers looked up at Nick and bit her lip, the silver-haired woman turned to Nick.

"May I help you, Chef?"

"Well it's nine a.m. and I was afraid I was late for the nine a.m. staff meeting that we have every weekday in this room at nine a.m. Fifteen minutes ago, Miss Sommers asked me not to be late for the nine a.m. meeting. Is that meeting still a go, or should I come back at a later time?"

"That will be all for now Chef St. Germaine, we know where to find you," replied the silver-haired woman.

"My sincere apologies, I guess I misunderstood Miss Sommers' seemingly unambiguous request." The two men — one was a light skinned African-American with very short, dark brown hair and broad shoulders, the other tall and lanky — looked at each other and shook their heads as if to say, "What nerve." Nick closed the door and told Stern as he passed, "Nice knowing you Daniel."

Melissa was a real crackerjack and loved by the members. Unfortunately, her standards were so high the staff only became frustrated when they couldn't reach them. She was probably too expensive for the new management company anyway, despite the fact she was doing a great job — but that certainly didn't carry much weight with this new group. Might as well go bake some chocolate cakes, Nick thought. He walked through the back hallway, but stopped when he reached the bottom of the stairs, turned to the back door and walked outside. It was a beautiful day. The cool of the morning was wearing off and Nick stood on the loading dock taking in the crisp air. He was certain he was next and hopefully, his arrogant display in front of the corporate folks was enough to seal his fate. If Sommers had purposely tried to make a fool out of him, well, he was just going to throw it right back in her court. Nine a.m. staff meeting, my ass! He had come here only five months ago because Jack Carrollton had sought him out. Nick had taken a year off after he sold the Stone Avenue Tavern, the restaurant he and Robin had built into a success. He spent time bonding with his son, Theodore, as the two of them tried to come to terms with Robin's passing. Nick didn't need to work like this, but Jack Carrollton's company was the operator, and Jack was a good friend of the restaurant. Nick knew he needed some purpose in his life, so he had agreed to take the job until the first Chef could return. If he didn't come back, then Nick would help Jack find a suitable replacement. Nick asked his son, who had just started his junior year at Greenville High, for permission to go back to work; he thought it would be good for both of them. Nick knew he had done a pretty good job here at Woodmont, especially considering the mess he had walked into.

The first Chef was Andrew Russell, who Nick knew through the business. Andrew was in good shape and roughly the same age as Nick, so it was a shock when Jack Carrollton called to tell him Chef Russell was diagnosed with cancer and needed a leave of absence. That night, Nick sat down with his son and discussed the job. Chef Russell's sous Chef had put in his notice two weeks prior to the cancer diagnosis, so the first few weeks at Woodmont could be brutal. He had a sous Chef and a couple of cooks in mind, but it would take two weeks for them to go through the hiring process. On Nick's third day on the job, the cook that claimed he was ready to be the sous Chef, Matt McCrary, showed up looking like he had just crawled out of a bar. Thirty minutes later Matt was bleeding from a self-administered cut in his right thumb. Nick walked over to him, put a hand on his shoulder and said, "Mr. McCrary, after the nurse gets a bandage on your thumb please get yourself over to the Lab Screen offices on Paris Drive, all accidents require a drug screen."

"Yes, Chef," replied Matt as he walked out of the kitchen and never came back. The next day, Woodmont's Director, Robert Dupin asked Nick to hold a staff meeting for his department, and Nick made an announcement.

"I'm not your drinking buddy, I'm not your friend, and I'm not your enemy. I'm your supervisor, your Executive Chef, your new Daddy." Later that day, Dupin responded that he *should* consider his cooks as his friends, and suggested he cook lunch for them on a weekly basis. "Mr. Dupin, right now, they are not taking care of the paying customers. When we reach that point, of course, but not at his time."

Nick left his meeting with Dupin thinking he probably hired Chef Russell because the Chef was able to pronounce Dupin's name without a hint of sarcasm. "Roh-Bear Due-Pahn." Dupin had no say in hiring him, and was somewhat resentful towards Nick. During their first interview, he assumed that Dupin could speak French, so he greeted him with, "Le bon matin, Monsieur Dupin." Dupin responded with an uncomfortable,

"Pleased to meet you."

A week later, Melissa was in Nick's office sharing a laugh about that initial exchange.

"Who the hell introduces themselves as, 'Roh-Bear Due-Pahn,' yet can't understand elementary school French?" Dupin thought he was a direct heir to the Bourbon throne, despite the fact he had to go back at least four generations to find an ancestor that actually resided on French soil. Nick imagined Russell and his cooks at some crappy bar, trading shots and drinking to "Monsieur Roh-Bear Due-Pahn!" Dupin had even created French-sounding titles for the department heads, going so far as to name Melissa's position Director of Divertissement, or diversions. Melissa could only laugh and wave off Nick as he repeated, "Je suis très heureux de faire votre connaissance, Monsieur Dupin." Growing up around New Orleans certainly had its advantages, one of which was learning the many languages that flowed throughout the city. Like any properly trained New Orleans Chef, Nick spoke a little French, some Italian and Spanish. He needed the Spanish to converse with the dishwashers and bus boys that came to the city looking for opportunity, French to chat with the Cajun purveyors, farmers, shrimpers and oystermen, and Italian to impress the pretty girls.

He smiled and shook his head as he looked at the new green of the oak trees set against the blue April sky. He had never been fired in his life and here he was a successful Chef, restaurateur and father, 41 years old and on the verge of being canned. He dropped to the ground and knocked out 40 pushups. He then walked to the cardboard recycling area and picked out enough boxes to hold his office's personal effects and headed upstairs to the kitchen, stopping at the men's room to wash his hands. He wrote his last name on the boxes, and then left them outside his office.

"Come and get me, Miss Sommers."

Ten minutes later, he was trying to get the cakes started when he noticed Amy Sommers and the African-American gentleman standing at the entrance to his kitchen trying to get his attention. Nick saw them out of the corner of his eye but ignored them; she would have to work for this. Amy gingerly tried to approach Nick, but as she did, he walked to the opposite side of the kitchen to retrieve a bowl and some measuring cups. He kept his back to her then smiled as he heard Xavier speak up,

"On your back!"

A busy kitchen was no place for the uninitiated. One had to move with purpose, or one was libel to be run over. You just didn't walk behind someone without announcing your presence. Xavier, his lead line cook and all of 225 pounds, had just walked behind Amy and hopefully scared the beejesus out of her. Nick could hear the click of Amy Sommer's heels on the tile floor as she walked up behind him. Heels in the kitchen! With any luck she would slip and land on her butt.

"Chef St. Germaine?"

"Yes, Miss Sommers?"

"Could I please have a few minutes with you?"

Nick looked up and saw the African-American gentleman standing at the entrance to his office.

"Yes ma'am." He followed her to his office trying hard not to admire her figure.

"Chef, this is Rivers Williams. Rivers is the chief operating officer of Creek Side Management."

Nick looked Rivers in the eye and extended his hand.

"Mr. Williams, good morning."

Rivers was wearing a custom-made light grey linen suit, a white silk shirt topped off with a light yellow paisley tie and a gleaming silver tie bar. He had a firm handshake and piercing green eyes. Nick offered them each a seat in his office, closed the door, dropped his Blackberry on the desk and sat down. Amy Sommers smiled and picked up his phone.

"Oh, I see you're a Blackberry fan as well. I have the new Impulse model, and I just love it." Nick glared.

"Did you ask me in here to chat about phones, or is there something more pressing the two of you would like to discuss?"

Amy's smile faded as she set his Blackberry down on the desk, sat up straight and turned to Rivers.

"Chef, we would like to put you at ease. Miss Sommers and I, as well as the residents of Woodmont, believe you are doing a fine job here and we would like you to continue in your present position as executive Chef. We would also like your dining room manager, Mr. Torres, and your sous Chef to continue with Woodmont as well. Tomorrow morning, we will have a meeting with our vice president, Harriett Baltz, and we will discuss our expectations, plans and goals for moving forward."

Nick looked directly at Rivers.

"And am I invited to this meeting with Harry?"

"It's Harriett."

Harriett Baltz! Good Lord, thought Nick. Can this possibly get any better?

"And have I seen Mrs. Harry-yet Balls? Was she downstairs earlier?"

Rivers was obviously listening to Nick's words over in his head. He squirmed slightly in his seat and tried not to look directly into Nick's eyes.

"It's Baltz and yes, that's correct, she was in the conference room," replied Rivers cautiously. Not that many years ago, Nick had made numerous television appearances as guest Chef on everything from the local morning news shows to Good Morning America. He had done more live-cooking demonstrations then he could remember and he knew how to control his demeanor in front of an audience. Perhaps he could have a little fun and get Rivers to lose his composure over that unfortunate name.

"And Harry-yet – or does she prefer Misses Baltz – or shall I refer to her as Harry-yet? She apparently has been asked to shave overhead and squeeze labor. Is that why Miss Montague was invited to leave, because I can promise Miss Montague was doing an excellent job, she definitely knew how to juggle the job and keep all the balls in the air."

Rivers pursed his lips together, rubbed his eyebrow with his right forefinger then turned to Amy looking for help. Nick thought he could quickly have the nattily dressed COO of this multimillion dollar management company rolling on his office floor clutching his sides in laughter. Amy had been observing this and knew exactly what was going on, two grown men behaving like 12-year-olds telling dirty jokes for the first time. For Heaven's sake, what would be next?

"Gentlemen, at this time we need to focus on a seamless transition to the new management company. Mr. St. Germaine, CSM wants you to continue as executive Chef with no change in your rate of compensation or benefits."

"And what change will there be in the amount of hourly labor I have available?"

"Chef, at this time I do not have those numbers available to me," Amy snapped.

"Do you, Mr. Williams – or perhaps I can caress a response from Mrs. Balls tomorrow morning?" Amy quickly stood up.

"Mr. St. Germaine, this will be presented and discussed at the proper moment. If there are no more questions for me or Mr. Williams, no doubt you have a big day in front of you and I believe we will adjourn."

They quickly left Nick's office and headed to the lobby. Rivers let out a sigh and as they moved through the kitchen, he looked back over his shoulder. Nick was standing outside his office watching them walk away. When Rivers looked back, Nick winked at him. As soon as they were out of the kitchen, Amy shook her head.

"Good Lord, how immature can this guy be? I'm telling you, Rivers, I think keeping him is a mistake, especially considering that exchange."

"Oh, I wouldn't go that far. He was asking some legitimate questions, and perhaps taking out some frustrations on his new employer in a light-hearted way. Let's not rush to judgment based on that one exchange, OK? Everything about him says he is a good fit for this place. Let's just give him some time and if he doesn't work out, then so be it. Fair enough?"

"Some time?" Amy looked at her watch.

"Oh, come on now, Amy. Please don't make this transition any harder for yourself than it already is."

"OK, I'll try."

Nick's Blackberry went off. It was a text from Melissa. "just let go." He put his phone in his pocket then ran downstairs to Melissa's office and found her and the tall thin gentleman, probably the corporate HR guy, standing over her. Nick walked into the office, held the door open, put his hand on the gentleman's shoulder.

"Would you excuse us please?"

"Oh, hey Chef. I'm Gerald Durkins, Director of Human Resources for Creek Side and boy, am I glad you're staying on. Listen, I love to cook. We should trade recipes because I cook a lot and … "

"That's great, Gerry, good for you." With his left hand, Nick pushed lightly on Durkin's shoulder and waved his right hand towards the door.

"Oh sure, listen, about those recipes."

"I'll have to give you my personal recipe website, Mr. Durkins." Nick closed the door, "www dot asshole dot com." Melissa smiled unevenly and reached out for Nick. They hugged softly and he could feel Melissa's tears on her cheek.

"I've always dreamed of being on unemployment."

Nick released her and asked if she had any plans.

"You mean, after I key Durkin's turd-brown Chevy Impala?"

"Oh come on sweetheart, don't roll in the gutter, OK?"

"I won't, I promise. I was just fantasizing." She reached up and stroked his face with her right hand. "It was great working with you, I'll miss you dearly." He took Melissa's hand in his.

"Can I do anything for you? Do you need any contacts here in town?"

"No, thank you, I really miss Tulsa and I really want to move back, you know, lots of family and old friends and I sort of have an old boyfriend that I would like to try and reconnect with. And don't you sneer at me Nick St. Germaine, there is nothing wrong with liking Tulsa."

"Yes ma'am, wouldn't dream of sneering at Tulsa. Can I give you a hand here?"

"No please, I really need to do this myself. This is something I want to remember. I'm going to open my own business when I get back home, my own event-consulting business and the more painful today is, the more determined

I'll be to succeed because I never want to see another Gerald Durkins again."

"So do you want *me* to key his car then?" Melissa laughed and wiped her eyes, reached out for Nick, hugged him.

"You're a good man. I'll keep you and Theo in my prayers."

"Thank you, Melissa." She released Nick and told him to get back to work.

"I don't want you standing at the back door when I walk out of here, OK?" He nodded his head and turned to the door. "Oh Nick?"

"Yes?"

"Please close the door behind you."

"Yes, of course." He opened the door, walked through the threshold and stood in front of it as Durkins looked for a way around him but he quickly closed the door behind him.

"She'll be done in a minute, Gerry."

Nick headed towards the staircase with Durkins in tow.

"Hey, listen, Chef, let me give you my email address and about your website?"

"Sure Gerald, first thing in the morning." Nick raced up the steps two at a time, leaving Durkins at the bottom of the staircase.

"Yeah, OK, some other time then, Chef?"

When Nick got to the top of the stairs, he met Amy Sommers walking with Robert Dupin who was obviously enamored of Sommer's good looks. Dupin offered an animated greeting, as if the two of them were best friends.

"Oh Chef, have you met the lovely Miss Sommers yet? She's your new boss, you know. Miss Sommers, Chef St. Germaine does a fabulous job here. I'm *so excited* that he will be staying on."

Spare me, thought Nick. He looked Amy in the eyes.

"Yes, Miss Sommers and I met at the nine a.m. staff meeting, didn't we? Now if you two will excuse me, I have some cakes to attend to."

Nick walked briskly to the kitchen, hoping he would not be followed. Damn, it was almost ten a.m. Tony had just walked into the kitchen and offered an easy smile.

"Hey babe, we still have jobs?"

"We still have jobs, Tony."

"*Sweet!* You meet the new boss yet?"

"Why yes I have."

"Let me guess: five feet five inches tall, 235 pounds, platinum blonde hair and lots of dangling QVC earrings, right?"

"Close enough, Tony."

"Ha! I knew it!"

"Alright, you mind getting to work? Looks like we will have a busy lunch and I have got to get these cakes in the oven."

"Yes sir, Tony has the helm."

Anthony "Tony" Torres was the first person that Nick had hired after taking over the hospitality department at Woodmont. Tony liked to say that his last name was Hilton, because he had worked for the hotel company since he was 18. Woodmont was only his second non-Hilton job, and he was pushing 35. Smart, efficient and quick on his feet, Tony was the perfect foil to Nick's shoot-first; ask-questions later style of management. Nick was certain that Tony was a three-dimensional thinker, often solving problems before they arose and Nick was somewhat jealous of Tony's management style. Tony had an easy smile and rarely got flustered. Even when faced with the most hectic of days, he sauntered around as if he was in a golf game. Tony was six feet and two inches tall with a Mediterranean complexion and thick, dark curly hair. His grandparents on his father's side were Spaniards that had immigrated to America, settling in New York where Tony had grown up. Often referred to as Mr. TDH for tall, dark and handsome by the widows at Woodmont, Tony Torres was, in his own words, constantly on the lookout for the future Mrs. Ex-Torres. Tony was really enjoying his time at Woodmont, even though when Nick hired him he had given Nick a verbal promise to stay for one year. Nick was pretty sure that Tony was going to stay longer. He just had to get him in the door. After about a month Tony had come to Nick and thanked him for the job offer and told him how much he was enjoying himself.

"Chef St. Germaine?" Nick turned around and saw Amy Sommers standing off in the corner.

"Yes ma'am?"

"May I have a word with you?"

Tony walked back through the kitchen as Nick and Amy were headed to his office. Nick closed the door and looked out his window and saw Tony's eyes practically pop out of his head as he caught a good look at Amy.

"I uh, need to apologize about the miscommunication regarding the staff meeting."

"Apology accepted. I have some cakes to get in the oven; may I be excused now?"

"It was my understanding that our friends from Charleston would be meeting with several individuals today but would not require my presence so I…" Nick cut her off.

"Miss Sommers, I have already accepted your apology so unless you can bake, may I please be excused?"

"Um, well yes, of course, by all means."

"Thank you Miss Sommers. I'll see you at tomorrow's nine a.m. staff meeting, correct?"

"Um well, we probably won't have that meeting, but we will have a ten a.m. meeting for the members to meet me, Rivers and Harriett and I would like you, Daniel, and Maureen there as well."

"And where will we have that meeting?"

"Well, in the Chicago Room of course."

"Of course, Miss Somers, shall I ask Franklin to have it set up in a classroom setting? You know, rows of chairs facing a podium, or have you done that already?"

"Oh yes, please do that Mr. St. Germaine. That would be fine." Amy walked out of Nick's office and headed to the dining room. As she walked away Nick added "and whatever staff we have left." Nick's Blackberry went off with a text from his son.

"hey pop u still have a job?"

"Yes,"

"gr8, lets celebr8 2nite! sushi with amanda?" Nick laughed and looked around the kitchen. His son was always on the lookout for a meal courtesy of Dad. "ur girlfriend so u buying?" Nick responded. "u keep ur job tho, ur party! luv u!" Nick smiled and shook his head. "maybe tomorrow, no promises tonite. ok?"

Nick looked around for Xavier.

"Hey X, your phone, I have to get these cakes rolling." Nick tossed Xavier the kitchen phone, which had a nasty habit of ringing at the most inopportune moments. Xavier caught the phone and glared at his boss, then looked around for someone else to pawn it off on. Nick smiled and said, "Thank you, love you." Xavier could only respond with a frown. Nick had always enjoyed baking and he was good at it, but when one baked, it had to be done with a minimum of distractions. He gathered several measuring cups and measuring spoons, two large bowls, a sifter and some rubber spatulas. Next he brought over dark chocolate pallets, eggs, butter, cinnamon, and cocoa powder. Woodmont's kitchen had a small baking area with a stainless steel table, a kitchen-aid mixer, dry spices and rolling bins of flour, sugar and pastry flour. He helped himself to a piece of El Rey dark chocolate, and let it slowly melt in his mouth. He measured out his chocolate on the electronic scale, covered the bowl with plastic wrap, and placed it over a pan of simmering water. Next, he measured out the pastry flour, cinnamon, cocoa powder, salt and baking powder and sifted it twice over a sheet of parchment paper. He placed the butter and sugar into the stand mixer, inserted the paddle attachment and turned on the mixer. Nick had removed the butter from the walk-in cooler. It was about 60 degrees, the perfect temperature. In a few minutes, the butter and sugar had formed a soft creamy emulsion. He cracked four eggs into a ramekin and added them one at a time into the swirling butter and sugar mixture, and then tippled in some vanilla extract.

"Hey Flo, would you mind bringing me that bowl of chocolate please?" Florence Smith was tall, thin and pale, Florence's physical appearance reminded Nick of a post-punk band's groupie, someone that listened to The Cure or the Clash. She set the bowl down and frowned.

"When I hit that lottery I'm gonna have you bake me chocolate cakes every day Chef, alright?"

"Yes ma'am, a new cake every day for millionaire Florence."

"Oooohhh-wee! I like the sound of that, Millionaire Florence!"

Florence was a perennial dreamer, certain that if she kept buying lottery tickets with the same set of numbers, the odds would eventually catch up to her and she would win big. Nick had wasted many hours trying to convince her that the lottery was a waste of her hard-earned money, but eventually he grew tired of the exercise. Flo was certain that her number was coming up sooner rather than later. Nick removed the plastic wrap from the bowl of chocolate and used a rubber spatula to fold the chocolate into a smooth paste, closed his eyes and inhaled its aroma. He looked around and quickly stuck his finger into the bowl and had a small taste. He closed his eyes as the chocolate's flavors of vanilla, spice, dark coffee and black plums rolled across his palette. He never tired of fine chocolate. The melted chocolate needed to be close to 80 degrees before it was added to the butter mixture; otherwise, it would cook the yolks. He spent a few minutes beating the chocolate with the rubber spatula, keeping it in motion by constantly folding it over on itself. Nick stopped to wash his hands, grabbed a tasting spoon and checked the temperature of the chocolate. When he was satisfied, he slowly added the melted chocolate to the mixer. When the chocolate was fully incorporated, he turned down the mixer's speed and then carefully added the flour a little at a time. He took care to stop and scrape the bowl every couple of seconds. His

Blackberry went off, but he ignored it. As soon as he added the last bit of flour, he removed the bowl from the mixer, scraped the paddle attachment of any batter, added a half-cup of warm water and then finished mixing the cake batter with the rubber spatula. When flour gets mixed with a liquid, the wheat proteins can become elongated and toughen up. Amateurs never seemed to understand the "do not over-mix" line often added to cake recipes, but it was something Nick had understood for many years. The first real Chef he worked for in New Orleans, Remy Passard, a thickly accented Parisian, had fried an egg for him prior to giving him a cake recipe. The egg was cooked over high heat and the white was brown, tough and crusty. Remy had asked Nick to eat the egg before embarking on the recipe, Nick obliged, pronouncing the egg tough and disgusting.

"Oui. Now make sure you do not do that to zee cake. Zuh protein in zee egg white has been mees-handled and consequently toughened up. Control zuh protein in zuh flour, do not let it day-velop and toughen, fold zuh batter slowly and stop mixing when smooth, oui? You handle zuh cake battah like she is your girlfriend, oui?" Then he smacked Nick on the side of the head with the rubber spatula. When Nick had asked him why he hit him, Remy replied, "So you remember zaht lesson for a ver-ree long time."

When Nick was satisfied with his batter, it went into four round cake pans that he had lightly coated with butter and flour. He divided up the batter then set the cakes on a speed rack next to the oven. He grabbed a silicone muffin mold, placed it on a sheet pan, sprayed it with the aerosol vegetable oil and then spooned the remaining batter into the 24 holes. He only needed 16 mini cakes, but he always liked to have a few extra. You never knew when you would have to bribe someone, and a warm chocolate cupcake could get you a lot of favors. He slid the cakes into the oven and set his timer for 30 minutes.

"Xavier! Florence! My timer!"

"Your timer," responded Xavier.

Nick washed his hands then looked at his phone. 10:30. He set the alarm on his phone for 30 minutes then checked the two text messages. One was from Theo which he skipped; the other text was from Sonya, the Director of Human Resources, which he opened.

"goodbye nick, just let go, will miss you."

"Shit." He looked around at his staff and wondered who he would be asked to lay off. He took off his apron, washed his hands again and walked to Sonya's office. Sonya worked up front along with Heather Williams, the administrative assistant in Robert's office. As Nick opened the door to the front offices, he saw Gerald Durkins standing over Heather as she unpacked her desk. She looked up at Nick and tears were streaming down her face. Heather always wore too much makeup, especially mascara, and her tears had dragged her mascara down the length of her cheeks. Heather was recently divorced and not four weeks ago had moved into a rental home. She had a seven-year-old daughter and a loser of an ex-husband. She did a heck of a job as administrative assistant, but apparently Durkins and everyone at CSM was interested only in the bottom line.

"Oh, hey Chef, we meet again. Say, is that a smear of chocolate on your Chef coat? Baking something chocolate maybe?" Heather turned and looked up at Gerald.

"Do you really have to stand over me and gloat like this, asshole?"

"Uh, actually, yes, I am supposed to stand here to protect any confidential information and property." Heather wiped her eyes and looked at Nick.

"I'm sorry for being so rude in front of you Nick, but if this corporate douche bag here doesn't back away from me."

"Heather, be strong, please. You're a good gal. You're going to recover quickly, you'll see, and Mr. Durkins here was just about to have a seat on the couch, weren't you, Gerald?"

"Uh, yes, I suppose I was Chef." Durkins walked across the room to the couch, had a seat and got on his phone. Without lifting his eyes from his phone he said, "Just let me know when you're finished young lady, so I can verify you're not taking company property."

Heather saluted Durkins with her right middle finger.

"Just give me one more minute, sweetie pie."

Sonya walked out of her office with a cardboard box and smiled at Nick, it was obvious she had been crying as well. She put her box down on the corner of Heather's desk and hugged Heather for a long time, then hugged Nick.

"Goodbye, Nick, take care of yourself."

She eased back a bit and put her right hand to his face.

"Thank you for all of the lovely treats you have made for me. I'll miss you and Theo. Please give him my best, ok?"

"Of course Sonya, and all my best to that maniac husband of yours. Do you have any plans? Will we be able get together before you all go?"

"Tampa is calling. Honestly, we've thought about it for the last year. Hector and I really miss Florida, lots of family and friends there, and how we miss the beach, the food, the music, and we can actually visit Cuba now and the fishing, Hector *really* misses salt water fishing. I'm going to miss my South Carolina friends, I'm going to miss you Nick but I'll be OK. I have Hector to look after me, right?" Sonya hugged Nick again, tighter this time then ran her hands up his arms to his shoulders and squeezed his biceps. "You really shouldn't work out so much, Nick. A body like this really warms up my Latin blood. I'll have to get Hector into a gym one day, or maybe get myself a *novio caliente* with a *fisico* like yours."

Nick was a bit taken aback that the ever-cautious, always fair Director of Human Resources would be so forward with him. In six months, he had never heard her utter one word that was not calculated, and here she was practically fondling him.

"Uh, ok Sonya, I'll remember that."

"Goodbye Heather, best of luck to you."

"Thank you, Sonya, thank you for everything." Heather wiped her eyes with her right forearm. Sonya released Nick, picked up her box and walked to the door.

"Have a good day, Mr. Durkins"

"Oh, you too Mrs. Chavez."

Durkins smiled and waved at Sonya as she walked out the front door. About a dozen staff members were waiting for Sonya. As she walked through the lobby, they hugged one another tightly and cried effortlessly. Heather looked at Durkins and glared at him.

"Are you almost finished Miss?"

"It's Williams, *asshole*. My name is Heather Williams, ok, and yes, I'm finished."

Durkins walked over to Heather's box and rummaged through it, lifted up an ink pen and asked her if it was company property.

"It will be when it's dangling out of your neck." Durkins dropped the pen back into the box.

"Have a nice day, Miss Williams."

Nick opened the door for Heather, who was met by several crying housekeepers and waiters that hugged her goodbye. Nick headed back to the kitchen. His cakes should be done in about 13 more minutes. As he walked into the kitchen, he asked Tony to grab all the waiters and bring them into the kitchen. He went to the oven to take a look at his cakes then asked all the cooks and dishwashers to gather up front for five minutes. Florence and Xavier were there, his sous Chef Kevin Randall had just walked and he had three dishwashers there as well. Tony came in with his three servers and one servers-assistant.

"OK folks, we have new masters as of today. Mr. Carrollton and his team are no longer involved in Woodmont. He has turned over Woodmont's operations to Creek Side Management out of Charleston and unfortunately, on their first day, they are letting a lot of folks go, Sonya, Heather, Melissa, I'm sure others that will be let go today. I *have not* been asked to drop anyone from our department and

Tony, Chef Randall and I have been asked to stay on. So please, let's focus on getting the job done, taking care of our people and one another. Thank you for all of your hard work. I sincerely appreciate it, and your customers do, too."

"Yes thank you for everything you all do, day in and day out," added Tony.

"Now, I know this is going to be tough. Some of our friends have been asked to leave through no fault of their own, but please remember that we have almost ten percent unemployment in our country. We need to be thankful we all have jobs and we need to take care of business, OK?" There was a general nodding of heads, but for the most part everyone looked discouraged, dejected and scared.

"Would anyone like to say anything?" Nick scanned the eyes of his crew and finally caught Florence looking at him.

"Florence?"

"I'm gonna miss Mr. and Mrs. Carrolton."

Most everyone agreed with Florence. Even though Woodmont had not even been open for a year, the Carrolton's had a soft spot for the food and beverage business and had gone out of their way to have a personal relationship with every one of Nick's crew. They signed birthday and get well cards, knew the names of their children, sent graduation cards, and had given advances on paychecks. In turn, the Carrolton's were rewarded with excellent service whenever they sat down in the dining room. Yes, Nick's staff was going to miss the Carrolton's but in the present business climate, the bottom line ruled and perhaps Jack had ignored it. It didn't matter now.

"Agreed, I promise we will all miss the Carrolton's and for today going forward, we need to focus on the future and concentrate on getting our jobs done with the utmost efficiency. These folks will look at the bottom line first before they consider everything else, so please, let's try to do our jobs to the best of our abilities. Tony, would you get one of those blank greeting cards out of your desk and pass it around so we can all sign it and get it in the mail to the Carrolton's please?"

Everyone nodded their heads, a few wiped their eyes. Nick looked at his crew and thought that the next couple of weeks will be tough on everyone.

"OK people, chins up. We have work to do, so let's focus and make it happen."

2

Nick heard a knock on the front door and as he walked to the front of his house, he saw a police car in the driveway. What are the cops doing here? His pulse quickened as he reached the door and opened it. A police officer was standing at his front door.

"Nicholas St. Germaine?"

"Yes?"

"I'm afraid your wife has been in an automobile accident. She has been transported to the Piedmont Memorial Emergency Room. Can I be of further assistance?" Nick's heart rate exploded as panic set in.

"What? Where? What happened? How, how, how bad is she? How is she?"

"Mr. St. Germaine, I apologize but that is all the information I have. Can someone get you to the Emergency Room?"

"*Robin!*"

Nick lurched out of bed gasping for air. His heart was pounding and he was bathed in sweat. He momentarily struggled to make sense of his time and place and as reality took hold, he got out of bed, staggered to the bathroom, doused himself with cold water then looked at his reflection in the mirror. He splashed himself with more cold water, dried off with a towel and walked back into the bedroom. He looked at the clock. 4:19. He turned on his light, threw himself down on his bed, put the towel over his face, crossed his arms over the towel and laid there for a few minutes. He sat up and reached under his bed, pulled out a shoe box and lifted it onto the bed, opened the box and pulled out some of the CDs that held family photos. He sorted through the tear-stained labels: Bermuda, 2006, Willamette Valley, OR, 2003, '95 Olympic trials, Wine over Water 2004, Montreal Grand Prix 2002, Shenandoah Natl Park, 2005, Austin, TX, 2001, Disney World Food & Wine 2000, NYC Christmas 1999, Charleston Food & Wine 2002. He took a deep breath and looked at the ceiling. "No, no, no! Don't torture yourself,

Nicholas! *Do not* do this." He placed the CDs back in the box and shoved it under his bed, wiped his eyes with the towel, made a pot of coffee and got himself dressed for the gym. He walked into Theo's bedroom just in case his son was awake but no luck. Theo slept like the quintessential teenager, sprawled all over the bed, mp3 player plugged into his ears and drool coming out of his mouth. He turned off the mp3, removed the ear buds, and then slowly ran his hands through his hair. "I wish I could sleep like you kid." He went back to the kitchen, grabbed a banana, an apple and a bottle of water, filled up a portable cup of coffee, grabbed his car keys then headed out into the early morning darkness. Two hours later, he was back home and was greeted with the smell of bacon and pancakes.

"That you, Pop?"

"Yeah kid, smells good in here. What's going on?"

"Made some breakfast for us." Nick walked into the kitchen, hugged his son and whispered good morning.

"Damn kid, did you grow last night? You must be six three now."

"You up early, Pop?"

"Yep."

"What time? The usual?" Nick poured himself a fresh cup of coffee. "Well, I slept in a bit today, but I still managed to get in a good workout, upper body stuff this morning. You should have come with me; you need it."

"Thanks, Pop. You know it wouldn't kill you to miss a day every once in a while."

"Thanks, I'll look into that."

"You have another nightmare?"

"Maybe."

"Well maybe you should think about going back into counseling?"

"*Why? So some dip-shit egghead that has never suffered in his miserable God-forsaken life can tell me how I should feel? No thank you.*" Nick glared at Theo who turned his back to his father and mumbled.

"Good morning to you too, Pop."

Nick took a deep breath and looked up at the ceiling.

"Jesus, Theo, I'm so sorry. Please forgive me. Please? Theo?"

Nick put his hand on Theo's shoulder. He could feel his son quivering. Theo turned around and faced his father, and they hugged one another as Theo quietly sobbed.

"You know what, you stupid old man I miss Mom just as much as you do. You don't have to go biting my damn head off just because I want you to get better."

"I know, Theo, I know," Nick whispered. They held each other until Theo could smell the pancakes burning.

"Damnit! Now look what you did! If you would just get some sleep once in a while, maybe I wouldn't burn the damn pancakes!" Nick wiped his eyes, laughed and shook his head.

"OK, I know you're a math whiz, but what the hell did you just say? Where's the plausibility of that statement, Newton?"

"Pop, just put the damn maple syrup in the microwave please."

"Yes, Chef."

"Sorry, Pop. So how bad was work yesterday?"

"Pretty scary, kid. I never had to go through that sort of corporate change before. It really made me miss the restaurant. New company comes in and people just get let go for no damn reason. We had some folks like Heather and Melissa that were doing a great job one day and then the next day, their butts are on the street through no fault of their own."

"Damn, Pop. They let Heather and Melissa go? What the hell for?"

"It gets worse. Sonya was let go too and they're going to move back to Tampa."

"Sonya, too? What the hell! That means Hector is going with her?"

"Well, they are married, Theo."

"Who am I going to go fishing with now? Did Sonya say when they are leaving?"

"Well, they own a house. I imagine it wouldn't be right away, but I don't know ... I'm sure it's not today, Theo. Surely you and Hector can fit in one more fishing excursion, wouldn't you think?"

"Yeah. I'll send him a message on the way to school. Damn this sucks, I'm gonna miss those two."

"Me too kid, me too. We should have them over one last time." Nick sipped his coffee and placed the syrup and butter on the table and poured two glasses of orange and carrot juice Theo had made earlier. They sat down and Nick smiled in amazement as Theo put six pancakes on his plate, six slices of bacon, and then proceeded to slice two bananas over the mound of calories before dousing it with Vermont maple syrup. "Look Theo, Mr. Carrollton wasn't making money the way he had projected and that money didn't belong to him. It belonged to the investors that financed Woodmont, and those investors want their money back – with interest, only schedule."

"Hhhmmm, you must explain this theory of interest to me, Master."

"How about we pray first, kid?" They bowed their heads.

"Heavenly Father, thank you for the food set before us, may it nourish and strengthen us. Please look after our good friends, especially those that were recently let go at from Woodmont. Thank you for the many blessings of this life; may we recognize and gratefully accept them. Thank you for my Dad, even though he can be short-tempered at times, and please help me live up to the standards that Mom set for me. May she always smile when she looks down on the two of us. In Jesus' name, we pray, Amen."

"Well said, son." Nick took a bite of pancakes and imagined Robin sitting next to him, smiling.

"OK, we all know all about interest, but the point is that Mr. Carrollton was top heavy in many areas and when the economy crashed, it affected people even at the socio-economic level that he was targeting. His break-even and profit projections suddenly were skewed and he had a staff that he personally had helped hire that he couldn't stand to part with. So now Woodmont's investor has sought out another management company, one with a history of frugality and fiscal responsibility, and they probably spent a month or so looking at every place possible to cut back and one of those areas is people. So the folks that stay will be asked to pick up the slack of those that got let go. The business of business can be pretty ruthless, sometimes. Melissa will be fine. She's going back home where she has support and wants to open her own company. Sonya is going back to south Florida. Heather ... Damn, I hope she has some cash saved up because someone like her, it's going to be tough to find a job, real tough. I'm certain Maureen is next. I doubt she lasts the week and frankly, I won't miss her one bit."

"Well Pop, at least you still have a job. You got a new boss?"

"Yep, got a new boss."

"What's he like?"

"Well, *she* is like a nurse."

"*Ha!* My old man has to report to a nurse; that is *so awesome!* Yes, please come into my office Chef St. Germaine, roll up your sleeve and place this thermometer under your tongue while we review your quarterly numbers. This is so sweet! Is she hot?" Nick looked at his son, took a bite of pancakes and then finished his juice.

"Did you put ginger in this juice?"

"Holy shit, Dad! She is hot, isn't she? Come on Pop, tell the truth. *Tell your wittle Theo all about her.*"

"Let's just say that the good Lord was very generous to Miss Amy Sommers." Theo laughed, put his hands behind his head and leaned his chair back on two legs.

"Pop reports to the hot nurse now. Hell, she even has a hot name. Amy Sommers, yeah, I like that. Just wait until I Facebook this one. Does she wear that funny white hat?"

"Don't you dare make one post about my employer, understand?"

"OK, OK. Dang, I was just joking anyway. So what's happening over there today?"

"Well, at ten a.m., the lovely Amy Sommers will have to negotiate her way through a member's meeting. She has to make the case for the future of Woodmont and explain yesterday's layoffs to our residents. I wouldn't trade places with her for all the money in the world. So this morning, I'll get to see what this gal is really made of." Theo let his chair drop back on all four legs, then moved his hands back towards his breakfast.

"Oh, gross!"

Nick laughed and shook his head. Theo could be such a sloppy eater. As he devoured his pancakes, he had coated his hands in maple syrup, and now he had syrup all over the back of his head.

"Damn, kid, you're growing up but you sure as hell aren't changing much!"

"Yeah, yeah, this is just perfect, and here comes my ride." A car horn tooted as Theo finished his pancakes in two gargantuan bites. He then jumped up and deposited his plate in the sink, quickly washed his hands, and then ran his wet hands and a paper towel through the hair on the back of his head.

"Maybe Amanda can take care of that for you. I wonder if she has ever tasted real maple syrup, or is she a Log Cabin gal?"

"Amanda is authentic as they come, Pop. I'm sure she prefers the real deal. She loves me right. How much more authentic can a girl get than Theo St. Germaine?" The car horn tooted again. "Gotta go, Pop." He grabbed his bag and gave Nick a quick hug and ran out the front door.

"*Love you!*" hollered Nick as Theo slammed the front door behind him. Nick looked down at his pancakes and whispered,

"I love you very much, son." The front door opened and Theo stuck his head back in.

"Love you too, Dad!" then slammed the door.

Nick sipped his coffee and looked at the family Christmas photo on the wall. Theo was five years old and even then he was tall for his age. He had Robin's blue eyes and blonde hair and when Theo was young he couldn't go anywhere without women running their hands through his hair. Now eleven years later Theo was six foot three inches tall and his good looks were capable of stopping any woman in her tracks. Nick cringed at the thought of the amount of trouble his son could get into but he was a good kid and with high aspirations. Nick finished his breakfast, cleaned the kitchen, showered, changed then picked out a CD for the 20-minute drive to Woodmont.

The Chicago Room was Woodmont's ballroom, and could hold 125 chairs arranged in a classroom style setting. At 9:50 a.m., it was overflowing. Amy had asked Nick and Daniel Stern to be there. She also had backup from CSM in the form of Rivers Williams and Harriett Baltz. Nick had arrived about ten minutes early and spent a few minutes in the lobby chatting and saying hello to the members, most of which were furious at the sudden change, appalled at the amount of people that were let go, and concerned that Nick and Daniel would be next. As Nick was talking to Mr. and Mrs. Hemmers, there was bang outside the front door. Nick turned and saw that Mr. and Mrs. Jensen had just nearly driven their golf cart through the glass door. They smiled and waved to the 30 or so folks they had just scared to death then walked in as if nothing out of the ordinary had happened. Nick shook his head, made a mental note to suggest to Penny that Mrs. Jensen have an eye exam, and then walked into the ballroom. The din of the room had a menacing tone to it. The members were talking in short clips and as Nick scanned the room, he saw lots of scowls, frowns and worry. They had every right to be mad. These were people that had sold their homes and a lot of their possessions so they could retire without anxiety. They paid a hefty move-in fee and after that, only one monthly maintenance fee. In return, they never had to pay a power or water bill, did not have to deal with home maintenance or cutting the grass, and had access to limousines, three dining venues, a movie theatre, walking trails, covered parking, a barber shop, swimming pool and even a spa. Woodmont also had a huge staff, and they received excellent benefits and were well paid. Nick looked at his phone, 9:57 a.m. and still no sign of Amy. Willie Armstrong grabbed Nick by the elbow.

"Well Nick, where's your new boss?"

Colonel William Armstrong was perhaps Nick's favorite resident of Woodmont. Retired from the Air Force, Willie had flown B-17 bombers in World War II, transitioned to a single seat P-51 Mustang and later an F-86 Sabre in Korea. He had lived all over the world and had seen many amazing sights. Like Nick, he had loved one woman unconditionally and completely, only to lose her. At 90, Willie's thin 6-foot-1 inch frame moved only with the aid of a tennis ball-tipped walker. Some days, Willie's joints were so uncooperative he relied on an electric scooter with a USAF logo on the back. Willie's silver hair and pencil-thin moustache were so thin that he often joked he was afraid to use a comb lest he yank out what remained. Nick looked into the lobby across the hallway just as the elevator door. Out stepped Amy, Harriett and Rivers. Nick chuckled and shook his head. One damn floor.

"Well Colonel, I see that her flight has just touched down so if you will excuse me, I have a minefield to walk through."

Willie patted Nick on the back and smiled and slowly turned towards one of the chairs that Franklin had just placed along the back of the room. As Amy, Rivers and Harriett walked in Nick and Daniel Stern moved from the back of the room to the front and stood next to one of the six chairs. Nick looked at Daniel and then at the approaching trio, and asked Daniel who was missing.

"Dang Chef, you didn't know Maureen got the axe this morning?"

As Amy and her entourage walked through the crowd to the row of chairs, Nick heard hissing coming from the back. He scanned the crowd and saw Doris Peters bent forward slightly, her right hand covering her mouth. Doris was one of Woodmont's widowers. She was 80 and her husband, Henry, had passed away only three months after they had moved in. Doris was from Milwaukee and although her husband had flown for Pan Am and had taken her across the globe many times over, she wore her blunt Midwestern attitude with pride. Doris stood five feet, seven inches tall. She had sharp blue eyes and long, wavy silver hair. Unlike a lot of Woodmont's octogenarians, she had not lost any bone density to osteoporosis and stood straight. Nick caught her eye and slowly moved his head from side to side. Doris sat up, folded her arms across her chest, and glared. Harriett and Rivers joined Nick and Daniel at the front. Rivers offered Nick a handshake and a wink. Amy was wearing a silver linen business suit with a knee-length skirt and a buttoned-up white blouse. Her hair was pulled back off her shoulders. She wore a different set of clock-faced earrings. At least the men in the room were quiet. Nick thought to himself that right here and now, he would see how far this woman had gotten on her good looks. Amy smiled at Nick and thanked him for being here.

"Good morning, Chef," whispered Rivers.

"Why do I feel like I am in front of a firing squad?" responded Nick. Rivers grinned then patted Nick on the back as Amy switched on her wireless microphone.

"Good morning. For those of you that did not meet me yesterday, I'm Amy Sommers, your new Director here at Woodmont." Several boos came from the back of the room, but Amy was unfazed. "On my left is Harriett Baltz, the vice president of Creek Side Management, and this is Rivers Williams, the chief operating officer. You all know your head of facilities, Daniel Stern, and of course Nicholas St.

Germaine, your Executive Chef." Nick took his seat and the rest followed. Amy remained standing.

"I have a quick question before I get started. Raise your hand if you were financially able to move in to Woodmont because you won the lottery." Amy scanned the room, but no one put their hand up. "Well, I already knew the answer to that one. I know this is a very emotionally charged time here at Woodmont, and every one of you was probably very close to Jack Carrollton. Jack is a good man, a gentleman and a visionary. He did an amazing job with the design, construction and opening of Woodmont, and I know everyone here will miss him. I want everyone to know that Jack has offered to help me in any way he can, and he wants this transition to be as smooth and seamless as possible. Please understand that Woodmont's business model was unsustainable and that the financial backer, First Colony REIT, and Mr. Carrollton were instrumental in choosing Creek Side to take over Woodmont's daily operations. Creek Side has committed to the financial security of Woodmont, as well as to its continuing prosperity. Please remember that Woodmont, as beautiful as it is and as receptive and welcoming as the staff has become, is still a business. It needs to attain fiscal responsibility and be run as any of you would run your business. Living in Woodmont is a reward for all of your years of fiscal responsibility, and all of you understand that, correct? No one is here because they won the lottery. You all were able to move in to Woodmont because you were successful business people or entrepreneurs and you were very careful with your money. Woodmont, in turn, needs to be careful with your money. You all are Woodmont's only source of income, and if we're not careful with your money, how does that reflect on management? How does that reflect on you? Woodmont will achieve sustainability and growth through Creek Side. Yes, we let some of the staff go yesterday and I am certain that they were all good people and will be duly missed. All of them are eligible for unemployment which in this country is fairly generous. Woodmont's staffing ratio was exceedingly high and with only 147 members, our staffing ratio was unsustainable. So please, bear with us. I know this is painful because you all have grown close to this staff. Every one of these people will be greatly missed, and I understand that. At this time, though, Woodmont needs to stop the hemorrhaging. Then, we can grow and prosper as you would want your own business to." Amy paused and scanned the room. Someone spoke up from the back.

"How many successful businesses have you run, young lady?"

"One."

Her response was greeted with whistles, head shakes and eye rolls.

"Creek Side is a successful and responsible operator and has rescued five developments that were in very similar circumstances that Woodmont finds itself in now. Creek Side manages 27 communities in 11 states and owns seven of those outright. Every one of those is financially successful, as Woodmont will become within one year. Mr. Williams and Mrs. Baltz were turn-around specialists in their own right before moving to Creek Side, so I have a lot of arrows in the quiver. I have a lot of confidence in Creek Side, and with Mr. St. Germaine and Mr. Stern, both former successful businessmen at my side, I'm certain that we can achieve our goals." Amy turned to Nick and Daniel and offered a glowing smile. Nick squirmed in his seat. *She has known me for exactly one day and now I'm her faithful, financially responsible sidekick? Really?* Nick smiled and nodded slightly, *might as well put on the happy face.* Amy scanned the room again. The tone had definitely changed from one of anger to perhaps begrudging acceptance. Nick was impressed, but still a bit uncomfortable. "At this time, Mr. Williams has a short PowerPoint presentation on Creek Side's history and standards, an overview of the other properties in our portfolio, and a short bio on our CEO, Thomas Muncie." Amy sat down next to Nick as Rivers stood up. Nick turned slightly to Amy and noticed beads of sweat on her forehead and upper lip. Her hands were shaking ever so slightly. She switched off her microphone, turned and caught Nick's eye.

"Good stuff, Miss Sommers," whispered Nick.

"Thank you, and please call me Amy."

"Yes, of course."

25 minutes later, Rivers had finished up his presentation and had offered to take a few questions. Nick watched Rivers and as he admired his ability to work the crowd, he wondered if this guy had ever held an elected position – he was that smooth and confident. Rivers answered about a dozen questions and when the tempo of the room had settled down, he offered the floor back to Amy.

"I know that you all have a lot of unanswered questions, but time will not permit the five of us to be up here for much longer, so I would like to ask each of you to bring their remaining questions to your resident council member, and that they in turn would filter then submit your questions to Rivers and me. I will publish a response to your frequently asked questions list, and it will be distributed to everyone. Today is Tuesday, so I would like to have this done and back in your hands by Friday morning. I have taken the liberty of having a form ready for your representatives, and I would ask those representatives filter out those questions that Rivers or I have already answered, or that the members have doubled up on. So I apologize. I have had you all in here for an hour. I know this is a stressful time but working together, we will get through this transition and build Woodmont into a thriving, successful and rewarding community that you all deserve. Thank you."

As the members filed out, Harriett introduced herself to Nick.

"Chef St. Germaine, Harriett Baltz, my pleasure."

"Likewise," responded Nick.

"Chef, listen, first of all I need to say that if you're rolling around an itineration of my name, I can promise I have heard them all and for many years, so don't bother."

"Yes ma'am."

"Serves me right for falling in love with a German fella named Baltz, correct?"

"If you say so, Mrs. Baltz."

"And Chef, please call me Harriett, understand?"

"Yes, of course, Harriett."

"Chef, here's my card. By the end of the week, our IT staff will have everyone's computer networked and all of the company email addresses will be there. If you ever need me, feel free to reach out to me. However, I believe you are very capable. Likewise, Miss Sommers and I would like to think that you can handle your department. Creek Side also has a pretty deep bench of support in Charleston. We have 26 other Chefs there who you can turn to. You will be getting some online training and introductions to your home office staff by this Friday. However, I am always there you should you need me, understand? I have visited Woodmont several times in the past six or seven weeks and always had a very enjoyable meal in the dining room. We look forward to seeing you grow and prosper with the company."

"Yes ma'am, and thank you very much."

Nick excused himself and headed back to the kitchen, saying good morning to the staff as he walked to the back of the kitchen.

"Good morning, Dodger, how's your lunch menu looking?" Bobby Dodge was a recent hire and his lunch cook. He was very talented but immature, especially considering he was 27 years old. Nick privately thought Bobby had the maturity of a 13-year-old and often wondered if his mother ever let him interact with other kids as he was growing up. Bobby was pudgy and stood five feet, eight inches tall with scraggly, tightly wound up black hair that Xavier joked he could scrub pots with. Bobby did not stand up straight. He leaned forward as one would in a strong wind.

"Chef? I got a question. If I want to brine some pork tenderloin, how long should it sit in the water? How'd ya'll do it at the Tavern?"

"So Bobby, is this for today, because it's almost 11?"

"No Chef, this is for tomorrow."

"So you're all set for today?"

"Dodger's got it covered, dawg."

"Please don't call me dog, OK? So you're going to brine how many tenderloins?"

"Well, maybe six or seven tenders. Sorry, Chef."

"OK, so you will need a gallon of water, put that in a pot and add a cup of salt, a cup of sugar or molasses, a big handful of thyme and parsley, some cut lemon, orange and garlic, and some peppercorns. Let it come to a simmer, cool it down and then throw the tenderloins in it for about four hours. You do it now and when you leave for the day, pull them out of the brine, OK? And you know what would be really cool, Bobby? Instead of water, start with tea, iced tea."

"Dang, Chef, now that's sounding bitchin'! Sweet tea-brined pork tenderloin, hell, yeah! Man, Chef why'd you ever sell your place. You shoulda hung on to it 'stead of coming to a retirement home."

"Yeah, well things happen, Dodger."

Nick excused himself and walked into his office. He sat down, turned on his laptop and scratched his head before looking at his to-do list. As he watched his computer come to life, he turned to the photo of Robin and shook his head. "Things happen." He leaned back in his chair and closed his eyes, and drifted off to the Stone Avenue Tavern.

Robin tossed the kitchen door open and caught Nick's eye. She was wearing a simple black cocktail dress and her blonde hair was pulled back over her shoulders.

"Sweetheart, I just sat an eight-top. I know it's almost ten, but it's some big spenders. You all good back there?"

"Bring 'em on, darling. They're just getting us closer to our week in Tahiti" Nick shouted across the kitchen. Robin leaned forward and smiled, her blue eyes sparkling. She blew him a kiss, turned and left the kitchen. Nick sighed and smiled at Xavier, who shook his head.

"You're one lucky man, my friend." Nick winked at Xavier and patted him on the back

"I know Xavier, believe me I know it."

Nick opened his eyes and sat up. He looked out his office window at Woodmont's kitchen and all of its stainless steel, industrial-sized equipment. He stood up and walked into the dining room, making his way to the corner where perhaps he would be out of sight. He opened a window and took a deep breath. The April wind raced through the new leaves, pushing a few puffy clouds across the crisp sky as a Carolina wren sang its trilling "tea-kettle" song. Doris Peters walked up and stood next to him, reached out with her left hand and took Nick's right hand in hers.

"I miss Robin."

A Mourning Dove cooed in the crepe myrtle that bordered the pond as Michael and Marsha Hemmers, slowly pedaling past on their matching bicycles, sent two chipmunks scurrying for cover.

"I really miss my Henry."

The breeze picked up and the dove steadied itself, flapped its rusty brown wings, turned into the wind and flew off. Nick heard the rumble of a diesel engine approach and guessed it was the Sysco truck. He had a hefty food delivery coming in this morning. When the air brakes hissed, Nick let go of Doris' hand and whispered,

"I have to go."

3

Amy packed up the work she wanted to take home, then made her way to the main entrance of the dining room and said good evening to Tony.

"Good evening, Mrs. Sommers."

"Please Anthony, it's just Amy and I'm not married anymore."

"Of course, Amy. My apologies and feel free to call me Tony, and how has your first week at Woodmont gone?"

"A bit scary, but so far so good, Tony."

"Table for one, or will you be joining anyone?"

"No, thank you. I just wanted to say hello to some of the members before I leave."

"Of course." Tony gently waved his right arm to motion her into the dining room. Amy placed her stack of papers and laptop behind the podium, then walked in and scanned the room. She guessed there were at least 70 members having dinner – with Nick standing in the middle of the dining room talking to a table of six ladies. Amy gently started making her way towards them. Some of the members were smiling at her, but others were frowning or looking away as she moved through the room. As she approached Doris' table, several of the ladies turned to face her. They were obviously enjoying the attention from Nick.

"Good evening ladies and gentleman."

"Good evening, Miss Sommers. Do you know everyone here?"

"Well I think so, but please feel free to refresh my memory. I have met a lot of folks in the last week."

"Certainly, Miss Sommers. We'll start with Doris Peters ... and this is Peggy Roberts, Virginia Rogers who we sometimes call Ginger, Susan Simmons ... and this is Beverly Stafford and Veronica Parker." As Nick introduced everyone, he walked behind them and placed his hand on their shoulders as he said their names. Several of the ladies reached out and patted Nick's hand, and as they did this, they simultaneously glared at Amy as if to say, "Back off!"

"I was just going over tonight's specials with the girls here, but I think they are about ready to order, so if you will excuse me." Nick winked at Doris as he stepped away from the table.

"He certainly is the charming one," Amy noted. Several of the ladies smiled and nodded their heads.

"And healthy, too," replied Doris Peters. With that, the ladies all giggled and held up their drinks as Doris cheered, "To Nick's good health!"

"Well, if I had a drink I would join you."

The ladies all laughed and Doris Peters raised her right hand and waved Amy away as if to say that this was their little inside joke.

"Am I missing something?"

She was greeted with more laughter and waves. The ladies composed themselves as Susie Simmons looked at Doris and squeaked, "Oh, why don't we just tell her our little secret?" Doris responded with a look that could kill, and Peggy Roberts followed suit.

"OK, what's this all about?" quizzed Amy.

Susie smiled and blushed. Doris Peters looked around the table and scanned her girlfriend's eyes, then looked at Amy Sommers and croaked,

"Honest Injun lady, this is just a secret between us girls, OK? Ya gotta promise this stays amongst us available women, deal?"

"Uh, well sure, why not?"

"Oh no, that's not good enough for me, lady" snorted Doris, as she picked up her menu and held it in front of her face. The rest of the girls followed suit. Amy just stood there in silence, the only ostrich without her head in the sand.

"OK, I vow an oath ladies, your secret is safe with me."

The menus all came down and the entire table was smiling again. Doris squinted at Amy and held out her right hand, pointed her bony forefinger at Amy and curled it back to say, "Come here." Amy made her way to Doris and partially knelt down next to her.

"Twice a week, our Chef swims in the pool and we sneak into Franklin's office and watch him." Susie Simmons fanned herself with her menu and the other ladies all giggled like teenagers. "Lemme tell you something, that's the best entertainment on campus for a single gal like me."

"Oh golly, Doris, I'm going to need a cigarette!" exclaimed Veronica Parker, and the ladies all giggled again.

"It sure beats watching 'The Sound of Music' in the theatre," chirped Beverly Stafford, leading to an eruption of more laughter.

"I'm gonna need my nitro pills!" laughed Veronica, mockingly clutching her heart. As the laughter settled down, Doris reached out for Amy Sommers' hand, squeezed it tight and glared at her. "You wouldn't want try to take that away from us now, would you, Mrs. Sommers?"

"Please, it's Miss Sommers and, uh, well, I guess no one's breaking any laws here, correct? And Chef St. Germaine's food is certainly delicious, yes?"

"Nick certainly is delicious," snorted Doris Peters, and again the table burst into laughter. Amy found herself embarrassed for falling into that one. Doris raised her double Old Fashioned. Amy glanced around the dining room looking for Nick, but he had already gone back into the kitchen.

"To our Chef! Long may he swim!" toasted Doris. The other ladies joined her in lifting their glasses. Amy wished them an enjoyable meal and excused herself. She saw Mr. and Mrs. Jensen and stopped at their table. They had a bottle of wine on the table, and they were obviously waiting for another couple.

"Oh, Mrs. Sommers, Mrs. Sommers, please join us. Please sit down, won't you? You know my wife, Mollie. You two have met, correct?" Jim moved one of the empty wine glasses towards the edge of the table closest to Amy.

Mollie hoisted the bottle of chardonnay and proceeded to fill the glass practically to the rim.

"Just one glass, surely you have time for that?"

Amy looked at the glass. Good gosh! That must be 16 ounces of wine. If she drank that, she would stagger out of here.

"Oh, thank you so much. You're too kind, but I'm about to drive home and I haven't had dinner yet."

With that, Jim tried to stand up to pull a chair out for Amy, but she asked him to sit back down. He was very unsteady and she was afraid he would tumble right over.

"So what news do you have today, Miss Sommers? What's the latest cutback? Are you getting the electricity bills paid on time?"

"Of course we are, and CSM is even investing in Woodmont. In fact, we're getting a bus for the members, and that's something you all have been asking about for a long time."

"Is it going to be a used Cheese Wagon from the public school system?"

"You know, that's not a bad idea. I'll bet we could pick up three or four for the price of what we were looking at." The Jensen's frowned and Mrs. Jensen shook her head. Amy chuckled.

"Oh come on, we're buying a brand new 15-passenger bus with a wheelchair lift."

"Well, that's good news Miss Sommers. Cheers!" Jim hoisted his glass to Amy and smiled at her as she excused herself and headed to Willie Armstrong's table.

"Good evening, Mr. Armstrong and Mr. De Soto. How are you two gentlemen this evening?" Willie Armstrong was sharing a table with Benjamin De Soto, a well-known real estate developer. Willie looked Amy in the eyes and offered a formal,

"Good evening, Miss Sommers." Benjamin looked Amy up and down and leered at her.

"That shore is a pretty color on you young lady," he rasped. Amy was suddenly very uncomfortable, and Willie sensed it.

"What Mr. De Soto meant was that you have an innate and lovely sense of style, Miss Sommers."

"Well, thank you very much, Mr. Armstrong."

"Colonel Armstrong, please."

"Yes of course, Colonel. I hope you two gentlemen have a fine evening." Amy excused herself and headed for the back door, smiling and thanking the wait staff on the way out. Benjamin De Soto watched Amy walk out of the dining room and when she was about ten feet away Willie kicked him under the table.

"*Ouch!* Shit old man, what did you do that for?"

"Mr. De Soto, could you not exercise even a little bit of decorum when in the presence of a lady?"

"Well damnit, Willie! I couldn't help it. She's so dang pretty, and you didn't have to kick me."

"Yes, I did. You Army types are all the same, no sense of restraint, no manners, no discipline. Now, in the Air Force ..."

"*Oh boy!*," barked De Soto, "here we go again! Listen here, Armstrong. Just because you buzzed around at 30,000 feet joyriding while I was knee deep in mud and blood doesn't give you the right to dump on the Army. You damn jet jockeys are all the same." Tony Torres approached the table and smiled.

"I see you two gentlemen are enjoying some light dinner conversation."

"*Oh bullshit!*" grunted De Soto. "Tony, tell me something. If you had to walk down a dark alley and you needed some muscle at your side, would you walk down that alley with fly boy here or me, the grunt that can handle himself in close-quarters combat?"

Tony looked at De Soto's wheelchair then turned to Willie, who moved at an agonizingly slow pace behind his tennis ball-tipped walker.

"Well gentlemen, I do believe I would be confident in both of your abilities to handle yourselves in a tense situation."

"Ya got no damn backbone, Torres!" grunted De Soto. Willie Armstrong chuckled and shook his head.

"Your days of marching through menacing dark alleys are behind you, Ben, but since you posed the question, I believe I would be pretty comfortable with Chef St. Germaine at my side. Wouldn't you agree, Mr. Torres?" Tony laughed, tossing his head back.

"Now that is something we can agree on gentlemen. Have a good evening."

Two hours later, Tony walked into Nick's office and sat down.

"Well Skipper, have you ever had to endure anything like this before?"

"No sir, never."

"Listen, this kind of thing happens in the hotel business. One day, you're working for Hilton. The next day, the owners want to convert to Holiday Inn. This new company obviously likes us and believes in us, so just keep your head down and play nice, OK? I gotta say, they'll probably ask you to lose some labor. Don't be surprised if they tell you to drop 40 hours from your payroll, so maybe you should start thinking about who you could live without so when that time comes, you're not hit from the blind side." Nick looked out the window at his three cooks that were finishing up.

"Forty hours huh? One full-time employee."

"Look at it this way, Nick. You could call around and find a restaurant looking for someone and that way when you go to Florence, Juan, Sleepy or Jimmy, you could already have a job for them. That way, it won't be so traumatic."

"That's a great idea, Tony. At least I would be prepared for the worst, correct?"

"Yes, sir. Hope for the best, but prepare for the worst."

"Hey, were you surprised that the new boss left at six? I would have thought that she would have at least stuck around to see what we're up to." Tony tossed his head back and laughed.

"Why would she do that? So she can let us see how little she knows about food and beverage? Come on, skipper. Better for her to smile and say 'Good night' and get the hell out of here. I would guess that in another 30 days, she may take an interest in what we're doing, but not now. She's a nurse, remember? And she has a couple of departments that need a lot more attention than we do."

"Good point, Tony."

"Who loves ya, babe?"

"You do, Mr. Torres." Tony stood up and ran his hand through his hair.

"OK, let's get out of here, skipper. We have some long days ahead of us and in 30 minutes, I have a date with a very pretty social studies teacher."

"School's in session, Mr. Torres?" Tony grinned.

"Yes sir, and she has a willing pupil."

"Alright, enough of this. You here Sunday, Mr. Torres?"

"Yes sir, I'll be here for Sunday brunch."

"OK, enjoy your day off. I'm going to try to have an easy day on Saturday. Theo has three kids he tutors on Saturdays, so maybe we'll have dinner together. I'll see you Sunday morning."

"Cheers, babe!"

The only meal service Woodmont offered on Sundays to its independent residents was a Sunday Brunch buffet available from 11 a.m.-2 p.m. Nick would typically serve three to four meats such as fried chicken, roasted turkey breast, baked ham or something more eclectic such as duck leg, risotto or leg of lamb. He also served plenty of mashed potatoes, stone ground grits, rice pilaf, several seasonal vegetables, bacon and sausage, an egg dish such as Benedict or a frittata, pancakes with a fruit topping, cold salads and fresh fruit, plenty of desserts and an omelet and waffle station manned by one of his cooks. On an average Sunday, they might see 125 guests through the buffet. Chefs typically use a Sunday buffet as an opportunity to get rid of leftovers. A favorite dish of Nick's was creamed chicken or a beef stroganoff. Creamed chicken could contain leftover grilled chicken breast or fried chicken and leftover vegetables. Add some chicken stock thickened with roux and heavy cream, place that dish on the buffet next to mashed potatoes or waffles, and you had a crowd pleaser that also helped out the budget. The challenge of leftovers was to make something appealing and tasty that did not look or taste like leftovers. That is the hallmark of a great cook. Any half-assed cook can grill a fat filet mignon, drizzle a red wine sauce over it, top it with a quenelle of thyme butter and call it a day, but it took a skilled pair of hands to see the possibilities in a hunk of leftover roasted turkey breast, some overcooked carrots, a dozen day-old baked potatoes and a thin Alfredo sauce. Nick had several guys that could do this, but Xavier was the best at it. Xavier James had grown up on a real farm and learned at an early age that nothing ever went to waste. Nick had that ability, and so did his sous Chef, Kevin Randall. Kevin was developing that skill in his most recent hire, Bobby Dodge. On this morning, Nick had Kevin with four other cooks: Jimmy, Xavier, Bobby and Alex, with Jimmy on the omelet station. "OK Jimmy, let's get you all set up for your adoring fans. It's ten fifteen, so let's get your mise en place outside, sir."

"My what Chef?"

"Mees uhn plahs. That's an old French term that means everything in its place, but cooks use that term to describe their prep for a given station."

"Yes, Chef."

"Jimmy, you don't sound so excited this morning."

"I'm fine, Chef." Nick and Jimmy began placing the ingredients he would need on a rolling cart. Jimmy had diced up sweet peppers, onions, mushrooms, tomatoes, to which he added Cheddar cheese, cooking oil, eggs, waffle batter and some pan spray for the waffle iron.

"Morning, babe!"

"Hey, good morning, Mr. Torres, I didn't expect you to be in for another hour."

Tony squeezed Nick on the shoulder, pulled him close then whispered, "Well, I figured I could either get an hour's sleep or just shower up and come on in, so here I am."

"Well OK then Mr. Torres, please spare me the sordid details."

"You know I don't kiss and tell, babe." Tony winked at Nick, then sauntered over to the coffee pot.

"Hey Chef, you coming?"

"Right behind you Jimmy, let's go." Nick and Jimmy rolled the cart out to the omelet station and began carefully placing their items where they would be needed.

"You OK, Jimmy?"

"Not really, Chef. I'm kind of nervous about all those layoffs. I'm afraid I'm going to get let go. This is only my second cooking job, and I think I'm probably your weakest guy here."

"Look Jimmy, I haven't been asked to drop anyone yet but if I am, I have already started looking around at other restaurants and hotels to see who has an opening. I wouldn't sweat it yet. Please try to worry about things that are in your control, OK?"

"Yes, Chef."

"So tell me, on this beautiful Sunday morning, what is in your control?"

"My omelet station?"

"Correct. So take care of your customers this morning, OK? Make every one of your omelets just as pretty as if you were making it for your own dear, sweet mother. Will you do that for me?"

"Yes, Chef. Thank you."

Two hours later, Nick was carefully walking through a full dining room. Woodmont's residents did not move with much vigor. Their average age was 81, and at least half of the residents used some sort of assistive device such as a cane, walker or wheelchair. When Nick was in the dining room, he was very cognizant of his pace. He was carefully making his way back to the omelet station to check on Jimmy when he saw Beverly Stafford waving to him from her table, so he walked over to say hello. Beverly was enjoying the company of two little boys, probably her grandchildren. Beverly was 83, a widow from Rome, Ga., whose husband had made a fortune as a cotton broker. Beverly was a very gracious, polished and had aged well. She could have easily passed for 65. She earned an MFA from Barnard College and had played an integral part in helping to rebuild Italy's museums after World War Two.

"Oh Nick, Nick, I want to introduce you. These are my grandsons. This is Matthew and Caleb. They belong to my son, Todd, who's somewhere around here. Boys, this is our Chef, Nick St. Germaine."

"Hello, Mr. Nick," said the younger one.

"Hey pal, are you Matthew or Caleb?"

"I'm Caleb and I'm seven, and that's my brother, Matthew, and he's ten."

"Oh, and Nick, this is my son, Todd." Nick turned around to say hello. He recognized Todd immediately, Touchdown Todd Stafford. Todd stood four inches taller than Nick. He had a protruding Adam's apple, a full yet trimmed beard that ran the length of his neck, wide shoulders, slightly bloodshot eyes and shoulder length, dark brown hair that he wore in a ponytail. Todd wore a turquoise bolo tie and a long sleeve black shirt. When Nick turned around, Todd cut his eyes and took another step closer to him. Nick instinctively backed up until he bumped into Todd's empty chair.

"Mother, your Chef and I already know one another, don't we?"

Nick pulled Todd's chair out for him.

"Yes, I suppose we do, Mr. Stafford."

"Oh, isn't that lovely son?"

"Lo Chef, oggi tutto sembra deliziosa."

"Grazie molte Mrs. Stafford."

"OK Mother, we don't have to show off for the help," Todd snapped as he eased himself into the chair that Nick was holding. Nick briefly imagined yanking the chair out and Todd falling to the floor, covering himself in roast turkey and gravy, scorching hot grits and grilled asparagus. "Well, now that everyone looks comfortable, if you will excuse me?"

"Si, si, naturalmente, Chef."

"That's quite enough, mother."

Nick excused himself and quickly walked back to the kitchen, washed his hands and then got a cup of water. He closed his eyes and took a deep breath. He repeated the move as he tried to get control of his temper.

"Hey babe, everything all good?"

"Yeah, sure, fine Tony. I'm fine."

"Bullshit. You look like you're about to boil over. Who was that at Mrs. Stafford's table?"

"Her son."

"OK, I figured as much, and?"

"Hey Tony, can you give Jackson a hand at the hostess stand, please? He's got two big parties he's trying to seat. Thank you!"

Tony turned and looked at Ally. She had her hands full of dirty dishes that she was dropping off at the dish station. Nick folded his arms and glared.

"You're needed in the dining room, Mr. Torres." Tony looked at Nick and quietly responded.

"Yes, Chef."

Three hours later, Nick was finishing up for the day. The Sysco order and the produce order were done, his weekly dinner special menu was finished, and String Bean was finishing up the kitchen floor. He picked up his to-do list and looked for a project he could complete in 30 minutes or so, and then sent a text message to his son.

"dinner at high cotton?"

"what's the catch pop?"

"thirty minutes of basketball with the old man, loser pays."

"easy money pop"

"see you at the gym in 60."

4

Nick walked into the Armory, the gentlemen's bar tucked into the corner of the clubhouse. The Armory was decorated with framed pin-up posters of Rita Hayworth and Betty Grable as well as famous football players from the '50s plus a framed portrait of a smiling George S. Patton and Dwight D. Eisenhower. Nick said good morning to the team. Amy looked up and smiled as he took the seat opposite her. She was wearing a red and white floral print sundress, topped off with an unbuttoned, thin white sweater and a silver necklace with a single diamond set in a teardrop pendant. The sundress exposed the top third of her bosom, and the diamond had settled in the valley between her breasts. The morning sun spilled through the Armory's windows. Amy's diamond sparkled in the light, calling to Nick as a rotating beacon at a fog-shrouded airport would to a lost pilot. Nick had to summon every drop of discipline to keep his eyes focused above her neckline. His son's words from several weeks prior crept into his mind: "Pop reports to the hot nurse now."

"Good morning, Nick. I brought some doughnuts for everyone. Would you like one?"

"Good morning, Miss Sommers. They look delicious, but um, no thank you. I'll pass, but I appreciate it."

Percy caught Nick's eye.

"Ya'll, speaking of delicious doesn't our boss look positively fabulous this morning?" Amy blushed and looked away from Nick, while several of the ladies agreed with Percy. "And where did you get that diamond? It's stunning."

Amy looked down at the pendant and lifted it up and held it between her right thumb and forefinger. Every pair of eyes was drawn to the pendant. Nick quickly looked over at Grant, who instead of looking at his new boss' ample cleavage had turned to Nick. Grant raised his eyebrows slightly as Nick bit his bottom lip.

"Percy, my mother gave me this when I turned 18. The diamond came from her mother's engagement ring. It's probably my favorite piece of jewelry." Amy let the pendant drop back in place as all the ladies in the room complimented her. Eyes up, eyes up, eyes up, Nick said to himself.

"OK, by my watch it is 9, so let's get started please. For those of you that have not met Cassidy Cummings, our new Director of Member Services, and of course Grant Hughes, our Director of Health Care. Cassidy just moved here from Austin, Texas, and Grant comes to us from the U.S. Navy in Bethesda, Maryland. Cassidy, please introduce yourself."

Cassidy was from Trinidad but had grown up in Houston, Texas and had the accent to prove it. She was six feet tall, caramel colored skin, long, dark brown hair and very muscular.

"Thank you, Amy. I spent three years at the Austin Spa as the wellness coordinator, and I loved it. I have a degree in exercise physiology from University of Texas, where I also ran track. As much as I love Texas, I really wanted to live somewhere with four seasons. Those Texas summers can be long and so hot. I have a friend that went into elder care and he said it was the most rewarding career move, he loved it, so here I am – and I'm looking forward to helping Chef St. Germaine get into shape." Nick winked at Cassidy as Amy rolled her eyes.

"Thanks, Cassidy. Grant, would you mind telling us about yourself."

"Certainly, Miss Sommers. Well, I am originally from Jacksonville, Florida, and I joined the United States Navy after two years of college. I spent 14 years with the Navy, first as a corpsman and later as a diver, but my goal was to be an officer, so the Navy helped me finish my degree. Eventually, I was accepted to Officer's Candidate School. I got my MBA from San Diego State and ended up in health care administration in Bethesda, Maryland. My folks moved to Hendersonville not too long ago, and Mrs. Hughes and I were visiting last month and reading the newspaper and just happened to see this position listed, so I applied. Beth and I were thinking about life after the Navy. We wanted to be closer to family and out of Bethesda, so here we are. I am very grateful to Miss Sommers for the challenge she has offered me, and I hope to exceed all of her expectations."

"Hoo-rah, baby!" exclaimed Nick as he stood up and offered Grant a high five from across the table. Grant quickly stood up, slapped Nick's palm and smiled back. Nick had met Grant during the interview process and had liked him immediately. Grant was a guy that had an air of immediacy around him, a no-bullshit type that would get things done. A far cry from the previous administrator, Maureen Sullivan, who strolled out of Woodmont every day at precisely five thirty, four thirty on Fridays, and was constantly looking for someone else to problem solve for her. Amy went around the room and made sure Grant knew everyone.

"Oh, and I'm also looking forward to helping Chef here get in shape." Grant patted his belly as Cassidy and Jessica snickered.

"Grant, this is Jeanine Perkins. Jeanine is our Director of sales, and this is Christina Jenson. She's on the sales team. You already know Penny, Alicia Tomeny is our social worker, you've met Jessica, this is Anastasia, our health and wellness coach, and of course, Lisa Simoneaux, Lisa handles admissions for Overbrook and lucky for you, she knows Medicare like the back of her hand." The ladies smiled and offered Grant and Cassidy their greetings and their assistance. Nick looked around the table and was thankful for Grant's presence. Daniel Stern was off today, so there were eight women at the table, Percy, the concierge, himself and now Grant.

"And Miss Sommers, I need to point out that with the arrival of Mr. Hughes to the team, the estrogen to testosterone balance at this table, while still way out of balance, has at least moved in the right direction." Percy looked up from his notes and placed the ink pen to his lips and winked at Nick.

"And just what are you trying to say, Chef?" Nick winked back at Percy as he thought about the changes Amy had made in a short period of time. Under the previous administration, the morning meetings happened only twice a week and were often rife with finger pointing and excuses. In the five weeks that Amy Sommers had been in charge, the staff meetings had taken on a tone of teamwork and problem solving. Everyone in the room was genuinely interested in success, and even though Woodmont had a long way to go to reach financial success, Amy truly believed this group could do it – and they in turn believed in her. Amy put her team first so that they, in turn, would put their people first. She was certainly much more capable than Nick expected, given how unsure of herself she was her first couple of days here.

"Nick, I took a stroll through the dining room on my way out last night. I must say it certainly looked like everyone was enjoying themselves. Your staff really makes things happen."

"Thank you, Miss Sommers."

"Nick, seriously, Amy is fine."

"Yes, of course."

"OK, if we can please switch gears. I want to share a story about my first day here and turn that into a commitment to you all, so if you don't mind, please humor me for a minute. That first day I arrived about eight and I was walking through Overbrook and came up on Chet Bannon as he was leaving the assisted living dining room. Chet was full of crumbs from his breakfast. We all know he is also a bit palsied, which makes eating challenging for him, but he had a grease stain on him, crumbs from a biscuit and a blob of jelly on his shirt. I did stop and introduce myself so I could clean him up, but I *should not* have had to. If our people were doing their job, he wouldn't have left the dining room looking like that. But it has to be more than that. They have to want to do their job not just because it's their job, but because it is wrong to let someone, anyone, leave a dining room looking like Chet did that morning. When things like that happen, it makes me wonder what else the staff is allowing to happen. So from today going forward, I need a commitment from my team and from the staff, from the housekeepers to the drivers and everyone in between, that everyone will clean up the crumbs. Those crumbs may take the form of a piece of paper blowing across our front lawn, someone needing help getting into a car, an Alzheimer's patient needing some extra time in the shower, or one of Nick's cooks taking an extra second or two to garnish a plate. We need to instill pride in our teams. Start catching them doing something right instead of wrong, and turning Woodmont into the community that I know it can and will become. Are you all with me? Who will help me clean up the crumbs today?

"Hoo-rah, Miss Sommers!" exclaimed Grant.

"Oh my. Well, if that means yes, then I say hoo-rah also," beamed Percy. Grant smiled and shook his head.

"Yes sir, Percy, that's an emphatic yes."

"Well, hoo-rah to you too, Mr. Grant Hughes."

Amy waited for the laughter to die down and thought to herself how the relationship between Percy and Grant would develop. Percy Bishop, a gay man that loved pastel ties with matching socks and Grant, the no-nonsense Navy veteran. Grant would have to have a very close relationship with the lead concierge, the first person most everyone met when they walked into Overbrook's front door. The rest of the team then took their turn giving updates and pledging their commitment to Amy's mantra. Nick tried to pay attention, but found he was drifting off. He had so much to do and, with maybe one or two exceptions, he would not see these people again until tomorrow morning. Nick looked at Amy and Amy caught his eye, but he quickly looked away. Nick smiled to himself and looked at Amy again, and she caught his eye and smiled back.

"Nick?"

"Yes ma'am?"

"Do you have any news for us?"

"Well, I am concerned about Colonel Armstrong. I don't think he is eating much of anything these days. Coffee in the morning and his meals often come back just barely eaten, although he claims that everything is fine."

"Nick would you like me to pay a visit to Mr. Armstrong? Maybe just a courtesy call and see if I can get anything out of him?"

"Yes, please Penny, would you? Other than that, Miss Sommers, I think we're good in hospitality. We're putting the finishing touches on our Memorial Day picnic, the staff has for the most part come to terms with the takeover, and Mr. Torres is getting the job done. The Dodger called out today, so I guess I am cooking today."

Grant offered Nick a puzzled look. "Who's the Dodger, Chef?"

"Bobby Dodge, one of my lunch guys. He's a really good cook, but he struggles with multiple bouts of the brown-bottle flu and can't seem to find the maturity he needs to succeed in life. He likes wearing a Dodgers ball cap, but I started calling him Dodger after that character in Dickens' Oliver Twist, the artful Dodger. You know, the one that was always dodging the authorities, the 12-year-old orphan that ran this children's underworld crime ring. You remember, right?"

"Oh, I remember trying to read Oliver Twist in high school, Nick."

"Of course, Miss Sommers. Oliver Twist's theme was social repression and the problems created by an unjust society. Dickens created the Dodger to lend an aura of authenticity to that novel. See, Dodger spoke in this carefully researched street dialect and ..." Nick realized that he was getting blank stares from most of the room. "Um, well, it's not that important."

"Nick, let's make sure we are tracking his absences, please."

"Yes ma'am, of course."

"OK, thank you, Nick. Good news people, we're getting a bus. Harriett has purchased a 15-passenger bus for us that will be arriving next week, and the corporate folks are going to put a unique wrap on it, maybe our logo or something similar. Cassidy, there's no need for you or any of the drivers to get a commercial license. This will be a white Ford with a wheel chair lift, an automatic, and it doesn't have air brakes. I believe the wrap will be done by someone in Atlanta, so we should see the bus by the end of next week."

"Amy, who's deciding logo placement?" asked Jeanine.

"I think that either Harriett or Rivers will, but I'm not sure. I do know that the I/T guys called and asked me if we had some stock photos they could look at, but other than that, all I know is we're getting a bus. That means we won't have to rent anymore, which will be great for the members. Cassidy, I want you and Franklin to go to the Verandas in Columbia next week. They have the same bus, and I want you to be familiar with this vehicle before it arrives so you can give the other drivers tips the day it arrives. Will you please make that happen?"

"Yes ma'am, that's a great idea."

"One last item, I'm going to host an all-staff meeting and since we have three shifts and so many employees, I want to have three separate meetings for each shift, maybe four. Here's what I'm thinking. In two weeks on Wednesday, we have a 7 a.m. and a 2 p.m. meeting. The following Thursday, we have a 3 p.m. and a 10 p.m. Our ballroom is open those days. The meetings should last about 30 minutes or so but I think with this schedule, everyone should be able to make the meeting. And last thing, I would like my department heads at all four meetings. Each of you will have five minutes for any topic you believe should be brought to the staff's attention. I'll want to approve your topic at least five days prior, which should give you time to make any adjustments. Any questions?" Daniel Stern spoke up first.

"Did ya say we gotta go to all four them meetins, Miss Sommers?"

"That's correct, Daniel. Each one of you will have five minutes to go over anything that you would like to convey to the entire staff, understand?"

"Yes, Miss Sommers, I understand."

"Thank you, Nick."

Daniel looked down at his notebook and shook his head.

"If there are no further questions, then that's a wrap. Have a great day everyone." Nick gathered up his clipboard and folder then held the door for everyone as they left. Amy was the last one to leave and as she was leaving, she caught Nick's eye.

"Nick, I remember trying to read Oliver Twist when I was in high school lit, but it sounds like you were one of those guys that set the curve in English class. You must read a lot?"

"I actually have a degree in English Lit, Miss Sommers, from Louisiana State in Baton Rouge."

"You have a degree in literature, Nick? I never would have guessed."

"Come on, Miss Sommers, I'll walk with you. May I carry something for you?"

"That's very kind. Would you mind holding my purse for me?" Amy held out her red and gold Marc Jacobs purse. Nick hesitated. Amy grinned, then handed him her black leather laptop bag. "That was a close call, boss. I almost took you up on that one."

"Oh, I seriously doubt you would have carried my purse, Nick."

"Well, I guess we won't know, will we?"

"So you're from Louisiana?"

"Yes ma'am, from Hammond. It's a small town on the north side of Lake Ponchartrain, maybe 60 miles from New Orleans."

"And have you always cooked?"

"Well growing up in south Louisiana, sure, everyone cooks." They reached the elevator and Amy stopped and hit the call button.

"Miss Sommers, if we take the stairs you may have a bit more time to pry some more information out of me." Amy looked at Nick, glanced at the glowing red call button then turned back to Nick. "Ok Nick, we'll take the stairs, but what I meant was have you always been in the restaurant business?"

"I guess so. In high school, I started washing dishes at the Jacmel Inn, the only nice restaurant in Hammond. Then I bussed tables and one night, the salad guy didn't show up. Chef Harry threw me on salads and I never looked back." They reached the bottom of the staircase and Nick had to resist the urge to bolt up the stairs two at a time. He let Amy take the first step up then matched her stride.

"So, what made you major in literature? I would have guessed you have a degree in business." Damn, this woman moves so slow he thought.

"My Dad was an oil engineer, he worked offshore a lot and, uh, he wasn't around much. My Mom was a school teacher, and I guess she was more of an influence on me. I suppose there was a time when I thought I would teach, but I had restaurant jobs during my college years and I really loved it. So did my Mom, because I cooked a lot at home. She was very proud of me when we opened the Tavern. How about you, Miss Sommers? Always been a nurse?"

"Honestly, it was something I dreamed about when I was a little girl. Whenever we played dress up, I was always the nurse." They reached the top and turned towards the office suite.

"When the boys in your neighborhood played army, did you ever join them so you could be the nurse and bandage their pretend wounds?"

"*Oh my gosh!* Yes I did." she said sheepishly. "So how long did you have the restaurant?" He opened the door to the suite of offices that Amy shared with Jessica and the sales team. "Eight years. Listen Miss Sommers, I really need to get going. Do you mind if I just drop your bag on this table?"

"Oh yes, that's fine, Nick. Thank you very much." Nick turned and headed out.

"You're welcome, Miss Sommers."

"And please call me Amy," she called, but he was already on the other side of the threshold and the door was closing. Jessica came out of her office and smiled.

"My gosh, Amy. Was Nick helping you carry your school books? You lucky gal."

Amy shook her head as she gathered up her things and walked into her office. "I wouldn't go that far. He asked, so I said yes, and we were having this pleasant conversation. Then as soon as I asked him about his restaurant, he dropped everything and ran. I'll have to remember that Jessica." Amy placed her morning collection of folders on her desk, then unloaded her laptop and plugged it in. "Amy, I'm sure that he still has a hard time dealing with all of those memories. His restaurant was pretty popular, and he and his wife were well known."

"He and Daniel were the only salaried positions that we kept on and honestly, I didn't even see Nick's resume when I was going through the initial process. I was just told that CSM wanted him to stay on, but I tell you what, Jess. That first day, he sure acted like he wanted to be let go. Then he called me fat and boy was I mad. I was certain we didn't need him around." Jessica put her hands on her hips and lowered her right eyebrow.

"Amy, Nicholas St. Germaine called you *fat* your first day on the job?"

"Well, um, not exactly. You see, he told me I should take the stairs."

"He told you that you needed to take the stairs?"

"OK, well he suggested the stairs over the elevator, you see, and I wanted to take the elevator."

"But it's only one floor."

"OK, so now you're calling me fat too? Thanks, Jessica!"

"Oh my, someone's insecure." Amy folded her arms across her chest, spun on her heels and faced the window.

"Amy Sommers, first of all you are gorgeous and no one in their right mind can label you fat. Second, just because Nick suggested you take one flight of stairs instead of the elevator, doesn't mean he thinks you're fat. You're really reading too much into that episode. Third, he's a seriously hot slice of manhood that I would like to keep around here, so please don't go getting any ideas, got it? Mr. Alexander has kind of let himself go in the last couple of years, and a girl needs some eye candy, right? Right, Amy?" Amy didn't move. "Um, ok, well then if you need me, I'll be in my office." Amy turned around and faced Jessica.

"Nick is pretty hot, isn't he?" They both giggled. "Oh my God, would you listen to us? I swear, we sound like a couple of high school girls. My apologies, Jess. Sorry if I came off a little insecure about my weight." Amy sat down behind her desk and started shuffling papers.

"I've been through the dining room a couple of times during off hours and have seen him just staring out the window. The first time I walked over to him and said hello and asked him what he was looking at. He said, 'Nothing,' and walked away without even looking at me. So now, if I see him doing that, I just leave him alone. He's doing a nice job, but I really need a team and I just don't feel like he's on the team. It's more like he's this separate part of the campus that everyone leaves alone because he's so intense and brooding. If he's staying, then he has to be a part of the team. He's going to have to realize that."

"He'll come around, Amy. Just be careful how you approach him on it."

"I know, Jessica, I know. That's going to be tough. I really need to think it through first. Listen, thank you so much for everything you do, but I have to get some work done here, OK?"

"Yes ma'am, me too."

5

Nick sat down at his desk and stared at his computer, then leaned back, put his hands behind his head and closed his eyes. At the end of April, Nick's kitchen staff had been cut by 60 hours, or one and a half full-time employees, or, as the corporate office preferred, FTE. FTE was the favorite term of bean-counters like Hamilton, who probably had never held a front-line position in his life. To Nick, an FTE was Xavier, a dedicated cook that would come in, get the job done and push himself even in the face of adversity. And as Nick was asked to cut his staff, the sales team started moving more folks in. Jeanine Cartwright took charge of the sales team and she never looked back. In the last 45 days, Woodmont had nine new residents move in. Overbrook was already full, but the independent side had room to grow.

Nick had to lay off Jimmy in mid-April, but found a position for him at a popular bistro downtown. Then Rich quit because the pace became too demanding but Rich never had much hustle in him anyway. Nick looked at his reflection in the glass and shook his head. He sat up, rubbed his face and thought about taking Theo out to dinner tonight. He picked up his phone and shot a quick text to his son, "dinner tonight at Stella? I'm buying." His days were now so full that time was flying. When Heather was let go, the departmental bookkeeping was transferred to the department heads which meant another ten to twelve hours of work per week. He thought about quitting several times, only to decide against it. This place kept him busy, kept his mind occupied and when he had a lot on his mind, he was not thinking about Robin. Might as well stick around and see how things turn out. His office telephone rang. It was Dawn.

"Chef your three o'clock interview just drove through the front gate."

"OK, thank you, Dawn." Nick had a part-time cook's position open and this applicant looked very good on paper. She was a young woman that had graduated from the local culinary school and worked in her last kitchen job for two years. Her culinary school instructors and her last Chef had given Nick very positive reviews. He didn't want this gal to have any surprises about the size and scope of this place, so he planned on giving her a full tour of the campus. Nick stood up and walked into the kitchen.

"Hey Kevin, Chrissy Monroe is on her way. I'm going to give her a tour before I bring her back here, you good?"

Kevin looked up from his cutting board and offered Nick a nod of the head. Xavier's mouth fell open as he pointed at the sous Chef, then over to Nick.

"Did Chef Randall just speak? Was that what I heard? Chef Randall, you can talk?" Seriously? Man, all this time I thought you were raised by a pack of wolves and now you've just blown that theory away. You can talk! Well, now you two can spend some quality time discussing the differences between rugby and Australian Rules football." Kevin glared at Xavier, then turned and looked at the clock on the wall.

"OK, OK, the clock's ticking. Please don't yell at me, Chef."

Nick grinned and shook his head as he took off his apron, popped a peppermint in his mouth and washed his hands. Kevin Randall and Xavier James had been with him at the Tavern in similar positions. Kevin was his Chef de cuisine at Stone Avenue the last year Nick owned it, and he stayed on with the second owner after Nick sold out. Xavier had been Nick's sous Chef. Kevin was the first person he called after accepting the offer at Woodmont, Xavier the second. The two cooks could not be more diametrically opposed, yet they worked together as if they were joined at the mind. Kevin was 5-foot-8 with long blonde hair that he kept in a ponytail and green eyes tucked behind round Harry Truman-style glasses. He was very quiet, shy and methodical. In his spare time, he played the guitar and ran marathons; his goal was to qualify for the Boston Marathon, which for his age (31) meant he had to finish a qualifying marathon in under three hours and ten minutes. He finished almost four minutes off in his last race. Kevin often handed out assignments to the kitchen staff on 4 x 6 note cards, and counted on Xavier to follow up and provide any vocal advice if required.

Xavier James was 6-foot-4, a barrel-chested African-American that had played college football for two years at Clemson until losing his scholarship to knee injuries. Xavier shaved his head daily, yet sported a different facial hair arrangement almost weekly. Xavier would take two days off then show up with a soul patch, a thick moustache or a goatee. Xavier had grown up on his parent's farm. His mom and dad owned a large commercial operation, but Xavier had convinced them to switch to organic farming methods at just the right moment in time. In five years, the James family farm had gone from just another corn and okra producer getting commodity prices to a sought-after label that supplied the local Whole Foods with beautiful heirloom peas – black-eye peas, pink-eye, lady, purple crowders, Texas cream and red zippers – along with patty pan and crook neck squash, okra, onions and collards. Nick had met Xavier when he showed up at the Tavern with a sample of the farm's harvest. Months later, when Xavier had asked Nick for a cook's position, Nick immediately took him up on the offer. Xavier wanted to have his own restaurant near the farm, but he didn't know the business. He hoped to glean as much information as possible from Nick so that when the time came to open the James Family restaurant, Xavier would be prepared. Nick knew he was very lucky to have both guys on his team. Before he left the kitchen, he reminded Xavier, Alex and Flo to please behave, because we don't want Miss Monroe to think she is interviewing at an insane asylum. Alex looked at Nick and responded,

"And why not?" Flo put her hands in the air.

"I'm leaving in 30 seconds, Chef, so you ain't got nuthin' to worry about from me, but Sleepy here is trouble."

Alex "Sleepy" Smith had cooked for Nick at Woodmont for three months and at the Stone Avenue Tavern for about two years. Alex was a 6-foot-1 goofball of a guy always on the lookout for a cheap joke. He was born with deformed eyelids, and the corrective surgery had left him with droopy eyes that gave one the impression he was either permanently stoned or had just woken up from a nap. He had carried the nickname "Sleepy" for many years, and didn't seem to mind. Nick took off his hat and headed for the front desk, checking his phone for an answer from Theo. "major accounting final on horizon pop, sorry."

"OK get it done kid," he responded.

"Good afternoon Dawn, is this Miss Monroe over in the far corner?" Dawn picked up her phone to answer another call, smiled, nodded her head, and said, "It's a great day at Woodmont. How may I help you?"

"Miss Monroe? Good afternoon, Nick St. Germaine." Chrissy Monroe stood up. She was a pretty brunette with short dark brown hair that Nick guessed was recently dyed, perhaps five-and-a-half-foot tall and dressed in a white blouse, black cowboy boots, and black denim jeans held up by an enormous silver, cowboy belt buckle. She said good morning, but Nick was drawn to the tip of a green tentacle tattooed on her neck, which of course meant she probably had an entire octopus etched into her skin. Well, she's definitely tough, he thought.

"So Miss Monroe, what do you know about Woodmont?" Nick asked. "Well apparently, not much. I knew this was a retirement community but honestly Chef, it's gorgeous. It's more like a Ritz Carlton." As Chrissy talked, Nick could not help but notice the silver tongue stud that bounced around inside her mouth as if it were a solitary piece of shiny popcorn in a hot-air popcorn popper. Why would a cook do that to their tongue, he wondered? They walked through the lobby and headed towards the soda fountain with Chrissy beside him.

"Then I'll start at the beginning. Woodmont is a CCRC, a continuing care retirement community. The buildings you saw up front are all independent living, or IL. Those are basically apartments for folks that are retired, well off and finished taking care of a house. We currently have 156 residents in IL, with access to three dining venues. The 1949 is our soda fountain, where we offer an old-school Steak & Shake-style menu. Then we have our main dining room, which serves lunch and dinner six days a week and a big Sunday brunch, but no Sunday dinner. On the other side of the dining room in the far corner is The Armory, basically our gentlemen's pub with darts, pool, cards and such. The men put some black and white pin-ups of Betty Grable and Rita Hayworth in there so I'm not going to include that room on the tour. We have dry snacks and a happy hour on Wednesday night that is pretty popular, but very seldom do we offer any hot food, just a lot of liquid refreshments." Nick walked through the swinging aluminum doors of the 1949.

"Cool!"

The black and white checkerboard floor held 12 round, chrome-accented, Formica-covered tables of four. The bar's surface was covered in Zinc and had a lovely patina to it. Behind the counter was a large mirror faced with wood shelving, on which rested an assortment of beer mugs, coffee cups, parfait glasses and tall milk shake glasses. The back counter had two Waring, triple-spindle milk shake mixers sitting in front of a white, subway-tile back splash.

Nick walked behind the counter while Chrissy took a seat in one of the red, vinyl-covered barstools.

"In here we keep eight flavors of ice cream. We serve malted milks, milk shakes, banana splits and sundaes. We also have our own soda water dispenser right here so we can make old-school egg creams and root beer floats. We have two local beers on tap. The '49 gets pretty busy on Saturdays when we can get a lot of grand kids in here, but our folks like this place, too. We have a separate menu for the '49, burgers, chicken salad, grilled cheese, club sandwiches, chili cheese fries and such. You know, what's funny is when our new owners came in – that's Creek Side Management – they gave us a wellness menu with six low-fat, high-fiber items, a vegetable stir fry, pork tenderloin with a green apple vinaigrette; no one wants that stuff. I mean seriously, if you're an 85-year-old millionaire, are you really going to be concerned about your cholesterol? Hardly. We sell more root beer floats in one weekend than we do any of those wellness items all year." Chrissy smiled and looked around. The table tops held squirt bottles of ketchup and mustard and little napkin dispensers that looked like old fashioned Coca Cola machines. The walls were decorated with black and white photos from the '40's and '50's: young men in white t-shirts with cigarettes rolled up in their sleeves, a young couple on a swing in a city park, smiling girls in poodle skirts in a dance hall, a fire fighter showing off his massive biceps in front of a fire station, Ford and Chevy hot rods outside of early drive-ins, smiling bare-chested young men on a beach, a pilot smiling in front of a fighter jet as he touched the name "Naughty Natalie" on the jet's nose.

"All of those photos are our members."

"Really?"

"Oh, yeah, the pilot is my buddy, Willie Armstrong, and that's him in front of his F-86 in Korea. The fireman is big Chet Bannon, who lives in Overbrook now. That's him in front of his station in Memphis. This couple on the swing is the Hemmers, and that's Central Park. Pretty cool, huh?"

"Yeah, very cool."

"OK, Miss Monroe let's go to the main dining room. Right this way, please." They left the 1949, walked around the corner past the hostess stand and into the main dining room.

"It's beautiful in here, Chef." The dining room was actually three rooms of slightly different sizes, each room separated from the other by a partial wall that extended out only about six feet. The walls were covered in lightly stained walnut paneling. The tables were covered in white cloth and topped with black napkins, shimmering tableware and neatly polished glasses. Each table was centered with a handcrafted bronze luminary that bore the outline of an oak tree. The east side of the room was bordered by eight-foot windows shaded by pine-wood blinds and cream-colored curtains. Each dining room featured a tray ceiling with plenty of recessed lighting. Brass wall sconces gleamed against the wood walls.

"I agree. Jack Carrollton, the developer, wanted to build something timeless. The floor is antique heart of pine that was reclaimed from several of our local textile mills. All the art work in here is original, too, and I believe all of the artists are Southern. That one over there may be my favorite; it's a peach orchard in the spring, one not far from here, maybe near Gaffney." Nick walked to the other side of the dining room and stood in front of the oil painting as Chrissy looked out the window at the pond. Nick took a deep breath as he stared at the peach orchard in full bloom.

Spring time was his favorite time to ride. He loved being out here with his wife and friends, and this was the perfect size group; there were only eight on this ride and everyone was in very good shape, so there was no one to slow the group down. The roads around Gaffney undulated; a few tough climbs and plenty of rolling hills that meandered through the orchards that were now in full bloom. It was one of those painfully beautiful days, acres of pink blossoms set against a brilliant blue sky with the high green and slate Blue Ridge mountains off to the northwest. The sound that a group of healthy riders averaging 20 miles an hour generated was unique, a blend of mechanical whirring and purposeful breathing made intermittent by the wind rushing across Nick's ears. The wind shifted from the northwest to the west, and they suddenly had a 10-mile-an-hour tailwind. Robin heard everyone talking about the orchards, so she launched an attack. She stood up on the pedals and took off, glancing underneath her left arm to see if anyone came with her. Pamela responded first, not to be outdone by the only other girl on the ride then Sam yelled out, "Attack!" to let everyone know that someone was off the front. Nick looked over his left shoulder to make sure there wasn't a car approaching, clicked up one gear, swung out into the road, moved his hands to the end of the bars, gritted his teeth and stood up on the pedals, setting off after his wife. Robin had wisely chosen a small valley to launch her attack and was now at the bottom of the uphill side, climbing towards a small rise perhaps a quarter mile in the distance. Nick was going for all he was worth, but was quickly distracted by the graceful, athletic figure of his wife. Her trim body was purposely swaying left to right, ponytail bobbing out of her helmet like a blonde metronome keeping time to her movement. Her calf muscles strained against her skin and her bottom – the envy of everyone else on this ride – bulged against the tight Lycra shorts. She had such a fluid motion every ounce of energy she generated was transferred to the road. Robin's Cannondale was soon putting distance on the rest of the group. Nick had latched onto Sam's wheel, and behind Nick was Jeremy. They soon caught Pamela and they continued to work together, each taking short, 20-second pulls at the front. It was no use. Robin had crested the climb and now had her head down, her upper body flush against the top tube of the bike, hands on the very front of the bars. She was pushing a big gear, probably pretending to be screaming towards the finish line at the Olympics. No one was going to catch her. Sam had just taken his pull at the front and as he slid past Nick, he yelled, *"Damn, that woman is so hot!* What does she see in a dope like you, St. Germaine?"

Nick gave up the chase, moved to the left of the road, sat up on his Bianchi, cupped his hands over his mouth and yelled as loud as he could, *"I love you sweetheart!"*

Sam looked over at Nick, laughed and put his right hand on Nick's left shoulder. "You're one lucky SOB."

"Chef?"

"Yes ma'am?" Nick looked over at Chrissy, who was at his left shoulder. Shit, how long had he been standing here?

"Uh, Ok, let's, uh, continue on downstairs please, Miss Monroe." Nick and Chrissy headed out of the dining room and down the staircase, stopping at the entrance to the Chicago Room. "This is our private banquet room, which we call the Chicago. Right now, there is a card game going on, so we won't go in, but it's pretty cool. Every month, we host a live dance with music and drinks. There's a dance floor and a great sound system and a nice wooden bar, and we even have a disco ball. The walls are done in trompe l'oeil style that gives you the perspective of being on a rooftop in the middle of Chicago and the lights can be adjusted to give it a day time or night time feel. It's so damn cool. OK Let's head outside, please." Nick opened the door and they walked across the parking lot to Overbrook. "As you can see now, Miss Monroe, this campus is shaped like a giant X, albeit the front part of the X is four stories high and this one in the back, Overbrook, is two stories and has plenty of right angles to it. I'll bet if you saw this place from the air it would look like a giant Lego spider with only four legs. Does that make sense?"

"Not really, Chef because spiders have eight legs and insects have six, I think hornets and such have four legs but they also have wings." Nick put his left hand up.

"OK sorry about that Miss Monroe. If seen from the air this place would not resemble a spider but perhaps a hornet with a rectangular body and no wings. Does that make sense?"

"Got it."

They walked into the back entrance, crossed through the hallway and exited on the other side so that Nick could take Chrissy into Overbrook's main entrance. "So this is our health care facility, or nursing home, Overbrook Station. The phrase 'nursing home' comes with all sorts of negative connotations, so I won't use it again. Overbrook is divided up into three different disciplines: assisted living, skilled nursing and memory care, and each of those is made up of two neighborhoods with a common dining room in the middle of each neighborhood. Assisted living has two units, Pelham and Hudson. A/L is for folks that can make their own decisions, but need help with the daily chores of getting dressed, going to the bathroom and moving around. Memory care is just like it sounds; that's where our dementia and Alzheimer's folks are. Our memory care unit takes up the entire second floor, it's on the same level as our kitchen, we have Hawkins to the right and Laurens is on the left side with a common dining room in the middle. That area is the reason why this building has so many right angles to it. The folks with Alzheimer's live in the moment so the memory care unit was designed with lots of turns to it, the hallways twist and turn so to our residents it always feels interesting, it's one more way to help fight boredom. It's much more interesting than long straight hallways. The memory care unit has locks on their doors because those folks need limited access otherwise they may just wander into another part of the campus. Skilled nursing takes up the two neighborhoods to the left of the entrance or on the east side and is divided into rehab and skilled care. Rehab is for folks that are probably on Medicare. They're 67 or older and are recuperating from surgery or some sort of accident and they need somewhere to recover. Those folks are here short term, anywhere from seven days to maybe three months. Skilled care is the biggie. That's where we take care of folks that have a variety of debilitating conditions plus some of these folks may have some form of dementia. They need help moving around, so there's a lot of wheelchairs, scooters or other assistive devices plus the folks that live there average 83 years old. The people working there are a very special breed of care givers, incredibly patient and kind." Nick opened the door to Overbrook just as Ronnie Jones was coming out. "Hey there, Ronnie, please say hello to Chrissy Monroe. Miss Monroe is interviewing for a cook's position here. Ronnie is one of our drivers and occasionally doubles as a tour guide."

"Hello Chrissy, pleased to meet you."

Chrissy smiled and returned Ronnie's greeting. They continued through the door, then Nick turned to the front desk. "And this is Percy, our lead concierge. Percy, this is Chrissy Monroe. She's interviewing for a cook's position."

"Oh, look at that tentacle on your neck girl. Who did your ink?"

"I got this one at the Five & Dime in Columbia. It's still a work in progress though. It's a giant green squid."

"Such as the one in '20,000 Leagues under the Sea?' " asked Nick.

"Um, as in calamari, Chef," Chrissy said, smiling.

"I see. OK, continuing on. Chat later, Percy." Percy smiled, winked at Chrissy and answered another call. "Ronnie's been here from the beginning, he's a really good guy. Percy has been here four months and he has done a great job, he is Grant's right hand man, and well, let me back up and say Grant Hughes runs Overbrook. He's our health care administrator. Maybe we'll run into him, anyway this is the lobby of Overbrook. If we turn to our left, we have our rehab unit, Augusta followed by Burgess. Then upstairs we have our memory care units, Hawkins and Laurens. If we turn to our right we have the assisted living neighborhoods, Pelham and Hudson." Nick led Chrissy towards the Augusta neighborhood and Nick introduced Chrissy to one of the nurses, a short, pudgy woman with caramel-colored hair that was brushed back over her shoulders, green eyes and a large silver cross around her neck. "Hey Penny, this is Chrissy Monroe. She's interviewing for a cook's position with us. Penny Rhodes is our director of nursing in Overbrook." Nick reached out and put his right arm around Penny's shoulder and gently scratched her back.

"Hello, Penny," smiled Chrissy. "Your hair is beautiful."

"Oh thank you so much. You know, Chrissy, we could use someone to look after Nick so he doesn't have to be here so much. You think you could do that for us?" Chrissy looked at Nick, then at Penny. "Just kidding, Chrissy, pleasure to meet you. You're going to love it here."

"Oh, uh, ok."

"Everyone good today, Penny?"

"Oh sure, just the usual grab bag of chaos and love, faith and healing. I'm going to do a lap outside the building, grab some sunshine and then jump back into the fray."

"OK, see you, Penny. Let's head this way please, Miss Monroe." Nick looked over his shoulder. "Penny has been here about as long as I have, and she is just brilliant. If Grant ever gets promoted or moves on, Penny would be a natural for that job. So now, let's turn to our right and we will head through Burgess." As they walked through the hallway, Nick smiled and said good afternoon to everyone they met, mostly folks that looked like they were at least 85. They moved about with a variety of assistive devices such as walkers, canes and wheelchairs. They were men and women in the twilight of their lives, recovering from their latest injury or sickness. As they were talking, Chrissy saw a woman with short, jet black hair walk up behind Nick, wink at Chrissy, and then wrap herself around Nick and squeeze until Nick begged for mercy.

"This is my baby right here, young lady, so don't get any ideas."

"And this is Candace who apparently dyed her hair black yesterday?"

"Maybe I did."

"Candace is also one of our RN's."

"Stands for really naughty," winked Candace. She whispered something in Nick's ear, causing him to blush then she strutted away.

"OK, Miss Monroe, let's uh … this is the … uh … skilled care facility, which unfortunately is where Candace works."

"I heard that, Nick," fussed Candace as she stuck her head around the corner and smiled.

"So Burgess is our skilled care unit, and we have folks that have a variety of ailments, plus they are usually past 75, plus some of them also have dementia. I know we have a memory care unit, but when one's dementia comes with additional conditions that prevent them from being able to walk, well then, they end up in skilled care. So in Burgess, we have folks that are typically wheelchair bound, may or may not have dementia, plus they typically have other medical conditions that require the attention of a nursing staff. That's where Candace comes in. She's the charge nurse in Burgess, and I promise that these are the best and most compassionate people on campus. They have to be. Now Augusta is all rehab and is very transitional; that's mostly folks that have had surgery and are recuperating and no longer qualify for a hospital bed. However, most are also on Medicare, so they are past 67. And since they are using Medicare, that's federal money. Once you climb into bed with the US government, well that means you open yourself to all sorts of federal inspection. So Miss Monroe, we have on average five health inspections per year, and the federal health inspection can last all day, or sometimes two days. So for this huge campus and all of those folks to feed, we have one kitchen that is kept spotless at all times. Our kitchen delivers three meals a day to all these neighborhoods. That's three hot meals. At this point, if you would like to run back to your car and never set foot in this building again, I will certainly understand." Chrissy looked down the hallway then back to Nick.

"May I see the kitchen now, Chef?" Nick smiled.

"Certainly, Miss Monroe, right this way."

In a few minutes, they arrived at the kitchen. Nick took her through the back entrance by the freight elevator.

"First stop is my office, and my rule is the door is always open – unless it is closed. If my door is closed, then please wait until it is open before knocking, OK? On our right side is the dish station and you can see that we have an enormous Hobart machine that sits in the far corner and it's manned by the hottest dish crew in town. "Diego! Esta es Chrissy Monroe, possible la nueva cucinar." Diego smiled and gave Chrissy a thumbs-up.

So on our back line, we have two convection ovens, a 48-gallon tilt skillet with manual tilt, a 28-gallon steam kettle, a blast-chiller and two full-size hot boxes. Up front, we have a Vulcan eight-burner range, a Blodgett steamer, a single convection oven, reach-in freezer, lots of cooler space, and my favorite, a wood-burning grill. While Chrissy was looking away, Nick sent a text message to Jessica, asking her to chat with Chrissy for five minutes. Nick never did a solo interview, but would often invite other members of the team to sit down with the candidate in order to glean a different perspective.

"Very impressive, Chef," said Chrissy. "I like all the equipment, and this place sure is clean." A very lanky man with a Marine's haircut and huge eyes approached them.

"And this is Kirby Hawkins, one of our full-time utility guys."

"Don't know anyone 'round here call me Kirby though. They all calls me String Bean, so if you pass muster with Chef here, you gets to call me String Bean, too, so long as you don't go making a mess in my purty kitchen, little lady."

"I like you, String Bean, oops, I mean, Kirby. Once I pass muster with Chef here, then you can call me Chrissy." Kirby nodded his head slowly.

"Deal, Miss Chrissy."

"Miss Monroe, shall we head to the office?" Nick offered Chrissy a seat and asked if she would care for something to drink.

"A Coke would be fine."

"OK, in the meantime, please complete this for me." Nick handed her his culinary quiz. It was a one-page sheet of 10 questions designed to gauge an applicant's basic food knowledge and desire. How many quarts in a gallon? What happens if you over-whip whipping cream? Describe the differences between braising and roasting. And then, Nick's favorite: tell me about a memorable meal. If someone described a meal that their grandmother cooked when they were younger then that was a big positive. If, however, someone described a meal at a chain restaurant or a steak house, then perhaps that person did not have an emotional attachment to their chosen profession. It was not necessarily a deal breaker, but probably signaled someone that saw the culinary arts as a job, and not a calling. Nick excused himself and headed to the soda fountain, brought Chrissy her soda, then walked over to Kevin Randall.

"Chef, I just asked Jessica to come in and chat with Chrissy, and then would you please follow up with your interview?" Xavier heard this, walked next to Kevin and looked over at Nick.

"Do you need me to interpret Chef Randall's series of grunts and squeaks into English for this young lady?" Kevin held his hand out to Xavier, palm up as if to say, "Stop!" and Xavier said, "Ok, ok, I know when to quit."

Jessica Alexander was Amy Sommer's first hire after she took over. Jessica was smart, clever, patient and had a wealth of knowledge in all matters concerning human resources. She was also five feet and eleven inches of female gloriousness. If someone told Nick that Jessica had once been a cheerleader for the Dallas Cowboys, he would have believed it. She was that much of a woman. Jessica bobbed into the kitchen wearing a knee-length, simple white linen dress, her flowing champagne-blonde hair bouncing off of her shoulders, heels clicking on the terra cotta floor. She smiled at Nick, Xavier and Kevin, and raised her left hand and offered the girl wave, her fingers moving quickly up and down then she headed towards Nick's office. The three cooks' heads glided right to left in unison, silently tracking Jessica's movement through the kitchen as she effortlessly parted the sea of mid-afternoon activity, leaving an estrogen laden contrail that quieted everyone in its path. Jessica knocked on Nick's door, introduced herself to Chrissy, closed the door then sat down in Nick's chair. She looked through the window at the three cooks, stood up and in one motion, dropped the blinds concealing the two women from view. Kevin Randall looked at Xavier and spoke up, "You were saying?"

"You know, I think that Miss Sommers is absolutely brilliant for hiring Jessica Alexander, absolutely brilliant. I really think Miss Sommers should win the Nobel Peace Prize for bringing Jessica in here, I really do. And I think we should vote for Mr. Alexander as hands-down the luckiest guy in the world." Xavier lifted the side towel off of Kevin's apron and pretended to wipe away tears of joy off his face.

"OK guys, back to work please. And Chef Randall, you know you're not supposed to wear towels, that's a potential Health Department violation, and now that Mr. James has sullied that towel with his bodily fluids, please destroy it. Kevin, let's see your menu for tonight. I want to see where we are, oh and when you talk to Miss Monroe, please try not to stare at her ink." Xavier smiled.

"Too late! I already noticed. I'll bet she has a pierced tongue, rides a Harley and watches pro football. Finally! Someone I can talk to."

"Miss Monroe or may I call you Chrissy?" asked Jessica.

"Please, Chrissy is fine."

"Has Chef St. Germaine given you a full tour?"

"Yes, he has. I think we saw the entire campus. It's ... uh ... pretty spread out around here."

"Yes, it is."

"And he has told you we are considering you for a part-time cook's position with a rate of pay at 12.15 an hour?"

"Yes ma'am, I understand that."

"Are you sincerely interested in working here at Woodmont?"

"Oh yes, of course. I would love to and I've heard very good things about Chef. I would love to be able to work here."

"What did you think of Chef St. Germaine?"

"Honestly?" smirked Chrissy.

"Yes, of course, Chrissy. It's just us girls in here, right?"

"Well, he's, uh, he's, you know, he's kind of hot," Chrissy covered her mouth and giggled. "I'm sorry. I can't believe I said that!"

Jessica smiled and leaned back. "It's OK, Chrissy, I'm sure you're not the first girl to say that."

"I'm sorry, let me try again." Chrissy stood up in her chair and smoothed out her blouse, adjusted her belt buckle, then sat back down.

"Mrs. Alexander, Chef St. Germaine is one of those people that someone like me would love to work for."

"And why would that be Miss Monroe?"

"Well, um, back when I was cooking at the Bijou, I can remember going out after work and us restaurant types, we tend to congregate after work and we all know one another. The ones that cooked for Chef St. Germaine, they were always a little different, higher up the totem pole, maybe. It's like there is a pecking order, you know what I mean? Even at a bar, when one of the Stone Avenue guys came in, you could just tell. They stood straighter than someone like me that was working at a tourist trap like the Bijou. Even the ones that worked at the Poinsett Station Grill were a bit jealous, maybe. They would never say it, but you could tell that it was there. I know his bartender, Kelly, and Kelly was always so proud to say that he worked for Nicholas St. Germaine. One night, I was at Big Joe's and I introduced Kelly to this guy, Dustin that cooked at one of the hotels downtown. When Kelly said he worked for Chef St. Germaine, Dustin was quiet for a minute and then said that if they ever needed a cook, maybe Kelly would put in the good word for him. That's the kind of reputation he had."

"I ate at the Tavern at least a half-dozen times, Miss Monroe, and I have to say it was just delicious. We always had a great time and it was so effortless. Does that make sense? It was always busy, but we were always taken care of, even though I was no one special."

"But everyone was special at the Tavern, and that was the beauty of it. Everyone was special to Robin and Nick when they walked through their front door. The one time I ate there, I was treated like the queen, and I was just a lowly cook. One of the wait staff recognized me and told Nick that a cook from the Bijou was there, and they treated me as if I were the Chef of the White House." Chrissy ran her hand through her hair and looked around the office. "You know, when his wife was killed it was like there was no sense of right and wrong in our world, you know what I mean? It was like this great chasm had opened up and swallowed up everything that was good. I cook to make people happy, that's why most of us do it. We express ourselves through our cooking, and Chef St. Germaine made lots and lots of people feel special and happy at his place." Chrissy lowered her eyes. "So how come he gets paid back with a mountain of misery? That just doesn't make any sense at all, does it?"

Jessica looked around for a tissue but there were none. She wiped her eye with her finger.

"No, Miss Monroe, it doesn't make any sense at all. Listen, I appreciate your time and I'm sure you'll be a great fit here at Woodmont. Do you have any questions for me?"

"No, ma'am."

"It was a pleasure chatting with you. Have a great day."

"You too, Mrs. Alexander."

Jessica left the office and saw Kevin Randall look up at her. "Next?" Kevin Randall nodded, put his knife down, washed his hands and headed to the office. Jessica walked up to Nick and kept her eyes low, because she knew they were still a bit misty.

"I like her a lot, Nick. I think she will do a fine job for you, and she is very excited about working for you." Jessica turned and walked out of the kitchen. Nick watched her walk away, and thought about how wonderful it was to have a beautiful woman stand close to him even if for just a minute. He felt a hand on his shoulder and he turned and saw Tony Torres.

"How you doing today, Skipper?"

"Fine, Tony, fine."

"Jessica is something else, isn't she?"

"Yes sir."

"So Chef, when are you going to get back out there?"

"Get back out where, Tony?"

"Come on, Chef, you need a date." Nick looked down and with his right hand, he spun his wedding ring around his left ring finger. "Maybe so, Tony."

"Chef, have you …"

"OK, I have work to do, Mr. Torres. Things to do, let's make it happen, please."

"Yes sir." Tony headed out to the dining room just as Kevin Randall came out of the office and caught Nick's eye. Tony offered a thumbs-up. Xavier watched Kevin, and shook his head.

"Chef Randall, have you been in there all this time drawing stick figures for that young lady? You cook here. You peel potato here. Chop carrot this way." Kevin picked up his Chef's knife, and with his right thumbnail, plucked the blade slowly as he glared at Xavier.

"OK, Chef, you don't have to lose your temper. Damn! Can't anyone around here take a joke?" Nick shook his head and headed to his office. He walked in, said hello to Chrissy, opened his blinds and sat down.

"So Miss Monroe, what do you think?" As he sat down, Nick saw one of his waiters, Jackson Mallory, approach from the left side of the kitchen and Sleepy approached from the right side. They met directly behind Chrissy Monroe, in full view of Nick. They bowed to one another, then Jackson held his right hand up in the air. Sleepy took Jackson's hand, and Jackson pirouetted under his hand while Sleepy grinned like the goof ball that he was. They bowed to one another, then continued on their separate paths. Nick focused on Chrissy. It would take a lot more than that for him to crack. Nick looked over the culinary quiz and went immediately to the last question (tell me about a memorable meal). Chrissy had written: I grew up in Cayce, SC, and in the summer time, my Mom always made a big Sunday supper, and it was nothing for her to invite five or six of our neighbors over who would also bring a dish and I come from a big family three sisters and two brothers so that table was crowded! I guess that's why I became a cook.

"My mom was the same way," Nick said. "She loved to have a table full of guests. Do you have a favorite recipe of your mom's?"

"Oh, she loved to make chicken and dumplings! She would butcher the chickens the day before and would trim off all the extra bits of chicken fat, put those in a pot with a bit of water and would render the fat on the stove. She would cool the fat and the next day, she would make buttermilk dumplings and would cut some of that chicken fat into the dumplings."

"Would she use baking powder or soda?"

"A little of both, but too much baking powder and the dumplings would be fragile and fall apart. Oh, and she threw in some freshly chopped parsley that we grew. Oh, and the gravy was full of carrots and onions and whatever vegetable she bought at the market or came out of the garden. We didn't have much money, but I didn't know it because we were always cooking something." Nick sat back and offered Chrissy a knowing smile.

"Miss Monroe, here's what will happen next. I will check your references, fill out the necessary paperwork, then forward that on to Mrs. Alexander. At that point, she'll authorize the background check and when that comes back OK, she'll ask you to schedule your drug screen, physical and TB test. If you so much as ran a red light in the last seven years, it's going to show up on your background check. Then Jessica will be the one that extends the offer, not me, OK? So if all that goes according to plan about three weeks from now you will spend a day in orientation, and then Woodmont will have a new cook. Any questions?"

"No, Chef, thank you very much. I won't let you down."

"The thought never entered my mind, Miss Monroe. I'll show you to the front door."

As Jessica came back into her office, she walked right past Amy.

"Jess, what's wrong?" Jessica sat down in her chair and reached for a tissue as Amy stood in her doorway.

"Well, I was interviewing an applicant for Nick and uh, she told me about Nick's wife getting killed and what an effect it had on her." Jessica reached for another tissue and blew her nose. Amy closed the door and sat down.

"Amy how does someone like Nick get up and go to work every day? If I lost Stephen, I'm not sure I could face much of anything for a long time. And Nick comes in here day after day. I would have moved away, so I wouldn't have to see the faces of people that knew what I went through. I couldn't take people whispering about me or looking at me and wondering how I was doing. This young lady said that when Nick's wife died, it cast a pall across the restaurant community in town. I'll bet Nick can't go anywhere without someone saying, 'Oh look, there's that guy that had that restaurant we really liked and then his wife got killed. Let me go ask him how he's doing.'"

Amy sat down. "I never went to his restaurant, I'm sorry to say. When I moved to Greenville, he had already sold the restaurant. Hell, even when I was married, Richard was more of a beer-and-steak guy and wouldn't have taken me to a place like that. It would have been an affront to his fragile manhood. I know Nick's restaurant was popular, but I guess I never thought about what an effect something like that could have on a community, much less on Nick personally. When my Mom died ... " Amy looked away and left her words hanging in the rapidly thickening air. Jessica wiped her eyes.

"Do you mind if I have some privacy, Amy? I'm gonna call Stephen and tell him how much I love him."

"That's a good idea, Jess. I have a report for Harriett that I should have turned in this morning." Amy got up and walked back to her office, closed the door and sat down. She stared out the window for a minute, then turned to the framed photo of her girls, Paige and Rebecca, and felt her eyes moisten. Her girls meant everything to her and unfortunately, they meant so little to their father. He rarely called them, often forgot important milestones in their lives, and had to be prodded to send a birthday present. Usually, it was just cash inside a card signed, "Love Dad." She set the frame down, looked out the window and listened to a mockingbird sing from the crepe myrtle, then turned to her laptop and set about finishing her report for Harriett.

Nick sat down at his desk and looked at the digital clock in the corner of the monitor as it flashed 8:39 p.m. The cooks had just left and the dish crew would be done shortly. He picked up the clipboard with the list of items he wanted to complete before the week was out.

Overtime Report

Cost menu for Marketing Dinner

Add new items to Point of Sale System

New Cleaning Schedule for Dish Crew

New Menu/Summer

Dessert Menu

Inventory Dishes for Overbrook

Schedule, two weeks, three weeks

Quarterly Performance Reviews/mid June

He tried to concentrate, but he was looking at too much work so he decided instead to hit the gym. He stood up, grabbed his gym bag and closed his door. As he walked out the back, he called his son. "Hey Pop, you done over there?"

"Yeah, you feel like hitting the gym? We could hit on the heavy bag or the speed bag or maybe play some hoops?"

"Sure thing, Pop. Meet you there in 15?"

"Roger that, kid. On the way." He threw his bag into his BMW wagon, yanked off his Chef's coat and threw it in the back seat, climbed in and closed the door, pressed in the clutch, made sure it was in neutral, and turned the key. The six-cylinder engaged with a satisfying growl and Nick tapped the throttle gently, engaged reverse, eased out of the clutch, drove into the mid-May evening and headed towards the gym.

6

Nick looked at his phone. 9:21 p.m. He was exhausted, having been on the job since eight thirty this morning, with still one more of Amy's damn meetings to muscle through. He looked around. The dish crew would be leaving in another five minutes, the produce order was done, and his kitchen was clean. Amy's staff meeting for the third shift would start at 10 p.m. Forty minutes to kill. He could catch up on some invoices, send Amy an overtime report or better yet, write an essay on how he could work less hours, a favorite topic of Amy's. She would constantly ask him to slow down and delegate some of his responsibility, yet in practically the same breath, she would ask him to spend an hour in Overbrook chatting with the new residents, walk the campus with her or work with Jeanine to make one of her marketing ideas come to fruition. Every minute that Amy asked of Nick meant one more additional minute spent in the kitchen trying to make up for lost time. So here he was, nearing the end of a 14-hour day. Amy would arrive shortly and tell him he looked beat, and then ask him to be on time for the 8:30 marketing meeting tomorrow morning. Amy, who strolled out of here at five forty five, five days a week and rarely worked weekends. "Gee Nick you sure have been working a lot lately. You really need to learn how to delegate." Christ! If he heard her say "delegate" one more time, he would scream. Nick could feel the tension rising.

"Lord God in heaven, *please* grant me patience with this woman!" Nick opened his filing cabinet, took out his gym bag and changed right there in his office. Black gym shorts, Under/Armour shirt and his white New Balance shoes, grabbed his Blackberry and ran downstairs to the workout room and practically leapt onto the treadmill. Amy would just have to look for him when she got here, and she said nothing about a dress code for the meeting. He would run three miles and then go directly to the third-shift staff meeting. Sure, there would be a few whistles and catcalls from the girls, but Nick wouldn't mind. Amy certainly would and how could he pass up an opportunity to make her blush? Fifteen minutes later, he had already put in 2.3 miles and worked up a delicious sweat when the lights blinked. A power surge? "No big deal," he thought. The weather was fine, so maybe somewhere nearby there was a traffic accident and someone had taken out a power pole, or maybe it was just Duke Energy fiddling with the grid, so he kept running. He grabbed his Blackberry to check the time but as soon as he picked it up, it rang with a phone call from Amy. He hit the red button and set it back down. A minute later, he received a text from Amy, so he opened it.

"u here?"

"Good Lord. Of course I'm here girl. I live here, remember?" he said out loud.

"Yes" he responded.

"n back elevator stuck betwen floor plz help"

Nick laughed out loud. "Serves you right for taking the elevator up one damn floor, woman." He jumped off the treadmill then washed his face in the bathroom. "On way" he responded and ran upstairs to find Michael, the night security guard. The lobby was empty. Nick called out, "Michael!" but didn't hear a reply. He dialed Woodmont's number and Michael answered.

"Good evening and thank you for calling.."

"Michael!"

"Yes sir, hey, is that you, Chef? What's up?"

"Where are you?"

"I'm way over in Overbrook. What's up?"

"Miss Sommers is in the freight elevator and it's stuck between floors. Please grab the elevator skeleton key and meet me there."

"Affirmative, Chef, on the way." Nick's Blackberry went off again with another text from Amy. "where r u?"

"coming" Nick replied back.

"plz hurry nick, i don't like this," responded Amy.

"shall I cxl ten pm meeting?" Amy responded with an angry face icon. Nick got to the elevator first, knocked on the door and called out, "Miss Sommers?!" He heard a muffled response.

"*Yes, of course I'm still in here!*" Michael appeared; he was already on the phone to the elevator company. He unlocked the outer door with the key and slid the door open to expose the elevator's mechanicals. The car had stopped on the way up, clearing perhaps 40 percent of the second floor. Nick tried to open the elevator car's inner door, but as hard as he tugged the door, it only opened about two inches. Nick put his face to the opening and called to Amy.

"Anybody home?"

"*Will you quit screwing around and get me the hell out of here please!*"

"Miss Sommers?" called Michael, as he covered up the phone with his hand. "Otis Elevator says they will be here in no less than 90 minutes, maybe 80, tops."

"I'm definitely cancelling that 10:00 p.m. meeting," said Nick.

"*Damnit, Nick. Do not leave me in here for that long!*"

"OK boss, give me a minute please. In the meantime, can I slide you a stick of gum, a candy bar or perhaps a stalk of celery, because a doughnut will not fit through this opening."

"*My God! You are such an ASSHOLE!*" shouted Amy.

Michael looked at Nick and winced. "Wow, she's really mad." He put the phone back to his ear and resumed his conversation with the Otis representative. Nick backed away from the elevator so he could think.

"Miss Sommers, Otis Elevator does not recommend doing anything until they get here. They said it's too dangerous to pull someone out of a stuck elevator, because the elevator may come on during an attempted rescue and cause severe bodily harm to the rescuee." Nick's Blackberry went off again. "gonna strangle u 2 as soon as u get me out".

"Sorry boss, but in the interest of your personal safety, I think that I should delegate this rescue to the authorities from

Otis Elevator. In the meantime, can I slide you a thin, grilled cheese sandwich?"

There was a long silence, then another text from Amy: "plz get me out Nick plz". Michael's cell phone rang. "Yes, Mr. Stern?" Michael backed away from the elevator to take the call. Nick began studying the door mechanism. Surely there was a way to open that inner door. After a few minutes and a few more "Yes sirs," Michael hung up the phone.

"Miss Sommers," called Michael. "I just talked to Mr. Stern. He said that in no way should we attempt a rescue, as it would be too dangerous and against all regulations regarding elevator stoppages. He asked that you sit tight until Otis gets here."

"Please, Nick," he heard Amy sigh. Nick stepped back towards the elevator and took a close look at the door's mechanicals. He found the cable that moved the door, followed the cable to a pulley, saw where the power was supplied to the door cable drive, then followed the cable to the left side of the elevator car and found a fat aluminum hook, roughly the size of a large serving spoon and shaped like the number 7. It was hooked to a stationary point on the left side of the elevator car. Nick followed the cable again and looked for anything that he might get caught on if he reached in. Satisfied that he wasn't going to get electrocuted or tangled, he cautiously reached in and carefully slid the hook up. He felt the tension come off of the inner door then applied a bit of pressure to the door. Just like that, the elevator door slid open and there was Amy Sommers, sitting in the far corner with her knees pulled up to her chest looking as if she was about to cry.

"Why so blue, Miss Sommers?"

"Please get me out of here, Nick," she pleaded as she jumped up and held her hands out to him. "Of course, boss. Michael, would you please go into the kitchen and roll one of those half-size hot boxes out here"

"Sure thing, Chef"

"Miss Sommers, I'll take your shoes and your purse, please." Amy smiled and gladly handed her black leather flats and matching handbag to Nick. "OK Miss Sommers, in a second, I'll reach down and grab you by the wrists – not the hands, but the wrists – and you're going to do the same to me. Then when I pull you up, I want you to put your feet on the wall of the elevator. Otherwise, you are going to bang your shins, OK? And no looking up my gym shorts!" Amy smiled and nodded.

"Here you go, Chef" said Michael as he wheeled the four-foot tall, stainless steel hotbox into the hallway. Nick and Michael placed it on the elevator's threshold, just in case the elevator did decide to go back down while he was pulling Amy out; this might buy him an extra second or two. When the hot box was in place, Nick took an athlete's stance, inhaled deeply, squatted down on his quads, leaned in and offered Amy his hands. She grabbed his wrists tightly and he grabbed hers. Nick started to exhale and then in one seamless motion, he stood up and easily lifted Amy out of the elevator, before she could even get her feet out in front of her. A breathless Amy Sommers ended up standing right in front of Nick, with her hands moving up from his wrists to his biceps. She closed her eyes, pulled him close, put her head on his shoulder and whispered, "Thank you."

"Well, um, I guess I will leave you two alone then," announced a somewhat nervous Michael as he headed back to the lobby. Amy stepped away from Nick, put her right hand on her forehead and called out to Michael.

"Oh, uh, thank you so much, Michael!"

"Anytime, boss. Always here for you." He offered Amy a salute, then headed off. Nick folded his arms across his chest.

"Mr. Stern is going to be mad at us." Amy twisted her hands behind her back, looked down at her feet then looked into Nick's eyes. "Thank you very much. I, uh, certainly did not want to wait for over an hour or more to get out of the, uh, elevator. Daniel will just have to get over it. And Nick, I, um, well, I apologize for calling you, well, for calling you an …asshole. I didn't mean it. I was just getting claustrophobic."

"You sure as hell did mean it," laughed Nick. "Why were you coming up here anyway? The meeting is downstairs."

"I just wanted a Diet Coke, that's all, and *Oh, damnit, the staff meeting!* Damn, you're coming correct? Damn. I probably look like hell. Oh, I need to brush my hair, I need a mirror. Oh Nick, where did you put my purse? Oh gosh, I'm going to be late. Nick, you will be at the meeting, correct?" asked Amy as she picked up her purse, then scrambled through it for a brush. Nick was pushing the hotbox back to the kitchen and looked back at Amy.

"Yes, of course Miss Sommers. I wouldn't miss it for the world."

"Will you have time to change?"

"It's nine fifty nine, Miss Sommers."

"Oh gosh, time to go!"

"Miss Sommers," called Nick, without turning around.

"Yes?"

"Stairs are to your right."

The stairs, thought Amy. She looked at the stairs, then back at Nick and had a funny feeling of déjà vu. "Yes, of course, Nick, the stairs. See you downstairs."

"Yes ma'am. See you downstairs." Five minutes later, Nick walked into the Chicago Room and headed to the front and his seat. There were probably 35 people there, 30 of whom were women, most of whom were certified nursing assistants (CNAs). As Nick walked down the center aisle, they gave him enough whistles and catcalls to rival a strip club. Amy could not help but smile as Nick approached. He was four inches taller than Amy and so handsome with his short, wavy, sandy blonde hair and olive green eyes, and was he ever in shape. Amy thought back to their initial meeting, when he was so rude to her and Rivers. He did a fine job here, but he was so melancholic. When he got upset, he just shut down, but Amy could tell he was smoldering by the look in his eyes. The fact that he was a widower certainly didn't help; Nick obviously had plenty of emotional issues that he was dealing with. After her first week, Amy had decided she would help him become a better manager and channel some of his energy into working smarter, instead of spending so much time here. Perhaps then she would earn his respect. She turned on her wireless microphone.

"Chef St. Germaine is modeling our latest uniform for the executive staff. His white New Balance running shoes are accented by black Nike gym shorts and a gleaming silver short sleeved Under/Armour shirt that is a half size too small." Nick smiled and nodded a thank you to Amy, and took his seat at the front next to Jessica, Cassidy and Grant.

"Is you and Mr. Hughes going to start dressing like that Miss Sommers?"

Amy smiled. "No Saffron, I'm just teasing our Chef here. I have to tell you that about 20 minutes ago, I was going upstairs to get a Diet Coke and the elevator broke down with only me in it." Daniel Stern walked into the room, and he glared at Amy as he headed up front. "Well, the people from Otis Elevator said they could not get here for an hour and a half, but our Chef was able to get me out in about 15 minutes." Amy turned to Nick, smiled warmly and blushed. "So thank you very much, Nick." Amy offered Nick her applause, and the staff joined in. Grant reached over and gave Nick a knuckle bump.

Saffron stood up and hollered, "Good thing it wasn't me in that elevator. I woulda dragged Nick in with me and shut that door, girl! Ninety minutes later ... *oh yeah, honey!* Rescue me baby!" Saffron held her flabby arms out wide, closed her eyes, did a little dance and snapped her fingers as the staff cheered her on. Nick smiled and just shook his head. Saffron was all of 275 pounds, and he briefly had an image of trying to pull her up and being yanked down into the elevator by her quivering mass. Saffron was very sweet and did a fine job, but she had very little decorum. A certified nurse's assistant made ten to twelve dollars an hour and had about eight weeks of training. Most of these girls were fairly low on the socio-economic scale, and had gotten their training through the local technical college using lottery money granted by the state. The turnover rate for the CNAs was horrendous under Maureen, and the good ones like Saffron were the exception. CNAs are the primary caregivers in a retirement community or nursing home, and if Amy Sommers was worth her salt, then attracting and keeping good ones should be her first concern. As Daniel took his seat, Amy smiled and said, "Thank you for joining us," then scanned the room.

"I was at a friend's house the other day and she was cooking a ham. She picked up a knife and chopped off a chunk of the ham, put it in the pot and put the ham in the oven. When I asked her why she did that, she said she didn't know, but that's how her mother always did it. She called her mom and asked her why she cut off a chunk of the ham. Her mom said that's the way her mother always did it, so my friend called her grandmother. "Grandma, why did you always cut a chunk off the ham before you put it in the oven?' Well, her grandma replied, 'So that it fit in the pot.' " Amy looked out at her staff. "Do you ever find yourself doing something over and over because that's the way you learned, and not because it's the best or right way to do it? Would anyone ever accuse you of chopping off a chunk of ham just to get it to fit in the pot?" Nick looked over at Daniel, who in turn looked at Nick, glared, shook his head and turned away.

"What you mean, Miss Sommers? You gonna cook us some ham?" Amy waited for the laughter to die down before answering.

"Saffron, what I meant was do you ever do something one way because that's the only way you were shown? Suppose someone showed you a better way or suppose you were to come up with a better way to do a certain task, something you have to do every day. Would you be interested?"

"Sure, Miss Sommers."

"What I don't want us to do is to do the same thing over and over just because that's the only way we know how. What I really need everyone in this room to do is start thinking about how we go about our daily tasks and assignments. What can we do better? What can we do differently? Saffron, I want you personally to think about breakfast. Is there something we can do differently if it will mean a better experience for our customers, our residents? If you could change anything about breakfast, what would it be?"

"I would cook the eggs and grits myself, Miss Sommers, because my folks in Hudson gets up at different times and those eggs sits in the steam table and get all nasty after about an hour. Why can't I cook my own eggs?"

"That's a great idea Saffron. Why don't you cook your own eggs?"

"I don't know, can I, Chef?"

"Well Miss Sommers, we would have to buy pans, do some Serve-Safe training with the staff, figure out how to cook eggs without splattering grease everywhere, and make sure we follow Health Department guidelines but sure, why the hell not?" Amy smiled broadly at Nick.

"Of course, Nick, why the hell not?" Amy turned to Saffron and clapped, and Nick joined in. Saffron stood up, turned to her coworkers and took a bow.

"Daniel, Grant, is there something we could do better, do differently. What would you change, if you could?"

"Not a thang, Miss Sommers" answered Daniel. Amy stared at Daniel, thinking how stubborn he was. Grant looked at his shoes. Amy turned and faced Nick, then looked back at Daniel.

"Daniel, how do we track maintenance requests?"

"Well Chef, ya'll ask for them to get fixed, and my guys fix them."

"But how do you personally know when stuff gets fixed?"

"My guys tell me when it gets fixed."

"Such as the hand sink in my kitchen that's leaking?"

Amy looked carefully at Nick and tried to convey a feeling of calm. Please don't embarrass Daniel in front of these people, she thought. Please Nick.

"I think what Chef St. Germaine is trying to say, Daniel, is how do you track your completion rate?" Nick nodded his head.

"That's correct Miss Sommers."

Daniel sat back in his chair, took his eyes off of Amy and looked past her shoulder at a wall sconce with a burned-out light bulb.

"Well honestly, Miss Sommers I guess I don't. No one ever asked me to."

"Well Daniel, why don't we start a completion log and that will give you something measurable, so when someone from corporate asks you how your maintenance guys spend their day, you can show them, you can track your request and completion rate. That also will help you so when someone asks for maintenance, you can tell them how long it will take your team to respond." Nick looked at Amy and offered her a sly smile. This girl really knows how to make things happen, he thought. When it was Nick's turn to speak, he addressed the problem of food cost. Chefs live and die by their food cost, and CSM had given him only $8.05 per person per day to feed the residents of Overbrook. And that was a hot breakfast, lunch and dinner every day, snacks, and a refrigerator full of milk, juice, bread, ice creams, butter, jams and jellies, cans of soup, and so on. Eight dollars a day! Nick had taken the time to remind everyone about the food that went to the individual kitchens in Overbrook, especially the snacks and beverages then asked the staff to treat the food as if it were a friend's wallet accidentally left behind at their house.

"Would you take your friend's money out of their wallet?"

Saffron shouted out, "How much money's in that wallet, Chef Nick?"

"Saffron, you're a wonderful, honest person, and I know you wouldn't take money out of your friend's wallet, right?"

"That's right, Chef. I was just fooling."

"So please treat this food as your friend's wallet. My food budget is very lean, and if all of us work together, we can stay in our budget. And if we can do that well that means more money for us in the form of raises and bonuses and things we need, such as pans to cook eggs in, right?"

"Hoo-rah, brother!" shouted Grant. Amy turned to Nick, smiled, then clapped. As the applause died down, Amy thanked everyone for coming then asked the staff to go back to their assigned stations and question everything they were doing then – then ask themselves could it be done better? As Nick was walking out, he felt a touch on the small of his back. He turned to his left and smiled at Amy.

"Thank you, Nick."

"For what, Miss Sommers?" Amy smiled, looked away then turned back to Nick.

"For today, for being there for me."

"You're very welcome, Miss Sommers."

"And Nick?"

"Yes ma'am?"

"Would you please call me Amy."

"Yes ma'am, of course. I'll see you in the morning."

7

As the team's morning meeting was about finished, Amy spoke up and reminded everyone that the new bus would arrive today. "That will be great, Amy. I'm tired of renting a dang bus every time we need to bring more than four people anywhere, and it should be interesting to see the color scheme our friends picked out. Amy, the transportation company said they would call me when they got into Greenville. I'll give you a heads up when they do that, OK?"

"Sure thing, Cassidy, thank you." Two hours later, a brand-new Ford 15-passenger bus pulled into the front entrance. Amy and Cassidy were standing at the front entrance when it pulled into the gates.

"Amy, why is it blue?"

The bus rounded the driveway, giving Amy and Cassidy a good look at the driver's side, which was covered with a massive photograph of Peggy Roberts and Susan Simpson dressed in their blue work out tights. The photograph was obviously taken during one of Anastasia's yoga classes, and then turned into a vinyl wrap which now graced the entire side of the bus. Cassidy gasped and all Amy could do was cover her mouth. Peggy was about 75 pounds overweight and she always covered up with a robe whenever she walked through the hallways in her swim suit or yoga outfit. Susan Simpson was thin as wire. She had lost both breasts to cancer years ago, and consequently had very little contour to her body. Like Peggy, she also wore a cover-up when on her way to her workouts. The photograph was taken from their right as the two women were performing the tadasana mountain pose, and they were both smiling at the photographer. As the bus slowed to a stop, the driver made a 180-degree turn – thereby exposing all of Susan and Peggy's glory to Woodmont's main entrance.

"Good Lord, Amy. There is no way on God's green earth that either of these women agreed to this, correct?"

"Holy Shit!" Amy and Cassidy quickly turned around and were met with a glaring Doris Peters. "Who in the hell did this to my friends, lady! You think this is funny, Sommers?" Doris, with her hands on her hips, had the look of a prizefighter before a match.

"Um, I, uh, I'm sorry Doris, but I can promise you that I did not authorize this. All I knew is that we were getting a new bus. Um, I can promise you that I will get to the bottom of this."

"Oh my God!" gasped Beverly Stafford as she walked by. The side door opened and the driver bounced out of the bus.

"Hi ladies! I'm Reggie Wilson from the Atlanta Bus Company. How do you like it? Just like the boss ordered, correct?" Reggie waved his right arm at the side of the bus. Even covered in blue tights, Peggy's thighs were flabby and dimpled with cellulite. Reggie then moved to the left side of the bus, which was covered in the sunshine yellow Woodmont logo, contact information and the slogan, "Start Living Today!" Doris glared at Amy and shook a fist at her.

"Not responsible, huh?"

"Ms. Peters, I can assure you that this gentleman did not get my permission to cover this bus with that photograph." Reggie Wilson scratched his head, looked at Amy's nametag, then opened up his manifest.

"Well, it says here that I am to deliver this bus to one Mrs. Amy Sommers, and that looks like you, so here you go. Here's two sets of keys, your owner's manual, and if you would just sign right here, please, I can be on my way. We even put your keys on a Atlanta Bus fob … got my number right there, when you're ready to get another one. My associate is right behind me ladies, so thank you very much for doing business with us, Mrs. Sommers."

Amy yanked the key out of Reggie Wilson's hand and hissed.

"Miss Sommers, thank you very much."

A white Chevy Impala pulled into the driveway with an Atlanta Bus Company logo on the door; Reggie jumped in as the driver slowed to a stop. He waved again as the Impala drove off.

"Oh No!" fussed Marsha Hemmers as she walked out of the lobby.

"You have some explaining to do lady; start talking," hissed Doris.

Amy threw the keys to Cassidy and barked, "Move this bus where we won't see it please." Benjamin de Soto emerged from the lobby and broke into laughter.

"Holy Crap! Ain't this something! I tell you what, Sommers, you guys are hitting on all cylinders. Ya'll just can't get out of your own way, can you?" Peggy Roberts walked out just as Cassidy was starting the bus. Amy turned and when she saw her, all she could say was,

"I'm so sorry, Peggy; I'm so sorry."

"Who would do this?" Amy thought Peggy was going to cry.

"Peggy, please understand that this is a terrible mistake and I will not let this bus off campus. If you will please excuse me, I need to make some phone calls to get this taken care of." Amy walked back into her office, closed the door and immediately called Rivers. Before he answered she received a call from Cassidy.

"Where the heck do I park this thing?"

"Hide it!" Amy responded. Rivers' phone went to voicemail. "Shit! Come on Rivers, answer your damn phone." Amy dialed Cassidy's phone, then stood in front of her window. "Amy, I can put this thing in the garage, but it's still going to be visible by the members."

"Well, how about on the north side of the campus? Where Daniel keeps the landscaping equipment, maybe on the other side of the security truck?" As Amy looked out her window, she saw the bus drive past as Cassidy searched for a suitable hiding spot. A group of ladies were out walking, and they stopped and pointed. "Good God, Cassidy."

"I know boss, we're stuck. No matter where we put this thing, someone's going to see it. If we drive it off campus, that's going to make it worse."

"Agreed. Put it in the garage, maybe up against the wall. Try to conceal it as much as possible, and I'll get to work on some damage control. When you get back inside, you need to coordinate with Daniel on getting that wrapper taken off. Let's make that happen ASAP, please."

"Yes, ma'am."

"I'll call Daniel right now and see if he can't get us a tarp or something like that to cover it up with. And when you get back to your office, please send out a campus-wide email asking everyone to stay off of that bus."

"OK, will do." Ten minutes later, Cassidy had parked the bus, dropped the keys on her desk and went off to look for Daniel. Five minutes later, Franklin walked in and saw the keys.

"Sweet! The bus is finally here." He turned and looked in the hallway, where Jim and Mollie Jensen were walking past. "Hey folks, you want to take a ride in the new bus?"

"Well certainly, Franklin. We have an hour before lunch, so why not? That OK with you Mollie, darling?"

"Let's go."

"Where you all going, Franklin?" Franklin turned to see Chet Bannon rolling up behind them. "Hey Mr. Bannon, our new bus is finally here and we're going to take a little road trip. You game?"

"Damn right! I'd love to get out of here for a bit." The three of them walked into the garage, with Franklin pushing Chet. They found the bus parked tightly against the wall of the garage. "I wonder why it's parked that way?" The Jensen's told Franklin they would stay put while he backed it out. Franklin pulled up and the Jensen's climbed on, then Franklin used the electric wheelchair lift to get Chet on board. In the garage's subtle lighting, no one noticed the massive pair of blue thighs that adorned the left side of the bus. Franklin carefully drove out of the garage, turned left onto the main driveway, and headed out the front gate.

"You know Franklin, when I first joined the Memphis fire department, we had a team of horses that pulled our fire engine."

"Oh, come on now, Mr. B, you're pulling my leg." Mollie smiled.

"Actually, it was wooly mammoths that pulled Chet's first fire engine." All four broke out into raucous laughter. Franklin turned onto Highway 101 and as he did so, he saw a car of teenagers laughing and pointing at them. Franklin just glared back. The next car that passed contained an elderly couple. As they drove past the bus, they stared and their eyes lit up. Now Franklin was concerned. He slowed for a traffic light as Chet mentioned the bus had a pretty good ride. The light turned green and Franklin pulled away smartly. "Plenty of giddy-up too, Franklin."

"Well, it's got a ported and polished 351 Cleveland, chrome headers, dual Holley 750s, domed pistons, a Hurst shift kit and two-stage nitrous injection." Chet laughed and patted Franklin on the back. "Hey, as long as we're trading bologna sandwiches, right?" Franklin's Blackberry buzzed, so he took a quick glance at it. Chet grabbed the phone from him.

"Not with us in here, buddy; both hands on the wheel." Franklin asked Chet to open his email. "Uh, Franklin, it's a note from Cassidy saying under no circumstances should anyone drive the new bus."

"Uh oh!" Another car drove past, two middle aged women and the driver looked at the bus, then shook her head.

"Oh dear," said Mollie. "I wonder if there's gas in it?"

"We have plenty of gas, Mrs. Jensen." Franklin wheeled into a grocery store parking lot and came to a stop. He asked everyone to stay put, then jumped out of the bus. He took a few steps back and looked at the driver's side of the bus. "Jesus, Mary and Joseph! How did I miss this?" Franklin's

Blackberry rang; it was Cassidy. Franklin shook his head and said hello.

"Franklin?"

"Uh, yes ma'am?"

"Where's our new bus?"

"Um, well, it's kind of in the parking lot of the Publix grocery store on 101. It has a really nice ride Cassidy, and Mr. Bannon thought the wheelchair lift worked flawlessly."

"Franklin Jones, you get that damn bus back here right this minute or I promise you'll be cleaning toilets for the rest of your Woodmont career!"

"Yes ma'am! On the way."

Amy Sommers had just gotten off the phone with Rivers when Dawn walked in with a long face. "Miss Sommers, we've received a couple of crank phone calls about our bus. They want to know who the hottie in blue tights is."

"Good Lord!"

"Well, Miss Sommers, they just called. I thought the bus was in the garage." Amy's Blackberry rang with a call from Cassidy.

"Bad news, boss. Somehow, Franklin took the bus out for a short drive and he's been up and down 101 with the Jensen's and Chet Bannon." Amy put her forehead down on her desk. "Oh my God, Cassidy, I should just start searching the classifieds for a new job right now."

"Amy, seriously, let's get that bus back and problem solve; this isn't your fault, OK?"

"I know, I know. Cass, once that bus goes back in the garage, I want both sets of keys in my office within five minutes, got it?"

"Consider it done, boss." Amy's email chimed with a note from Daniel Stern. "I will have a full-size tarp ready tonight, please ask Cassidy to park the bus out back and we can cover it ASAP." Amy typed a quick thank-you and hit send. "Cass, change of plans. Put the bus out by the garden, park it parallel to the sidewalk with the girl's photo facing away from the street, and Daniel's going to cover it tonight, OK? Then bring me those keys, please."

Doris, Peggy and Susan sat in Peggy's apartment, trying to console her. Susan Simpson held her hand.

"Shall we get Hemmers on this? Marsha told me he was a ruthless attorney in his day; let's get him on it." Doris groaned.

"We don't have that kind of time, gals. We need to do something, and do it fast. We can't let these numbskulls walk all over us like this. I have an idea, but Peg, I'm leaving you out of this. When that Sommers gal finds out what happened, you're the first suspect, so you ain't involved, got it?" Doris picked up her cell phone and sent a text to Veronica. "Meet me at the Armory in ten."

"Let's go, Susie, we got a job to plan." Susie Simpson and Doris met Veronica in the Armory ten minutes later. Cassidy parked the bus next to the garden and brought both sets of keys to Amy. Cassidy told Amy that one of Mr. Stern's maintenance guys would cover the bus with a full-size tarp before the end of the day. At four p.m., just before Daniel left for the day, he asked Stanley to go to the nearest Home Depot, purchase a full-size tarp to cover the new van and make sure it happens before six. Stanley purchased a tarp big enough for a full-size van, but not nearly big enough to cover a 15-passenger bus. It was six thirty by the time Stanley gave up and decided he would return the tarp in the morning, purchase an appropriately sized tarp then cover the bus. His wife was making fried chicken for dinner, and there was nothing worse than cold fried chicken.

8

Doris and Veronica approached the concierge desk. "Dawn, we need you, oh, please hurry! Susan has fallen in the bathroom, please come help right away!" Dawn jumped up from her desk and followed Veronica into the bathroom. As soon as Dawn got up, Doris sat in her chair and opened her Outlook. She opened an email box and addressed it to maintenance. "Please bring a six-foot ladder to the vegetable garden by six p.m. today. Mr. Hemmers needs to trim his hanging flowerpots. Ladder can be picked up tomorrow morning, thank you." Doris clicked "Send," then got up and walked away, headed to the 1949 just as Dawn, Veronica and Susan came out of the ladies room.

"I just dropped a roll of toilet paper. Why would you think I fell? I swear, you're such a worry wart, Veronica."

"Well, at least everyone's OK, and that's all that matters ladies." Dawn headed back to her desk, relieved that it was all a misunderstanding. Doris walked up to the bar and found Jackson polishing glasses.

"Three vodka martinis, please. A little dirty with two olives each."

"Yes ma'am."

"What have you been up to, Miss Peters? You're grinning like the Cheshire cat."

"Me? Oh please, Jackson. I'm just trying to waddle through another dull day in this den of inequity." Veronica and Susan walked into the 1949. Doris turned to face them, offered them a big thumbs-up and all three broke into raucous laughter as Jackson set the three martinis in front of them. "I thought we would celebrate with a little potato juice, ladies." The ladies pulled the barstools out and hoisted their glasses to Jackson, who placed his palms on the bar, furrowed his brow, then eyeballed each one of them.

"OK, just what are you ladies celebrating? The air has a hint if illegality to it, and you three are going to talk."

They smiled, hoisted their martinis to one another, clinked their glasses, then drank. Doris shot hers as if it was lemonade on a hot summer day, then wiped her lips with a beverage napkin.

"OK gals, I'm going to go get a nap. We have a long night ahead of us. And if anyone blabs to this young man, they're going to have to deal with me, got it?" Jackson, Veronica and Susan watched Doris saunter away from the bar.

"OK ladies, spill it. What're you all up to?"

"Oh Jackson, you must keep this quiet," whispered Veronica.

"Deal."

"We're going to do some modifications to that new bus tonight."

"Thank God! Do you need any help?"

"No, we have it all taken care of. Just keep it quiet and cross your fingers."

"That's a deal, Miss Parker." Jackson lifted a glass of club soda and toasted Veronica and Susan. "To good fortune," he said.

Five hours later, Doris knocked on the door of Veronica's apartment. A minute later, the door opened and Veronica whispered, "Password."

"Oh, cut the secret agent crap and open the damn door, will ya!" barked Doris. "Well, you can't be too careful when you're planning a crime like this one," whispered Veronica. "Why the hell are you whispering? If I have to turn up this hearing aid, it's going to whistle like a teakettle, and the then entire county's going to hear us coming. Where's Susan?" The toilet flushed and the door to the bathroom opened. Susan walked out wearing a long yellow-and-blue Iris print dress. "Oh, what the hell's with Doris Day here? I said to wear black, and you look like you're going to the damn Easter parade."

"Oh dear Doris, I just don't look good in black. Besides, I wanted to dress up. This is all just so exciting." There was a knock on the door. Doris looked at her wristwatch, then turned to the door.

"Veronica, it's almost eight thirty. Who's coming over at this hour?"

"Well dear, I may have invited someone else to give us a hand."

"Oh, for the love of Pete!" groaned Doris. Susan opened the door and there was a smiling Peggy Roberts wearing black pants, a black sweatshirt, a reflective yellow runner's vest and white running shoes. "*Oh heavens to damn Betsy!* Shall we just call the cops right now and spare them the foot chase? Would anyone like to carry a torch while we're at it?"

"Oh, come on Doris, ease up please. Peg, you look wonderful."

Doris glared. "Listen, can we just break up this little fashion show and get going?"

"Yes, yes, of course, Doris. Do you have the razor?" Doris reached into her pocket and produced a pearl-handled Roberson straight razor.

"Henry sharpened this thing every Sunday, and wouldn't you know, he died on a Monday, so it's still sharp as a tack. Let's go, but Peg, you gotta drop that vest, please."

"OK, for you, I'll do it."

"In the middle of all this dress-up, did anyone else remember their flashlight?"

"Oh, I did Doris," smiled Veronica, "See?" Veronica had taped two small flashlights to the front of her walker. She reached down and turned one on, smiled proudly, then turned it off. Doris rolled her eyes.

"Peggy, I think you should put that vest back on so that Grandma Andretti here doesn't run over you on the sidewalk." The four of them headed out, with Veronica pushing her walker. They slowly walked to the side elevator so they could avoid the front lobby. When the elevator opened on the first floor, they all stuck their heads out and looked around, then quietly moved towards the back door. The wait staff was still in the dining room cleaning up; the sound of the vacuum cleaner echoed through the hallway. When they reached the back door, Doris reached into her pocket and produced a rubber door wedge, opened the back door, then slowly bent down and stuck the wedge in the door to prop it open. As she stood up, she put her right hand on the small of her back. "Jesus Christ, that's a long way down. Someone else is picking this thing up when we come back." Doris turned on her flashlight, Veronica turned on hers, and they slowly followed the sidewalk around the pond and headed towards the garden. The sidewalk was well lit from the luminaries that were about 30 feet apart and the pathway lights that had been placed every 12 feet.

"Oh, my! It is so lovely out here at night" cooed Veronica. "Perhaps we should come out here more often. I had no idea how much decorative lighting Mr. Stern had out here. I don't think that I even need my headlights."

"I sure do miss mine," Susan said with a sigh.

Doris reached for Veronica's hand. "Just keep moving, Grandma, we'll admire the landscaping on the way back." Veronica was slightly out of breath by the time they reached the bus, so she turned her walker around and sat down. Doris walked over to the greenhouse and sure enough, there was the ladder propped up next to the greenhouse door. She carried the ladder to the bus and set it up right next to the rear wheels, looked at the massive photo of her and Peggy and grimaced, then patted her right pants pocket just to make sure the razor was still there. She reached in and pulled out the razor, then handed it to Susan.

"OK sweetie, you're going to hold onto this until I get up on this thing. If I fall while I am doing this, you better get out of the way so you don't get cut."

"Oh please, don't say such awful things, dear."

"The rest of you keep your eyes open for Michael. Let's hope he stays on schedule." Doris climbed up the ladder then asked for the razor. Susan handed her the Roberson blade, Doris opened it up and carefully sliced the appliqué from the top to about the middle, then turned the blade and continued at a 90-degree angle as far as she could reach. She did it again and then a third time. With each pass, she left about a two-inch gap from her previous cut. She handed the blade to Susan. "OK sweetie, your turn. See how much damage you can do at the front of this thing." Susan took the blade by the handle and began making diagonal cuts across the front of the appliqué. Doris cautioned her not to cut too hard or they would scratch the paint. Doris pulled out her eyelash tweezers, gripped the edge of the appliqué and tugged. To her relief, the appliqué started to come off. She pulled hard and was rewarded with a 12-inch piece of the photo, but it quickly tore.

"Crap! I thought it was all going to come off. How you all doing up there?"

"Oh dear, it's not as easy as I thought it would be. This can't be glue holding this thing on. It doesn't feel sticky."

"Well, soldier on gals. If we can't get this thing off, maybe we can screw it up enough to send a message." The appliqué was coming off, but only in thin pieces. In 15 minutes, they had only removed about five percent of it. Doris climbed off the ladder and backed up to look at it. Peggy and Susan stood next to her. Most of Peggy's arms and butt and Susan's flat chest were still there. Doris walked back to the photo, wiped off the Roberson with her left thumb and forefinger, and carefully carved around Peggy's waist. She then switched to the tweezers and tugged on the edge of the offending photo, but was only able to remove a piece the size of a paper towel. She held the piece up to the streetlight and smiled; she had removed about half of Peggy's butt.

"Here you go, sweetheart. Don't say I never risked prison for your butt." Peggy smiled. The front of the bus was suddenly bathed in light from a car approaching on the opposite side. "Oh crap! It's the cops! Hide gals," Doris squawked. Susan, Doris and Veronica ran towards the back of the bus. Peggy steadied herself on her walker and switched off one of the flashlights, but when she looked forward, she lost her spatial sense of vision. Doris came out of her hiding place to help Peggy but as the car got closer, Peggy fussed,

"Just leave me!" The vehicle slowed down and Doris did as she was told and ran towards the back of the bus. The truck drove past, and Peggy recognized the white Dodge that Michael used for his nighttime patrols. He drove past at a steady 20 miles an hour. As he did so, Peggy headed to the sidewalk to put some distance between her and the bus. Michael drove past and headed towards the corner of the Overbrook building, slowed down for the stop sign and turned to his left. As he did so, he thought he saw a shadow in his rear view mirror. He came to a stop and looked out the left window. Sure enough, there was one of the residents walking down the sidewalk. Michael rolled down his window, then reached for his flashlight and shone it out the window. Peggy's reflective vest sparkled like a slow moving disco ball.

"Oh crap, the warden's caught Peg," groaned Doris.

"We should all just give ourselves up," whispered Susan.

"Don't you dare! Let's just see what happens."

"*Miss Roberts?* What are you doing out here?"

"Oh, good evening, Michael, is that you?" Michael had gotten out of his truck and approached Peggy Roberts. Fortunately, when the vest had lit up, it distracted Michael's vision away from the bus that was maybe ten feet behind them. "Yes ma'am, it's me. Are you taking a walk?"

"Oh, why yes, I was. I was trying out my new modifications to my walker. You see, I have added some head lights, see?"

"Oh yes, ma'am, that's very clever. Are you, uh, going to be walking much farther tonight?"

"Oh no, Michael. I was just headed back to my room. I guess I didn't realize how far I had gone."

"Well can I give you a lift back to McBee? It's quite a walk, or I can just walk with you."

"Oh well Michael. A lift back to the front of McBee would be just lovely. Thank you so much."

"Yes ma'am, let me go grab the truck." Michael turned to the truck as Peggy looked over her shoulder. If he points the truck at the bus, he will surely see the ladder in the glare of the headlights. "Oh Michael, would you just walk me to your truck. It's such a fine evening."

"Oh sure, of course, Miss Roberts."

"Weren't you in the Navy, Michael?"

"No ma'am, the United States Coast Guard. I was stationed in Savannah, Georgia, with the Lowcountry Lifesavers."

"Well, how about that? Now were you a helicopter pilot or a rescue swimmer?"

"No ma'am, I was a seaman and I served on the Maria Bray out of Savannah, Georgia. I remember this one time we had to ..." Doris, Susan and Veronica listened as they watched from behind the bus. Michael helped Peggy into the cab of the truck and put her walker in the back. As they drove away Doris remarked,

"Well, that Peg's a smart cookie. I swear, if that were me, I would have asked him to throw me in the back instead of riding up front and having to listen to one more story about the Coast Guard. If someone ever falls into that 12-inch deep pond of ours, we know who to call. Come on girls, let's get home." Veronica and Doris put the ladder back against the greenhouse, while Susan picked up the pieces of the appliqué. They headed to the back door, stopping to throw the pieces into the dumpster first. When the elevator reached the lobby floor, they carefully exited and looked around for Michael, but there was no sign of him.

"Alright ladies, let's get some shut eye. I'll see everyone for lunch tomorrow. And if Ma Barker needs to get bailed out tonight, I'm gonna come knocking on your doors for the dough, OK?"

"Ma who?" asked Veronica.

"Oh, never mind sweetheart, let's go to bed." Doris slowly walked to Peggy's room, looked up and down the hallway, then knocked on her door. Peggy opened the door and smiled. "You OK, sweetheart?"

"Oh yes, of course. Michael thought I was just taking an evening stroll. I was so afraid that he was going to turn that truck around and see what we had done."

"Well, that was a stroke of genius to ask him about the Coast Guard."

"Oh wasn't it though? Doesn't he love to talk about the Coast Guard?"

"Alright sweetheart, I'm going to turn in. Goodnight."

The next morning, Amy's staff had assembled in the Armory for the morning meeting. Nick strolled in right at nine and Amy asked him to close the door. Nick did as he was asked, then took a seat to the left of Franklin, who offered him a knuckle bump. Nick responded, then stretched his arms out a bit, put his right arm across the back of Franklin, patted him on the shoulder, then reached down and pinched Franklin on the butt. Franklin flinched, then turned and winked at Nick and blew him a kiss.

"As soon as Nick and Franklin can get control of their testosterone levels, we can start the meeting."

"Yes ma'am. Please carry on, Miss Sommers, and feel free to ignore Chef Alcatraz here."

"Well, good morning everyone, and happy Thursday." Nick smiled and said good morning but inside, he winced at the thought of wishing anyone a happy Thursday. "If you all don't mind, I would like to ask Daniel to start as he has some interesting news. Daniel?"

"Last night, someone vandalized our bus. A razor was used to attempt to remove the vinyl graphic wrap, but they were not successful. Nevertheless, the vinyl wrap has been basically destroyed. So I'm going to conduct an investigation, and Miss Sommers will decide legally what our next step will be. It's going to be fairly easy to find the culprits, maybe take me ten minutes leafing through the security footage. Then we'll decide how far we proceed with this." Nick couldn't help but smile. He leaned back and looked at the ceiling and knew immediately that Doris Peters was to blame.

"Do you find this amusing Nick?"

"Why, yes I do Miss Sommers, and thank you for asking."

"Are you serious?"

"Figures," mumbled Daniel Stern.

"Miss Sommers, did anyone get permission from those ladies to have their likeness placed on the side of that bus? A bus that was meant to routinely travel off campus as a rolling advertisement for Woodmont? Did any of them sign a model's release? Did either of them agree to have that photo placed on that bus?"

"Well, uh, I can't answer that question right now. I would assume yes, but I can't say for sure."

"Well I can, and the answer is no. *No one* ever asked their permission verbally or contractually. I know, because I asked them. CSM leafed through our photos and decided that a photo of some of our residents doing yoga would be perfect for the side of the bus. So Peggy Roberts has to see a ten-foot high photo of herself in tights and according to Miss Roberts, her butt in tights looks like a 50-pound sack of cottage cheese. Her words, not mine, thank you. Can we do a better job of humiliating one of our residents? *Doubtful!* Honestly, Miss Sommers, I think those ladies did a good job of cleaning up the crumbs."

Amy was suddenly red with embarrassment.

"Miss Sommers, Mr. Stern, do you really want this episode to go any further? Legal proceedings? *Really?* And what happens when the newspaper finds out? Do you really want that much negative publicity? Do either of you realize how much press a story like this could generate? Disgruntled retirees deface bus with razor blade, film at five, six and ten. Let's face it Miss Sommers, they won." Amy blanched at Nick's words.

"Perhaps our esteemed Chef does not realize how much that vinyl wrapping process cost, and it came out of *my budget.*"

"Perhaps Mr. Stern *does not* realize the amount of negative publicity this could generate could cost us 20 or 30 times the cost of that ridiculous wrap."

Amy sat up, pursed her lips and rubbed her forehead with her right hand, then looked around at her team. Cassidy gently shook her head as if to say no, while Jessica looked away. Amy turned to Grant, who shook his head no. Penny also shook her head no, as did Jeanine and Christina. Amy looked up at the ceiling, exhaled loudly then turned to Daniel.

"Daniel, let it drop, please. Rivers has given me permission to submit my own design for the bus, and in the meantime, we'll just drive around a plain, white bus. I don't want to know who vandalized our bus, although I have a pretty good idea. Let's let this one go people, OK?"

"Miss Sommers, all I need is ten minutes to find out who did this and then … "

"Daniel, let it go, please. *Understand?*" Amy scanned the room as everyone nodded in agreement. Daniel's energy evaporated, he shook his head, looked at his notebook, looked across the room at Grant then mumbled.

"Yes ma'am, I understand."

Twenty-five minutes later, Amy adjourned the meeting. Nick held the door for everyone, but Amy took her time gathering up her papers and laptop, making sure she was the last one to leave. As she was crossing the threshold, she stopped and looked at Nick. "Um, Nick, I uh, need to say thank you for allowing cooler heads to prevail. You were right, I was wrong."

"It's OK, Miss Sommers. I know you were very upset and what they did was disrespectful of private property as well as illegal. But they had every right to be mad."

"I agree, Nick, and please feel free to call me Amy."

"Yes, ma'am."

"Have a great day, Nick."

"You too, Miss Sommers."

9

Nick looked at his phone. 8:25 p.m., the blessed end of another 12-hour day. Maybe he could go to Northampton and grab a glass of wine, or go for a run with Theo. It was late June, and the sun was still up for another 45 minutes or so. He was almost done here, Xavier was finishing up sweeping, and String Bean and Jose would finish mopping. Nick was wiping down the line, and the last thing he did was run a dry towel under the wood burning grill to wipe up the soapy water. As he moved his left hand under the grill, the metal edge sliced into the knuckle of his right forefinger and opened up a cut about four inches in length.

"Son of a Bitch!" he yelled. The pain shot through him and for a second or two, Nick was afraid he would pass out. He grabbed a clean cloth and applied pressure while holding his hands over his head. He quickly found a glass rack to sit down on and put his head between his legs. Xavier heard him cry out and came around the line.

"You OK, boss? What happened? Let's take a look." Nick took the towel off his right hand long enough for Xavier to take a look, and the blood flowed out of the wound unabated. "Damn Chef, how did you do that? You're gonna need some stitches. Get downstairs to see the nurse, please."

"Damn, damn, damnit!" declared Nick. "I was just about to leave, too."

"Stop your whining boss and go see the nurse will you? I'll finish this up."

"Yes sir, Xavier, off to the nurse." Nick took a deep breath, steadied himself, got up and walked downstairs to Burgess and said hello to Candace.

"Oh Nick, just what have you done to yourself?" said Candace as she caught a glimpse of the blood-soaked cloth. Nick sat down in one of the dining room chairs, while Candace brought over her first aid kit. "OK, let's see what we have here." She put on a pair of latex gloves, placed a clean towel under his hand then carefully poured sterile water over the cut so she could remove the paper towel. Nick grimaced and sucked in a deep breath. "Oh golly Nick, look what you've done. How did you do this?"

"I was just cleaning up, that's all. Moved my hand underneath that crappy grill to wipe up some soapy water, and did this."

"Oh sweetheart, I don't know if I can fix this. I can't do stitches here. I can try some Steri-strips, but I don't think that's going to do the trick."

"I really *do not* want to get stitched up tonight, I really don't. I just want to go get a drink."

"Well, you may not have a choice. I can see your knuckle. You've cut entirely through the epidermis, and it probably won't stop bleeding without stitches."

"I'll be fine, Candace. Can you just Steri-Strip it?"

"Sweetie, there's no honor in stupidity, besides, when was the last time you had a tetanus shot?" He tried to think. It must have been seven or eight years.

"*Damn.*" Nick looked up at Candace and frowned. Candace smiled at Nick and placed her right hand under his chin.

"Sorry, Sugar. I would drive you if I had someone that could cover me, but third shift isn't in for another 90 minutes. Let me find somewhere you can go. You just sit right there and look scrumptious, OK?"

"Yes ma'am." Candace called an after-hours medic, Triage/12, then wrote out some directions and gave them to Nick.

"Here ya go sugar, they're only about a ten minute drive from here and they're expecting you, OK?" About 15 minutes later Nick walked into the reception area of Triage/12. It was practically brand new and very modern, full of steel, glass and cut stone. The receptionist looked up at Nick as he walked in.

"Chef St. Germaine?"

"Yes, how did you know?" Nick smiled.

"Uh, your white Chef coat with your name embroidered on it was a dead give-away. I just have a bit of paperwork for you to fill out, and then the doctor can see you." Nick filled out the obligatory forms, turned them in then was shown to an examination room.

"Good evening. How are you, Chef?" announced a stocky red haired, red-mustached gentleman.

"Good evening, Doc," replied Nick.

"Oh, no, I'm the nurse, David Miller. Dr. Giansante will be in just as soon as I clean you up and get a look at this, OK?"

"Oh, sorry, my apologies."

"None needed. It happens. A lot of us have pre-conceived notions of what a nurse or doctor should look like."

"Let's take a look and get you cleaned up. How about you take off your jacket and I'll get your BP and pulse." Nick removed his Chef coat and placed it on the table next to him. David put on a clean pair of gloves then set about filling a bed pan with sterile water. When he placed Nick's hand in the water, it quickly blossomed red. David then poured Betadyne in the water.

"Does that hurt?"

"No sir, all good."

"OK then, let's just sit here. You will definitely need maybe half a dozen stitches and a little red-headed bird told me you could use a tetanus shot too, correct?" Nick just nodded his head. David placed the cuff on Nick's upper arm and read his blood pressure and took his pulse. "118 over 64, excellent, and a heart rate of 56, that's really something. Candace and I rode in the same ambulance as EMTs while we were in nursing school. She texted me and said I should take good care of her favorite Chef. Us redheaded nurses, well, we're such a rarity we really need to stick together."

"Thank you, David."

"Good evening, I'm Doctor Giansante." Nick sat up straight and smiled. Doctor Giansante. She was five-foot-ten with long dark-black hair that curled well past her shoulders, a stunning smile, big brown eyes, full red lips and high cheek bones. She finished washing her hands, put on a clean pair of gloves and turned to her patient. Nick glanced at her nametag: Lynda Giansante. Maybe a little Italian was in order, Nick thought.

"Sera buon medico, Giansante"

"Ah, buona sera a voi," replied Dr. Giansante. "Come avete fatto questo?" Damn. Her Italian was impeccable. Now he was in trouble. Nick listened to her words again in his head. Fatto questo, what have you done? Is that what she said?

"Su una griglia?" Nick hesitated.

"Are you sure?" quizzed Lynda, knowing she had caught this guy flat-footed trying to impress her with his modest Italian. "Yes ma'am, I was cleaning the grill and I guess I was in a hurry."

"I see, and when was the last time you had a tetanus shot Mr...."

"St. Germaine, Nicholas St. Germaine and it's been a while, seven or eight years, maybe a bit longer." Lynda turned to David and nodded slightly. David responded that he was one step ahead of her.

"Doctor, Mr. St. Germaine is the Chef of Woodmont where my friend, Candace, works."

"Is that so? I understand that Woodmont is beautiful and the food is excellent."

"Correto!"

"And where did you pick up your Italian? Dove hai imparare l'italiano?"

"New Orleans, a city of many languages. I cooked in, uh, ho cotto in un ristorante italiano, Vincenzo's. It was in Metairie just outside of New Orleans. Vincezo Piccone was the Chef and owner and the busier we got, the more Italian he used to direct the kitchen. So if you wanted to work there, you had to learn Italian, or at least enough Italian to survive in the kitchen."

"Questo sta andando a male senore," Lynda cautioned as she prepared the needle of lidocaine. Nick took a deep breath and exhaled, slowly bracing himself for the pain. He closed his eyes and suddenly Robin was sitting next to him, her head on his shoulder, whispering in his ear how much she missed him and how foolish he was. Lynda inserted the needle into the cut and started working the lidocaine around the wound. The lidocaine burned like battery acid as it moved through the soft tissue of his hand. Robin held Nick close, twirled her fingers through his hair, and softly whispered that it would all be over soon. Lynda reinserted the needle and pushed the last of the painkiller into the wound. She looked at Nick's face and noticed tears weeping out of his closed eyes. She put the needle down then told him she was done.

"Tissue?" Nick opened his eyes, accepted the Kleenex and wiped his tears away. She was used to strong men flinching and fussing when she gave them lidocaine. This guy held perfectly still, but looked like someone had just shot his favorite dog. "Mi dispiace," Lynda offered.

"I'm okay, I'm okay," responded Nick. "It's nothing."

"So tell me, what's your favorite thing to cook?" smiled Lynda. David was opening a sterilized suture kit as she was blotting the cut clean. Lynda glanced at his left hand looking for a wedding ring and there it was, a thick band of shining gold. Too bad, she thought.

"Whatever makes the doctor happy."

"No, no seriously, what do you really like to cook?" queried Lynda.

"OK, whom am I cooking for?"

"Well, let's say someone special, Mrs. St. Germaine perhaps." Lynda inserted the tiny curved needle into the flap of skin and pulled the suture tight. David turned his head and coughed loudly. Nick just bit his bottom lip and closed his eyes, wishing that Lynda would have skipped the lidocaine and kept her mouth shut. It would have been less painful. Lynda looked at David, and he glared at her while gently mouthing, "Widower". Oh no, thought Lynda, what have I said. "Perdonarmi" she whispered while trying to concentrate on the sutures. His wife was dead, he was a widower. Damnit, me and my big mouth.

"It's OK doc." Nick took a deep breath, looked up at the ceiling and exhaled as he pushed the tears back. Lynda tried to smile. Damn, this guy was close to exploding into tears. Damn.! What would she do if he just started bawling right here? Offer another tissue? Lot of good that's going to do, maybe he can hold it together. She focused on the needle. The examination room had never been so quiet.

Nick breathed deeply, fought back the closing darkness, cleared his throat and turned his attention to Lynda as she gracefully closed the cut back together. You can do this, he thought to himself. Soon he was admiring her touch with the diminutive needle. David offered him a cup of water, which he gladly received. "You don't have anything stronger, do you?"

"Well, I could put some rubbing alcohol and Betadyne in it that would definitely be stronger." The mild laughter helped the tension ease out of the room. Lynda finished up the last of the six stitches and glanced up at Nick. He sure was good looking, with his sandy brown hair and those sad, green eyes – and did he ever spend a lot of time in the gym. Too bad I didn't get to take his blood pressure, she thought. I would have put that cuff way up there and maybe spent an extra second or two wrapping it around his biceps.

"OK, how about that tetanus shot now, David." David moved towards Nick with the syringe, but Lynda interrupted. "Here, I'll do it." Lynda took the syringe from David and swabbed Nick's left arm with alcohol. "Hopefully I won't break this needle," she smirked. "Here comes a little stick." As Lynda pushed the syringe's plunger Nick thought to himself: I wonder what makes her happy?

"Che marche lei felice? Damn, uh, Ciò che fa felice?"

"italiano cattivo," responded Lynda with a wicked smile as she deposited the used syringe in the sharps container.

"Bad Italian makes you happy?" Lynda winked at Nick. Whatever darkness was there five minutes earlier had parted and he was smiling again. Lynda cleaned up the leftovers from the suture kit and asked David for an appropriate bandage. She held his right hand in her left hand, and gently covered the wound while giving Nick some care instructions.

"Now Nicholas, if you see a lot of redness or swelling in this area..." She was almost caressing his hand but because of the lidocaine, Nick couldn't be sure. Was she flirting with him? Damn, if he had known this was going to happen he would have asked her to skip the painkiller. He imagined himself 15 minutes earlier telling Lynda, "Hey Doc, you sure are gorgeous. If you plan on hitting on me later, then let's skip that lidocaine, please. That way, I can tell if you're interested in me or you just have a really delicious bedside manner."

"Nicholas, are you paying attention?"

"Oh, uh, yes. We were talking about uncontrolled swelling."

There was an uncomfortable pause as they stared at one another. He certainly didn't mean to drop a sexual innuendo, but that's exactly what it sounded like. Nick's mouth was slightly open and Lynda realized she was holding his hand. "Nicholas, if you see redness and swelling around *this area,* then please come see me again, OK?" Lynda pointed to his injured hand and parsed out her words as if she was talking to a five-year-old.

"OK Doc, I get it. If I don't heal properly, I'll call you."

"No, you will come see me, not call me. Are you sure you're listening?"

"So when *should* I call you?" Lynda smiled, then turned her back to him to write out a prescription and asked him if he needed anything for the pain. "No, thank you." She turned to Nick and handed him a pamphlet on wound care, a prescription for hydrocodone and her business card.

"Here's a scrip for a pain killer, just in case. Here's my card. It has our operating hours on the back, so if you think you are not healing properly then please make a return appointment. Make sure you take note of our operating hours on the back of my card." Nick glanced down at the card in his fingers and flipped it over. There, in black ink, she had written, "Medico Lynda Giansante, 546-9096, per favore di chiamare." Damn, thought Nick, per favore, that's please, but what was chiamare? No matter; she had just given him her number. Nick beamed and held up her card. "Yes ma'am, I will follow these instructions to the letter."

"Thank you for paying attention, Mr. St. Germaine, and have a lovely evening." The look on Lynda's face could have melted a popsicle. She turned and left the room as Nick gathered up his Chef's coat then headed home.

10

Tony Torres walked into the 1949 to grab a cup of fresh coffee to start his morning and found Nick chatting with Willie Armstrong. "Morning, Skipper. Good morning, Colonel."

"Hey, Tony Torres! Top of the morning to you, sir. How's my favorite dining room manager?"

"You're awfully chipper this morning, babe. Everything ok? You get that job offer as Chef at the Playboy Mansion?"

"Well, if that's so, then count the Colonel in, too. You're going to need a personal valet at the mansion, right?"

"Mr. Torres, am I not entitled to my happiness?"

"Yes sir, of course. Hey, what happened to your hand? Come here, Chef."

"It seems our esteemed Chef needed a little balance to his humors, so he drained a pint off last night." Tony lifted Nick's right hand. "Damn babe, that looks like it hurt."

"No worries, Mr. Torres, the pain was worth the reward." Tony picked up his coffee and gave Nick a puzzled look. "How so, Skipper?" Nick pulled Lynda's card out of his pocket, held it up for Tony to read, then flipped it over. As Tony read Lynda's note, his eyes popped open. "Damn, Skipper. I don't read Italian, but that's some sexy penmanship and that's her phone number. Way to go!" Willie squeezed Nick on the shoulder. "That gal is in for a treat, wouldn't you say so, Tony?"

"Absolutely, Colonel. You tell your son, yet?" Nick looked away. "Not yet, Tony. Maybe later tonight at the gym."

"Good morning, gentlemen. There certainly are a lot of happy voices coming out of here. What's all the excitement about?" Tony turned towards Amy and lowered his voice. "Oh, pardon us, Miss Sommers. It was nothing." Tony looked away and Willie took his hand off of Nick's shoulder. "Good morning, Miss Sommers. Our sincerest apologies; I was just telling these two young men about the time Naughty Natalie and I strafed a whore house in Berlin and all these German SS officers came running out with their pants around their ankles. I would have shot every damn one of them one my second pass if I could have stopped laughing long enough to aim straight. Later that night, Natalie's gun camera film was shown to sellout crowds at bases all over England." Tony smirked and looked away, while Nick looked down at his coffee and bit his bottom lip. The interest and smile quickly faded from Amy's face. "Well, that sounds interesting. I'll just grab a Diet Coke and get going. Nick, I'll see you at the meeting."

"Yes ma'am, of course. See you in ten minutes." Amy helped herself to a soda and quickly walked away. As she passed the 1949's threshold, the three men could barely contain themselves. Tony Torres cracked first, and quickly covered his mouth with a beverage napkin.

"Colonel, you are priceless, you know that?"

"Well actually Nick, I know exactly what I'm worth. When I was shot down for the third time, I was rescued by the French resistance and was traded for two cartons of Lucky Strike cigarettes, four pair of panty hose and 12 Hershey's bars. So you see, everything has a price, even me." Tony broke into hard laughter and gently patted the Colonel on his back. "You troublemakers are going to get me into hot water with the boss and I happen to like working here, so if you two will excuse me."

"Of course, Mr. Torres, I appreciate everything you do for us here. The Dodger has a good-looking lunch menu today." Tony walked into the kitchen muttering, "Whore house in Berlin."

"Thanks, Colonel. I really don't need Miss Sommers prying into my life."

"Oh, come on now, Nick. She wasn't prying, but she didn't need to hear all of that. Listen, I think Miss Sommers is doing a fine job here and she is a lovely person."

"She is lovely, isn't she? Colonel, how are the members taking to her?"

"Honestly Nick, she was faced with some tough decisions and has handled herself pretty well, wouldn't you say so?"

"Yes sir, I agree. When I found out she was a nurse, I thought she would last maybe four weeks, but here we are. It's late June, and she is really getting the job done. I have to say I have actually learned a lot from her. She is incredibly patient and has given me a few lessons, tips in managing my people, almost as if she was coaching me and not bossing me, you know what I mean? I think she's doing a fine job, Colonel. Between her and Grant, they have really transformed Overbrook. That staff down there is night and day over Miss what's-her-face had ... Damn, I can't even remember that gal's name that was running Overbrook. Oh well, it's not important. You know what's a shame, though? Her little girls are so pretty and their Dad never sees them. How's that possible, Colonel?" Willie scrutinized Nick. "You still talking about Miss Sommers, or what's-her-name?"

"Oh, sorry Colonel, I was talking about Miss Sommers. I was in her office one day and saw the photos on her desk, but there's not a photo of him anywhere. I asked her about her girls, and she sort of volunteered some info about her ex and what a loser he is and how he rarely calls or sees them." Willie slowly nodded his head and stroked his thin grey moustache.

"I see. That is a shame, isn't it? A fine woman like that should have a good man to share her life with. So Nick, where are you going to take your doctor?"

"You know what, Colonel? She's in pretty good shape."

"Of course."

"So I'll probably ask her to go for a run or a ride, see how she likes to keep in shape, you know, something she's comfortable doing and later, I'll take her to dinner at Northampton."

"That sounds like a good plan, Nick. Just try not to compare her to anyone, OK?"

"I'll try Colonel. I'll try."

"OK Nick, you have a meeting to get to and I could use a walk in the sun." Nick stood up straight and looked Willie in the eyes. "Thank you, Colonel."

"Anytime, Nick." Willie winked at Nick before slowly shuffling off behind his tennis ball-tipped walker. "Off I go, into the wild blue yonder, flying high, into the sky."

Forty-five minutes later, Nick walked into his kitchen. "Dodger, how's the world treating you today?"

"All good, dawg!"

"Dodger, please don't call me dog."

"Yes, Chef."

"You need a hand with anything? You and Flo OK?"

"Yes, Chef."

"OK, I'm going to take a walk through Overbrook then. I'll be gone about 30 minutes or so."

Nick checked his email, grabbed a cup of water, put on a clean apron, and then headed downstairs, saying good morning to the residents and staff as he passed through the hallways. When he got to Hudson, he saw Chet Bannon and Beatrice Campbell, who were just finishing their breakfast.

"Hey Chet, Beatrice! How are you two doing this morning?"

Beatrice was 84 and had been a talent scout and agent in the Nashville music business for many years. She loved to talk about the early days of country music, and Chet was always one to listen to her stories. Her room was decorated with photos from her younger days, many of which included country music legends such as Earl Scruggs, Gene Autry, Johnny Cash and Chet Atkins. Beatrice had not aged well; the last few years had been hard on her. In the last couple of months, her hair had thinned significantly, her eyesight was fading and she had recently fallen, leaving her with a nasty bruise on the left side of her face. Her skin slid loosely across her bones, and she was full of age spots. Nick rarely saw anyone visit her and last week, Amy had mentioned that she was appropriate for hospice. That meant she probably had less than six months to live. She was a very proud woman and never left her room unless she was dressed as if she were headed out on the town. The CNAs spent a lot of time helping her pick out clothes, jewelry and brushing her hair.

"Oh, good morning, Chef. I was just telling Chet here about the first time I heard Roy Clark play. Please do sit down."

"Sure Beatrice, I would love to."

"You see, Roy Clark was playing guitar for Hank Penny's band. They were in Vegas playing at one of those hotels, the Nugget, I believe it was. I just happened to be in Vegas and my, my! I was just absolutely enthralled. Chet, did you know that Roy Clark had won the national banjo championships not once, but twice?"

"I don't think I did, Miss Beatrice. I'm not surprised, though. That is one talented man, and funny, too."

"Well, did you know that Roy also tried to make a living as a boxer? Can you imagine? A talented musician like that, a boxer? Suppose he had permanently damaged one of his hands in a fight? We all would have been deprived of some really amazing music, and the world would have been a less happier place. Anyway, Hank Penny did sort of a comedy routine when he played, and Roy really studied his style. Roy learned a lot about comedy, as well as music, from Hank. You know Roy Clark hosted the Tonight Show for Johnny Carson many times? Did you know that, Chef?"

"Yes ma'am, I used to watch the Tonight show when I was a kid. Always loved staying up late with my Mom and watching Johnny, but that was usually only on a Friday night that she would let me stay up that late. That was a treat."

"Did your Dad not care for Johnny?"

"Well Chet, honestly, my Dad wasn't around much."

"Oh." Amy Sommers was walking through Hudson. When she heard Nick's voice, she stopped just before the entrance and listened in. "Bea, you sure do look lovely this morning. Tell me about this dress you're wearing."

"Oh my, Nicholas, you do know how to talk to a lady." Beatrice lifted her right hand to the bruise on the left side of her face. "And me with this awful bruise on my face. You do say the sweetest things."

"That little bump? I hardly noticed it, Bea. Besides, it would take a lot more than that little bump to tarnish your beauty." Beatrice blushed. "You know, Nick, when I was a young lady, there were many times when I would walk onto a stage to introduce one of my musicians. When I stood in front of those lights, all the men in the audience would whistle and cheer and the ladies would all clap."

"Of course they did, Bea. They still would, right, Chet?" Chet smiled then wolf whistled at Bea while Nick clapped. Beatrice blushed and smiled, carefully stood up while steadying herself with her walker, slowly lifted her right arm and said, "Ladies and gentlemen, Miss Brenda Lee."

Amy walked in, stopped then took a bow as Chet and Nick clapped. "Sing us a song, Miss Sommers!" cheered Nick. Amy smiled and sat down with the three of them. "If I had a voice as pretty as Brenda Lee's, I would. How are you two doing today? Bea you look like you're enjoying all this attention from these two very handsome gentlemen." Amy turned to Nick and smiled, as he quickly looked away. "Oh, I certainly am, Miss Sommers." Beatrice slowly sat back down as Nick stood up and offered his hand, just in case she needed it. "Oh thank you, Nick. Miss Sommers, when my son takes me back home, I am going to miss your Chef terribly. Perhaps you could spare him a few days to come and cook for me in Nashville? My son is moving into a very large house, and I'll have my own master bedroom."

"I would be happy to come and cook for you in Nashville, Bea. Have your people call my people, OK?" Nick winked at Chet. "Now, if you all would excuse me, I have several reports to conjure up for Miss Sommers and the folks at our home office. Beatrice, Chet, if I don't see you two again, have a wonderful day. And Miss Sommers, I'm certain I'll see you again before the end of the day."

Nick stood up, took Beatrice's hand and kissed it, then turned and left the room. Beatrice blushed again and brought her right hand to her chest, exhaled then looked at Amy. "Our Chef does say the kindest things." Amy smiled and agreed as Saffron walked in, said hello, and reminded Beatrice that it was time for her medicine and a blood pressure check. "Oh Saffron, must you spoil our good times?"

"Sorry Miss Bea, but we wants you to be healthy when the Grand Ole Opry comes looking for you, right?"

"Well, I suppose you're correct."

"Well speaking of work, I need to get going as well. " Amy excused herself and walked through the rest of Overbrook checking up on everyone.

Two hours later, Amy walked into the kitchen for a drink and saw Nick sitting in his office, typing away. She walked over and knocked lightly on the door. Nick looked up and smiled. Amy opened his door and took a seat opposite his desk. "How's your hand, Nick?"

"My hand? It's fine, a little tender maybe, but I'm fine." He reached over and closed his laptop.

"Are you keeping it dry?"

"Yes ma'am, trying my best."

"Nick, that was awfully sweet of you to spend time with Beatrice."

"Thank you, Miss Sommers. You know, her son never comes over. In the nine months I have been here, I think he's been here once. He didn't even make it over for Mother's Day. She's not moving into that big house he built, either."

"I know. Honestly, I don't think she'll be with us much longer."

"I've noticed the changes. She has gotten so unsteady lately and her skin has gotten so loose, I keep asking her to eat. I'm trying to cook something special for her every chance I get, but she's on so many medications that it's probably robbing her of her appetite. She did ask for some chicken noodle soup so later, I'm going to make a big batch and Saffron can put some small portions in the freezer for her." Amy looked at Nick and thought to herself that this could not possibly be the same smart-ass that was so immature to her and Rivers her first day on the job.

"Miss Sommers, were you going to say something?"

"Oh, um, no Nick, just thank you. That was very kind of you to say those things to Beatrice, that's all." Nick put his ink pen down. "Miss Sommers, when was the last time a man paid any attention to Bea? Her husband died seven years ago, and while she may have a wonderful retirement home to live in plus great care and attention, well, some people just need a little bit of special attention every once in a while, don't you think so?" Amy thought to herself how long it had been since a man paid her a sincere compliment, took her to dinner, held her hand or opened a car door for her. "You're right, Nick. Some people need special attention every once in a while. Now, if you would excuse me, I too, have reports to conjure for the home office, plus a very full schedule, and there's nothing at home for supper tonight, so I'm really pushed for time." Amy stood up and opened the door. "Thank you, Nick."

"For what, Miss Sommers?"

"Well, just thank you."

"You're welcome, Miss Sommers."

"And Nick, do you think you could call me Amy?"

"Yes ma'am, of course, oh, and Miss Sommers?"

"Yes, Nick?"

"I love those little clock faced earrings you wear. They're very unique and they look great on you." Amy smiled and realized she was about to blush, so she quickly excused herself and made her way back to her office.

Three hours later, Nick went looking for Tony Torres and found him at the podium. "Hey Tony, I'm missing some invoices for your last two wine purchases."

"No worries, babe; they're in my office. Look in the right side of my desk in that invoices folder. There's probably a liquor invoice in there, as well."

"How we looking tonight? Busy?"

"Of course, I was just counting reservations. Looks like we may hit 105 to 110."

"Damn. I guess I'm on the line again, so much for taking Theo out to dinner. All done with lunch?"

"Yeah, 58 covers for lunch, and Mrs. Stafford is the last table left in the dining room."

"Who's she with?"

"Her son and grandkids."

"Shit, I need to go."

"Oh Nick, Nick, you remember my son, Todd?" Nick summoned up his discipline, then turned and smiled warmly at Todd and Beverly as Caleb and Matthew raced past. "Yes, of course, Beverly. Todd, how are you?" Todd Stafford walked to within eight inches of Nick, stared him down then thrust his hand out so Nick could shake his hand.

"Mighty fine, Chef, mighty fine, I shot my first buck of the season yesterday, and can't wait to taste those venison steaks on the grill."

"I wasn't aware it was deer season yet."

"It's not," Todd said smugly.

"How's your lovely wife doing, Chef?" Nick searched Todd's eyes for an answer. Was he trying to be an asshole, or did he honestly not know that Robin was gone?

"Mrs. Stafford, can I offer anyone a mint?" Beverly and Todd both turned to Tony, who was holding out the jar of starlight mints that he kept on his podium. Tony shook the jar until the mints rattled.

"Oh, thank you so much, Tony."

As Todd reached for a mint, Nick backed away. "Well folks, I need to be going. You all have a fine day." Nick retreated to the safety of his kitchen.

"Hey boss, what are you doing here? I thought you were watching the All-England Cricket Championships over at that wine bar you like?"

"Funny, Xavier. Don't you have some parsley to chop?" Nick banged through the kitchen, shoved his way through the stairwell door, trotted down the stairs then walked out the back door. He stopped when he got behind the maintenance shed. *"Fuck that worthless piece of shit, Stafford!"* He looked around for something to hit, but saw only concrete, trees and cars. He dropped to the ground and started doing push-ups. His arms began burning when he hit 56, but he kept going. At 62, his abs became tight and at 68, his deltoids and triceps were on fire. When he hit 73, he was barely able to return to the horizontal position. He let himself drop to the ground, caught his breath and rolled over and looked up at the sky. He put his right arm over his forehead to shield his eyes from the sun. He used to love summertime. What's not to love about summer in upstate South Carolina? Three hours from the beach, an hour from the Blue Ridge Mountains, more amazing produce than a cook knew what to do with, baseball games to go to, hikes up Looking Glass, lots of bike rides and micro brews to enjoy on the back patio of the Tavern after closing time.

Robin stuck her head in the kitchen. "Hey sweetheart, there's a guy out here with some white nectarines for sale. You want to take a look?"

"I love nectarines! Hell yeah, I want to take a look."

"I thought you loved me?"

"I do love you, sweetheart." Nick wrapped his arms around Robin and pulled her close, nuzzled her ears with his nose, then slowly whispered, "I love you, Robin St. Germaine." His whispers set off electrical impulses that coursed through her body. She reached up and put her hands on his face and they slowly kissed. Nick's hands glided down her back to her bottom just as Xavier walked into the kitchen.

"Oh come on, you two! Haven't ya'll got in enough practice for the National Face Sucking Championships? I mean really, I have work to do here. Will you all go out back, please?"

"Yes sir, Xavier, sorry."

"Someone has to get some work done in this place, you know."

"Chef, you OK?" Nick opened his eyes to see Xavier standing over him.

"Yeah, Xavier, I'm fine. Why?"

"*Why?* You're out here lying on the sidewalk staring at the sun, that's why. Listen, if you need to take off, just ask Sleepy to work a double. He's only got 32 hours this week."

"Yeah, I know, but the boss is fussing at me already. I ran almost 15 hours over last week."

"Then tell her to get her pretty little self on the salad station tonight. You can't keep pushing yourself like this, Chef." Nick rolled over and stood up, dusted off his Chef coat and started walking towards the door.

"I'm fine. Come on, Xavier, let's get to work." Xavier patted Nick on the back.

"You sure you're OK?"

"I'm fine, Xavier. Let's make it happen." Nick stopped at the bathroom then hustled back into the kitchen.

"Hey babe, I was looking for you."

"Yeah, well I had to go to the bathroom."

"Uh, huh; boy, that Stafford guy is something else. What a tool."

"Yeah, what a tool, hey, thanks for distracting him, Tony."

"Listen Skipper, anything going on between you two I should know about?"

"I really don't want to talk about it, Tony. Can we just pass on this subject?"

"Listen Nick, if this guy is gonna keep coming around, well, maybe you should come clean with me." Nick looked for a way around Tony, but Tony moved in front of him and blocked his path. *"Look, he's just the biggest fucking creep in the state of South Carolina, that's all. Satisfied, Tony?"*

"Whoa, slow down boss. This is Tony Torres you're talking to, remember?" Nick looked around, then turned his attention back to Tony and exhaled. "Sorry Tony, let's go into my office."

"Sure thing, babe." They walked the 20 feet to Nick's office and Tony closed the door. "Touchdown Todd

Stafford, basically a washed-up has been. Last I saw of him he was the Athletic admin at the university. He used to come into the Tavern, always so obnoxious, what a scumbag. Well, one day, and this was years ago, he starts showing up with women other than Mrs. Stafford, and one was his administrative assistant. This goes on for a few months, and rumor has it that this girl tells him she wants a ring and demands he ditch his wife. So what does Stafford do?"

"Fires her?"

"Bingo! So she goes to the university's board, tells them everything and of course, the university ends up firing *him* for screwing this gal. Then, his wife rakes him over the coals in a very nasty divorce. He was some hotshot football player way back when for South Carolina, Touchdown Todd they called him, so he's somewhat of a minor celebrity around here, so that makes the whole thing fodder for the media."

"OK, so I guess now he's cuddling up to mommy because cash is an issue?"

"I'll bet you've hit the nail on the head, brother. I had to escort him out of the Tavern one night. This was a few days after the paper ran a big story about his troubles. He came into the bar and Kelly only sold him one drink, but he must have had a few on the ride over because 20 minutes later, he was hammered and belligerent. So Kelly politely cuts him off, Robin offers to call a cab for him. Well, he grabbed her on the butt and says something like, "I'll ride this home.""

"Oh boy, you two didn't come to blows, did you?"

"Not quite. One of my waits stuck her head in the kitchen and yelled for me to come out to the bar but by the time I got out there a buddy of mine, Dave had already taken care of business. Dave's a Clemson grad that just so happened to be a part-time boxing instructor, and he showed no mercy on a washed up Carolina tailback that groped his friend's wife. Dave had this jackass on the floor with one foot on his neck and his wrist twisted behind his back, and Kelly had already called the cops. Good Lord, that rivalry is pretty serious shit. So when I found out what happened, I picked his sorry ass up by the belt loops and tossed him into the parking lot just as the cops showed up, and of course his ass went right to jail for drunk and disorderly conduct. Anyway, after that, he fell off the radar for a while. That was maybe three and a half years ago. I've heard Beverly talk about her son, Todd, maybe once or twice, but I never put two and two together."

Tony laughed and shook his head. "Yeah, that Clemson-Carolina shit is hard core. Look skipper, I think it's best that you go to the boss on Monday morning and tell her this just to get it all on the table. In the meantime, please steer clear of this guy. I like working for you and want you to stick around, but if you so much as look at this guy with crossed eyes, he'll have a case, understand? That's the way it is in the corporate world, so please mind your manners around him? Got it?"

"Sure, whatever, Tony."

"Am I getting through to you, skipper?"

"Yes, Mr. Torres," groaned Nick.

"Good man. Who loves ya, babe?"

"You do, Mr. Torres."

Amy looked at the time. 5:54 p.m. Damn! She sent a text to her girl's sitter saying she was on the way and quickly received a response: "they wanna know what's 4 supper." Amy gathered up her laptop and the folders she wanted to bring home and stuffed them into her shoulder bag. "I'm going, Jess. I still have to pick up a pizza or something for the girls, so I'll see you tomorrow."

"Goodnight, boss!" Amy closed her door and as she walked past the front desk, Dawn stopped her.

"Miss Sommers, this is for you." Dawn pointed to a large paper bag on the floor next to her desk.

"What is it?"

"Well, it smells like your dinner." Amy leaned over the bag and was met with aromas of roasted chicken, bacon, Brussels sprouts, thyme, garlic and freshly baked bread. There was a sticky note on the bag that read, "knew you were pushed for time". Amy looked back at Dawn, who lightly sang, "Someone must like you." Amy stood up, turned towards the kitchen, then looked back at the bag and thought about how late she was. She lifted the bag, reached out for Dawn's hand and whispered, "Thank you for keeping this between us girls, Dawn." Dawn winked at Amy and answered her phone.

"It's a great day at Woodmont. This is Dawn."

Two and a half hours later, Nick's crew was finishing up for the day. He checked his phone for messages and saw one from Amy. "thank u 4 dinner, who told u I love Brussels sprouts?" Nick looked up and smiled.

"What're you grinning about Chef?"

"Nothing, listen Chef Randall, I'm gonna take off, OK?" Kevin shooed him away with a wave of his right hand. Nick walked to his office, took off his Chef coat, changed his shoes and then turned off the light. He hesitated, turned the light back on, sat down at his desk, turned on his computer, and then typed up an email to Amy regarding the incident with Todd Stafford, did an internet search for Todd Stafford, found several links to stories detailing his past, attached them to the email, and then hit send. He turned off his computer, turned off the light, and then headed home.

11

Amy reached out for her Blackberry. Damn, it was 5:49. She had assumed that since her girls were away with her sister for an impromptu trip to the beach, she would naturally sleep late. However, the house was just too quiet. She rolled around for a few minutes, but her mind raced with thoughts of work and everything she was hoping to accomplish in the next few days. What the hell, might as well get to it. An hour later, Amy was unlocking the door to her office. She consulted her daily to-do list and spent ten minutes planning out her day. She planned to be on campus right up until 8 p.m. She could even have supper here; if she walked into the dining room, surely some group of residents would ask her to join them. Amy spent the next few minutes looking at overtime reports and schedules and noticed that Grant had scheduled extra time for a couple of his folks. Maybe this was an oversight, but she still typed up a quick email asking Grant to take a look and offer an explanation. Everyone else's schedules looked good. Next a quick scroll through the marketing calendar looking for upcoming events that she thought she should attend. After that, Amy looked through the emails from the corporate office looking for something to put on the list for the day. Most of ones she read were from Harriett asking for specific actions or paying her a compliment. Harriett never missed the opportunity to offer some encouragement. Amy did see one from the head of marketing asking for comments on the recent sales luncheon. She banged out a quick email with her concerns and suggestions, hit reply then looked at the time, ten after seven. Continental breakfast went out at seven a.m. She could use a cup of coffee and with any luck, there might be some doughnuts. Perhaps she could snatch one without the wait staff catching her. She stood up and took a quick stretch, reminding herself that she really should join a gym. Long days of sitting through meetings and staring at her laptop would quickly catch up to her, if she wasn't careful.

She walked into the 1949 and to her delight saw a sliver tray of freshly delivered Krispy Kreme doughnuts.

"I should do this more often," she said to the Jensen's. The three of them briefly chatted while helping themselves to coffee and doughnuts. She said hello to the other members already there and headed back to her office. As she passed the stairs, she decided to head out back and take in the morning sun while enjoying her doughnut. As Amy trotted downstairs past the entrance to the ballroom, she heard a handful of animated voices coming from around the corner. She took a look and saw Doris and her group headed towards the pool, but no one was dressed for a swim. She looked at her Blackberry. 7:16. She looked around but saw no one else, so she finished her doughnut and headed off to investigate. She rounded the corner to the pool entrance and saw two walkers outside of Franklin's office. The lights were off, but she gently opened the door and offered a tentative "Hello?" She was greeted with guilty looks from the two Susan's, Doris Peters, Peggy and Ginger Rogers. They all stared at Amy with open mouths. Doris was wearing a pair of paper 3D glasses and eating a bag of popcorn, her right hand frozen halfway to her mouth. Ginger had a pair of gold opera glasses around her neck, which she used to peer at Amy. Doris grabbed Amy by the hand and spoke up.

"Well, don't just stand there, lady. Get in here and be quiet, and don't touch that light switch."

"What on *earth* are you all doing in here?" asked Amy as Doris dragged her into the office by her left hand.

"Lady, are you gonna be quiet or do I have to pull out my brass knuckles?" Amy looked through the pool observation window and it all made sense. Nick was swimming in the pool, and the ladies were watching. She took a step towards the window to get a better look, but several hands pulled her back. "Not so close Sommers, or he'll see you!" fussed Doris.

The window was off-set at a 30-degree slant and since the office was about four feet higher than the pool, Franklin's office offered a good view of the entire area. Nick was freestyle stroking through the water, his muscular arms rising up, stabbing through the frothy water, hands pointed forward, fingers together, feet steadily kicking. As Amy watched Nick, she remembered the comment card she had read the day before she walked on campus. "Chef Nick looks great in swim trunks," and even though he was moving quickly, it was obvious why the ladies were here. Nick looked great in swim trunks.

"Oh, Miss Sommers, do back up. Otherwise, Nicholas is likely to see you," pleaded one of the Susan's.

"Yes, of course." Amy took two steps back from the window.

"Popcorn?" asked Doris. Amy looked at Doris, who had removed her 3D glasses and was holding out the bag of popcorn. Amy looked at the bag of popcorn, then at a smiling Doris Peters and whispered.

"I shouldn't be in here. This is wrong."

"Can you just sit still and enjoy yourself?"

"No, I'm sorry, I shouldn't be in here." Amy reached for the door when Ginger squeaked.

"Oh no, he's getting out!" As they attempted to duck out of sight, Amy heard so many old bones and joints creak and groan in protest it sounded like someone snapping celery stalks. "Oh Jesus! Ouch! Crap!" they all groaned. Slowly their heads rose up to just above the desk as they cautiously looked out the window. Nick had gotten out of the pool on the near side and was toweling himself off not eight feet away. Amy was stuck. If she opened the door to go, Nick would see her leaving. She would have to stay put. Ginger lifted her opera glasses.

"He's put a bit more definition on his deltoids, gals." Amy turned and looked at Ginger, who in turn looked at Amy. Ginger blushed, turned back to the window and put the glasses back to her eyes. "I'm a retired doctor you know; I can't help noticing such things, Miss Sommers."

"Whose turn was it to count laps?" demanded Doris.

"Mine, but I swear he only did 18," responded Peggy.

"Oh, you are getting old. Miss Sommers, I think you should send Peggy Einstein here to memory care tomorrow," she quietly rasped. Peggy reached over and pinched Doris on the waist. "Ouch! Will you cut that out? I was only teasing, and can I just enjoy the show here, please? I'm getting a THO."

"What's a THO?" Amy quietly asked. "A tittie hard-on, lady. Sheesh! What rock did you grow up under?"

"If I had any, they would be hard. Damned cancer!" chimed in Susan Simpson. Amy could not help but giggle, but deep down she was embarrassed. This episode would surely make its way out to other members, as there were few secrets at a place such as Woodmont. Nick finished toweling off and headed to the shower, listening for the whispers as he walked past Franklin's office. As he did, he was certain he smelled a new perfume. He opened the door to the men's locker and smiled as the door closed behind him. Amy stood up and helped the others do the same, then quietly asked everyone to please keep this to themselves (though she knew it was pointless). She excused herself and as she was walking away, Peggy asked her if they should call her for the next showing. "No thank you, ladies." Amy picked up her coffee and headed back upstairs. 90 minutes later, she and her team assembled for the nine a.m. meeting. As they got down to business, Amy found it difficult to focus. Nick sat not five feet away from her. She had a lot of respect for him; he knew his business, took care of his staff and went to great lengths to make sure the members enjoyed themselves. And she had sat there in a darkened room spying on him like a 13-year-old girl. She felt awful. 30 minutes later, Amy was asking everyone to have a great day as they gathered up their stuff and headed out.

"Nick, um, may I have a word with you, please?"

"Yes ma'am, of course." He sat down at her table and waited patiently as the others filed out. He thought to himself that Amy's perfume certainly felt familiar. When they were alone, Amy looked at Nick and tried to apologize.

"Nick, I ... uh ... I am ... uh, not sure how to say this."

"Did you enjoy the show, Miss Sommers?" Amy was mortified. She put her head down in shame.

"Nick, it was not my intention to spy on you. I saw the walkers outside Franklin's office, opened the door to see what was going on, and was dragged in. I knew immediately what I was doing was wrong, but apparently you got out of the pool early, so I was stuck. I told the ladies that I should not have been there. Please don't think that I'm some sort of deviant. I'm just a victim of circumstance. You have my sincerest apologies. It won't happen again, and I'll ask the ladies to stop as well."

"*Whoa!* Slow down, boss. Please don't be so hard on yourself." He leaned forward. "Look, if you tell Doris' group that they can't watch me anymore, you're just going to get his thing blown out of proportion, right?" Amy slowly nodded her head in agreement. "And you certainly don't need any negative press, right?" Again, she nodded. "And I can swim so long as I am out by eight. That's when the classes start, right?"

"Yes, you can keep swimming, Nick," she replied, cautiously.

"OK, stop worrying about it boss, water under the bridge, right?"

"Of course, water under the bridge," agreed Amy, softly. She picked her head up, adjusted her glasses and looked him in the eyes. "Nick, may I ask you something?" She hesitated. "Never mind." He reached across the table for her hand and held it for a second or two.

"No, feel free to ask." Amy looked down at his hand as his thumb stroked the top of her hand twice before he pulled his hand back. "You want to know how I knew you were there, correct? I smelled a new perfume as I walked past Franklin's office, and when I sat down with you, your perfume came back to me. That, and the fact that you couldn't look at me during the meeting, I sensed your embarrassment and, well, I just added up two and two. No big deal." Amy just shook her head. The more she got to know Nick, the more she appreciated his intellect and intuition.

"Well, that wasn't what I was going to ask you."

"Well, then fire away. I have another seven or eight minutes for you." Nick leaned back, put his hands behind his head and offered Amy an easy smile.

"Why do you work so much? You're always here, you have a son, you should really have a life outside of Woodmont." The smile faded from Nick's face as he let his chair drop onto all four legs, and put his hands down on the table in front of him. Amy reached out for Nick's hand, but he pulled away. "I'm sorry, Nick. I shouldn't have asked you that."

"No, no, you're right, Miss Sommers. I am always here and I work too much. Uh, listen, when I, uh, got through my wife's funeral and all the attention died down, I, uh, sort of floundered around for about a year. Theo and I moved to a smaller house to put some distance between us and those memories. I sold the restaurant and spent a lot of time with him, but he's practically a man now. We have a great relationship, but he has his friends, he's gonna be a senior soon, school and basketball keep him pretty busy. He studies a lot and practices a lot, even in the summer, and he uh, tutors younger kids in math. He's a good kid, he uh, doesn't want to disappoint Mom, you know?" Nick briefly looked up at Amy, wiped his eyes on his shoulders then looked back down at his hands. "And uh, so when I'm home, it's easy to uh, get blue, and I end up, you know, feeling lonely and uh, melancholic, and I don't like that so I go to the gym or go to work. I need a lot of distractions to get me through the day because when I'm home, a lot of times it's just me, the cat and memories of Robin."

"Forgive me for asking Nick," as she offered him a tissue.

"No, no, no need for apologies, Miss Sommers. I keep these folks happy, and they in turn provide plenty of distraction for me. Perhaps you haven't noticed, but a lot of our people have gone through a death, too, because of their age. Why do you think I spend so much time with Doris and her friends? I know they're twice my age, but when I'm with them. Well, we have something very painful that binds us together, and they tend to look after me. When a friend of mine asks me how I'm doing, well, they uh, *they really don't want to know the truth*, because they can't fathom losing their wife or husband. They really don't want to know what I'm going through." Nick thanked Amy for the tissue, wiped his eyes then wiped his tears off of the lacquered table with a quick circular motion. "When Doris or Peggy stops me in the hallway and asks me how I'm doing or offers me a hug, they know exactly how I'm doing. They sense I'm having a really crappy day and memories of Robin are swirling around me. They've all lost their husbands and know exactly what I'm going through. That's why I'm here. It's as if I work at a club for widows. I fit in pretty good here, Miss Sommers, I fit in pretty good. May I go now, please?"

Amy nodded her head, wiped her eyes and whispered one more apology. She felt so stupid. Why couldn't she have sensed that? It all made perfect sense, but here she was with a damn degree in psychology, and she totally missed that one. Suddenly, her diploma felt as useful as a wet paper towel. She gave Nick a good head start before leaving the room. She had definitely worn out her welcome for the day.

Nick glanced at the clock on the wall. 5:35. Dinner to Overbrook was done and delivered, he had three cooks for the dinner shift and only 90 reservations, plus Mr. Torres was up front. Maybe he would call it a day and grab dinner at Koji with Theo. He looked at his to-do list and wondered if he should knock out a project for Amy first. Nick's phone buzzed with a text message. He didn't recognize the number, but the subject line said, "it's Lynda," so he opened it up. "It's Lynda G hey Nick, want to go for a run on the swamp rabbit? meet me there in 30? medico lynda g" Damn. He looked at his hand. It had been five days since he had cut himself, and he was planning on having Candace pull the stitches in the next day or two. He turned and looked at the clock again. "How did she get my number?"

"Who?" Nick looked back at the clock then turned to Chef Randall.

"You OK, Chef?"

"Uh, yeah, I think so. Chef Randall, would you mind if I, uh, take off?" Xavier looked up from his cutting board.

"Chef, you know that the Ralph Lauren Polo Championship highlights don't start until eight p.m. Why you want to bail out on us now?"

"Well, I've just been invited to go for a run on the Swamp Rabbit with a beautiful physician." Xavier stood up straight, put his hands on his cutting board and lifted his right eyebrow. "Shirt on or shirt off, Chef?"

"Oh, come on Xavier, give me some credit, please. You guys OK if I take off, yes or no?" Kevin Randall waved his left hand as if to shoo him away. Xavier wasn't budging. "Shirt on or shirt off, Chef?"

"Xavier, if our relationship is going to grow, she's going to have to get to know me as a person first, and only after accepting me as a man of intellect and courage will I take my shirt off in front of her." Xavier shook his head. "Chef, you won't be 50 feet down that jogging trail, then you're gonna ask her if she appreciates badminton as an Olympic sport. She's gonna look at you like you got two heads, and your shirt's gonna come flying off!"

Chrissy put her hands under her chin and batted her eyes at Xavier and breathlessly said, "Oh, I've never watched Olympic badminton before, but maybe we can watch it together, if you take your shirt off!"

"Alright, enough of this people. I swear I am going to report every one of you to Jessica first thing in the morning." Xavier put his arm around Nick and patted him on the right side of his face, then kissed him on the cheek.

"Get out of here please, and have a good time, OK?"

"Yes sir, and please don't ever kiss me again Mr. James." Xavier smiled broadly and wagged a thick finger at Nick.

"Ah, but now you won't have any tension over your first kiss on this date!" Chrissy high-fived Xavier. Nick could only shake his head and smile.

"I'm just going for a run; it's not a date, OK?" He responded to Lynda with, "I'll be there doc." Lynda quickly responded with a smiley face icon. Nick went into his office, closed the door, dropped the blinds and changed into his running clothes. He had a choice of two shirts, both short sleeved Under/Armour, one silver and one fire-engine red. He put on the silver one, then changed his mind and switched into the red one. He stuffed his work clothes into the gym bag, laced up his shoes and opened the blinds. As he walked out of the office, Xavier, Kevin, Chrissy and String Bean whistled at him. He smiled and waved, then ran down the stairs and out the back door. He met Amy also walking to her car.

"Well, hey Nick, you headed to the gym?"

"Uh, no ma'am, I'm actually going for a run with a friend."

"Oh, how far are you going?"

"Um, not sure, maybe three miles, maybe less. Do you run, Miss Sommers?"

"Not really. I used to, but I haven't done it on a regular basis in a few years. Sometimes, I do aerobics at this small studio in the mornings and I like to walk with the girls in the evening, try to keep them active, but that's about it. I would love to take up running again though, um, Nick, about this morning ... "

"Water under the bridge, Miss Sommers, OK? Anyway, here's my car. I'll see you tomorrow morning."

"Yes, of course, have a good run, Nick. Tomorrow we need to talk about that email regarding Todd Stafford, OK?"

"Yes ma'am, thank you, I'll see you tomorrow."

Nick got in his car, threw his gym bag in the passenger seat and started the engine. He tapped the accelerator pedal gently, adjusted the rear-view mirror and caught a glimpse of the red shirt he was wearing. He shook his head and changed back into the silver one. "That's better." Nick slowly drove through the parking lot, passing Amy who was still walking to her car. He offered a slight wave, and she smiled. As Nick drove past, he glanced in his rear view mirror and admired her figure. "Miss Amy Sommers, with such a lousy exercise regimen, how do you stay so gorgeous?"

As Amy watched him drive past, she sighed and said to herself, "And please call me Amy."

12

"Morning all," said Nick as he walked into the Armory. Jeanine, Lisa, Jessica, Grant and Amy were already there. "How was your run yesterday, Nick?"

"Fine, Miss Sommers."

"How far did you go?"

"Not far. Maybe three miles."

"Nick, do you run with a group?"

"Not usually, Grant. I ran with a friend yesterday, just down the Swamp Rabbit Trail."

"I should start running with you, Nick. This Carolina lifestyle doesn't agree with my waistline."

"Don't blame your expanding waistline on this fine state, buddy. Why don't you try a salad in lieu of a cheeseburger, once in a while."

"OK, you're right, Nick, totally my fault. If I bring a change of clothes, maybe we could run one day, maybe say, five p.m. or so?"

"I suppose I could take pity on a United States Navy veteran and humor you. Sure, Grant. I always keep a set of gym clothes with me so any time. Afternoons are best for something like that. But I warn you, I don't run to sight see." Nick looked across the table at Amy. She was wearing a sarong-style, royal blue sundress, her favorite diamond pendant and a new set of clock-faced earrings. She looked down at her notes, and her hair rolled off her shoulders. She reached up with her left hand, pulled her hair back and then sat up straight, catching Nick looking at her, and smiled at him. "If I held up a mirror, could you tell me the time, Miss Sommers?" She looked at her phone.

"8:56."

"Thank you." Nick looked over at Grant, who shrugged his shoulders.

"What is it, guys?"

"It's nothing, Miss Sommers." The rest of the team slowly made their way in and settled down. "OK folks, by my phone it's nine, so let's get going. I have my girls with me, so I am going to try and get out of here at noon. Grant, would you like to start us off please?"

"Yes ma'am. My biggest challenge right now is pharmacy. Our present provider just isn't getting the job done. I can't tell the residents that we don't have their meds. I've done some research and have received quotes from several, and would like to switch to PharmaStar. They have a great reputation locally, and I have been impressed with their company."

"Grant, don't we have a signed agreement in place with our present pharmacy?"

"Yes ma'am. However, I've tracked their missed delivery times, documented every one of them and by their own standards – promised and signed off on by their regional veep – they are already in default of their contract. I can kick them out tomorrow, and they will have no recourse."

"Hoo-rah, baby!" Nick leaned across the table and offered Grant a high five. "I knew Mr. Hughes was an O/C anal-retentive geek the first day I met him."

"Yeah, thanks Nick, I think."

"Don't mention it, Grant. I'm full of compliments today." Amy looked at her notes, then across the room at Lisa Simoneaux. "Lisa, do we have any admissions today?"

"Yes ma'am. Mr. Cecil Middleton is coming into Augusta today. Does anyone remember hearing his story on the news a few weeks ago? He and his wife were hit by a drunk driver, a young girl, only 18. His wife died at the scene and he suffered multiple injuries and has been at Piedmont Memorial. They were married for 40-some-odd years. He'll be here sometime around noon." Nick looked down at his hands and wondered where this conversation would lead.

"I remember reading about that," said Jessica. "The newspaper article quoted him as saying he was very concerned about the young girl, because this was something she would have to live with for the rest of her life." Nick kept his eyes down, put his left elbow on the table, rubbed his scalp and thought that any second now someone was going to suggest that we move on. "He actually met that girl a week later and offered his forgiveness, not three days after his wife was buried. Can you imagine?"

"Lisa, that is so amazing that someone can suffer such a terrible tragedy and offer so much forgiveness." Grant coughed loudly several times, and when Amy turned to Grant, he cut his eyes to Nick. Amy's eyes opened wide as she realized what was happening. Amy quickly interjected "and Mr. Middleton will need plenty of therapy, correct? We have him all set up, Grant?"

"Yes ma'am, we're all set."

"OK, moving on people. Jessica, do we have any interviews this week?"

"Yes ma'am, we have several CNAs coming in for second interviews this afternoon. Grant, I have these scheduled in the library at 1, 1:30, 2 and 2:45."

"Thank you for setting those up, Jessica. I'll be there."

"Maybe I'll pop in and give you a hand, Grant."

"That would be great, Amy."

"Nick, do you have anything on your calendar today, any events that we need to know about?" Nick kept his head down and pretended to flip through his notes.

"No, ma'am." Amy looked over at Grant, who made a slight twirl with his right forefinger as if to say, "Keep moving." Fifteen minutes later, the meeting had broken up and Amy was telling everyone to have a great day. Nick left quickly. After most of the team had left the room, she picked up her papers and laptop, then looked over at Jessica and shook her head.

"How could I have been so brain-dead, Jess? We just sat there talking about Mrs. Middleton being killed in a traffic accident, as if Nick wasn't even in the room. How could I have been so stupid?"

"Amy, don't beat yourself up. You weren't being insensitive. That kind of thing is going to come up in a place like this, and when it happens, it is going to have to be discussed. That's the nature of our business, you know that."

"I know, but I feel so awful."

"Do you want me to talk to Nick about this so that he knows we weren't being insensitive?"

"No, honestly, I think that I would prefer Grant to handle that one. Nothing personal, Jessica, but I believe Nick and Grant have a pretty good bond."

"Of course, that makes more sense. Come on, let's get to it. I have a long day ahead of me."

Nick made his way to the kitchen, said good morning to the Dodger, Flo and Jose, then looked at his calendar of events and his to-do list before taking a look at the lunch specials. The produce delivery was just coming in, so Nick verified the delivery, then signed for it.

"Dodger, tell me about this dish, chicken with onion relish, please?"

"Chef, I got a bone-in chicken breast that I'm gonna grill, and I was gonna make an onion relish with finely diced leeks, red onions, Vidalia onions and shallots. Gonna brown that in a little olive oil, then hit it with some white wine and champagne vinegar, reduce that, then add a touch of honey, some salt and finish with chopped parsley and chopped chives. That sound pretty dang cool, or what?"

"Yes sir, that sounds good. Don't forget to cool your relish before you add the herbs, otherwise you are going to lose those herb flavors right away."

"Yes Chef, will do."

"And Dodger, are you not worried that everyone's gonna order hot dogs today and ask for a double dose of that relish?"

"Well, I suppose that could happen, right?"

"Just make sure you have at least two cups of relish, and you should be fine."

"Yes, Chef."

"You know what would be cool, Dodger? If you took some honey and sugar-cane vinegar, mixed those two together in a small pot, whisked in some whole butter then used that as a finishing glaze." Dodger smiled at Nick, and they bumped knuckles.

"Morning, Skipper!" Nick turned and smiled as Tony approached. Tony put his right arm across Nick's shoulders, pulled him close and said quietly, "Heard you had a date yesterday," then rubbed Nick's head.

"Not exactly a date, brother, but I was certainly in the company of a beautiful physician for a couple of hours. We just went for a run then shared some gelato. That was it." Amy walked into the kitchen, smiled and chirped, "Good morning, Tony!"

"Good morning, Miss Sommers!" Tony turned away from Amy and tugged on Nick's Chef coat, dragging him into the office.

"So, where did you two go?"

"Well, we met downtown and we ran about a mile and a half on the trail, then turned around."

"OK, stop right now, Nick. What was she wearing?"

Nick grinned and looked Tony in the eyes. "Let me tell you something, Dr. Lynda Giansante is in *very* good shape. She was wearing three-quarter length black tights and a sleeveless pink Lycra top, and I promise that woman probably has 19% body fat. There is not one ounce of extra anything on her. A couple of times on the run, we had to switch places because of walkers or kids, and when she was in front of me, damn is that bottom of hers round! I had to keep reminding myself to keep my head up. After our run, well, we had gelato and chatted a bit. We didn't talk about anything earth-shattering, just small talk, med school, food, favorite restaurants and such. Then I had to get going, and we agreed to do it again soon."

"What do you mean, you had to get going?" Nick looked away. "I, uh, I had to go. I had things to do, you know?"

"OK, sure I understand, skipper. Good for you, baby steps, brother. Listen, I have a dining room to take care." They walked out of Nick's office and Tony patted Nick on

the back. "Yes sir, things to do. Thank you, Mr. Torres."
The kitchen phone rang and Dodger answered.

"Yes sir, understand."

"Chef?"

"Yeah, Dodger?"

"DHEC just pulled through the front gates."

"Perfect!" Nick groaned sarcastically. "And I thought today was going to be a great day. *Mr. Torres!* Please send someone behind the bar and make sure we're clean. Flo, Dodger, let's make sure we're all good please. No wet towels lying around. Hey String Bean, we're gonna have a health inspector in here in about five minutes. Let's shine it up, please, and I want fresh soap and sanitizer buckets out, lids on our garbage cans, and if that three-compartment sink is even slightly dirty, please drain it and leave it empty!" Nick quickly walked to his office. On any given day, he could have any number of reasons for the Department of Health to show up. Any business that sold food to the public received a routine inspection at least twice a year, and those lasted about an hour. A nursing home such as Overbrook, with three different levels of care, should expect to receive at least four to five inspections per year, and those could easily last all day. Plus, Overbrook accepted Medicare. That's federal money, so this could be a federal survey, and those held all the promise of a 48-hour long colonoscopy. His only federal health inspection had lasted two days, and there were three inspectors poking through every inch of the campus. Nick looked at the two Chef coats hanging up in his office. He could put on his short-sleeve, black coat and show off some muscle, just in case the inspector was a woman. That might help distract her, and perhaps she would be a bit lenient. If the inspector was a man, well, most state employees tended to be in lousy shape and Nick wouldn't want to make anyone uncomfortable. His other option was his white, long-sleeve, embroidered Egyptian cotton coat. Better not risk it, so he decided to go with the white one. He pulled the pen and thermometer out of his pocket and quickly yanked off his Chef coat, set it on the chair, and reached for the white coat.

"Uh-hum."

Nick turned around. Standing at the threshold of his office was Amy Sommers and her two girls, Paige and Rebecca. Rebecca was smiling, and Paige had her mouth open. Nick was wearing a ribbed tank-top undershirt, so he quickly pulled on his white coat.

"Uh, sorry, my apologies, Nick. I just wanted to introduce you to my girls. This is Paige and Rebecca."

"No wonder Mom's always talking about you," smirked Rebecca. Amy popped Rebecca on the side of her arm. "Rebecca, where are your manners?" Nick knelt down a bit, smiled and poked Paige in her stomach.

"You must be Paige. Your Mom talks about you all the time, too. She says you're so fiery that you eat your chocolate chip cookies dipped in hot sauce. Is that true?" Paige was five years old, with dark brown hair like her mother's that was twisted into a pony tail. She was holding a Barbie doll; her eyes sparkled as she twisted her arms behind her back and grinned.

"No, Mr. Nick, that's not true." Amy's phone rang, so she answered it. Nick stood up.

"Your Mommy's about to say a naughty word, girls."

"*Shit!* Understand."

"Told you so," smiled Nick. Paige looked up at Nick, put her right hand over her mouth and smiled. He winked back. "Nick, we have a survey crew from DHEC that just drove onto campus. Do you need anything from me?"

"No ma'am."

"Girls, I'm sorry but the two of you are going to have to head back to my office and entertain yourselves and please forgive me for saying that word. I better not catch either of you talking like that!"

"Hey boss, how about if I bring them down to the theatre and they can watch *Sound of Music* or *Mary Poppins*?"

"Thank you so much, Nick. That would be great."

"Oh, yeah! I love *Mary Poppins!*" Paige cheered.

"Sure, what's not to like about someone that can clean up a room with just a swish of her magic umbrella, right?" Nick looked at the scar on his hand. "I wish I could do that here sometimes. Come on, girls. You need something to drink before we go? I have spoiled milk, warm carrot juice or hot tea. Which would you prefer?"

"You're just being silly, Mr. Nick. I want a Coke."

"Tell ya what, young lady. Since Coca Cola is caffeinated and your mother has gone back up front to meet our visitors, how about if we stick with fruit juice for now, and switch to the caffeinated stuff later. Apple, orange or cranberry, girls? And we gotta make it fast. We wouldn't want our DHEC friends to find unlicensed children in my kitchen; I would be in deep doo-doo." Nick poured two glasses of juice, then ushered Paige and Rebecca out the back door and down to the movie theatre. Once inside, Rebecca started sorting through the DVDs and picked out *2012*. "Let's watch this one please, Nick. It's PG-13." Nick looked at the box and shook his head. "Sorry Rebecca, but I promised someone *Mary Poppins*, and I would prefer you call me Mr. St. Germaine, OK?"

"Only if you call me, Becca."

"You got it, Becca. Let me guess, you're 13, right?" Nick looked at his phone: 10:02 a.m. "I'll make you a deal, girls. If your Mom is still here at lunch time, I'll make you the prettiest lunch you've ever seen, OK?"

"OK, Chef Nick. I like my lunch with chocolate milk, please?"

"That's a deal, Paige. OK ladies, here we go. Mary Poppins on the eight-foot surround-sound screen in three, two, one."

"Walt Disney presents."

"Paige, are you gonna read all the opening credits?"

"Julie Andrews."

"*Paige?* I swear, my little sister can be so ... "

"You two sweethearts enjoy yourself, OK? Chef Nick is needed upstairs. Cheerio, ladies!"

Nick rushed back upstairs and tried to think positive thoughts, but a survey team could really ruin your day. In a health-care facility's kitchen, it was not enough to serve tasty, properly prepared, nutritious food. There is also a load of paperwork that went along with virtually every piece of equipment. All the refrigerated or heated equipment required logbooks, and the cooks had to record the units' internal temperatures three times a day. Wash and rinse temperatures and sanitizer levels were also recorded thrice daily for the dish machine and the three-compartment sinks. On top of that, every bit of food delivered to Overbrook had to be within proper temperature ranges, and those temperatures had to be recorded. If something was sent out hot, it had to be served at a minimum temperature of 141 degrees. Cold food, such as potato salad or fruit salad, was served at a maximum temperature of 41 degrees. However, the food could not leave Nick's kitchen at those temperatures and expect to remain at those temperatures, because it took time to deliver that food, set it up, plate it and serve it. Anything hot needed to be at a minimum of 170 degrees when it was loaded into the hot boxes, in order to still be at 141 by the time it was served.

Nick's biggest challenge was controlling the quality of the food that went to Overbrook, because it sat so long at high temperatures. A grilled, boneless, skinless chicken breast presented a special problem because by the time it was served, it would have very little moisture left in it. The best thing he could serve was a creamy casserole dish, such as chicken and dumplings, beef stew or lasagna – something forgiving that could sit at a relatively high temperature with very little loss of moisture. If the day's menu called for grilled, boneless chicken breast with no gravy ... well, that was what Nick had to serve. He could offer the gravy on the side but by law, he had to follow his menu. If a resident complained about dry and tough grilled chicken, Nick had a few options.

He could cook the chicken as close to delivery time as possible, he could request a new menu item from the nutritionist, or he could add something to the menu that was a bit more user friendly – but that option could negatively impact his food cost.

The residents were well within their rights to complain directly to the Department of Health and Environmental Control and if they did, a DHEC inspector would eventually show up and ask Nick, "What are you doing about these complaints?" If DHEC received a complaint about dry chicken after it had already made a visit, that could actually mean the potential of a monetary fine for Woodmont. Nick had to constantly keep up with the tangle of rules, potential violations and documentation that the federal government required. He ran a tight ship, he constantly checked his logbooks and his crew was always cleaning something because when DHEC walked in, you wanted to be ready. The kitchen's five-minute warning was used to do some last-minute tidying up; first impressions were everything to a health inspector. If an inspector walked in and saw a dirty floor, you could count on them to poke a flashlight into every nook and cranny. A survey team would also look through employee tuberculosis vaccination records, medication-distribution records, cleaning schedules, the drivers' safety records and their vehicles' maintenance logs, employee training schedules, and on and on. No one on campus was safe.

The kitchen door opened and Amy Sommers walked in with a slightly overweight gentleman carrying a metal binder and wearing a white lab coat. He was wearing grey Haggar slacks, white socks, brown loafers, an orange Clemson tiger-paw tie and a short-sleeved white shirt. Nick quickly looked at his crew to make sure no one was wearing a Carolina Gamecocks hat. Nick walked up, smiled and offered his hand.

"This is our executive Chef, Nicholas St. Germaine. Nick, this is Darryl Smithfield. Darryl is here from DHEC to perform a kitchen sanitation inspection today."

"I see you're a Clemson fan, Darryl. Aren't they looking good? That Dabo Swinney has been a God-send hasn't he? Let's hope they can keep up their momentum through the rest of the season."

"Amen to that, brother," replied Darryl as he carefully washed his hands. Nick glanced at Amy and winked at her. "Mr. Smithfield, do you need anything else from Miss Sommers?"

"I don' think so, Chef."

"Miss Sommers, I'll take care of Mr. Smithfield. If we need you, I know where to find you." Amy smiled, thanked Nick, turned and walked out of the kitchen. As Darryl dried his hands, he watched Amy walk away.

"Maybe just her phone number." Nick furrowed his brow and gave Darryl a look of disapproval. With one little politically in-correct comment, Nick suddenly had Darryl Smithfield at a distinct disadvantage.

"Mr. Smithfield, shall we get back to the business at hand, please?"

"Uh, yeah, sure." Darryl put his hairnet on and pulled his pen out of his pocket. Nick was now in control.

"Shall we start with the walk-in coolers?" Nick guided Darryl Smithfield through his two walk-in coolers, the walk-in freezer and the dry goods storeroom.

"Everything appears to be in order, Chef."

"Thank you, Mr. Smithfield. Now, if you'll follow me this way to the dish machine." Darryl had no choice but to allow Nick to guide him around the kitchen as if he were a puppy dog on a leash. After about 40 minutes, Darryl pronounced the kitchen satisfactory. He did find some dried cake batter on the large mixer and suggested to Nick that it was time to get the hood filters cleaned, but other than that, there was nothing to complain about. "Chef, if you will direct me to the skilled nursing facility, I need to check those kitchens as well. Thank you for your time."

"Of course, Mr. Smithfield, right this way." Nick pointed Darryl in the right direction, thanked him for his time, washed his hands, and then thanked everyone in the kitchen for their efforts. "You guys have the cleanest kitchen in Greenville County, hands down. Thank you, very much." Nick returned to his office and shot a quick text to Amy.

"Looks like a 97 or 98 for the main kitchen." She replied quickly with a smiley face icon then "didn't know u were a Clemson football fan."

"I'm not," he replied.

"Hey Chef, mind giving me a hand?"

"Sure thing, Dodger. What do you need?"

"Well see, my girl's outside and she kinda wants to kick me out of her life, so, uh, can you cover for me for five minutes?" Nick shook his head and thought to himself how pitiful this relationship must be if Bobby thinks he can save it from disaster in only five minutes. "I can spare 10 minutes Dodger; go make it happen."

"Thanks, Chef."

"Hey Sleepy, what do we need for the line?"

"A cook without any baggage?"

"Anything else?"

"A quart of black-eye pea salsa?"

"You got it."

An hour later, Nick took a walk to the theatre. *Mary Poppins* was just ending.

"Hey girls, how was the show?

"It was great, Mr. Nick. I'm really hungry now, is it time for my pretty lunch?"

"Paige is always hungry."

"Well, you two are in luck. How about if we adjourn to the dining room for a special meal? How would you two feel about having lunch with someone that was the Queen of Hawaii?"

Rebecca frowned. "Hawaii doesn't have a queen."

"Well, not any more. After this lady's rule ended, Hawaii said no more monarchs, and they begged to be let into the United States."

"Sure, Mr. Nick!"

"OK girls, let's go." They reached the bottom of the staircase and Paige looked back up. "That's *a lot* of stairs, Mr. Nick." Rebecca passed them both and trotted up quickly.

"That *is* a lot of stairs, Paige, but if you hold my hand, I think I'll be OK." Paige reached out and held Nick's hand, and they went up one step at a time. "Almost to the top, Paige. Thank you very much for holding my hand. You're a very brave girl." As they got to the top of the stairs, Amy walked past, leading Paige to yell,

"Mommy!" Amy looked down as Paige waved to her.

"I'm helping Mr. Nick be brave." Nick winked and thanked Paige as they reached the top. "Mr. Nick is cooking lunch for the Queen of Hawaii today, and he said we can eat with her."

"*Really?* The Queen of Hawaii, huh?"

"Miss Sommers, you really should get out of that office of yours every once in a while." Nick looked at his Blackberry. 12:15. "Hey Tony, is Doris Peters in yet?"

"Yes sir, she just sat down with Mrs. Hollowell."

"They have any space at their table?"

"Yes sir, it's just the two of them and they're at a four-top. Shall I show these two lovely ladies to the queen's table?"

"Please do, Tony. OK girls, shall we adjourn to the dining room? Miss Sommers, if you will excuse us?"

"Um, well, OK. I have to check on our inspectors down in A/L." Nick, Tony and the two girls walked up to Doris Peters' table and said hello. "And just who would we have here, Nick?"

"This is Paige and Rebecca Sommers, the daughters of the lovely Miss Amy Sommers, and I have promised these two a lunch with the Queen of Hawaii. Ladies, this is Mrs. Peters and Mrs. Hollowell."

"Is that so? Well gals, pull up a chair please and join us." Nick and Tony each held a chair out as Paige and Rebecca had a seat. "You see girls, my Henry was the first Pan-Am captain to land a Boeing 707 in Hawaii, and boy oh boy, was that ever a big deal! And back then, wives could ride along all the time. Let me tell you what, gals: I was royalty like you wouldn't believe, queen of Hawaii for a day. Have you two ever been to Hawaii?" Nick picked up the menus and softly told Doris, "You ladies won't need these."

"Did you get to wear a crown, Miss Doris?" asked a breathless Paige Sommers. Nick excused himself, went into the kitchen and asked Dodger for some help with a VIP meal.

"How about if we send them each a BLT salad to start with?" Nick grabbed his biscuit cutter and a loaf of white bread and cut four circles of white bread. He asked Dodger to put them on the grill with some melted butter, and top them with a slice of cheddar cheese. Next, he set up a big pot of water and placed it over a hot flame. He asked Sleepy to finely chop a big handful of iceberg lettuce and toss that in a bowl of apple cider vinaigrette. He finely chopped a few pieces of bacon as Jackson came by and asked what Doris' table was having for lunch. "First course is a salad, Mr. Mallory. Let me know when they have beverages and you're ready for them."

"Yes, Chef. Give me maybe three or four minutes."

"Perfect." Nick slowly cracked four eggs and carefully dropped them in the now simmering water. He tossed the lettuce with the ranch dressing, placed the four rounds of cheese toast on four salad plates, placed a thick slice of beefsteak tomato on top of the melted cheese, then placed the biscuit cutter on top of that and carefully pressed the lettuce on top of the tomato slice. He carefully lifted the biscuit cutter, pulled the poached eggs out of the water, blotted them dry, and then placed a soft poached egg on top of each salad, garnished with the chopped bacon and some sea salt. Nick told Jackson he was ready. "Pretty cool, Chef. I hope those little girls are adventurous." Jackson carried the four plates out, carefully serving each. "Bacon, Lettuce and Tomato Salad, courtesy of Chef St. Germaine."

"Wow!" exclaimed Paige. "Totally cool!" replied Rebecca. As soon as the salads left, Nick ran to the cooler and pulled out two pineapples, then shot a quick text to Amy.

"Your girls have any allergies I should know about?"

"just to homework ;)" she replied.

"Dodger, throw me a pork tenderloin on the grill please." Nick peeled and cut the pineapple in small dices, then tossed them into a sauté pan. He turned up the heat and pulled two sweet potatoes out of the steam table. He quickly peeled and placed them into a bowl, mashed them, and added some brown sugar, a dash of dried ginger and a squeeze of fresh lime juice. He turned to the cooking pineapple, gave it a quick toss, squeezed in some fresh lemon and a splash of white wine, and turned down the heat. He then added about a teaspoon of tamari sauce and a quarter-cup of honey. "Dodger, how's that pork looking?"

"Looking good, Chef. Who you cooking for?"

"The Queen of Hawaii, Dodger, who else?"

"Sorry, Chef. Stupid question."

"Dodger, give me 16 bias slices of pork please."

"Yes, Chef."

Nick took four rectangular dinner plates and placed a scoop of the sweet potatoes on the plate. Using the underside of the spoon, he dragged the potatoes across three inches of the interior of the plate. Nick shingled the pork slices on top of the potatoes, then carefully placed a small amount of the cooked pineapple on top of each slice of pork. When he was done with all four plates, he heated up the remaining pineapple, strained it, swirled in some whole butter, and carefully poured the sauce across the plate, finishing it with a few leaves of mint and a sprinkle of crushed macadamia nuts. Jackson picked up the plates, stole a quick look at Nick and said, "Running this place should come with a fringe benefit or two, right, Chef?"

"I agree, Mr. Mallory."

Five minutes later, Nick went to the table and asked everyone if they were having a good time. Paige stood up on her chair and reached out and gave Nick a hug then asked, "Miss Doris, did you eat like that when you were the Queen of Hawaii?"

"Oh, of course. Lots of pineapple and pork in Hawaii, and most of it came with rum."

"What's rum, Miss Doris?"

"Only the most wonderful, terrible stuff you can imagine young lady, but that's a story for another day." Doris smirked at Nick.

"Chef Nick, can I come back tomorrow, please?"

"Paige, don't you have any plans this summer? You can't hang out here all summer."

Rebecca wiped her mouth and turned to Nick. "We're supposed to go to the beach again in two weeks and I have basketball camp and summer camp with church. We may go to Asheville for a weekend, depends on how much work Mom brings home that weekend. Lunch was delicious, Mr. St. Germaine." Nick looked over at Doris and winked. "Thank you, Becca. So you play basketball?"

"I do. I want to make the school team this year; I'll be in eighth grade."

"What position do you play?" asked Doris.

"Small forward, sometimes shooting guard. I want to play point, but I need more practice dribbling."

"Our lunch was delicious, Nick. Maybe you have a future in this business, right?"

"Thank you, Doris. Lunch is on me, girls. Would anyone care for some peach upside-down cake? Maybe with a little vanilla ice cream on it?" Nick excused himself, sent a quick text to Amy to let her know the girls were about to have some dessert then prepared four plates of peach cake. She replied, "thank u will round them up soon."

Thirty minutes later, Tony came into Nick's office. "How did our DHEC inspection go Skipper?"

"Very well, Mr. Torres. Looks like we should get a 98 or maybe a 97. He was happy, the place looked good, most everything was in order, so no worries. Plus that dope made an ill-timed comment about Amy and after that, I had him by the short hairs." Tony leaned forward in his chair. "What did he say?"

"He watched her walk away then asked me for her phone number."

"Holy shit! You're serious?" Nick sat up straight. "I glared at him then asked him to keep it professional and at that point, he was *all mine,* brother – not that I needed any help, but when those guys come in, every little bit helps."

"So you had him on the leash after that."

"Damn right, plus he doesn't need to be drooling over the boss. This isn't some singles bar." Tony leaned back and nodded.

"Amy's girls sure are cute." Nick leaned back in his chair, put his hands behind his head and offered Tony an easy smile.

"They are, aren't they? The little one, Paige, is certainly charming."

"You sure were comfortable with them, skipper. Too bad they don't have a Dad in their life."

"No kidding, that is too bad." Tony nodded and rubbed his chin. "OK, I have things to do. I need to get out of here at a decent time tonight. I have a date with this senorita that works for Pedro Hernandez Tequila."

"She a sales rep?"

"Nope, she's the hottie in the tequila poster wearing the cactus bikini."

"Ouch! OK, be careful tonight, brother."

"Yes sir, I guess throwing all that salt over my shoulder finally paid off!"

13

Nick opened the door to his office, sat down and opened up his computer, and then looked at today's schedule. 9:45 a.m. He had five cooks on today, including Chef Randall and Tony, and there were no special events today or tomorrow. Maybe he should take the day off. Was it Thursday? What would he do? The weather was nice. Maybe he could take a long bike ride, but he preferred to ride with a group and it would be tough to find someone right now – but no problem if he waited until the afternoon. Theo would be at his basketball program until seven tonight. He looked at his phone and scrolled through his contacts and rolled across Lynda Giansante's number. It had been four days since they had gone for their run.

"Lynda Giansante," he said out loud. "John sahn tay," he said it a little bit slower. "Doctor Lynda Giansante. Hello Lynda, it's Nicholas St. Germaine. Yes, very well thank you. Lynda, I would love to take you to dinner tonight; what time shall I pick you up? Lynda, hey Nick St. Germaine here. Listen, how about you and I grab some dinner tonight? Great! What time?" A date, it was time for a real dinner date with Lynda. He looked up at his computer, then caught a glimpse of Robin smiling at him from the framed photo. He looked back at Lynda's number, reached over and carefully placed the photo face down. "Sorry, sweetheart," he whispered. He closed his eyes, took a deep breath, counted to 20, and then looked at Lynda's number and hit dial. She answered on the second ring.

"Hello Lynda, it's Nick St. Germaine."

"I know who this is, silly boy."

"Oh, um, of course, sorry."

"Nick, will you quit apologizing and ask me out to dinner, please? I'm between patients and my time is short."

"Well, uh, sure, Lynda. Will you have dinner with me tonight at Northampton, please?"

"Yes, of course, I would love to, Nick."

"Oh, uh, are you sure that's OK?"

"*Nicholas!* I just said yes, now you're supposed to tell me what time you're going to pick me up."

"Yes, of course, seven OK?"

"That's perfect, Nick. I'll see you at seven."

"Wonderful, see you then."

"*Nick?*"

"Yes, Lynda?"

"Would you like to know where I live?"

"Oh yes, I suppose that would help, right?"

"Listen, I have to get into my next appointment, will text you at lunch time, gotta go."

"Oh, OK, Lynda." He exhaled, set his Blackberry down, closed his eyes, and leaned back in his chair. His heart was pounding, he had broken out in a sweat, and tasted bile. He got up and walked into the bathroom, splashed cold water onto his face, rinsed his mouth out, dried off and smiled at his reflection. He thought about Lynda. She was certainly beautiful and smart as a whip, but what else was there? She was in shape. She was excited about being in his company, but she was also a bit impatient. So what? She basically worked in a freestanding emergency room, so she probably had to be impatient. "It's just dinner, it's just a dinner date, don't let her rush anything," he said out loud. "I have a date with Lynda Giansante. I can't stay guys, I have a date with Doctor Lynda Giansante." He walked back into his office, closed the door, sat down, leaned back in his chair and closed his eyes. "Hey Tony, listen, if you don't mind I'm going to take off. I have a date tonight with that beautiful doctor friend of mine." There was a knock on his door. He looked up and saw Tony Torres, so he motioned him in.

"Morning, Skipper" smiled Tony as he sat down in one of Nick's chairs.

"Morning, Tony".

"Damn, boss, you OK? You look a little washed out. What's up?" Nick realized that he had been talking to himself while Tony was at the door.

"Well Mr. Torres, I, uh, I can't stay, because I have a date tonight."

"Way to go, Skipper! With the doc? Where you two going?" Tony reached across with his left hand, pulled the door closed and looked back at Nick. He noticed the framed photo of Robin was face down.

"Yeah, taking her to Northampton tonight."

"So you have a reservation then?"

"Shit!"

Tony leaned back and laughed. "Listen skipper, why don't you take the day off? We don't really need you today, nothing big going on and you need some time to get your beauty rest before your date. Go on and get out of here, please."

"Only if you promise me that this conversation stays in this room?"

"Of course, boss, of course," smiled Tony. Nick stood up and took off his Chef coat and hung it up on his coat rack. He was wearing a grey Nike gym shirt. "Damn skipper, what are you benching these days?"

"Uh, well, I don't know. Maybe 250 or so? I don't really keep track."

"Oh, right. You look like you've put on an inch across your chest in the last month. I'll bet your doc is strictly interested in your intellect."

"Sure, thanks Tony."

"Damn, here comes Amy." Tony looked over his right shoulder, and then turned to his left as she passed behind him. Amy Sommers was wearing a white knee-length skirt and a shimmering pink silk blouse with gleaming gold buttons and a white jacket. The jacket was unbuttoned, and her blouse displayed just a bit of cleavage. "Eyes up," Nick said out loud. Nick motioned her in as Tony stood up and opened the door.

"Hey guys, good morning. Can I join you two?"

"Yes, of course. What's up, boss?" asked Nick as they all sat down. "Nothing really, I was just looking for a Diet Coke and saw you two and wanted to say hello." Nick furrowed his brow. "So where's your soda?"

"Well, uh, I guess we're out of Diet Coke." Nick smiled. "You know that stuff is really hard on your kidneys, right?" Amy groaned and put her head down on her left palm.

"Nick, would you or Tony *please* show me how to fix the soda dispenser so I can get a damn Diet Coke?" Tony and Nick laughed, Amy lifted her eyes above her palm and smiled.

"I'll do it, Mr. Torres, since I'm getting out of here. Will you please check in with the Dodger and get his lunch menu straight?" Nick stood up and held his left hand out, palm up, to Amy. "My darling, if you will come this way, I will be happy to explain the intricacies of the modern soda fountain." Amy looked up at Nick, smiled warmly, took his hand and stood up.

"Did you say you were taking the day off, Nick?" He walked into the dry storage room and tapped the box of Diet Coke.

"Fountains use concentrated syrup that gets mixed with water then carbonated at the dispenser head. The syrup comes in these cardboard boxes, so we just need to remove the empty box and install a new one, and we're all set. The syrup's inside a thick plastic bag. Do you mind if I take the day off, Miss Sommers?"

"No, of course not, Nick, and really, Amy is fine." He squatted down and picked up the box, and Amy couldn't help but watch his biceps flex. "How much does that box weigh, Nick?"

"Oh, not much, maybe 40 or 50 pounds, never really thought about it. Why?"

"No reason. So what did you have planned for today?"

"Well, since you asked, I have a date."

"Oh." Nick carried the box of syrup towards the rack and set it down. "Here's our empty soda box. Would you mind unscrewing that receptacle? You sounded disappointed when I told you I have a date."

"*What?* No Nick, heavens no, of course not. Why on earth would I be disappointed? Why would you say that? I'm happy for you, sure, I'm happy. Please go and enjoy yourself tonight."

"Thank you, Miss Sommers."

"Seriously Nick, please call me Amy? OK?"

"Of course." Nick removed the empty box and installed the fresh one. The carbonator made a series of quick gasps as the syrup was pulled towards the soda fountain. "Does that sound mean I can have a Diet Coke now?"

"Yes ma'am."

"Oh great. Thank you so much, Nick."

"My pleasure."

"Nick?"

"Yes ma'am?" Amy put her hands behind her back and looked down at her feet, then lifted her eyes to him. "I, uh, I want you to know that if you ever need to talk to me about anything, my door is always open for you. I mean that. And I think you're doing a fine job here. I never apologized to you for the terrible awkwardness that occurred on our first day together, but I need to now. I'm sorry you thought you were going to be let go. I'm certain that day came with a lot of anguish and angst, and for that, I apologize. I hope that you will stay here and grow with the company."

"You did apologize that day, so please don't sweat it further. And you're right, there was a flurry of emotions that day, and I'm certain that most of it was not your doing."

"What do you mean most of it?" quizzed Amy. Nick broke into a wide grin.

"Just teasing, Miss Sommers, I hope to stay here for a while, too, and I think you are doing a fine job as well. However, I'm 41, I'm pretty sure I'm finished growing." Amy smiled and blushed, then looked back down at her feet. "You're blushing, Miss Sommers. How about if I get you that Diet Coke, so we can stop apologizing to one another and get on with our lives?" Nick walked to the soda fountain with Amy in tow. He filled up a styro-foam cup, put a lid on it, and then inserted a straw. "Here you go, boss. One freshly drawn Diet Coke." Amy took the cup from Nick and smiled.

"I hope you have a wonderful time tonight, Nick." Tony came around the corner as Amy turned and walked out the front door.

"Fat old stubborn nurse, huh?" Tony said under his breath.

"OK, so she's a beautiful, charming, smart and compassionate nurse that happens to be doing a very good job here. We can agree on that, right?"

"Yes sir, she is *beautiful*."

"You have a one-track mind, Mr. Torres, you know that?"

"Yes, I do." Tony squeezed Nick on the shoulder. "Now please get the hell out of here."

"Yes sir." Nick headed back to his office, grabbed his gym bag and car keys and made his way to the stairs. When he hit sunlight, he found Kelly's number and called.

"Hey Kelly, you guys have a table for two tonight, seven p.m.?"

"Nick, you want a table? *For two?*"

"That's right. I want a table for two."

"I hear ya, brother. Table for two at seven, anyone I know?"

"Jeez, I hope not," laughed Nick.

"Alright boss, I got ya covered. I'll put you in Christina's section, ok?"

"Thanks Kelly, thank you very much." As Nick was almost to his car, he saw Penny getting out of her van. "Hello Penny, how are you on this beautiful morning?"

"Hey Nick, I'm well, and what about you? Are you leaving?"

"Yes, gonna take the day off."

"Good for you Nick; any plans? It's such a beautiful day."

"I, uh, I actually have a date, Penny."

"*Oh my, Nick.* Oh, that's great. Are you excited?"

"Yes ma'am, and very nervous. This will be my first."

"I know, Nick. Listen, just try to relax and have a good time, and let it go at that. Not that you need my advice, right?" Penny reached out and hugged Nick. "Thank you, Penny. Thank you very much."

"You're welcome, Nick." He headed towards his BMW wagon. As he unlocked the car, his phone's text message alert went off. He put the gym bag in the back and eased into his seat, closed the door, pressed in the clutch and started the engine. He selected neutral, then looked at his phone. It was a text message from Lynda. "mcbee mills condos, just buzz me, L". She added an icon of a female smiley face blowing a kiss. His heart rate jumped, and he pushed his right foot to the floor. The six-cylinder surged towards the red line.

"Oh, shit!" He pulled his foot off the accelerator pedal and quietly apologized to his car. He responded to Lynda with a thumbs-up icon. Nick set the phone down on the console and smiled, tapped the throttle, eased into reverse, and headed out of the parking lot. Now he just had to tell his son that he was going on a date. He turned towards Highway 101 and waited for the light to turn green. How would Theo take this? Would he see it as an act of dishonor against his mother's memory? Would he storm out of the house? Would he be happy, disappointed, furious? Nick was pretty sure that Theo would be happy for him and would want to know all about Lynda, but he could not be certain. Theo was very conscious of his mother's memory, and he prayed every night that he would not disappoint her. The light turned green, Nick engaged first gear, eased onto 101 and accelerated through fourth gear. What if Theo is upset with him? What would he do, cancel the date? No, he thought about what Penny said, so he would ask Theo to understand that this was just a first date, just dinner, and that he was not seeking a replacement for Robin's memory. It was just dinner, nothing more.

Nine hours later, Nick pulled into the McBee Mills parking lot. Ever since he left his house, his palms had been sweaty. Theo had given him a handkerchief to carry, and he had used it several times on the short drive over. Nick had stressed over how he was going to tell his son, but when he finally had mustered up the courage, Theo's response was, "Cool." He gave his dad a high five then asked him if he wanted to go for a run.

"Uh, sure, son, let's go for a run." Nick shook his head as he retreated to his bedroom to change. He put on his running shorts, grabbed his shoes and ducked into the bathroom to urinate, then washed his hands and looked in the mirror. He had literally made himself sick over how he would tell his son about his date.

"Let's go, old man!" Theo yelled from the front door. As they left the house, Theo asked, "Nervous?"

"How far we going, kid?"

"Let's do the three-and-a-half mile loop. You need it."

"Three-point-five it is, and damn right I'm nervous."

"No doubt she's a few years younger than you?"

"No doubt."

"Shit, my old man going on a date. I'll be waiting up, OK? I want you home by ten."

"Sure thing, kid, home by ten."

"And don't even think about bringing her in the house. Not on your first date, got it?"

"Wouldn't think of it, son. I do have my standards, you know."

Nick trotted up the stairs to the front door of McBee Mills condominiums, scanned the names for Lynda Giansante, took a deep breath, and rang the buzzer.

14

Nick handed Xavier back his lunch menu. "Looks great Xavier, appreciate all you do here, now if you will excuse me

I have a meeting to get to." He picked up his clipboard and laptop and headed out of the kitchen, just as Amy was walking in with an empty cup in her hands. She was wearing a charcoal grey pencil skirt and a white sleeveless linen blouse, and her favorite diamond pendant sparkled against the fully buttoned up blouse. Her hair was pulled back off of her shoulders and she was wearing a different set of clock-faced earrings.

"Good morning, Nick."

"Good morning, Miss Sommers. May I pour you a cup of coffee?"

"No, thank you, I'm going to have a Diet Coke."

"You know, Miss Sommers, as your certified culinary health specialist, I must remind you how hard that stuff is on your kidneys." Amy finished drawing her Coke, reached for a straw, stuck the straw in her soda, then turned to Nick and slurped loudly.

"Were you talking to me?"

"Uh, no ma'am. I'll see you in the Armory in a few minutes." Amy winked at Nick, turned around and walked out of the kitchen. Nick watched her walk away, admiring her figure. As Amy headed out of the kitchen, she glanced in the mirror that Tony had put up for the wait staff to use and caught Nick looking at her. She smiled as Nick quickly looked away. Five minutes later, Amy's team was assembling for its meeting.

"Good morning, people. Happy Wednesday, everyone!" Amy walked into the Armory with a stack of paper and her laptop, and plopped them down at the nearest seat as Grant held the chair out for her. "Thank you so much, Grant. Everyone ready to have an amazing day?" Happy Wednesday? thought Nick. I wonder if she was a cheerleader in high school?

"Happy Wednesday, Miss Sommers," replied Nick as the rest of the staff followed suit.

Twenty-five minutes into the meeting, Amy took over. "OK, folks, here's something I need everyone's thoughts on.

One of the many issues when caring for Alzheimer's patients is the wandering or Sundowner's Syndrome. Nick, in case you don't know, as Alzheimer's progresses, one of the symptoms is the desire to wander when the sun goes down. It's a form of anxiety. The reasoning is not clear but honestly, I think it's based in a desire to be active. Our folks in the memory care unit have been very active for a long time and there's a rhythm that they get used to. Now that they are suffering from dementia, their rhythm has been severely affected. So I want us to start looking for ways to ease the wandering."

"Could they not help clean up the dishes, Miss Sommers?"

Grant nodded his head. "That's great, Nick. We're doing some stuff like that now. Some of our folks will set the tables or fold napkins, and they may fold napkins three or four times over." Cassidy scratched her head.

"You know, Amy, when my son was little, if he was fussy, Reggie would take him for a car ride, and that usually would settle him down."

Franklin chimed in. "That's not out of the question. We have enough drivers and the bus. Honestly Amy, I don't think all of our folks would respond to that, but maybe some of them would. Certainly worth a try, though.'

"Boss, I always sleep better if I've exercised before dinner. I know with a lot of these folks that may not be possible, but could we not walk them up and down the hallway, play some sort of game or get them in the pool? *Hey,* what about the Wii? There's some games on that system that may be appropriate. How would that go over?"

Amy smiled as she rolled the suggestions around in her head. "All good stuff here guys, all good. Cassidy, we need to start taking some notes on this, so we can really see what is and isn't working. This is going to be ongoing, our dementia patients may respond today, but may not respond next week. We will have keep track of this, so Grant and I have created notebooks for each Memory Care resident. The girls in the Haywood and Laurens neighborhoods will be taking notes on wandering, and when we see results, it's going to be noted. Right now, I believe we're having the most trouble with Mr. Fillmore and Mrs. Hendricks; if we can see a reduction in their wandering that will be huge."

"Miss Sommers, are the girls in Memory Care going to time the wandering? How are they going to verify and track all this?"

"Nick, right now we take extensive notes on the Memory Care unit. Most of them have for a long time, and that evening activity is all part of the progression of the disease. But not all of our dementia patients have pronounced evening or night-time wandering. So to answer your question, yes, we already track this, but it is not actually timed with a stop watch. We use time frames and some anecdotal evidence, but some of the girls are better at describing the evening activities of our patients. So for now, we are going to use a time frame, Mrs. Jones wandered from 11:15 p.m. until about 11:45 p.m., and was in a nervous state or an excited state, something along those lines. Like I said, it's going to be a work in progress."

"So how about if I make a chart for you, say with ten or twelve adjectives that can be used to describe the wandering, something the girls can quickly circle. I'll make it a fairly large font, and then I can write a cheat sheet that they can use to familiarize themselves with each adjective. Would that help?" Grant stood up, reached across the table and offered Nick a high five. "Hell yeah, brother! Damn right, that would help."

"We could even put a large clock on this form so the girls could make hash marks on the clock, instead of actually writing out the time."

"Franklin dang Jones! Way to go, Idaho!" Grant offered Franklin another high five as Amy beamed. "I'm buying doughnuts for all of you tomorrow, I am *really proud* of my team right now."

"No doughnuts for me, Miss Sommers, but I do enjoy a freshly squeezed orange and carrot juice every once in a while." Amy rolled her eyes as Grant smiled at Nick.

"Miss Sommers, I like mine covered with that waxy, fake chocolate syrup and those little sprinkly things that cause cancer in lab rats. Chef Wheatgrass here can bring his own sweet potato juice tomorrow morning."

"That's a deal, Mr. Hughes." After the meeting adjourned, Nick went straight to his office, put on his Chef coat and found Bobby Dodge sulking in the walk-in cooler, staring at the produce. "Hey Dodger, how you looking for today?"

"I dunno, Chef, I'm trying. See, me and my girl, well, we was fighting last night and maybe she kinda walked out on me again." Jesus Christ, thought Nick. Here we go again.

"Come on Dodger, we have work to do. You need me to write today's specials, or can you get it done?"

"I'll get it done, Chef. Dodger will get it done."

"OK, thank you. It's nine forty, let's make it happen. Let's shake it off and focus on what makes us happy, and I do believe cooking really cool stuff makes you happy."

"Yes, Chef." Nick walked out of the cooler, found Florence, and asked her to make sure she prodded Bobby to keep moving. "Chef, when I hit my number, I'm not gonna worry about no one no more. Just Flo and my dollars."

"Yes, ma'am. Maybe you'll invite me to one of your parties after you hit that number."

"Morning, babe!" Nick turned around and smiled as Tony Torres hoisted a steaming cup of coffee in his direction. "Good morning, Tony Torres, how's your world this morning?" Tony walked up to Nick and grabbed him by the sleeve of his Chef coat, dragged him into his office and kicked the door closed.

"OK, Skipper, let's hear it. How was your date?"

"We had a really good time last night."

"Yeah, yeah, elaborate, please."

"Well, the guys at Northampton hooked us up pretty good. Five courses, matching wines; Lynda is somewhat of a foodie, so she has good knowledge and appreciated her meal."

"And so what did you all talk about?"

"Food, cooking, med school, Italy, the whole Chef culture, work, a couple of times I had to redirect her, because I really didn't want to talk about the Tavern. It was obvious she's somewhat smitten with the whole restaurant thing; she thinks it's all pretty sexy."

"She's right."

"Sure, it is pretty sexy, but I'm not doing that again. At one point, she even said something to the effect of if I had a restaurant it would be an authentic Italian trattoria like the ones I went to in Liguria."

"I *love* that idea, Skipper!"

"I'll give her your number, then."

"I would take you up on that, but I already have a future Mrs. Ex-Torres in mind."

"Your social studies teacher?"

Tony furrowed his brow and with a puzzled expression asked, "Who?"

"The tequila model?" Tony winked. "Yes, of course, I knew that," replied Nick, sarcastically. "Hey, I thought we were talking about me anyway?"

"You're right. So you two had a good time then, right?"

"Yeah, we had a great time, we really did. Finished our dinner, walked around downtown, threw a penny in the fountain and made a wish then."

"And then?"

"And then I brought her home, kissed her good night, and here I am." Tony sat up straight and nodded his head slightly.

"Theo cool with all this?" Nick leaned back and put his hands behind his head.

"Well, honestly Tony, I was a hell of a lot more nervous about this than he was. You know what? That kid told me I better be home by ten."

"Ha-ha! Good for him! And were you?"

"Nine fifth-eight brother."

"Good for you, Nick, good for you."

"And did she try to drag you inside her place?"

'Well, since you asked… "

"Ha, I knew it! That girl's an animal."

"You can't say that now, Mr. Torres. Just because she grabbed my butt once or twice doesn't mean anything, OK?"

"I think when you're ready, Doctor Lynda Giansante is gonna rock your world, brother." Tony's words eased out of his mouth as if he were describing a bottle of 20-year old Bordeaux to a table of wine connoisseurs.

"Well, in three weeks, Theo is headed to a basketball scouting camp in Chapel Hill. He's gonna be gone for a three-day weekend and he's travelling with a group of players and coaches, and that just might be the perfect time to have her over."

"You gonna ask Theo's permission?"

"I don't know, maybe."

"Damn skipper, I was kidding."

"Oh, right, right, of course. OK, I have a busy day, Tony. I have a project to do for the boss, something I promised her this morning. Tomorrow's end of the month and I have a boatload of accounting to do plus prices to update for June inventory, plus you need to update your wine list and bar inventory, plus the Hemmers are having their anniversary in the ball room this weekend, and I have a massive prep list for that, plus Dodger will probably call off tomorrow morning."

"OK, slow down, skipper, you're getting me depressed. And why do you think Dodger's gonna call off tomorrow?"

"He was fighting with his girl and she walked out on him, so he'll probably have a good case of the brown-bottle flu tomorrow morning. He's already had one too many in the last six months, and if he does call off, it's going to have to be at six, since he has to be here at eight. I need to sit down with Jessica and pull applications for cooks. I don't see this guy lasting much longer. Now, if I can only find the time to look over apps, make appointments, interview, schedule second interviews, shit, sometimes I really miss Heather. These guys in Charleston, you think any of them ever held front-line positions in their life? I mean, we're constantly balls to the wall, then one little hiccup and the people that you pay to think and manage are suddenly your dishwashers and parsley choppers." Nick looked out his office window as Sleepy and Chef Randall walked in and saluted Nick.

"Amen to that, brother. And yes, I think Hamilton probably worked his way through his MBA degree by washing dishes and cooking. That's why he has such intimate knowledge of the amount of muscle it takes to run a place like this." Nick turned to Tony, who smiled sarcastically.

"OK, it's getting deep in here. Will you get to work, please?"

"Yes sir, Skipper. Tony has the helm."

"Atta boy, go get 'em." Nick smiled as Tony left his office, then he turned to his laptop and fired off a quick email to Jessica asking her to pull any cook's applications that were posted on the company job site. Nick opened up his online thesaurus, entered "agitated," and set about making the chart for the CNAs that worked in memory care. An hour later, he had a legal-size chart with a heading on top for date, the resident's name, the neighborhood, and the staff member's name. He listed, "bothered, concerned, annoyed, tense, irritable, jumpy, edgy, troubled, mad and hysterical". He added a round clock face on the very bottom, printed it off using a landscape orientation, then went to Christina's office and pulled out one of her legal-size, three-ring binders. He made a dozen copies of his chart, ran them through the hole punch, placed them in the binder, then put the binder in Amy's mailbox. He stared at the binder for a minute, then rummaged around for a sticky note. When he found one, he wrote on it, "who loves you?" He placed the note on the binder, hesitated, then removed it and threw it away. Nick wrote out another note, "my pleasure", then threw that one away. On his next note, he wrote, "here you go Boss". He held that one up, stuck it on the binder then walked back to the kitchen.

An hour later, Nick was on the back line making chicken and rice soup. He had about five pounds of raw chicken that he was reducing to a fine dice on a cutting board.

"Nick?" He turned around. Amy was standing about 10 feet away, clutching the binder he had made. She smiled, squeezed the binder to her chest.

"Thank you, very much."

"You're very welcome, Miss Sommers." Amy turned and walked out of the kitchen. Xavier folded his arms across his chest, lifted an eyebrow and stared at Nick. "Yes, Xavier?"

"And just *what in the hell* was that all about, Chef?"

"I did a favor for the boss, and she came to say thank you."

"Oh really, that's what she was saying? *Thank you?*" Xavier shook his head. He picked up the head of celery off of his cutting board, squeezed it tightly to his chest and giggled, "Oh thank you, celery, thank you, thank you, thank you, celery!" Nick shook his head and went back to making his soup.

15

Nick heard the knock on the front door and as he walked to the front of his house, he saw a police car in the driveway. *What are the cops doing here?* His pulse quickened as he reached the door and opened it. A police officer was standing at his front door.

"Nicholas St. Germaine?"

"Yes?"

"I'm afraid your wife has been in an automobile accident. She has been transported to the Greenville Memorial Emergency Room. Can I be of further assistance?" Nick's heart rate exploded as panic set in.

"What? Where? What happened? How, how, how bad is she? How is she?"

"Mr. St. Germaine, I apologize but that is all the information I have. Can someone get you to the Emergency Room?"

"Robin!"

Nick lurched out of bed, gasping for air. He reached across the bed for his wife. As reality took hold, he turned on the light on his nightstand. He pulled a pillow to his chest, buried his face in it, squeezed his eyes shut, and let the tears flow. His vision blurred as he cried out, "*I miss you so much Robin.*" After a couple of minutes, he wiped his eyes on the sheets and got out of bed. He walked over to the bookcase and looked at the series of framed photos of Robin. One was her passing under the finish line, her right fist pumping the air, as she won the Charlottesville Road Race. In another, Robin and Nick were on Tybee Island, Nick holding seven-year-old Theo on his shoulders. Another framed memory was from their honeymoon in Belize. Nick held each photo, tracing Robin's outline with his right forefinger before carefully setting each frame back in place. He rubbed his head, paced his bedroom, then got back in bed and put his hands in his head.

He rubbed his forehead and looked at the ceiling. "Come on Nick, don't do this! *Do not do this!*" He looked at his wife's side of the bed, grabbed a pillow, threw it at the photos, scattering them to the floor. He got out of bed and screamed.

"Why the hell couldn't you have just stayed home? You didn't have to go to the goddamn store!"

He clutched his sides, and the tears started again. He picked up the pillow and squeezed it to his chest, quietly sobbing. "Why couldn't you have just stayed home, sweetheart? I would have made dinner for you, I would have made dinner." He dropped the pillow on his bed and staggered into his bathroom, splashed cold water on his face and dried off with a towel. He stared at his reflection, walked into his bedroom and looked at his clock radio. 4:41. He checked his Blackberry for text messages but there were none, so he tossed it on his bed. He scratched his head and looked around then knelt down next to his bed and prayed for forgiveness and the courage to face another day without Robin. "One more day, Lord, help me get through one more day, please." He sat down on his bed and looked at the clock radio again, got up and made a pot of coffee, got dressed for the gym, grabbed a banana, an apple and an orange, and headed out.

About an hour later, Nick was finishing his workout with a 15-minute turn on the heavy bag. He was bathed in sweat and short of breath. He looked across the room at the clock. 5:56 a.m. He bit into the Velcro strap that held the glove on his wrist, peeled the strap off, placed his right hand in his left arm pit and tugged until his glove came off. He pulled off the other glove then headed for the locker room. He opened his locker, reached in for his Blackberry and sure enough, he had a text message from Bobby that he didn't even bother opening. *"That little fucking loser!"* He threw the phone into the locker and the battery popped out. He grabbed his soap, towel and shampoo and headed for the shower.

Thirty minutes later, Nick was in the kitchen prepping lunch. Sleepy had come in to do breakfast, so the two of them had to prepare lunch for Overbrook and for the line. They had a long list to prep: two soups, 12 broccoli and cheddar quiches, meatloaf, three salad dressings, mashed sweet potatoes, rice pilaf, and two pans of sugar-free brownies. Nick decided that at nine, he would send a message to Kevin Randall asking him to come in at 11. Kevin could get on the line while Nick did prep for dinner. At 8:45, Nick sent a text message to Amy. "sorry won't make morning meeting dodger called off." Five minutes later, Amy walked into the kitchen.

"Have you talked to Bobby this morning, Nick?"

"No ma'am."

"Are you going to?"

"No ma'am, he called off; said he didn't feel good. What else is there?"

"Have you been tracking his absences?"

"Yes ma'am."

"OK, I sense your frustration, Nick. Please sit down with Jessica at your earliest convenience and let's see where we are with Bobby. We need to follow company protocol, OK? I'll let her know what's going on. Oh, and don't forget about the video conference we have at five today."

"Yes ma'am, and the dining committee meeting and the July fourth picnic and the marketing lunch menu for Tuesday and the labor report and the fall festival committee meeting." Amy folded her arms and cut her eyes at Nick.

"Are you finished, Mr. St. Germaine?"

Nick walked to the hand sink, washed and dried his hands, responded with a curt, "Yes ma'am," then headed to the produce cooler, leaving Amy standing in the kitchen. When the door to the cooler closed, he exhaled loudly and tried to remember why he had gone into the cooler. He looked around, then picked up a case of sweet potatoes, carried them to his prep table, pulled out his Blackberry and sent a text to Kevin Randall, asking him if he could come in early. Nick mumbled to himself, "And don't forget about your date with Lynda."

Eight hours later, Nick was in the conference room waiting to join the monthly Chef's video conference. Most of the other Chefs were already online, but not the corporate office. Nick sat and stared at the screen. The door opened and Amy walked in, so he stood up and held a chair out for her. She thanked him. Nick sat down and continued staring at the screen. "How's your day gone, Nick?"

"Fine, Miss Sommers." Nick looked down at his hands then turned to Amy. "Forgive me for being rude this morning, boss. I had a ton of stuff to do and I just knew Bobby was going to call off today. I just knew it." Amy reached over and placed her left hand on top of his.

"It's OK, Nick, I understand."

"I'm sorry," he whispered, slowly pulling his hand away. The 6x4-foot video conference screen started to pixilate and, one by one, dropped off individual callers. Amy stood up and exclaimed, *"Damnit!"* Within 30 seconds the screen was black. Nick stood up and picked up his clipboard. "Well, I guess we're off the hook. If you will excuse me, I have a date tonight." Amy's phone went off with a text message.

"Hold on, Nick, I have a message from Harriett. She says to please be patient, give us 30 minutes, and we'll try again." Nick looked up at the ceiling and exhaled. "I'll see you in 30 minutes then."

Nick's phone buzzed with a text message from Lynda, which he quickly opened. "where we going tonight lover?" Nick looked at Amy, then walked out of the conference room and trotted back to the kitchen. He was supposed to pick Lynda up at 6:30. If he left Woodmont by 5:30, he could be on time. He had a 20-minute drive home, had to clean up, get dressed, then get Lynda. He had tickets to see Bruce Hornsby; downtown would be crawling with people and if he were so much as five minutes late, that could throw the whole evening into jeopardy. However, he would hate to have Amy in the video conference without him. It would reflect poorly on her, and to CSM, image was very important. Amy was doing a great job and the two of them were getting along, but if he let her go into that conference solo, he was certain that Hamilton or Harriett would assume that Amy was having management issues with Nick. He texted Lynda – "six thirty doc, got tix to bruce hornsby" – and she quickly responded with a kissy face icon.

Twenty minutes later, Nick went back to the conference room. Amy was already there. "Listen boss, I, uh, kind of have a date tonight. I promised my friend I would pick her up at six thirty. If I leave now, I'll just barely make it." The video screen crackled to life as Harriett appeared. "Oh, hello Amy, Nick, and how are the two of you doing? Amy, I have to tell you I love the reports I get from Woodmont. Your numbers are moving in the right direction, and I hear lots of positive comments about the food and service. Plus Amy, your turnover rate has dropped significantly."

"Thank you, Harriett" they both answered. "Listen Nick, do you think you could do something special for me?"

"Sure, Harriett, what is it?"

"You think you could spend a couple of days at our community in Decatur, Georgia? We have a new Chef there, and he could use a hand learning some of our online systems. Amy, could you live without Nick for a few days?" Amy turned to Nick and smiled, looked down at her calendar, then turned to the screen. "I'll make do."

"Nick, could you be there next Thursday and Friday? We'll cover your mileage, pay you fifty dollars per diem and put you up on property plus Decatur has some pretty good places to eat."

"I agree Harriett, Decatur has some great restaurants." Amy scribbled "don't forget about your date" on a piece of paper, and then passed it to Nick.

"Thank you," he whispered.

"Amy, maybe you should think about going with him. Jason, their Director, has been with us for a long time and he's a real crackerjack. I'd love for you to spend a day or two with him." Amy's eyes opened wide and she turned to Nick then quickly turned away. Nick looked down at his clipboard as Amy opened up her calendar and started turning pages in one direction, then the other. "I, uh, I have, um, something planned with the girls. I was, uh, going to … "

"OK, well maybe next time Amy."

"Sure, Harriett, uh, next time." Amy fiddled with her purse as Nick wrote out "Decatur Georgia" several times. One by one, the other properties came back on line. "You need to go Nick," Amy whispered.

"Yes, I suppose I do." Nick quietly got up and walked to the door. As he opened the door, he looked back at Amy. She turned and looked at him, smiled warmly and whispered, "Good night." Nick returned her smile, then ran to his car.

"Morning, Skipper!"

"Hey, how's my favorite dining room manager?" Tony walked up to Nick, threw his right arm around Nick and dragged him into the office.

"So how was your date last night, brother?" Nick took a seat as Tony closed the door. Kevin Randall walked past the office, turned to the window as he walked past, and nodded. "Chef Randall's in awfully early. What is it, 10:30 or so?"

"Skipper, am I going to have to beat this information out of you?"

"Sorry, Tony." Nick leaned back, put his hands behind his head and smiled. "We had a really good time last night, the concert was great, Hornsby still sounds amazing, we had a great time. The concert lasted two hours and after that, we went to Soby's and had a few snacks and a couple glasses of wine, and then I took her home."

"And then?"

"And then I went home. Sorry brother, I'm not going to rush anything. She did ask me about my, uh, my wedding ring, though."

"Oh boy. What did she say?"

"She asked me if I have ever thought about taking it off."

"OK, fair enough, right? That's a legitimate question, Skipper. Has anyone else ever asked you about it?"

"Maybe."

"Maybe? Listen to you-who?"

"Well, my son, two counselors, Robin's sister, my sister, my cousin Lynn, Kelly, uh."

"So were you upset when Lynda asked?"

"Uh, not really upset, but maybe disappointed. I thought it was a bit presumptive of her to ask me so soon in our relationship."

"Nick how many women have you dated since Robin passed away?"

"Well, uh, just Lynda."

"Right, and I think you like this lady, so if I were you, I wouldn't read too much into that. This was your third or fourth date and she obviously likes you, so I think that question is fair game. She probably needs to know that you are emotionally ready for a relationship. Let it go, skipper."

"OK, OK, Mr. Torres. This from the man that can't remember if he's dating a teacher or an engineer."

Tony leaned back and winked. "I can remember. It's you that can't." Nick leaned back and scratched his head.

"OK, point taken. Listen, I sat down with Jessica earlier regarding the Dodger's call off yesterday and he basically got a final warning, so if you know anyone that could fill his shoes, then send them our way, alright?"

"Yes, sir. Why wasn't he canned?"

"Well, Jessica and Amy both thought that according to company standards, he deserved a final warning and a second chance. Dodger basically promised them the moon and the stars, and maybe Amy fell for it. I don't like the idea of having to depend on him so much, but this damn company runs their labor so lean, I don't have a choice. It's going to take me a month to get the right pair of hands in here, and I'll bet that in that time Dodger gets hammered and leaves me hanging yet again. And guess who gets to cover his shift when that happens?"

"Yeah, I know, these guys at CSM run it on the knife's edge, but hell, skipper. You don't need to work like this. Why do you stay here?" Nick looked out at his kitchen, then turned back to Tony. "Don't know, Tony."

"Nick, you got any more plans for the doc?"

"I think Saturday morning, I'm going to take her on a bike ride to that café in Traveler's Rest then I'll have to beat it back here for dinner. I need to be here by two. When that girl is off, I mean she is off. She turns the company phone off and she just drops all of the pressure of work. She really doesn't understand why I have to work like this."

"Look Skipper, I know you have a lot on your plate and the pressure here is intense, but try to leave a few scraps for your lady, OK?" Nick's phone went off with a text message from Amy, which he quickly opened. "Fall festival meeting in fifteen in Armory".

"I'm working on it Mr. Torres." He responded to Amy, "i'll be there miss sommers".

"Tony, you do know that Amy is planning an outdoor fall festival for the first week of October, correct? We'll have a cookout, live music, a basketball-shooting contest, a lot of games and such. I would love to surprise Amy with our Wheel of Fortune set-up. Man, she would love that. Remember the first month you were here, we did that in the Chicago Room and our folks loved it? So will you dust off that wheel then, and make sure it spins?"

"Sure thing, Skipper. So what do you have planned for the basketball contest?"

"Well, I'm hoping Theo comes over and stages a shooting contest, then a winner take on Theo. Maybe we could sell five shots for a dollar, and the proceeds could go to Amy's favorite charity?"

"Sounds great, Skipper. Listen, I have a dining room to take care of, I have things to do."

"Yes sir, Mr. Torres; best get on it." Tony stood up and leaned on Nick's desk. "Hey skipper, you think we could get Jessica to dress up as Vanna White?"

"Mr. Torres, you have a one-track mind, you know that?"

"Yes, I do!"

Eight hours later, Nick was in the thick of a busy night. He had three cooks on the line and he was expediting. As Kevin Randall finished plating up an order, he would place the tickets in the window. Nick would pull the ticket, then pull each plate, add any necessary condiments, then have Ally run the food to the dining room. Every night, they tried to have one server whose sole job was to run food and bus tables. Nick looked at the clock between tickets, 7:20. Another 20 minutes or so, and he could get out of here.

"Nick! I need you out here right now! It's Mrs. Stafford!"

Nick asked Jackson to finish plating the order, then yelled at Kevin, "Get a nurse up here right now!" He rushed into the dining room and found Beverly Stafford lying on her left side on the floor, screaming in agony. "Beverly, can you hear me?"

"Oh God, Nick, it hurts so bad. Oh God, Nick! Oh, God!"

Virginia Rogers was holding Beverly's hand; Nick took the other one.

"Nick, I think she's broken her hip. She lost her footing and fell. Her hip probably let go before she hit the floor."

"Beverly, we have a nurse on the way." Nick looked around and saw Ali. "Call 911 right now please, Ally."

"I already have Chef." Nick asked someone for a seat cushion and he carefully put it under Beverly's head.

"Oh God, I can't breathe it hurts so bad!" Beverly squeezed Nick's hand so hard that two of his knuckles cracked. "Beverly, if you can scream, then you can breathe. You're not going to suffocate, sweetheart, so just hang in there for another minute or two, OK? Keep squeezing my hand, OK?" Nick looked up at Ginger. "Anything we can do, Doc?" Ginger just shook her head. "She needs some morphine and she can't be moved until then. Hip fractures like this painful. She's just going to have to wait it out. I doubt we have morphine downstairs."

Candace and Saffron showed up with a trauma kit. "The nurse is here Beverly, OK?" Candace knelt down and carefully ran her hands across the top of Beverly's hip.

"How you doing, Beverly? Does this hurt?"

"*Oh please, don't touch me. Please stop, stop … it hurts so much. Please do something, please!*"

"Candace, don't we have something for her? Morphine or something like that?" Candace shook her head. "Nick, we aren't licensed for those narcotics." Nick squeezed Beverly's hand. "You're gonna have to hang in there for a few more minutes sweetheart, OK?" Candace took her blood pressure, pulse and oxygen levels.

"We just have to keep her comfortable until EMS gets here. If we could get her to sit up, we could get some Tylenol in her, but I wouldn't want to twist her around." Nick turned and saw Ally. "Ally please run up to the front desk and when the ambulance pulls into the front, will you run and let us know?"

"Come on, Beverly, talk to me. Tell me about your grandsons, please."

"*No Nick, it hurts too much to talk.*" Nick looked at Candace, who tried not to smirk.

"Miss Beverly, I don't think you've stopped talking since we got up here!" Beverly opened her eyes and glared. "*OK, Saffron, I'll just lie here and scream then.*" Ally showed up and knelt down next to Nick.

"Mrs. Stafford, the ambulance just pulled through the front gate. They'll be here in just a minute, OK?" Moments later, the EMTs came rolling into the dining room, pushing a gurney and carrying several metal boxes.

"Guys, our patient is an 83-year-old female in good health, BP is 167 over 110, pulse is 84, O2 levels are good, probable pathological fracture of the right femur." Candace handed Mrs. Stafford's medical records to the EMT. "Here's everything the ER will need to know."

"OK, thank you, uh … "

"Candace. I'm the charge nurse." In two minutes, the EMTs were cleared to give Beverly a shot of morphine. "Beverly, how you feeling now?"

"Oh, I feel great, Nick, how about you?" Candace looked over at Nick and winked.

"Morphine is amazing," she whispered. The EMTs carefully moved her onto the gurney as Nick squeezed her hand and told her she would be OK. Candace reached out for Nick's hand as Mrs. Stafford was loaded onto the ambulance.

"Nick, as the only department head on campus, you need to call the family member and let them know what's happened to Mrs. Stafford." Nick had a brief glimpse of Todd answering the phone. "OK, thank you Candace."

Nick walked up front to retrieve the booklet with all of the resident's contact information, took his phone out of his pocket and called Amy.

"Hey Nick, how are you?" Amy sounded excited to get a phone call this late.

"Good evening, Miss Sommers. My apologies for calling but, uh, bad news. Mrs. Stafford probably has a broken hip. She fell in the dining room. Virginia Rogers was there, and she was sure that her hip snapped before she fell. Anyway, the EMTs have just taken her to the ER, and I'm about to call her family member and let them know what happened."

"Oh no, was she in a lot of pain?"

"Yes ma'am, she got some morphine about two minutes after the ambulance got here, but she was in agony before that."

"OK, have you notified her power of attorney?"

"Not yet, but that's next on the list. Hopefully it's not her son."

"I understand. If it is, I'll be happy to make the call for you, just let me know. Is there anything else I can do for you, Nick?"

"No ma'am, I just thought you would want to know."

"Yes, of course, Nick, I'm always here for you and, uh, *the residents*, I'm always here for the residents, and if you ever need to call me, I'm here for you, too, OK?"

"Yes ma'am, thank you, Miss Sommers." Nick hit the red button on his Blackberry, then leafed through the contact book hoping he would not have to call Todd. Much to his relief, Beverly's daughter Beth was listed as the primary contact. He dialed Beth's number and waited for her to answer. Five minutes later, Beth was on her way to the ER. Nick walked into his office and filled out the report on Beverly Stafford, emailed a synopsis to Amy, copied Grant, and hit send.

The next morning, Nick was in the Armory 10 minutes early. He sat down, opened his laptop and looked at his calendar.

"Good morning, Nick." Nick looked up and smiled as Amy walked in. She was wearing a flax-colored business suit with a lapel jacket, knee-length skirt, and a white linen pullover blouse. "May I sit next to you, Nick?" Nick sat up straight and smiled.

"Yes, of course, Miss Sommers, you, uh, look quite lovely this morning."

"Thank you, Nick. Candace was correct about Mrs. Stafford. She has a broken hip, she's going to have a long recovery, at least seven to ten days in the hospital, and then we'll need to try and find a spot for her in Overbrook. At her age, it's a long shot that she will be able to return to an independent lifestyle. Do you mind if we talk about Todd Stafford now?" The smile faded from Nick's face and he looked away. "Yes ma'am, that's fine."

"Sorry, Nick, but we really need to discuss this. Listen, this is a direct family member and he has visitation rights. We can't ask him not to come here just because of something that happened a year or five years ago. As long as his mother says she wants to see him, then we need to honor that. I understand that he has a rather unsavory past, but we're not in the position to deny him the right to visit his mother."

"Unsavory? This guy is pure trash and he's going to gradually cause more trouble. I think he's probably on coke."

"Nick, are you listening to me?"

"Yes, ma'am, I understand. I *have* been professional to him, but I thought you should know that he has a sordid past, and that the two of us have sort of crossed swords."

"I didn't say you weren't being professional, Nick. I was just reminding you, that's all. A place like this, well, we're always going to have to deal with a difficult family member; it's inevitable. People get very fussy over how their loved ones are being treated when they're paying this much money. Listen, just be careful about getting into a one-on-one situation with Mr. Stafford. If he gets upset and raises his voice with you, then walk away. Tell him you'll get someone else, or if he asks to see you, then *do not* do it alone. Take someone else with you, understand?"

"Sure, of course, Miss Sommers."

Amy reached out and put her left hand on his right hand. "Nick, are you sure you're paying attention to me?" He turned his hand over, squeezed her hand, and looked Amy in the eye.

"Yes ma'am, I understand." The door to the Armory opened, and Amy quickly drew her hand back. "Hey, good morning, Grant. How's your world today?" Grant walked in, smiling as he always did. Jessica, Cassidy and Christina trailed behind him.

An hour later, Nick was chatting with Tony. "And don't forget that Theo is away this weekend, I have a date tomorrow, and I'll probably turn my phone off as soon as I walk out of here tonight."

"Don't worry, brother, we'll be fine. I thought you were gonna take Saturday off as well?"

"Well, I wanted to, but it's really tight on Saturday and we are going to be busy. Kevin and Xavier are going to need me, and everyone else is maxed out on hours already."

"So what do you have planned for tomorrow night?"

"Just dinner, that's all."

"Just dinner? Where you taking her?"

"A new place I've heard about. Listen Tony, I got things to do here and Theo is leaving first thing in the morning. This is probably the last step in his scholarship quest; he really wants to get into UNC and if he impresses the right folks this weekend, then I think he's a shoo-in. He's gonna be with some teammates and his coach, plus there's some other kids from a few other schools going as well, so I want to spend some time with him tonight."

"With that kid's skills and good looks, they'll fall all over themselves to sign him up, boss."

"This isn't a beauty contest, Tony, and it's his grades that will get him in. He's pushing a 3.85 right now, and that's damn good. Honestly, he could probably get enough scholarship money to stay in state and get a free ride, but he wants to try and make the NBA, so I think UNC would be a great fit. As long as he keeps his grades up, I'm OK with it. He really needs that degree, though. Getting on a pro team, man, you have to have so many things go right. That's such a long shot."

"It's good to have goals though, Skipper, no matter how lofty. Alright, I have to get moving, time to make it happen." Tony patted Nick on the back and headed towards the dining room.

16

Nick looked at his clock. 5:44 p.m. Lynda would here in 30 or 40 minutes. The Prosecco was chilling, the vegetables were cut and the short ribs in the oven, the kitchen was clean, wine glasses were standing at the ready, Theo would not be home until Sunday afternoon – and Nick didn't have to be back at work until 2 tomorrow. He picked up his Blackberry, thought about turning it off then decided to set it to vibrate. He took a quick look around for any photos of Robin that he may have left out then headed for the shower.

Thirty minutes later, he heard a car door close. He opened the front door about the same time Lynda walked up. "Wow." Lynda was wearing a tight. turquoise-and-white print strapless dress that showed off her body to its fullest.

"Well, are you going to invite me in or are you just going to stand there taking in the view?"

"Lynda, would you please come inside?"

"Yes, of course, I would love to." As she walked into the house, she ran her a fingertip over his chest. The electricity she generated caused Nick's abdominal muscles to fire and a shiver to run up his spine. Lynda surveyed his house, admiring his craftsman-style furniture, and then walked over to the kitchen. He obviously had hired a cleaning service, because there was no way two guys kept a house this clean. She turned to face Nick and put her right hand on her hip. "Are you going to close the door?" Nick realized he hadn't moved since Lynda walked in. "Oh, yes, the door." He looked around outside before closing the door – for what, he wasn't sure – and noticed Lynda's red Mini in his driveway. He hoped it had a five-speed, not an automatic.

"What a cute bungalow you have, Nick. How long have you and Theo lived here?" She sat down on one of the stools that bordered his kitchen and placed her handbag on the counter. She noticed the assortment of wine glasses perched on the counter, everything from champagne flutes to brandy snifters.

"About a year. We love it here, too. North Main is a great neighborhood, very vibrant, close to downtown, and you never know who will drop in for dinner."

He picked up a remote control, pointed it at his bookcase and turned up the music just a bit. "Oh, I do love Norah Jones," cooed Lynda, "and the aromas in here are divine. If that's my dinner that I smell, I just might stick around for a while." There was a basket of food items on the counter. Cherries, raspberries, plums, peaches, yellow and green zucchini, a couple of vanilla beans, cinnamon sticks and some chocolate bars were neatly arranged in a muslin-lined basket. Next to that was a small white ceramic bowl of freshly cut peaches, with a couple of cocktail forks nearby. A small vase that contained two red roses, freshly cut rosemary, lavender and thyme, stood guard nearby. Nick walked into the kitchen and opened the refrigerator.

"I hope you like sparkling wine."

"Champagne?"

"Prosecco."

Lynda removed one of the lavender stems, closed her eyes and ran it under her nose. "Mmmmm, one of my favorite scents. Lavender is so wonderful." Nick smiled. He had read many times that lavender is the scent that women find the most arousing. He poured two flutes of Prosecco, and offered one to Lynda.

"A noi, I love sparkling wines, and this Prosecco is delicious. What are we drinking?"

"Mionetto, one of my favorites. Crisp and delicious. I hope it's OK to have with your medication?"

"And just what medication do you think I'm taking?"

"You have obviously overdosed on your gorgeous pills today." Lynda rolled her eyes, shook her head and sipped her Prosecco.

"I hope you're a better cook than comedian."

"Would you like to know the best way to drink Prosecco?"

Lynda gently tossed her hair back and nodded. He walked from behind the kitchen counter and stood directly in front of her. She reached out to him with her left hand, and moved her fingertips from his chest down to his abdominal muscles, counting each ripple. Nick took her left hand in his, and she stood up. He took a generous sip, then put his left hand on the small of her back, pulled her close, and moved to kiss her. As their lips met, the Prosecco flowed from his mouth to hers. She swallowed every bit. She moved her lips up to his ear and whispered,

"Are your knees as weak as mine?" They kissed again. Lynda could still taste the Prosecco on his lips.

Nick thought how wonderful Lynda's body felt against his. Her full breasts, her tightly toned back and arms, the curve of her hip as his fingers gently traced her outline was intoxicating. He set down his flute of Prosecco, reached for a cocktail fork and stabbed a peach slice, then offered it to Lynda. She pressed her left hand against his chest and pushed back a bit, smiled at him, and gently bit into the peach. Flavors of honey, citrus, clove and chamomile slipped across her tongue as the late July peach offered up its full glory. He took another sip of Prosecco and they kissed again. The peach, Prosecco and Nicholas St. Germaine flavors wove together, and the effect was stunning. Lynda had never experienced foreplay like this before, and she had not even been in his house for 15 minutes. She moved her lips to his ear.

"Tell me this is all leading up to multiple orgasms, because the suspense is going to kill me."

"You have to eat your vegetables before you can have dessert."

She reached down and gently squeezed his swollen penis.

"So che voglio per il dessert," she grinned.

He reached for a raspberry, and offered it to Lynda. They kissed again, and Lynda's hands moved to the top button of Nick's shirt. She quickly opened the first two buttons, kissed his chest, then moved her hands to his waist and started to unbuckle his belt. Nick reached down for her hands and pulled them up and kissed them.

"What's the hurry? I have dinner for us, and we have nowhere to go."

"Lei e correto, of course. Piu Prosecco?" asked Lynda, dangling her empty glass.

He filled their flutes with the sparkling wine and as she drank, he asked her to dance. She put her glass down and moved to him. They kissed again, and she asked for another peach. Nick obliged her, and as she swallowed the succulent fruit, they kissed again. She put her arms around his neck, he wrapped his arms around her lower back, and they slowly swayed to the music as Lynda sang to him. Nick lifted her left arm and gently twirled her out, then pulled her back to him. She reached up with both hands and caressed his face.

"A girl could sure get used to this kind of treatment." She moved her hands down the front of his chest to his abdomen, and could feel his muscles tingle. "How much more of this can you take, Nicholas St. Germaine?" He kissed her again then whispered,.

"The zucchini is ready." She laughed and threw her head back, and caressed his swollen penis with her left hand.

"Yes," she giggled, "the zucchini *is* ready."

Nick smiled and winked as he returned to the kitchen, opened the oven and pulled out a roasting pan of thickly cut zucchini. He neatly arranged two small plates then picked up a small, soft wedge of cheese and a paring knife. He carved several small slices of cheese onto the warm vegetable, added a twist of fresh pepper and some fresh chopped chives, spooned a red pepper sauce across the plate then set the plates down in front of the two bar stools. "The zucchini is ready, my darling." Lynda approached the stool as Nick poured two glasses of white wine.

"And what are you pouring me, now?"

"Jon David Sancerre, a 2007. Monsieur David himself personally assured me that this would be the perfect wine for my beautiful physician and that after only one sip, she would be mine."

"Well, you can tell Mr. David that you had me at Prosecco," she smiled. "Mmmmm, what kind of cheese is this? It's divine."

"Comte. It's French, a raw milk cheese that's made near the border of Switzerland by sex-starved farmers. Since they are so emotionally unsatisfied, they pour out their frustration into their cheese."

"Do you have a degree from Bullshit University, or are you self-taught?" Lynda smiled as she bit into the cheese and zucchini.

"Definitely self-taught," he winked. Lynda sipped the wine. The roasted zucchini, warm cheese and the slightly acidic wine were a dreamy combination.

"Oh my gosh, Nick, please tell me you eat like this all the time."

He laughed. "You're implying that I cook at home. Sorry, Sweetheart, but I work like a dog, sometimes six days a week usually, and I wouldn't dream of cooking like this for my son. He's only 17, you know. I'm sure there's laws to prevent a father from teaching his under-age son how to seduce women through cooking."

"Nick, why do you have to work so much? If we're going to make this work, Dr. Giansante is going to need plenty of personal Nicholas time."

"I know, Sweetheart, and I promise I am going to work on that." They kissed again and finished the zucchini. Nick had to summon up all of his discipline to move to the next course, and not throw her over his shoulder and dash into the bedroom.

"And now comes the sex?" she cooed.

"I believe it's time for some breast," said Nick, as he deposited the plates in the sink.

"*Finally!*" declared Lynda, as she stood up and practically knocked over her stool. Nick opened his toaster oven and produced two fat duck breasts, placing them on the wooden cutting board. "Duck breast, my darling."

"Oh, Nicholas St. Germaine, you do know how to tease a girl, don't you?"

Nick flipped the breast over and looked for the direction of the meat's grain. He then turned the breast fat side up and sliced long, thin bias slices, carefully fanned the slices on two white rectangular plates, and then lifted a small saucepan off the stove and quickly spooned the pinot noir-based cherry sauce over the slices, before finishing up with a sprinkle of fleur de sel and some freshly picked lemon thyme. Nick held out a fork for Lynda and then offered her a plate of duck. She took the plate of duck, closed her eyes and brought it close to her nose, inhaling deeply. The aroma of black pepper, thyme, warm fat and glowing cherries filled her senses. When she opened her eyes, Nick was offering her a glass of red wine.

"Oh Nicholas, you are so wonderfully cruel." She lifted a slice of the duck, swirled it in the sauce and placed it in her mouth, closing her eyes again.

"Oh my gosh, *so wonderful!*"

"Pinot Noir?" She gladly took the wine as the setting sun began to shimmer through the westerly facing windows. "And what are we drinking?"

"Garretson Pinot Noir, from Southern California. I cooked at the vineyard several years ago."

"And let me guess, the grapes are harvested and squeezed one at a time by the sex-starved Garretson brothers, and they put all of their sexual frustration into their wines, and that's why this Pinot Noir is so amazing?" Nick laughed.

"Well, there are two Garretson brothers, but I have no idea how sexually satisfied they are. However, I think the phone number of the vineyard is on the back of the bottle. Shall we call them and ask?"

"*Absolutely not!* We will finish this amazing duck, and then retire to the bedroom. Agreed?" Nick raised his glass to Lynda, and they toasted. Norah Jones' voice softly flowed through the house. Lynda bit her last slice of duck and took another sip of the wine as Nick offered her a ripe cherry.

The cherry's bright acidity rolled across her palette and softened the duck fat that she had just swallowed. She took another sip of wine, and strawberry, allspice, white pepper and cherry flavors gently cascaded across her palette.

"Have another sip, please," Nick suggested to Lynda. As she did, Nick held the vanilla bean to her nose. "Now close your eyes and breathe deep." She closed her eyes, inhaled the vanilla bean's aroma and swooned.

"Oh my, Nicholas, I think I just had my first orgasm."

Lynda finished her glass and stood up, as Nick walked from the kitchen to her side of the counter. He picked up a linen napkin and tenderly wiped her mouth. She put her arms around his waist, and they gently swayed to the music. Nick put her face in his hands and as they kissed, he moved his hands down to her hips, then back up to her waist and the small of her back, then gently across her tight, round bottom. "The short ribs can wait," he whispered. She eased back a bit to look into his eyes, then brought her hands behind his neck and pulled his lips to hers. Nick inhaled deeply, then moved his right arm from her back to the front of her thighs and held on to her shoulders with his left arm. He gently eased down on his quadriceps, moved his right arm behind her knees, and lifted Lynda Giansante's 118 pounds off of his kitchen floor and into his arms. Lynda quickly gasped, then smiled and kicked off her shoes. As he carried her past the counter, she reached out and grabbed his glass of Pinot Noir. Nick laughed as he carefully walked across the house to his bedroom, eased her through the threshold of the bedroom door, and carefully laid her on his bed. Lynda held the glass steady the entire time. Nick lifted the glass out of her hands and placed it on the nightstand. He unbuttoned his shirt and pulled it off, as she bit into her right forefinger and smiled. She sat up, kneeled on the bed and reached out to Nick, moving her hands across his muscular chest and arms. As she kissed him on the chest, she took off his belt and unzipped his pants. He backed away from her, stepped out of his loafers, and let his linen pants drop to the ground.

Lynda giggled as he climbed onto the bed and perched over her body. She moved her hands across his chest, then to the back of his neck and lifted herself to his lips. They kissed again as Nick reached underneath her and held her tight as he rolled to his left. She was now on top of him and she sat up, reaching behind her and unzipping her dress. Nick helped the dress slide off of her shoulders, but she had to lift herself up to shimmy the dress down to her feet. Nick laughed, and scooted it off the bed with his toes. He pulled her close and as they kissed again, he moved his left hand down to remove her panties. Nick performed the same toe routine to get her panties off of her feet. She sat up on him and smiled, threw her head back and gently stroked his chest. She worked her hands down to his shorts, scooted back a bit and pulled off his underwear as he lifted his bottom off of the bed. She laughed and twirled his shorts over her head, then threw them across the bedroom. She sighed, then slowly kissed Nick on the chest and traced his muscles with her fingers, then gently caressed his swollen penis. She rolled on the condom that Nick had just handed her, moved her hips up and over him, and guided him in while she closed her eyes and gasped, "Oh Nicholas!" in satisfaction.

Nick turned to his nightstand and grabbed a small bottle of baby oil and rubbed it into his hands, reached up and softly caressed her shoulders, arms and breasts. Lynda opened her eyes and smiled, leaned down and nuzzled his ears with her nose, then bit him on the ear lobe as her hips moved to the rhythm of the music. Nick moved his hand to the small of her back and pulled himself up, then ever so slowly whispered.

"Lynda Giansante, you are so beautiful." His whispers set off electric impulses that coursed through her spine, and she tingled all over. She closed her eyes, threw her head back, and giggled as they moved in unison. She then leaned forward and Nick laid back down as Lynda softly moved the ends of her silky hair across his face and chest, then threw her head back again.

"Oh, Nicholas, you are so amazingly yummy." Nick sensed that she was close to orgasm. He sat up and moved his hips off of the bed, and she squealed. She smiled, tossed her head back, and closed her eyes.

"Open those beautiful eyes of yours please, Sweetheart."

"I'm trying, baby"

Nick whispered, "Lynda, I want to look into your eyes when you come."

She grinned, "Start looking."

Nick sat up, wrapped his arms around her and held on tight. Lynda looked into his eyes, ran her hands through his hair, grasped his face and shouted,

"Oh, Nicholas! Oh my! Oh, Nick! Oh no, Nick!"

Several minutes later her heartbeat began to slow, Nick pulled her close and kissed her, then slowly whispered, "Mmmmmm, Lynda Giansante." He rolled her over and propped himself up on his elbows, and gently stroked her face with his right hand. He kissed her lips, neck and ears, then slowly moved down to her breasts as his left forefinger traced the outline of her hips and stomach. Her abdominal muscles tingled and quivered, and she giggled. Lynda ran her hands across his back, lightly tracing the contour of his muscles with her fingernails.

"Oh, Nicholas," she sighed as she felt his penis beginning to swell. "Shall we make love again, or retire to the kitchen for pot roast?"

"They're short ribs, and the longer short ribs cook, they more tender they become. I vote for another orgasm. All those in favor, say aye." She lifted her head up and playfully bit him on the right ear, then whispered,

"Aye".

He reached over for his Pinot Noir and saw the clock radio. Damn, it was almost nine. He had forgotten how great sex can make time stand still. He took a generous sip of wine, then shared another wine-drenched kiss. They made love again, and when they were finished, she laid her head down on his chest, draped her arms across him, and they both drifted off to sleep.

There was a knock on the front door, so Nick got out of bed and walked to the front of his house. He looked outside and saw a police car in the driveway. What are the cops doing here? His pulse quickened as he opened the door and saw a police officer.

"Nicholas St. Germaine?"

"Yes?"

"I'm afraid your wife has been in an automobile accident. She has been transported to the Greenville Memorial Emergency Room. Can I be of further assistance?" Nick's heart rate exploded as panic set in. "What? Where? What happened? How ... how ... how bad is she? How is she?"

"Mr. St. Germaine, I apologize but that is all the information I have. Can someone get you to the Emergency Room?"

"Robin!" Nick jerked himself up out of bed, gasping for air. His pulse must have been in the 140s.

"Oh, sweetheart, what's the matter?" Lynda asked. "Were you having a nightmare?"

He looked at Lynda and quickly got out of bed. His eyes were wide open. Confused, he ran into his bathroom, closed the door and looked into the mirror. He forced himself to take deep breaths and gain control of his breathing. He turned on the hot water. There was a slight knock on the door.

"Nick? Are you OK, baby?"

"Sure, Lynda, give me a second please?"

"OK, sweetheart." He washed his face with soap and warm water, toweled himself off, shut off the water, turned off the light, and then walked back into the bedroom. Lynda was sitting up in bed with the glass of wine.

"Sweetheart, are you OK? You were having a nightmare."

"I know, I know," he said as he climbed back in bed and asked her for a sip of wine. He took a generous sip, as Lynda curled herself around his torso and moved her left hand across his chest.

"Anything I can do?"

"You already have."

"Nick, you called out to Robin."

"I know, Lynda. I'm so sorry."

"It's OK, Nick, but I have to ask you something."

"Sure, anything, ask away."

"Have you been, you know, have you been with anyone since she passed away?"

"No."

"Serious?"

"Yes, of course I'm serious." Lynda squeezed him tighter and pulled herself on top of him, sat up and took his face in her hands. She wiped away the tears that had started to run down the sides of his cheeks.

"I'm so sorry. Please forgive me, Lynda."

"Oh, don't be so silly, there's nothing to forgive." She leaned down and kissed him, kissed his cheeks, kissed his salty tears, then kissed him on the lips again. Nick's penis started to swell as he returned her kisses and brought his hands up to her face. "Nicholas St. Germaine, you cannot be serious." Nick smiled and winked at her. God, she was so beautiful.

"I'll bet you've never gotten a speeding ticket in your life, have you?"

Nick rolled her over.

"Mmmmmm, three's my lucky number and yes, for your information, I have gotten a speeding ticket Mr. Smart Ass, and I also made straight As in high school, college and most of med school, but right now, I would like another orgasm, so would you mind concentrating?" Nick smiled at her and blew the hair out of her eyes.

"Si mia bella signora," he whispered, "un orgasmo per Medico Giansante a destra fino."

Thirty minutes later, Nick walked into the kitchen and pulled the short ribs out of the oven, lifted the lid and inhaled. He had prepared the ribs with lots of garlic, shallots, black and white pepper, carrots, fresh bay, thyme and some cabernet sauvignon. After four hours in the oven, the short ribs were certainly tender. Lynda walked up behind him wearing a pair of his work out shorts and a t shirt and slid her arms across his abdomen while she took in the aroma of the short ribs.

"Oh my, Nicholas, I am starving. Shall I set the table?" He turned slightly to his left and kissed her, then turned and faced her. He wrapped his arms around her waist, then slid them under the shirt and kissed her again. Lynda sensed that he was getting aroused again.

"Easy there, tiger. The good doctor needs to get her strength back, OK? Nick, would you be a sweetheart and retrieve my bag in the back seat of my Mini? Please?"

"Sure thing, Doc. While I'm doing that, would you open that bottle of wine for us?"

"Mmmmmm, absolutely. Let's see, Whetstone Syrah. I suppose there is a double entendre you would like to utter first?"

"No, ma'am. I just happen to like Jamey Whetstone's wines. Excuse me whilst I retrieve your bag, darling." Nick walked outside as Lynda unlocked the car with her remote. He opened the back of the Mini and lifted out her overnight bag. Before he shut the door, he glanced at the shifter. Sure enough, Lynda Giansante drove a standard transmission, not an automatic.

"I may be in love," he said out loud. "Here you go, sweetheart. Shall I just put in the bedroom?"

"Mmmmmm, yes, please. Oh Nick, this wine is, I don't know what to say, it's amazing. Tell me you know this Jamey guy and you're planning on whisking me away to his winery." Nick stood next to Lynda, lifted his glass, swirled the wine across the globe of the glass, lifted it to his nose, and inhaled deeply.

"Mmmmmm, black pepper, dark plums, dark chocolate, maybe a bit of cinnamon." He took a long sip, let it sit on his tongue for a few seconds, then reached out with his left hand and caressed Lynda on her bottom. "Wow, you're right. *This is* amazing!" Lynda swatted his hand.

"Will you cut that out? I thought we were going to have some short ribs?" Nick took another sip of wine, turned and winked at Lynda as she reached out and pulled him close. They shared a Syrah kiss then Lynda whispered, "Nick, I am *really* hungry." He gently caressed her hips.

"So am I."

Lynda sat down as Nick prepared two plates of short ribs that he finished off with some whipped Yukon gold potatoes, a splash of truffle oil, and a few leaves of fresh thyme.

"Oh Nick, this is just so scrumptious. You are *so amazing.*"

"Thank you, Sweetheart. And how is my cooking?"

"And *so naughty.*"

"Thank you, Doctor."

"What shall we do tomorrow?"

"Sorry, Sweetheart, I have to work tomorrow. I have the morning off, but I need to be in by two."

Lynda dropped her fork, and it clanked against her plate. "*Damnit Nick*, you can't be serious? Do you really have to work tomorrow?"

"And Sunday. Come on, Lynda, please. Let's just enjoy our time together, please?"

"Yes, yes, of course, Nick. Would you fill my glass, please?" Lynda exhaled loudly, dipped her finger in her wine, and slowly ran her finger over the wine glass' rim. "Why don't you schedule yourself off, next weekend? We could run off somewhere?"

"Can't, sweetheart. My schedules are done for the next three weeks. Besides, I have Theo to think about."

"OK, OK. How about the next time you write your schedule, you can give yourself a weekend off. I can do the same, and we can fly away to a beach. It is summertime, remember?"

"I'll see what I can do, but I have a son, remember?"

"Yes, of course, but he would understand."

"I suppose so. It's a deal, Sweetheart. Until then?" Nick raised his glass. "Until then, lover."

17

Nick looked at his phone and saw a text message from Lynda, so he opened it up. "sorry for snapping at you lover apologies." She added a kissy face icon. He deleted the message and put his phone back in his pocket. It had been two weeks since she had spent the night with him, and in that time he had cancelled two dates and one run with her.

Tony Torres walked into the kitchen and sauntered over to Nick.

"Hey Skipper, what are you doing here today? Thought you had a date with the doc?" Nick looked up from his cutting board.

"Well, I did, but we have 90 folks in the Chicago this afternoon for that family reunion, and we didn't have the manpower to pull that off, so here I am."

"Yeah, I understand, Nick, but did she?" Nick pursed his lips and gently shook his head.

"No." Tony patted Nick on the back.

"Anything I can do?"

"No, thank you, Mr. Torres."

"When did you tell her?"

"Yesterday. We didn't have any big plans. A bike ride around town, catch an early supper, then take in Shakespeare in the Park, but she was still pretty upset. But hell, I can't have the Bradshaw's banging on Amy's door Monday morning complaining about their family reunion. They only moved in four weeks ago. Mr. Torres, I noticed that you've been on six-day schedules yourself for the last two weeks. When do you have time for your girl?"

"We broke up."

"Well, she's an engineer. Surely she understood your work commitment, right?"

"An engineer? Come on, skipper, I was dating a Pilates instructor."

"Right. Uh, I knew that." Nick put his knife down.

"You know, Tony, two weeks ago Lynda and I had a great weekend, but when I told her I had to work the next day, she damn near bit my head off."

"A great weekend? Skipper, she was only there for one night, right? That's hardly a weekend. You really need to make some time for her. I thought you were going to take her away for a weekend or something." Nick looked down at his cutting board.

"I know, I know. I'm trying, but I can't put everything on Kevin's shoulders. I even quit wearing my ring to try and satisfy her, but she's just been somewhat impatient with me. That hospital system she works for, she only works 48 hours a week, and when she's off, that's it. They really take care of their doctors, because they know the stress level can be intense, but these people we work for. "

"Skipper, she needs time with you, understand?"

"Yeah, I know. I'm trying."

"Listen to you. Ya gotta make it happen. You know the weekends are tough around here, take her out on a Monday or Tuesday when your schedule is a bit lighter. Have Kevin pull every Tuesday, or something like that."

"Kevin's wife is already fussing at him for the hours he's putting in."

"Oh."

"Alright, Mr. Torres, enough of this belly aching. I have some parsley to chop and a Sunday buffet to prep for tomorrow. Looks like I'm gonna be here until nine or nine thirty plus I gotta figure out how I'm going to make this up to Lynda."

"You wanna grab a beer or a glass of wine later? I'm buying."

"Deal, Mr. Torres."

Eleven hours later, Nick was negotiating the crowd as he walked down Main Street. The sidewalks were packed, people just looking for something to do. When he and Robin were looking for a space for their restaurant, their Realtor was adamant they go to Main Street. Robin, however, believed that in just a few years, Main Street would become a victim of its success. Her thinking was Main Street itself would soon become the attraction and eventually, the foot traffic might dissuade the serious diners and she didn't want to compete with dozens of other restaurants. They settled instead on Stone Avenue, and as Nick jostled his way through the crowd, he realized that Robin's gamble was accurate. Main Street was bustling but not everyone was looking for a great meal, a lot of them were just out, looking. Nick opened the door to McGuire's Pub and saw Tony already at the bar. Someone patted him on the back as he walked in. "Hey, Chef." Nick turned and smiled, but he didn't recognize the voice's owner.

"Who was that?" asked Tony as he handed Nick a beer.

"Uh, I don't know."

"Saved you a seat."

"Thanks, brother. Good hustle today, Tony. Plenty to do, but we got it all done."

"Thanks, Skipper. Jake poured you a frosty Thomas Creek ale. Cheers!" Nick hoisted his glass. He had been on his feet all day and was sore and exhausted, yet the anticipation of the 36-degree beer in his hand was bracing.

"Oh, that's good. Thanks, Tony." Tony squeezed Nick on the shoulder.

"You doing OK?"

"Yeah, fine Tony. Why?"

"Well, I don't know, you have a pretty good job -- an ass-busting job — but I think you like working there. You have a really good boss, a hot girlfriend, a son that will probably get a free ride to a top-tier university, and money's probably not an issue for you."

"Well, my hot girlfriend is not going to put up with this job lunch longer. So what's your point, Tony?"

"I don't know. You seem awfully distant, lately. You sure you're OK, Skipper?"

"Hey Nick, how you been, brother?"

"Good, Jake, how 'bout you? You're looking good, man. You like tending bar over here?"

"Yeah, sure boss, it's all good. It ain't like the Tavern was, but it's good, though. How you been? Life's treating you OK? Looks like you're keeping up with your workouts."

"Yeah, I'm fine, Jake. The gym keeps me out of trouble, but so does Mr. Torres here."

"OK, let me know if you two need something." As Jake tended to his customers, Nick ran his hands through his hair and looked around.

"You know what, Tony? It's been almost two years since I sold the Tavern. I miss it, I miss the excitement, but I also miss being relevant, you know what I mean? Cooks like our Chrissy Monroe used to come in for dinner over there just to see what we were up to, to try our specials, see who we were buying from. For years, it was as if the Tavern made a difference in this town, you know? We were part of what made this town cool and interesting. And now, sometimes when I'm out, I see the faces of folks that used to come in for dinner. I recognize them as a customer, but that's it. They smile at me or say, "Hey, Chef," or, "Hey, Nick," but I'm not sure who they are. My memories of the Tavern and those eight years that Robin and I had together are fading. I can't even bring myself to look at our old photos or menus. It's just too painful."

"You saying you want another restaurant, Skipper?"

"I don't think so. When Theo gets into college and *if* that kid starts playing college basketball, I want to be able to go see his games whenever I want. I don't think I want to be tied down to another restaurant. I guess I'm just realizing that I lost a lot more than Robin. I lost my sense of purpose. I need to *do* something." Nick picked up a beverage napkin and wiped his eyes. Tony squeezed him on the shoulder as Jake walked past and casually dropped a couple of beverage napkins in front of Nick. "Jake always was pretty observant. He was my best bartender, after Kelly, of course. Sorry,

Tony. Listen to me babble on. I guess I'm just feeling sorry for myself."

"Of course. Skipper, I gotta tell you I like being a part of Woodmont, and I like working for you and Amy. She's a good person and it's a lot of fun, but I can see where you would miss the restaurant. Maybe if you and the doc open that Italian place she's talking about, I'll work for you."

"That won't happen. She doesn't understand what it takes to run a restaurant, and I'm not sure she's right for me. You know, I really like working for Amy, too. She really has turned Woodmont around. I liked Jack, but there wasn't a whole lot of team work there under what's-his-face. It was all so disjointed. Amy's been there, what, five, almost six months, and it's night and day. She's got all of us focused on the success of Woodmont. She's something else, isn't she?"

"I thought you said you lost your sense of purpose?"

"What's that, Tony?"

"Two more Thomas Creek's, Nick?"

"Sure thing, Jake, but that's it for me. I can't sit here all night and feel sorry for myself. Plus, I got some omelets to flip tomorrow morning."

"You got it, boss. I'll keep an eye on you." Jake drew two more Thomas Creek ales and nodded, "These two are on me."

"Thanks, Jake. Thank you very much."

"Nick, you gonna open another restaurant any time soon?"

"I don't know, Jake."

"When you do it again, I'm your guy, got it?"

"You know it, Jake."

"Look Tony, I don't need another therapist. That's what my son is for."

"Come on Nick, I wasn't recommending therapy. But you did say you said you needed purpose, and then told me you have purpose."

"OK, Tony, OK. I like working for Amy and I think she's wonderful and, yeah, I like being at Woodmont, but what I don't like is the corporate control. I wonder if Harriett knows she's burning me out? You think those folks have any idea how hard we're working?"

"Why don't you tell her?"

"You know I'm not a whiner."

"Damn, you're hard-headed, boss." Nick took a long sip of beer.

"Look Tony, I need to figure out if I'm destined to labor in obscurity in this retirement community or if I want to be back in the action again. If I'm going to be working this hard, then I really should work for myself."

"So you *do* want another restaurant."

"I don't know, Tony, I don't know. Honestly, I couldn't do it alone. Theo will be in college soon, and, uh."

"OK, skipper, I think I understand now." Tony patted Nick on the back and squeezed his shoulder. Nick stood up, left a five-dollar bill on the bar, and nodded to Jake.

"I have to get going, Tony. I'll see you Tuesday morning. Enjoy your day off, and thanks for the beer."

"Any time, babe."

Nick tapped the gas pedal then looked at his phone. 8:49 a.m. Would Amy frown at him when he walked into the Armory five minutes late? He hated the thought of all those eyes turning to him as he walked in to the team meeting, and he certainly didn't want to disrespect Amy. The opposing light went from green to yellow, so he engaged first gear. He looked up and down the crossing highway, saw no approaching traffic, and eased into the gas until he had the engine turning at 1500 rpm's. His light went green, and he smoothly disengaged the clutch. Nick's BMW leapt away from the intersection and raced past 35 miles an hour. He eased off the gas, clutch in, engaged second gear, eased out of the clutch as his right foot pressed hard on the gas. Third gear, 55 mph. He looked as far ahead as possible for a cop, searching the oncoming traffic for that thin light bar sitting on top of a dark-blue Chevy sedan. He glanced in his rear view mirror for the grill of a white Crown Victoria that sat just a bit too low. He engaged fourth gear and flew through a yellow light. If he stayed on 101, he would have one too many traffic lights to contend with. If he took Highway 256, he had fewer lights, but it was a two-lane road with few passing lanes. If he got lucky, it could save him a few minutes. He downshifted into third gear, tapped the accelerator to bring the revs up, tugged on the wheel for the left hand turn onto 256, pressed hard on the gas as the speedometer swept past 60 miles an hour and the highway straightened out. The road ahead looked clear. He just might be on time.

Nick opened the door to the Armory and said good morning. "Good morning, Nick, you're just in time. Happy Tuesday, everyone!" Amy was practically singing her welcome.

"Miss Sommers, you certainly have a pretty voice and happy Tuesday to you, too." Amy grinned, and looked down.

"Thank you, Nick." Grant looked across at Nick and lifted an eyebrow.

"OK folks, let's get going. Grant, would you mind leading us off please?"

"Yes, of course."

An hour later, Nick was going over his daily schedule when Tony walked in.

"Hey babe, you're looking good today. Don't you have a date tonight?"

"Yes, I do. Lynda and I are going to see a tango band from Argentina at Furman. Got my tux in the car."

"A tux? You two gonna dance?"

"Yes sir, she's coming over here at six thirty to pick me up."

"I didn't know you can tango."

"Well, I've been practicing with Theo. It's amazing what you can learn on YouTube these days."

"You two getting along OK, then?"

"Well, sort of. I can't keep cancelling on her, so I'm trying hard to honor our time together. I sort of surprised her with this tonight, told her yesterday."

"So who's on tonight? We're gonna be busy, 115, maybe."

"Chef Randall is here, along with Xavier and the Dodger."

"Well, as long as everyone is here, we should be fine, Skipper."

"Don't you go jinxing me, Mr. Torres. OK, I have a lot to do today before I can get out of here. Meetings and reports and more reports, and then I have to help these guys get ready for tonight. Shower up and change, so I can walk out of this kitchen no later than 5:50 p.m."

"OK skipper, let's get moving then."

Nick looked at the clock on the wall – 3:11 p.m. – then picked up his clipboard to check his progress. He still had three beef tenderloins to clean, a compound butter and a soup to make, two salad dressings, and 24 crèmes brulee to get done. "Crème brulee, first. While that's cooling, beef tenderloins cleaned. The two dressings, and no soup gets done after the tenders, then dressings."

"Hey Chef, I, uh, hate to disturb your monologue, but Bobby was supposed to be here at three, and, uh, there's no sign of him."

Nick stopped and turned to Xavier, then pulled his Blackberry out of his pocket. Sure enough, he had a text message from Dodger, which he quickly opened. "feelin crappy aint gonna make it today." Nick's blood pressure spiked. He threw his hat at the wall, glared at Xavier, and he came close to throwing his phone across the kitchen. *"Damn that little shit!"* Xavier put his head down and kept working. Nick put his phone in his pocket, stormed out of the kitchen, banged his way out of the back door, ran down the stairs and out the back door then shouted, *"Son of a bitch!"* He texted Bobby, "If you choose to call off you are finished here, understand?" A minute later, his phone rang. Of course, it was Bobby.

"Dang Chef, why you gotta do me that way?"

"Dodger, if you don't get your butt in here tonight, you're done, understand? This is a decision you are making, not me, so don't blame me for your failure to take your job seriously. You had your final warning already, remember?"

"But Chef, I don't feel good, I don't think I'm gonna make it." If Bobby didn't get in here then Nick would spend the night on the line and not in Lynda Giansante's arms and if Nick called out on Lynda, well that may be it for the two of them.

"Bobby do you understand what you are saying here, you have 35 plus hours of vacation you are about to lose plus any potential employer will ask for a reference and you won't get one from us."

"But Chef, I really don't feel good. I can't make it tonight, sorry man." Nick hung up his phone and put it in his pants pocket, lest he throw it across the parking lot. His rage boiled over and he looked for something to hit. He ran across the parking lot onto the foot path and continued into the wooded area. He stood behind the fattest oak tree he could find then screamed:

"Sonofabitch! Hiring that kid was the biggest mistake I have ever made in my entire fucking career! Bobby Dodge doesn't have the backbone of a FUCKING SNAIL!"

Nick desperately wanted to punch the oak tree, but the energy he had expended allowed him to think just clearly enough to know he would break his hand. He ran his hands through his hair, and scratched his head hard. He looked around to see if anyone else was nearby, then thought about Lynda. Would she understand yet again? If so, how would he make it up to her? Bobby would get fired in the morning, but that would only make Nick shorthanded for another 14 to 21 days, so that meant Nick would be pulling doubles for the next two or three weekends. *"FUCK!"* he shouted again. This place was killing him. He walked from behind the oak tree and started jogging on the trail.

What the hell was he doing here? He had an investment account with 1.4 million dollars in it. Not quite enough to retire on, but he sure as hell didn't need to bust his ass for this ungrateful bunch at CSM. Tomorrow morning, he would turn in his resignation. This was the last straw. He wanted to fire Dodge a month ago, but Amy had insisted on a counseling session. What the hell for? If a CNA called out sick, Miss Amy Damn Sommers sure as hell didn't have to come to work to cover that shift, so what the hell did she care? But when a cook or dishwasher called off, Nick was somehow supposed to keep everything clicking without incurring any over time and without using a temporary staffing agency. *Screw this place!* He turned around and started jogging to the back door. Lynda would be furious, but perhaps once she heard he had turned in his notice, maybe that would smooth things over.

Nick walked back inside the building, ran upstairs then stopped outside his office to look at the schedule. Was there anyone he could call and get in here? Alex was the logical choice, but he had specifically asked for today off because he and his girl were going to Asheville. Kevin and Xavier were already working tonight, Flo was already at 38 hours, and Chrissy was at 39 hours for the week and he needed Juan for the rest of the week. He should call Amy and tell her that she has just been awarded a night on the line, let her come in and do the cold side. Fat chance! Maybe the answer was to redo tonight's menu. If he could change a few things up to make it easier on the guys, they could get by without him. All he needed to do was be out of here by six, so he could shower and change. Shit. He forgot about Mrs. Peterson's private dinner for 16, right at damn seven o'clock.

"Chef?" Kevin Randall was standing behind him. "Yes, sir?"

"You know I would take a bullet for you, so please, we really need you tonight." Kevin turned and walked back to the front line. Damn, there goes his temper again, threatening to cloud his thinking. He decided to just get to work, send a text to Alex if case he didn't end up going to Asheville after all, and email the salary folks and ask for help. Maybe Grant would come in and do the cold salads, and that might be enough. He walked into his office, dropped and did 40 pushups, sat down at his computer, and emailed the department heads:

"I'm suddenly down a cook for tonight and if I cancel on my lovely physician one more time she may cancel our relationship, is anyone available to work the salad station tonight for me please?" He sent a text to Alex: "any chance you didn't go to hippie town and instead would cover for me tonight?" Then he did the only logical thing, and that was get back to work and get ready for the night. There was still plenty to do. Ten minutes later, he received a text from Amy, "can't you call someone in?"

"Seriously, boss, like I didn't *damn* think of that already?" He shook his head and hit delete. About five minutes later, he got a text from Grant: "sorry bro in Columbia with kids, wish I could help." Shit. Five minutes later, he got a message from Sleepy. It was a photo of him holding up what looked like a 64-ounce beer. The caption read, "cheers from hippie-town." Shit. Nick looked at the time. 4:55. His evening with Lynda might as well have been a marble that he was chasing down a steep hill. He kept working and prayed for a miracle. Is there something he hadn't thought of? Another 15 minutes and he figured it was time to let Lynda know. He walked to his office and called her but she didn't answer, so he left a short message. "Sorry sweetheart I have a problem over here and I may be delayed until seven forty five or so, will do my best to get out of here at the earliest possible moment. Call me please, OK?" Shit. Nick got back on the line and tried not to think about what Lynda had planned for him tonight. Five minutes later, his Blackberry went off. It was a text from Lynda. He opened it, and all it said was, "seriously?" He responded, "had a cook call off and a big night in front of us, please darling, 8:15 at latest, xoxo". A minute later, he got another text from Lynda, "again" was all it said. Damnit. Nick kept working, kept chopping, tried not to think about what this meant to his relationship with Lynda, tried not to blame this on Amy, but it didn't seem to be working. An hour later, the kitchen door practically exploded as a furious Lynda Giansante burst into the kitchen.

"Nicholas St. Germaine! We had a date! Just what the hell are you trying to do to me?!"

The two cooks and wait staff stopped in their tracks as they took in the full beauty of Lynda. She was wearing a tight black, mid-thigh-length dress with thin shoulder straps, diamond stud earrings, a thin gold necklace, and probably nothing else. Jackson, a man that since the age of 16 preferred the company of other men, was scraping off plates at the dish station and even his eyes popped open. Nick quickly walked from behind the line and approached Lynda. She backed away and put her hand out, palm up, as he got close.

"Sweetheart, I'm so very sorry, but just give me another hour and a half and I can get out of here, right guys?" Nick turned to his guys and Xavier spoke up.

"Yes ma'am, just give us 90 minutes with your man here, then he's all yours." The mechanical chatter of the Aloha printer broke the silence as it spat out a ticket for an eight-top with lots of special requests. Xavier read the ticket out to Kevin, who in turn started putting steaks on the grill. Lynda let out an exasperated scream, threw her hands over her head, turned around and stormed out of the kitchen. Nick, red with embarrassment, walked back to the line.

"She'll be OK, you'll see. I'll catch up to her after I leave." The cooks nodded their heads and kept cooking, the Aloha printer kept chattering, the waiters kept coming for their food. Nick struggled to focus on the tickets and the process of cooking. Eighty-five minutes later, service had finally slowed to the point where he could say his goodbyes. He walked off the line and immediately texted Lynda. "Where shall we meet?" He grabbed his bag and ran downstairs to take a shower. He prayed that any second now, his phone would go off and Lynda would have forgiven him. He was in and out of the shower in less than five minutes and he immediately looked at his phone. Nothing. He dried off and changed, almost falling over because he was hopping around like a scalded frog trying to put his pants on. He picked up his phone again. Nothing. He dialed her number and her voice mail picked up: "Hi, you've reached the newly available Lynda Giansante that no longer dates Nick St. Germaine, please leave me a message."

Nick sat down on the nearest chair, put his head between his legs and scratched his head. Lynda was right, he was an idiot for letting her go. He should have just left; Xavier and Kevin would have found a way to make it happen. He was a self-centered workaholic that was certain that nothing good could happen without him. He texted his son, "what r u doing tonight?" He trudged back upstairs to the kitchen to look at tomorrow's menus, spent a few minutes looking through his coolers, and then sat down in the office and called the produce company. He left his order on their voice mail, and as he hung up the phone, Xavier came in and sat down.

"Can I help you, Xavier?" Xavier shook his head and rubbed his face.

"Chef, you're a good man, you know that? I mean seriously, you're a good guy. You gave Bobby a chance, offered him some responsibility and I'm sure you probably want to throw him off the roof right now just to see if he would fly, but you gave him a chance, OK? Your girl, well, it's a shame she can't or won't understand that. And honestly, Chef, who treated you worse tonight, her or Bobby? I mean, she was hot and all. Damn, she was really hot, Chef. But who does she think she is to drive over here just to embarrass you in front of your staff? Come on, Chef, what the hell is up with that? My friend, that was way worse than what Bobby did, *way worse.*" Xavier got up and walked out of the office. Nick leaned back in his chair, then turned to his computer and thought about catching up on a schedule or next week's menu. He looked at his phone and sent Theo another text: "wanna grab a burger?" Nick turned back to the computer to look over some emails.

Theo responded, "thought you had a date?"

"yes or no kid?"

"sushi and it's a deal, u buying?"

"10-4 sushi koji in 20?"

"koji in 20"

Fifteen minutes later, Nick walked into Sushi Koji on Main Street and found two spots at the sushi bar. Chef Koji smiled and waved.

"Hello, Chef Nick, very honored to have you with me tonight. You have a date, or just you?"

"My son will be joining me, so I hope you have a lot of shrimp ready." Nick felt a slap on his back as Theo sat down next to him, said hello to Koji, asked for green tea, and then carefully bent down and looked over the kaleidoscope of fresh seafood behind the glass case.

"Chef, I believe Theo has grown since he was last here. Maybe six-five now?" Theo looked up and smiled.

"Six-three point five." Nick put his right elbow on the bar and rested his chin in his hand. He watched Theo as he carefully studied the seafood. He saw so much of Robin in him, his sunflower blonde hair, his twinkling blue eyes, his natural athleticism and his innate desire to make the people around him happy. Nick sat up and looked across the restaurant then sat up straight.

"I'm putting in my notice tomorrow." Theodore didn't even bother to look at his dad.

"Why, that place too tough for you, old man?"

"No, that's not it at all, Theo."

"Then why? Thought you needed a challenge. That's what you told me not six or seven months ago."

"OK, thank you very much, Theo. I've been there almost a year, so are you going to look at the menu or just fuss at me?"

"Then what are you going to do, sit around the house and mope? Look at old photos of mom or maybe help me with my calculus? Nothing doing Pop, you're staying put."

"Since when are you my therapist?"

"Hey, that's a great idea, I could charge you $150 an hour just to talk to me. Seriously, that's a really great idea. Chef Koji, may I please have three of your best shrimp rolls, whatever you would like to make, two tuna rolls, then how about some pork soba noodles? Chef St. Germaine here will just have a glass of warm milk."

"Alright, that's enough, kid. Koji, how about some miso soup, an order of mussels, and how about a roll with the yellow tail, and an eel roll, please. And will you make sure Mr. Smart-Ass here gets the check." Koji smiled and winked at Nick.

"Maybe I just have him sign check and when he gets to NBA, he can pay me then. With interest, of course."

"Hey, that works Chef Koji, all for it," smiled Theo.

"NBA? Listen kid, you better concentrate on mathematics and keep that NBA dream as backup plan Number three, OK?"

"Oh, come on, Dad. We gonna go over this again? I was just kidding, OK? You gonna tell me what happened tonight, or do I have to beat it out of you?" Theo sipped his green tea and waited. "I had to cancel my date with Lynda and she, well, she, uh, came into the kitchen and pretty much chewed me out in front of my crew."

"Oh shit, you serious, Pop?"

"Yup."

"Well the heck with her, then. She doesn't deserve you anyway then, does she?"

"I guess you're right, kid."

"*You guess?!*" Theo sat up straight, shook his head, and then took a long sip of tea. "Come on, Dad. Did you really think you were going to meet Miss Perfect the first time out? Why did you open up to this girl so soon? You bent over backwards for her, threw yourself at her feet, and now look at you. I swear, I don't think you saw past her good looks. And don't *even* tell me what happened when I was away two weeks ago." Nick took a sip of beer, scratched his head, then turned to Theo.

"You know what, kid? I have the weirdest feeling of deja-vu. This sounds a lot like the conversation we had when your first girlfriend told you she only wanted to be friends."

"Yeah, that was Mindy, Mindy Hayes. I was 13, eighth grade, the whole school knew it when she dumped me – not that it had any sort of permanent effect on me."

"Right. Didn't mean to imply that it did."

"You gonna be able to let this go or what, Pop?"

"Guess I don't have a choice, do I?" Koji placed a platter of sushi in front of them.

"Chef, I have some of my own pickled ginger tonight, just for you. And look, fresh wasabi root from California." Nick looked at his son and raised an eyebrow. Theo raised his tea to Koji and smiled.

"You know what, Pop? Sometimes it's pretty good hanging out with you."

"Thanks, kid."

Nick was the last one in for the staff meeting, so he closed the door behind him. He offered a quiet, "Good morning, everyone," found the nearest empty chair, kept his eyes down and had a seat. Amy had already started the meeting and true to form, she was going around the room asking her team to bring everyone up to date on any news or events that have happened or will happen in the next 24 hours. Nick kept his head down and tried to listen, but everything sounded so trivial. Another urinary tract infection, complaints about the landscaping, the marketing folks bringing Mr. and Mrs. So and So for lunch. When Amy turned to him, what was he going to say? Thank you, boss, for screwing up the first relationship I have had since my wife was killed. He could feel the tension rising, so he started making a fist and releasing it, doing that over and over. Then he thought about what his son had said last night. Are you going to be able to let this go?

"Nick, do you have anything for us this morning?" asked Amy.

"No ma'am, nothing to report," he replied as he kept his eyes down. Amy looked around the room for help, but no one offered.

"OK people, let's have a great day." As Nick got up, Grant put his hand on his shoulder and gently asked if he could have a minute.

"Sure thing, brother." Nick sat back down and Grant pulled up a chair on Nick's left as the rest of the team was filing out.

"I heard about last night. Anything I can do to help?"

"Well, I guess the whole world has heard about it. You want to buy me a beer tonight?"

"You know it," smiled Grant. "You're a good man, Nick. You know that, and you really know how to take care of business. The folks here really appreciate all you do, but I need to say that no matter how hot that gal is."

"She's pretty hot, Grant."

"Yeah, yeah, we all know it. Listen Nick, my point is that if she really cared for you, she never would have treated you like that in front of your staff. Most everyone here cares for and respects you. I mean, how would you feel about me if I stormed into your kitchen and started yelling at you like she did?"

"Well, maybe I would deserve it?"

"Oh, *come on*, you sure as hell didn't deserve that."

"OK, maybe she overreacted, but damn, Grant, we were really getting along."

"Seriously Nick, are you listening to anything I'm saying? If the two of you were getting along, then she would have understood, don't you think? You ask me, I think she just was all about your body." Grant squeezed Nick on the shoulder. "Damn, Chef, you do have a pretty hot body here, you know that?" Nick managed a smile and shrugged his

241

right shoulder to throw Grant's hand off. Grant stood up and grabbed him by the shoulders. "I mean, seriously here, Fabio, you need to slow down, you're giving the rest of us guys here a pretty significant complex. We're all starting to doubt our own masculinity." Nick stood up and looked at Grant.

"Maybe you're right about Lynda. My son said as much last night."

"Of course I'm right, brother. I mean, can you imagine Jessica yelling at you at the top of her lungs, right in the kitchen? Who treats someone they love like that? Come on, Nick, you got some cooking to do and I have some folks to take care of. I'll call you about seven thirty, and we'll catch that beer on me, OK?"

"Thank you, Grant."

"And hey, Chef, you can't blame Amy for this. She asked you to give that kid a chance, you did, and that's it. You offered him a chance to prove his maturity, and he decided he wanted to remain a child. I'll see you about seven thirty."

"Sure thing, Grant, and thanks again." Grant winked and walked out of the room, leaving Nick alone with his thoughts. He closed his eyes and thought about the first night he and Lynda made love and how wonderful and perfect that evening was. He then flashed to the image of her barging into the kitchen and yelling at him like he was a parking lot attendant that had just scratched her new car. Nick was devastated and confused. He had confided in Lynda, shared many secrets with her, and just when he needed her to be understanding and patient, she had exploded into a fiery rage. Damn, he was going to miss her. Thoughts of her body flowed across his imagination, the smooth warmth of her skin, her perfume, the silky feel of her hair.

"Oh hello, Nick, how are you this morning?" Nick snapped out of his daydream and turned to find Willie Armstrong and Jim Jensen walking in. "Hey, good morning gentlemen, what are you two troublemakers up to?"

"Well, I'm gonna take a few dollars off of the Colonel here. Apparently he thinks he can shoot pool, so I'm gonna give him a few lessons." Willie smiled mischievously.

"Hotshot here thinks I played tiddlywinks when I was in the Air Corps."

"Well, if there's money about to change hands, then I better beat it. I think that's probably against company policy, and I have a long day ahead of me. Good day, gentlemen."

Nick walked out of the Armory and headed to the kitchen. Kevin Randall was in today to cover for the Dodger. "Chef, how you looking? What can I do for you?" True to form, Kevin Randall already had a list of things he needed him to do, number one being, "hire a new cook."

"Well, I need to take a quick pass through Overbrook. Be back in 20, OK?" Nick made his way downstairs, walking slowly and telling everyone he saw good morning. When he got to Augusta, he heard someone playing the piano. "Hey, Candace." She stopped and turned, smiled and walked up to him, held him by the waist and looked at Nick with pouty eyes.

"Heard you're available? Anything I can do for you?" Nick took her hands.

"Good news travels fast, doesn't it?"

"Sorry, Sugar, but the fit that girl threw, everyone knew by the next morning." Candace reached up with her right hand and stroked his face.

"You know where to find me." Candace walked back to the nurse's station. "Candace?"

"Yes?"

"Who's that playing the piano?"

"That's Mr. Middleton, Cecil Middleton. He's the guy who was-"

"I know, Candace, I heard his story. Thank you." Nick walked over and sat down on the nearest chair and listened to "Claire de Lune." When he was finished, Nick thanked him. "I love Debussy. Thank you, that was lovely."

"Did you know his first name was Achille? Achille Claude Debussy. Cecil Middleton, my pleasure." Cecil held a thin hand out and Nick shook his hand carefully. "You're our Chef, Nick, correct?" Cecil was in a wheel chair, and he had braces on both legs and some slight bruising on his arms. His grey hair was short but fairly thick, his face was round yet thin, and he wore black glasses with thick lenses.

"Yes, sir."

"My wife and I ate in your restaurant several times. It, too, was very lovely."

"Thank you."

"My wife and I were both musicians, and when I close my eyes and play, it's almost as if she's still here, sitting next to me." Cecil wiped his eyes. "Does it ever get any easier?"

Nick exhaled slowly. "Eventually the good days will outnumber the bad, but that doesn't mean the bad days can't be really bad. They just get further apart. It's best to stay busy, to keep yourself occupied."

"I see. Do you think about her often?"

"Every minute of every day. It helps, though. It sounds crazy, but it's true, I often see her smiling, walking next to me, holding my hand. I hear her giving me advice or asking me to slow down and think. It gets tough when you're alone, though, especially at night. It gets real tough."

"Thank you, Nick." Cecil took his glasses off, wiped his eyes again and massaged his fingers. "Do you like Beethoven?"

"Yes, sir."

Cecil stretched out his fingers then began to play Beethoven's "Moonlight Sonata."

18

Amy closed the door to the Armory and apologized for being late. "Sorry folks, I had a phone call I couldn't dodge, is everyone here? Uh, who are we missing? Is Nick here?"

Grant spoke up. "I saw his car outside, Amy."

"Well, let's get started. I'm sure he'll join us soon enough. Grant, would you like to lead off? And let's keep it short and sweet; it's a beautiful day, and I know we're all excited about the festival."

Thirty-five minutes later, Amy made her way to the kitchen. She looked around and saw Florence, Xavier and Chef Randall, but didn't see Nick anywhere. Xavier walked up to her.

"He's in the dining room at the far window. He really shouldn't be here today, but there's a lot going on." Amy thanked Xavier and walked into the dining room. Sure enough, Nick was at the farthest corner of the room. He had the window open, and his arms folded across his chest. She cautiously looked around. Seeing only Jackson off in the distance, she quietly walked over to Nick and stood next to him on his right side. Together, they looked out the window. About a minute later, Nick whispered, "I promised myself I wasn't going to cry today. Guess I'm no good at keeping promises."

"I wouldn't say that."

Nick wiped his eyes on his shoulders and put his hands in his pockets. Amy looked out at the pond, surveyed the landscaping, and waited. The breeze picked up and loosened the leaves from the surrounding trees. Palettes of red, orange and gold twisted across their field of vision and fluttered to the ground, racing across the concrete and floating in the pond.

"Two years, Miss Sommers, it's been two years today." Amy moved a bit closer then gently reached over for Nick's right arm. She slipped her left hand around his right wrist as he took his hand out of his pocket. Amy laced her fingers through his.

"Please don't ask me to go home. I really need to be busy today."

"I wasn't going to," she whispered, as she squeezed his hand.

The wind settled down. Nick looked up and watched an airliner silently stitch two narrow contrails across the sky. Amy squeezed his hand again, and stroked the top of his hand with her thumb.

"I need to get going Miss Sommers, thank you." Nick let go of her hand, turned towards the kitchen, and walked away.

Two hours later, Nick pushed the outdoor grill into place, turned on the gas and hit the pilot. With a satisfying, "Whump!" the grill ignited. "OK, Xavier, we have burgers and dogs ready, all of our accoutrements are here, and the cotton candy machine is ready. Miss Monroe will be down here shortly, correct?"

"Acoo-tree-what? You gonna start speaking English any time soon, or should I purchase that subtitle package that ESPN Five keeps trying to sell me?"

"Sorry, X. Lettuce, cheese, tomatoes, pickles, buns, mayo."

"We got all that; why you asking?"

"Never mind, X." Nick looked out at the shimmering red, gold and green leaves as they fluttered against the azure sky. "You know what, Xavier? It's too bad winter is right around the corner, because October is such a great month. So full of pretty sights." Nick turned to face Xavier, who rubbed his belly.

"It reminds me that Thanksgiving is around the corner, and that there's still lots of football to watch. Chef, you gonna stay here for Thanksgiving?" Nick looked down at his feet.

"Not sure, Xavier; may try to go see my sister's family or she may come up here, don't know yet." Kevin Randall walked up.

"Chef, you need anything else, because I need to get the snacks into Chicago for the game."

"All good, Mr. Randall, let's make it happen. Hey X, Kevin, while this grill is heating up, let's go check out the wheel, OK?"

"Sure thing." The three cooks walked into the Chicago Room. At the far side, Tony was squirting WD-40 on the wheel's gear. "What do you think, boys?" Daniel Stern's guys had built a pretty realistic puzzle board wall, decorated with strands of Christmas lights strung along the wall's borders. The puzzle board was eight feet wide and six feet tall, with three rows of rotating squares. "The puzzle board has these rotating, three-sided blocks; two sides are plain, the other green with a Velcro square attached to it. So we have six phrases, and for each game we roll the proper amount of blocks to the green side, which gives us the blank letters. Daniel picked up these letters at the Ace Hardware, and glued a small amount of Velcro to each one. We have four sets of the entire alphabet, so plenty to go around, plus extra of the more common letters. Then our Vanna places the proper letter right onto this Velcro square as the contestant makes their guesses. Pretty cool, huh?"

Jessica walked into the Chicago room wearing a flowing, sunflower-yellow, one-shoulder, floor-length dress that was gathered over her right hip by a shimmering rhinestone clasp. The three cooks stared motionless as she glided across the floor, reached for a handful of letters, put her right hand on her hip, twirled in front of the puzzle board, then spelled out D _ R-K-S. Nick laughed and said, "Vanna, I would like to buy a vowel. I'll take the letter O for two hundred dollars, please."

"Don't we get a spin on the wheel first, Mrs. Alexander?" whimpered Xavier. Nick gave Jessica some applause then turned to his cooks.

"Ok, we have work to do. Jessica, you look splendid, right guys?"

Kevin Randall averted his eyes and stumbled over his words as he mumbled, "Oh, uh, yes, Chef." Kevin and Xavier silently walked out of the room and headed back to the kitchen.

"Why are those two so scared of you, Jessica?"

"I think they're probably just poor spellers, Nick."

"Miss Jessica!" Paige Sommers bolted across the floor of the Chicago room and ran to Jessica, who knelt down to give her a hug. "You are *extra* beautiful today, Miss Jessica!" Paige turned and ran at Nick. "Chef Nick!" Nick knelt down and gave her a hug. "And you look like a Chef, Chef Nick!"

"Thanks, Paige. And what are you doing out of school at eleven in the morning?"

"We're on our break, Chef Nick, so I don't go back to big girl kindee-garton until Tuesday, first thing in the morning."

"Well, is that so? Is your mother here?"

"She's in her big office, Mr. Nick. Will you walk me upstairs to go see her?"

"I have a better idea; would you like to see the big kitchen where I cook all of the food?"

"Sure, Mr. Nick."

"Hey Vanna, I'm going to take Paige to go see her mom via the kitchen. We're all ready to go; Chrissy will have hot dogs and burgers ready by noon. You need anything?"

"No, thank you, Nick. I'm going to stay down here. Our first game is at twelve thirty and we've had a lot of folks sign up to play."

"Who's gonna be your Pat Sajak?" Jessica pointed to the Chicago's entrance as Grant walked in, wearing a brown suit and a blue tie. Grant patted his belly.

"Pat Sajak is about 20 pounds overweight, right, Nick?"

"Uh, 25, maybe?"

"OK, that's enough out of you, don't you have some burgers to grill?"

"Yes sir, let's go, Miss Sommers." Nick held his hand out, and Paige ran to him and took his hand, just as Chet Bannon rolled into the Chicago. Paige jerked to a stop and looked carefully at Chet.

"Well, hey there, young lady. Who you got here, Nick?" Nick knelt down and folded his arms across his right knee.

"Chet, this is Paige Sommers, Amy's daughter. Paige, this is Mr. Chet Bannon." Chet recognized the look in Paige's eye, so he stroked his beard slowly and asked her if she was a good little girl. "Yes, Santa!" Chet winked at Nick and laughed.

"Well, that's not the first time I've been mistaken for that guy from the North Pole. I'll tell you what, Miss Paige Sommers, since I like your mom so much, well, I just might see if I can put in a good word for you with Mr. Claus, OK? I see him every year at our Fat Guys with Beards convention."

"How about that, Paige?" Paige looked at Nick, then turned back to Chet.

"Thank you," squeaked Paige.

"Jessica ... Oh my, don't you look wonderful today?"

"Thank you very much, Chet. Do I look like Vanna White." Jessica held her arms out and twirled. The Jensen's walked in and smiled, followed by Ben De Soto and Willie Armstrong. Chet rolled next to Jessica and spun his wheelchair 360 degrees, as Willie clapped and cheered.

"Show off!"

Nick took Paige by the hand and headed towards the stairs. "Mr. Nick, how much cotton candy are you going to eat today?"

"I hadn't thought about it until just now, Paige. How much should I eat?"

"Do you know how much cotton candy will make you sick?"

"Well, I think so."

"Eat less than that, OK, Mr. Nick?" Nick threw his head back and laughed.

"Shall we take the elevator, Miss Somers? The stairs are being cleaned right now."

"Only if I can press the button."

"Well, you're gonna have to get there first then." Paige looked up at Nick, dropped his hand and bolted for the elevator call button. Nick gave her a head start, then sprang off after her. Paige reached the button first, turned and smiled.

"I win, Chef Nick!" Nick held his right palm out, and she slapped his palm.

"OK, Paige, you get to press the button." Paige looked at the button, then turned to Nick.

"I'll let you do it, Mr. Nick." He looked down at Paige and pressed the call button.

"That's the nicest thing someone has done for me in a long time, Paige. Thank you very much." Five minutes later, they were walking into the lobby just as Rebecca came out of the front office.

"Hey, Mr. St. Germaine."

"Hello, Becca. Are you two going to help out today?"

Paige put her hands on her hips and spoke for the two of them.

"Yes, we are, Mr. Nick. Mommy promised I could help twirl cotton candy and scoop ice cream." Nick walked into Amy's office, holding Paige's hand.

"Well Paige, I see you found Chef Nick." Paige let go of Nick's hand, ran across the office and threw herself into Amy's lap. Rebecca's attention was diverted outside as someone taller than the window walked past.

"Who on earth was that?" asked Rebecca.

"Um, probably, my son." Theo walked into the front door and stopped at the concierge desk, just as Nick knocked on the glass and motioned him into Amy's office. Rebecca stood up and slowly whispered to her mother, "*O-M-G.*"

Theo was now six feet, four inches tall. He was wearing red Greenville High sweat pants and a Mickey Mouse basketball jersey. Nick opened the door for him, and as he walked through the threshold to Amy's office, his curly blonde hair scraped the top of the doorway.

"Hey, kid! Miss Sommers, this is my son, Theodore. Theo, this is my boss, Amy Sommers, and her daughters, Paige and Rebecca."

Six years ago, Nick and Robin were driving home from a friend's restaurant in Abbeville, crossing through a lightly populated corner of Anderson County. It was late, almost 10 p.m., and Nick was driving fast. A deer, a fairly good sized buck, had sauntered across the road. When it heard the sound of Nick's car, it lifted its head and looked down the road, only to be blinded into immobility by four high-intensity halogen lights. At 65 miles an hour, Nick had perhaps a second and a half to stab the brakes and crank the wheel to the left without hitting the buck and staying on the road. As their Audi drifted towards the buck, Robin's eyes and the buck's eyes passed a scant 24 inches apart. Both sets of eyes were wide open, motionless, and fixated on one another. As their Audi roared past funneling blue tire smoke, the buck cut to the right and leapt off the road. Thirty seconds later, Robin had caught her breath and Nick broke the silence. "Now I know the true meaning of that saying."

"Which one?"

"A deer in the head lights."

As she stood looking at his son, Nick thought Rebecca had the same look in her eyes as that buck did all those years ago.

"Hey, good afternoon, I, uh, came to help out with the festival. My Dad asked me to host a basketball shooting contest." Paige jumped off Amy's lap as Amy stood up, and introduced herself.

"You're really tall, Mr. Theo," exclaimed Paige.

"Yes, I am, Little Miss Half-Pint." Amy sat on the corner of her desk.

"Theo, did you know Rebecca plays basketball, too?" Theo turned his attention to Rebecca.

"OK, that's very cool. What position do you play, Rebecca?"

"Basketball. I play basketball for a, uh, basketball team," mumbled Rebecca. Theo turned to his Dad.

"Rebecca plays forward for her school team, isn't that right, Rebecca?"

Rebecca stood still and nodded. Theo turned back to Nick, then looked at Rebecca.

"Very cool, Rebecca. Uh, listen, if someone can just point me in the right direction, I'll set up the goal and get out of your way. Dad, I borrowed Ricky's truck and I'm kind of double parked out there."

Paige jumped out of her mother's chair.

"Can I help you, Mr. Tall Theo?" Theo looked at Amy, who nodded her head yes.

"Sure thing, Half-Pint. Let's go, and you can call me, Theo." Theo walked out of the office with Paige running next to him.

"You take really long feet steps, Theo." As Theo left, Rebecca put her right hand on her forehead.

"Oh My God, what did I say?" Amy sat back down in her chair, put her right elbow on her desk then rested her chin on her palm.

"You said, 'Hello, my name is Rebecca Sommers, very pleased to meet you.' "

Nick laughed, and shook his head.

"And then you curtsied just like Princess Kate would have done. Don't sweat it, Becca, he gets that a lot. Fortunately, he has his mother's good looks. Well, I came up here to deliver Paige, but she's run off again, so I guess I'll adjourn for now. Are you going to get outside today, or maybe play Wheel of Fortune, Miss Sommers?"

"I'll be down there at some point, Nick. All this never stops, even on days like today." Amy waved her arm across her cluttered desk.

"Yes ma'am, I understand. I need to get back to work, too, so I suppose I'll see you downstairs."

Thirty minutes later, the festival was in full swing. Grant and Jessica had a crowd in the Chicago playing Wheel of Fortune, Cassidy had lined up a beach music band, and Chrissy had the grill full of hot dogs and burgers.

"Hey, little Miss Sommers. You ready for me to show you how to make cotton candy?"

"Yes, please, Mr. Nick!"

Beverly and Doris walked up as Nick and Paige reached the cotton candy machine. "Chrissy, have you met Paige Sommers?"

"Yes, I have. Hey Miss Paige, what's shaking bacon?"

"Nothing but the leaves in the trees."

"OK, so you two have definitely met. Chrissy, would you mind if I show Paige how to roll cotton candy?" Nick took a paper cone then poured a bit of sugar into the center of the machine's rotating head. As it spun, it ejected ethereal strands of spun sugar that quickly cooled on the sides of the aluminum bowl. Nick took one of the paper cones and twirled it in his hands while spinning it around the inside of the bowl. In a matter of seconds, he had a fluffy cone of cotton candy. "See Paige, there's nothing to it. Ok, now it's your turn. I'm gonna hold you over this bowl. Here's a paper cone, and all you have to do is roll it around the candy, and it's going to stick to your cone. Then you just keep turning it, OK?"

"OK, Chef Nick, lift me up." Nick poured a bit more sugar into the head, and cotton candy soon began to billow around the inside of the bowl. He reached down and grabbed Paige, and held her over the bowl of shimmering spun sugar. Paige threw her paper cone to the ground, stuck her arm into the swirling sugar and rotated her arm through the bowl, screaming with delight. Nick couldn't help but laugh. He moved her over the circumference of the bowl as she coated her arm in the fluffy green sugar. In only a few twirls around the inside of the bowl, Paige's arm was coated in cotton candy, from her hand to her elbow. Nick was laughing hard as he reached over and took a bite of the cotton candy then Paige did the same.

"Paige Sommers! What have you done?!" Nick spun around. Of course, who had walked up but Amy? Nick had Paige in his arms, she had a huge glob of cotton candy wrapped

around her right arm, and Nick had it all over his face and Chef's coat. Amy glared as Nick set Paige on the ground, lowered his eyes, and mumbled an apology.

"Sorry, Miss Sommers. Totally my fault."

Amy cut her eyes at Nick, bit her bottom lip, then burst into laughter at the sight of the two of them.

"Good Lord, would you look at yourselves?"

"Smile!" Doris Peters snapped a photo. "Oh my gosh, Nick, who threw the two of you into the floss?" Nick looked at Paige and Paige looked at Nick and they both pointed at one another, Paige pointing with her cotton candy arm. Amy put her hand over her mouth as she laughed.

"She's leaving here in your car, not mine." Paige realized that her mother's anger had disappeared, so she ran off screaming,

"I'm gonna show Miss Jessica my cotton candy arm."

"Sorry, Miss Sommers, I'll get her cleaned up."

Amy was smiling as she walked up, stood next to Nick and put her hand on his shoulder. "No, don't worry about it, Nick, I'll take care of it. It won't be the first time I've had to clean up one of her messes. I came down to watch Theo. He and Franklin have decided to have a game; Christina has been selling tickets at five dollars each."

"Tickets?" quizzed Nick.

"Sure, a green one means you're betting on Theo, a red one means you're betting on Franklin. All the money goes to the Alzheimer's fund, so everyone wins. I think right now, Franklin has sold more tickets – maybe 50 to 35 – but not many folks have actually seen Theo yet. That may change in a few minutes." Nick looked across the parking lot. Theo had taken off his sweat pants and was warming up. He had brought about 15 balls with him, and he was casually shooting long shots from well behind the three-point line. Cassidy was behind the goal, passing the balls back to him. "They're supposed to start in about ten minutes."

"That gives me a few minutes to clean up." Nick excused himself and ran up to the kitchen, and immediately headed to the pot sink. Xavier frowned.

"Heard you got in trouble with the boss." Xavier held out his phone as he walked past, and the evidence was there. Chrissy had snapped a photo of Nick holding Paige over the cotton candy machine.

"Oh, boy." Xavier laughed out loud and patted Nick on the back.

"Chef Randall, would you please get one of those disciplinary forms out of the office, so we can write up Chef Juvenile Delinquent here?" Kevin smiled and shook his head.

Nick pulled off his Chef coat, then stuck his arms into the pot sink.

"I knew that Monroe girl was no good the day I laid eyes on her." Xavier laughed heartily, and patted Nick on the back. "So my son is going to go one-on-one with Franklin in about ten minutes. You should get downstairs and watch him, he's really something."

"Seriously? Damn straight I will. Chef in about ten minutes, I'm gonna run off and watch Theo get schooled by my brother, Franklin, you mind?" Kevin looked at Xavier, and shrugged his shoulders. Nick finished cleaning up and made his way to the parking lot. Franklin was perhaps two inches shorter than Theo, but he was thicker and 12 years older. Cassidy had chalked off half of a basketball court, and at least 60 people were already watching. As Nick made his way to the court, he came upon Willie Armstrong.

"Nick, your son certainly is handsome, but where did he get his height from?"

"Couldn't tell you, Colonel. His doc thinks he's still got another inch or two to grow. Between his clothes and his appetite, he damn near bankrupted me, but he's a good kid. Another seven or eight months, and he'll be taking off for college." Nick turned to Willie as Willie put a hand on Nick's shoulder. "Willie, I'm not sure what I'll do with myself when that happens."

"You'll figure it out, Nick."

Cassidy picked up a basketball, blew a whistle, motioned Theo and Franklin next to her, and shouted out the rules as Rebecca picked up the remaining balls. "We have a few rules here at Woodmont." Cassidy stepped on Franklin's toe, and Franklin shouted, "*Hey!*"

"We do not step on toes!" shouted Cassidy. She then turned to Theo and poked him in the ribs, doubling Theo over. "Absolutely NO poking in the ribs!" Cassidy then turned to Franklin, grabbed his earlobe and yanked on it.

"Ouch!" shouted Franklin.

"No tugging on ears!" shouted Cassidy before turning to Theo, grabbing the back of his shorts and quickly yanking them up. "And absolutely NO wedgies!"

"*Hey, cut that out!*" screamed Theo as he swatted Cassidy's hand. The audience clapped, laughed and cheered.

"Well, now I think we understand the rules. First one to 15 is the winner, three-pointers count as threes, possession changes after a basket, ball goes back to the chalk circle at the top of the court. Cassidy put the whistle in her mouth, blew hard, then tossed the ball up in the air and ran. Theo reached out for Franklin with his left hand, and pushed off as he launched himself up for the ball. Theo grabbed the ball with his right hand and as he came back down on the pavement, he drove to the goal with Franklin on his left shoulder. Six feet from the goal, Theo drove his left knee down hard, yanked his right knee up, elevated to the goal and brought the ball up with his right hand as Franklin went for the block with his left. As Theo began to drop back to the pavement, he brought the ball down, moved it to his left hand and gently tipped the ball into the basket. The members cheered as Theo trotted away from the goal.

Cassidy passed the ball to Franklin, who stepped into the chalk circle at the top of the court. Theo backed up a bit to give Franklin some room, then started backpedaling when Franklin drove at him. Theo cut off Franklin's dribble, forcing him to pick it up and try a fall-away jumper. Theo rose to block it, but the ball left Franklin's hands and arced smoothly in the air, snapping the net as it passed through. Cassidy passed the ball to Theo, who dribbled back to the top of the court as Franklin taunted him. Theo stepped into the circle then drove hard to the right side of the court as Franklin moved to try and cut him off. Theo passed the ball between his legs to his left hand and drove back to the left. Franklin could only watch as Theo burst past him and dunked the ball with his left hand, putting his hands on his hips and shaking his head.

"Damn, he's good," mumbled Franklin.

Cassidy picked up the ball and passed it to Franklin, who was now glaring at Theo. Franklin cautiously dribbled from the top of the court, slowly walking as Theo playfully tried to swat at the ball.

"Let's see what you got, Frank! Come on, baby, let's see what you got!" Franklin winked at Cassidy, who blew her whistle. Amy pushed two wheelchairs onto the court as the crowd erupted into laughter.

"This should even the odds out a bit." Amy ran off the court and stood next to Penny, who was next to Nick. Franklin laughed out loud and cheerfully plopped himself into the nearest chair. Theo's mouth dropped open. He put his hands on his hips, looked at Amy, shook his head, then turned to Nick, smiled, and climbed into the other wheelchair. As Theo rolled a quick circle to the cheers of the residents, he realized that there were at least 15 people watching the game from their own wheelchairs. Franklin rolled to the chalk circle and then onto the court, all the while dribbling the ball with his left hand. Theo banged into Franklin's chair, but Franklin picked up the ball and tucked it into his lap as he backed up and then rolled away from Theo. Franklin beat Theo to the right side of the goal, then quickly shot and scored. Theo frowned and rolled back the chalk circle as Cassidy passed him the ball. Theo reached out for the ball, but it bounced past him and right into Chet Bannon's hands. Chet rolled over to Theo in his new electric scooter, handed him the ball, then asked if he needed some help. Franklin pointed to Ben De Soto.

"OK, if he gets Chet, then I want Ben."

Franklin rolled over to Theo and quietly offered, "Don't throw that ball to Chet, hand it to him. He'll never be able to catch a hard pass from you, understand?" Theo nodded as he made his way to the chalk circle.

"Franklin's ball!" shouted Cassidy. Franklin rolled onto the court then banged his way past Theo, handed the ball to Ben who steered his scooter to the goal as Theo blocked Franklin. Ben eased the ball up, then shot from the left side. Franklin quickly rolled to the opposite side and caught Ben's rebound, quickly putting it back into the net then they high-fived one another.

Penny's pager went off. She pulled the pager off her hip pocket, looked at it, and then turned to Amy.

"Gotta go, Amy," she said, as she quickly trotted to Overbrook's entrance.

"Need me?" shouted Amy. Penny turned to Amy.

"It's nothing, Amy. I've got it." Nick turned to his left and smiled at Amy, who in turn took a step closer to him. Amy put her right hand on Nick's shoulder and leaned into Nick.

"Theo's so athletic."

"He is, Miss Sommers, thank you. I promise he doesn't get that from me. His mother was an amazing athlete and, well, he's quite gifted."

"You must be very proud of him."

Amy let her hand slowly drift off of Nick's shoulder before turning back to the game.

"I am, Miss Sommers. In two weeks, I'm taking him for a meeting at North Carolina. It looks like he may get a basketball scholarship to UNC."

Amy turned to Nick and placed her hand back on his shoulder, as Nick put his hands behind his back.

"Oh my gosh Nick, that is amazing. That is so amazing. You must be thrilled." She squeezed his shoulder.

"Yes ma'am, we both are. I'm going to go with him, I'll probably need four or five days off, if that's OK."

"Yes, of course, Nick, of course." She slid her hand across his back, and Nick turned to her and smiled.

"Thank you, Miss Sommers." Ten minutes later, Cassidy took the court and pronounced the Alzheimer's association as winner of the game. Theo, Franklin, Chet and Ben all got a big round of applause.

Four hours later, the festival was over and the staff was cleaning up. Nick sat down in his office, and looked at his list of projects. He picked up his phone to see if he had any messages, scrolled through the photos in his phone, and opened one that Lynda had taken of herself when they had gone out to dinner. He looked into her eyes for a minute, then deleted the photo. He scratched his head and turned back to his list, just as Franklin knocked on his door.

"Hey Chef, that son of yours is something else. He would have waxed my fanny if we kept going like we were, and *holy crap!* UNC scholarship? Chef, that's amazing, I mean, amazing."

"Thanks, Franklin. Yeah, we're all pretty pumped. I guess now I can take his college savings and ... uh ... "

"And what?"

"Honestly, I don't know. Get season tickets at the Dean Dome maybe?"

"What's he gonna do with a math degree, Chef?"

"Whatever he wants; climate research, aerodynamics, CAD/CAM design, algorithm design, analysis, computational fluid dynamics, the possibilities are endless. Honestly, he wants a shot at the NBA, but that's a serious long shot. I mean, the odds are against him in a big way. It's something like a 40-in-10 million shot for a really good high school player to make it as a starter in the NBA. So he's going to get his degree, and hopefully get a potential employer to pay for his master's degree. At least he's smart enough to know he

259

doesn't want to stand on his feet six days a week, like his old man."

"Amen to that, brother. Hey, Chef, looked like you were having a good time with that little Paige and all that cotton candy. What a sweetheart, huh?"

"I guess everyone has seen that photo by now, right? OK, sorry Franklin, but I gotta get moving. I got 30 minutes left here then Theo and I have some plans."

"Yeah, me, too. I have several projects I'm working on, too. The fun never stops right, Chef?"

"Amen."

"Hey Jessica, can I come in?" Jessica looked up from her computer and motioned Cassidy in. She closed the door behind her. "We got a lot of compliments about the Wheel of Fortune game; you and Grant were great."

"Thank you, Cass. Hey, did you see the photo of Nick and Paige Sommers?"

"Yes I did, Honey! Are you thinking what I'm thinking?" Jessica turned and scowled at Cassidy.

"I'm thinking we keep out of this. I have enough to do around here without playing matchmaker to the boss, OK?"

"Yes ma'am, my apologies." Jessica put her elbows on her desk, interlaced her hands, put her chin on her fingers and smiled. "But after work, if you want to buy me a drink, well then we can talk about *whatever* our little heart's desire, now can't we?"

Cassidy smirked. "Meet me at Starbuck's at 6:15?"

"Girl, that's a deal!"

19

Amy unlocked her office door, plopped her collection of folders on her desk, and sat down. It was eight thirty, she had a nine thirty conference call with Rivers, and she wasn't ready. She booted up her computer then remembered that Nick was back on campus today. She stood up and paced her floor, thinking she should walk over and see him, but then remembered her conference call. Maybe she could just pop in for just a second, but what if he wasn't here yet, and one of the cooks saw her looking for Nick? But so what? Nick worked for her, and she had a right to know if he was in yet. But what if he was there and she's a bit too happy to see him? Would she be able to control her demeanor? Or worse, suppose he's not excited to see her? Then what? She continued pacing her office. She looked out her window. It had been seven days since she had seen Nick. Seven days. Maybe she would wait until he came to see her. Surely he would walk over and say hello to her, right?

Nick sat down in his chair and looked at his desk just as Chrissy came out of the walk-in cooler. She saw Nick in his office and walked over. "Hey Chef. How was North Carolina?"

"It was great. Looks like Theo has his scholarship. How's things been here with Kevin and Xavier running the show?"

"All good, Chef. OK, things to cook, gotta get moving, glad you're back."

"Can I do something for you Miss Monroe? Looks like the boss may miss our morning meeting, so I may have some spare time at nine thirty."

"Give me ten minutes, and I'll let you know."

"Yes ma'am." Perfect, thought Nick, that's ten minutes I have to ice my knee. He walked over to the supply shelf, pulled out a freezer bag and filled it with ice, walked back to his office, sat down, and held the ice pack on his right knee. While in Chapel Hill, he had tripped on a morning jog and had twisted his knee. It was nothing a few days of Advil and ice couldn't fix, though. Nick turned to his laptop and started a to-do list, then looked at the emails as they dropped into his in-box. Damn! Kevin apparently did not look at any emails while he was gone.

"Good morning, Nick. Do you have a second for me?"

"Oh, hey, good morning, Miss Sommers. Don't you look lovely this morning." She was wearing a grey wool suit with a knee-length skirt, a black turtleneck sweater and black stockings.

"Thank you, Nick. How was your trip?" Nick turned away from his laptop to face her, and the bag of ice fell to the floor. "What was that sound?"

"Oh, just a bag of ice."

"Are you ok? What are you icing?"

"Just my knee. I'm fine, though."

"Well, let me take a look, please."

"No, that's not necessary. Seriously, little bit of ice, and I'll be fine." Amy stood over him, crossed her arms, and frowned.

"Yes, ma'am." He rolled up the right side of his pants leg, and Amy knelt down and felt his knee while Nick told her how he had twisted it during a run. Amy felt for swelling, ran her hand down the back of his leg and felt his hamstring, then tried to feel for a swollen tendon or fluid behind the knee cap. She gently moved the knee-cap back and forth then had him roll up the other pant leg to compare the size of the other kneecap. She got on her Blackberry and called the nurse's station, asking for an Ace bandage to be brought up.

"Well, you definitely have some swelling. There's fluid behind the knee cap, and it doesn't take much fluid there to prevent these quad muscles from firing. I'll bet you're favoring it, maybe limping a bit, and that's just going to make it worse. I'm going to wrap it, but while you're working and standing up, you need to make a conscious effort to fire that muscle, flex your quadriceps and work on keeping it in use. And before you go, I want you to go see Anastasia. She can give you a stretching routine that will keep this thing from causing you too much trouble."

There was a slight knock on the door. Nick and Amy looked up as Candace walked in with an Ace bandage.

"OK, Miss Sommers, what have you done to my sweetie?" Candace had dyed her hair again, it was a soft reddish-orange.

Amy stood up and smiled, and thanked Candace for the bandage. She returned to her kneeling position as she unwrapped the bandage.

"Don't you think that would be easier if Nick wasn't wearing any pants?" smirked Candace. Nick looked up.

"You're incorrigible, you know that?"

"That will be all, Miss Chapman, thank you," responded Amy flatly.

"Just trying to help." Candace said with a smile as she winked at Nick, then held her right hand up to her face, thumb and pinkie extended, and mouthed, "Call me," then turned away and headed back downstairs.

"You know she is only interested in my intellect, right?"

"Right."

"Are you going to ask Jessica to counsel her?"

"Probably not this time, but if it gets to be a problem, then yes. She will need some counseling."

"Did you miss me?" Amy stopped and looked up at Nick while she held his right knee in her hands. Her heart rate jumped.

"Yes, Nick, I did miss you," she quietly replied.

"I missed you, too."

Amy was slightly embarrassed and felt her face redden. She took her eyes off Nick and tried to focus on the process of wrapping his knee, but she was a bit uncomfortable as she secured the Ace bandage. "Nick?"

"Yes ma'am?" She looked up at him.

"You should ice it three or four times a day for the next 48 hours, no more than ten minutes at a time though, understand?" Nick felt a sudden sense of relief.

"Yes ma'am, it already feels much better. Thank you, Miss Sommers."

"OK Nick, I'll see you at the meeting."

Ten minutes later, Nick walked into the Armory for the morning meeting as the team got down to business. "Nick, did you hear that Beverly Stafford moved into the rehab unit. I seriously doubt she's going to go back to her apartment. Best-case scenario, she will move into Hudson in maybe ten days."

"Penny, has her son visited her yet?"

"Oh boy, has he ever? I swear, I think he comes over just to make trouble."

Grant nodded his head then spoke up. "Nick, that guy is something else. He's really first class. You would think a fall from grace, such as the one he went through, would make someone humble and repentant, but not this guy. What a piece of work. I'm pretty sure he has substance-abuse issues."

Jessica looked around the room. "Folks, we need to be very careful how we handle Mr. Stafford. As your human resources specialist, please do not get into any verbal altercations with him. If you sense he is getting upset, always make sure you have another employee with you, a witness, OK?"

Penny caught Jessica's eyes. "I swear, Jessica, I think he had been drinking the last time he was here. That was three days ago, Nick – plus his facial muscles were doing this weird jerky motion."

"Face dances?" Grant asked. Nick and Grant exchanged knowing looks of disgust. Grant looked across the room at Amy.

"I don't see a positive outcome for this, I just don't. I need to do a little research on this issue, Amy, just in case things get worse."

Thirty minutes later, the meeting broke up. Nick decided he would visit Beverly, so he made his way to the rehab unit and knocked on Beverly's door. Doris Peters was already there. Beverly was in bed, her head slightly elevated. She looked like she had lost 15 pounds, weight she could not afford to lose.

"Hello, Nick, where the hell have you been?" croaked Doris.

"Hey, Beverly, Doris… how you two doing?" Beverly turned her head slightly to face Nick, and tried to smile. She looked like she had aged five years since Nick had seen her. Nick pulled a chair up to the side of her bed, and reached out for her hand.

"Bev, glad we have you back here, so you can get better. A hospital is no place to get well, too many sick people." Bev offered a faint smile, and squeezed Nick's hand. "Shame on you for coming to visit me when I look so awful, where's your manners, young man?"

"Sorry, but I was just passing through. Can I do anything for you?"

"I could use some Scotch." Nick winked at her then turned to Doris. "You sure no one else has brought you any yet?" Doris swatted him and mouthed "Asshole."

"Beverly, can I fix something special for you? We have some turkey soup upstairs that's not on the menu. It's got rice and peas in it; how does that sound?" Beverly looked at Nick and smiled. "Yes, that would be lovely." Nick patted her hand and stood up. "Nick, I need to apologize for my son's behavior. He's been having a tough time lately. He was such a good boy. I don't know where I went wrong. And now, I don't know … I just don't know."

"No apologies needed, Beverly. You want that soup now or at lunch time?"

"The sooner the better, Nick, and something for my sitter here, too, please." Nick turned to the door.

"Naturalmente, signora. Ciao." Nick walked out of the room, then sent a text to Chrissy and asked her to send a hot quart of turkey soup to Augusta. He got an immediate response: "will do". Nick looked around, then headed to the assisted-living facility and spent about 30 minutes chatting with Chet and the rest of the residents.

Four hours later, Nick was in his office, trying to decide which project he would move to the top of his list when Amy knocked on his door. "Knock, knock." He smiled and invited her in.

"May I sit down?"

"Of course, please. Can I get you a Diet Coke?"

"No, thank you, Nick. Um, listen, Harriett has asked us to go to North Carolina and spend a few days looking at some of the other properties."

"Seriously?"

"Well, she thinks that you and I could learn something, see something new, maybe pick up some efficiencies that we could bring back here."

"You do know that efficient is not a noun, correct?"

"Excuse me?"

"Never mind. OK, when does she want us to do this? Late January, I hope."

"Uh, actually the first week of December."

"*What the hell! December?* Can I not get a break here? Doesn't anyone in this company realize what it takes to run this damn kitchen? And now I have to go sightseeing in North Carolina at the busiest time of the year? And that means I'll miss another of my son's basketball games." He realized he was practically yelling, and Amy was frowning at him. Nick took a deep breath and tried to relax. He glanced at his phone; it was already after two, three hours before dinner had to be ready. Nick closed his eyes, took a deep breath and slowly exhaled. No use fighting this one. If Amy and Harriett thought this was a good idea, he was going along for the ride. "OK, when?"

"How about Tuesday morning the third? We would fly out to Wilmington and stay at the Topsail Beach Community. They have several guest suites on property. Brent, the Director at Topsail, has already set aside two rooms for us. We can visit the Surf City and Holly Ridge properties, as well as spend some quality time at Topsail, then fly home Thursday morning."

"Can we at least rent a decent car? Could you get us a Mustang GT with a five-speed? In black?

Amy frowned. "You know how CSM hates to spend money."

"Yeah, yeah, so I guess we're flying Greyhound, then right?"

"Don't give them any ideas, please."

"Yes ma'am. You sure we can't put this off until, say June, when it's just a bit warmer?

"Sorry, Nick."

"OK, I'll give my son the news later today. What are you gonna do with your girls?"

"My brother and his wife already said they would take care of them. There's no real big events that week. It's the week after that we really get busy. The office in Charleston will take care of flights and the car and we get our per diem in advance, so it's a date, then?"

"OK, Miss Sommers, it's a date, but I get to pick where we have dinner at least one night, OK?" Amy smiled and stood up.

"Deal.." Amy held out her hand and they shook. Nick watched her walk away then turned to his computer.

Two weeks later, Nick was sitting in the Woodmont parking lot a few minutes after seven, waiting for Amy. It was cold, too cold for Nick. The high in Greenville would only reach 45 that day, and the highs along the beach in North Carolina would be in the low 50s. Amy had offered to drive to the airport and Nick agreed, hoping that she at least had a comfortable car. He parked his car in his usual spot and sat there listening to NPR, then texted Amy: "here at back lot". He wondered what kind of car she drove. He thought about her, how she dressed, and the fact that she had two daughters and started going through different minivan choices before settling on a white Honda Odyssey with a tan leather interior. He would probably have to move a Barbie doll off of the seat when he got into the car.

"I should be driving," he said to himself as he settled back in his BMW's leather seat and closed his eyes. He reached out for the shifter and gently caressed it, easing his left foot onto the clutch pedal and moving his right foot over the accelerator. Nick imagined the two of them in his car as he down shifted for an interstate entrance ramp. The six-cylinder sang as he went from fourth to third gear, stabbed the brakes to bleed off a bit of speed, and then eased onto the ramp at 45 miles an hour. Nick caressing the wheel into the turn as Amy reached for the Jesus bar over her shoulder and begged him to slow down. He focused on his line and kept his eyes level as the g-forces increased, gently applying a bit of power as the nose of the car reached for the highway. He floored the accelerator, snatching fourth gear as the speedometer edged past 60 and then 70, as he rocketed through the morning traffic.

"I should be driving," he mumbled.

Fifteen minutes later, Amy pulled up next to him in a black Jeep Grand Cherokee, splattered with mud.

"So much for the minivan," he laughed to himself.

Nick got out of his car, smiled and said good morning, then and retrieved his bag from the car. Amy opened the back of her Jeep and held the tailgate door open for Nick as he tossed his bag in the back. Nick asked Amy how she was doing on this beautiful morning.

"I'm well, and yourself?" Nick smiled.

"You look great this morning." The sun was just coming up and she was wearing a black wool, knee-length skirt with decorative stitching, a lilac V-neck cashmere sweater and a black jacket. Amy blushed, smiled at him and closed the tailgate.

"Thank you, shall we?"

"I figured you for a minivan. I guess I don't know you as well as I thought."

"A minivan? Please. My husband bought me a Dodge Caravan the first year we were married. I swear I should have strangled him right then and there."

"How long were you two married?" asked Nick, as he settled into the seat. Amy pointed the Cherokee towards the exit and headed out onto Highway 101.

"Eight years, although in dog years, it was 56. I had my psych degree, then went into nursing school at the University of Tennessee – *Go Vols!* – and he was getting his law degree and had committed himself to the Army. Richard convinced me he was going places. He had his 20 years in the Army all figured out: Italy, Japan, Washington, D.C. I guess I was mesmerized by the idea of being married to an officer, and I thought that life would be exciting and we would travel across the world and live this amazing life. After he got out of OCS, damn if he didn't get sent to Anniston, Alabama, and then to Alaska. Serves me right for letting him suck me in. I was young and impressionable, and he was handsome and a smooth talker. All he was looking for was a pretty face to escort him to his official embassy functions that never materialized, and I was certainly not cut out for life in Alaska.

"Did you live in Alaska, Miss Sommers?"

"No, thankfully, but I did visit him twice, and he was able to get time off. But it was still tough on us. It took me a couple of years to figure him out, and by then, we had Rebecca. I tried to stick it out for her, I really did. But then he screwed up big time, and that was enough for me. When I signed the final divorce papers, I cried myself stupid. Paige was just 11 months old, and I felt so awful. I knew I had made a big mess of the first part of my life, and I had to devote myself to my girls. I decided to set a strong example for them and help guide them through life. I wanted to try to make a real difference, and it made sense for me to get into elder care after struggling to find somewhere decent for Mom."

"Well, I would say you found your calling. I think you're doing a great, job Miss Sommers." She turned to Nick and smiled warmly.

"Thank you." Amy headed towards the entrance ramp of the interstate at a whopping 25 miles an hour, chopping unevenly at the wheel as she turned into the clover leaf. As far as Nick could tell, she was looking maybe five feet in front of the Cherokee. He closed his eyes and wished he was driving. "Did you get enough sleep?"

"Oh no, I'm sorry, I just closed my eyes, that's all. So how did your car get so muddy?"

"Oh, my Dad has a house near Lake Murray. He's got two horses and when we visit. Well, sometimes his driveway is a bit sloppy, or maybe we drive to the far side of his property on this rough gravel road. So I put it into four-wheel and we spin and slide across the mud. The girls just love it. We all bounce around, splash mud and rocks, and the girls scream, 'Go faster, Mom!'"

"So you like your Jeep, then?"

"Oh, sure, it has good towing capacity and I occasionally pull a horse trailer over some bumpy roads. It has very good clearance and short angles at the front and back."

"Perfect vehicle for a beautiful nurse, exactly what I pictured you driving."

"Liar," she smirked.

"So did you bring a swim suit?"

"*A swim suit?* Nick, come on, it's December."

"Sorry, Miss Sommers."

"Were you serious, Nick?" He looked away and mumbled, "Not really."

"I really want to spend some time at these three properties and to learn as much as possible. I'm going to excel in this position, but I'm also a single mom, so I simply can't live at work. I have to know what I can and can't do at home, and it's somewhat of a struggle right now. I'm afraid I spend too much time reacting, and not enough time planning. I have someone that takes care of the girls from 3 until 6, and I just can't leave them with her any longer than that. I just can't. When I was hired, I made it clear that I was a mother first and foremost, and CSM understood that I would be off campus by six p.m. five days a week. I can't pawn the girls off on my brother often. He has a big family. It's OK once in a while, but it's really hard on everyone."

"This company must have wanted you in a big way."

"Yes, they did, but that doesn't mean I was going to take this position for granted. I really want Woodmont to take the lead in innovative senior care, and yeah, I know that sounds like a monumental task."

"It is," responded Nick.

"Yes, it is, but I'm up to the task, and it's something I believe in. Do you believe me? Do you believe we can be leaders?"

"You know I'm just a cook, right?"

"Oh please, Nick, give yourself some credit."

"OK, I'm a pretty good cook."

"Oh Nick, listen to yourself."

"And I did bring a swim suit, because I was hoping to get into the surf. I'm a pretty good cook that likes to play in the salt water, but unless we're on the beach at high noon, I'm afraid the water is going to be too cold for me. From the sound of it, you plan on being nowhere near the beach at noon, correct?" Amy looked at Nick and winked, rolled down her window to retrieve her parking ticket at the entrance to the long-term parking, and then started looking for a spot near the front. Nick pointed to the furthest reaches of the lot and said, "I see one over there."

"Seriously, there is something not right about you. Don't you ever look for a short cut?" Amy relented and parked away from the front. Nick grabbed both bags and hoisted them over his shoulders, one on each side. Amy protested and reminded him that her bag had wheels.

"Where's the fun in that?" They made their way into the terminal, then to the long escalator that went to the check-in area. Nick watched the line of passengers slowly shuffling to the bottom of the escalator, then looked over at the vacant stairway next to the escalator, and then turned to Amy. She looked at him and just shook her head. Nick headed towards the stairs, grabbed a firm hold of their bags, bounded up the stairs two steps at a time, and quickly got to the top of the stairs. He stood there, looking down at Amy.

"Let's go, boss, we got a plane to catch!" he hollered. Amy shook her head, put her left hand on her forehead, and looked down. "Is he yours?" asked a well-dressed woman next to Amy. "Yes, he is."

"Some guys just never grow up, do they?" the woman replied. They shared a laugh as the escalator deposited them at the top. Two hours later, they were headed to the car rental kiosks of the Wilmington airport. Amy and Nick checked into Pocketbook's Car Rental and were given directions to the lot. Nick was shocked to hear that they would be driving a car from the subcompact group. They walked through the lot, passing cars that were lined up according to price. They passed the specialty cars like the Mustangs, a Buick Lucerne, and a Cadillac CTS, then the full size sedans such as the Crown Victoria and Chevy Malibu. Finally came the minivans, mid-size sedans and the compact cars, such as the Chevy Cobalt. At the furthest end of parking lot they finally found the subcompacts, the smallest and cheapest category of car available for rent.

"You have got to be kidding me! A Fuji Echo! This thing was made in Lilliput, for Pete's sake. Can't this 100 million dollar company not afford a little splurge on their hard-working salary folks every once in a while?"

"I swear I only understand half of your references, Nick. I'm just a nurse. Please tell me where on earth is Lilliput." Nick glared.

"Didn't you pay any attention in high school lit?"

"Are you going to be this ugly the entire trip, or is this your good side?" asked Amy, as she threw her bag into the tiny trunk, slammed the trunk then walked to the driver's door. Nick followed her.

"Damn, boss, please forgive me. I'm really sorry. Look, the company has sent me on a wild-goose chase at the worst possible time, and I'm not happy about it. I would rather see one of Theo's basketball games then do this, but, hey, at least we're together. My apologies, seriously, let's make the best of this trip, OK?" Amy had her back to him with her arms folded across her chest. He put his hands on her waist and gently turned her around to face him. "Please accept my apologies, Miss Sommers." Nick put his right hand under her chin and gently lifted her chin until he could see her eyes. "May I buy you a doughnut?" Amy broke into a gentle smile.

"Sure, let's go get a doughnut." He hugged her and whispered another apology. His touch gave her a quick flash of goose bumps, and she shivered.

"Are you cold?" Nick asked. She had her arms around his waist and her head on his shoulder.

"Oh no, I'm fine." Amy sighed, released him and backed away, feeling wonderful and awkward at the same time.

After stopping at the nearest Krispy Kreme, Nick and Amy headed down Interstate 140. Nick explained to Amy who Jonathan Swift was and why "Gulliver's Travels" wasn't exactly a children's book.

"So, you see, Swift was actually skewering early 18th-Century England and France, and in particular, their governing bodies. The chapter in which he describes Lilliputians that crack their eggs on the big end, the so-called big endians, and those that crack their eggs on the smaller ends, the little endians, well, he actually pokes great fun at the political and religious upheaval of the late 15th Century, in which the entire country was forced to switch religions because of Henry the Eighth." Amy looked over at Nick and practically groaned.

"Thanks, Nick. I, uh, never knew that. How about we listen to the radio now?" She quickly turned on the radio and started searching for something to prevent another history lesson. She found a local station and Plain White T's *Rhythm of Love*. Amy started to hum, then reached down and turned up the music and started to sing along.

Nick looked at Amy, and she looked back and winked at him. Suddenly, he was very uncomfortable. What was going on here? Was this trip really Harriett's idea, or was it Amy's from the start? Was she trying to get a couple of days alone with him? Was this whole trip Amy's plan to get him into bed? Damn, now he was getting mad. The whole thing started to make sense. He sat there in the passenger seat of this impossibly tiny car and fumed. Should have stayed in Greenville, he thought to himself. Amy looked at him again.

"Please smile Nick; I thought you said we were going to enjoy ourselves."

Rhythm of Love ended, and Nick reached for the radio mumbling, "No more Top 40, and I'll smile, OK?" He scanned a couple of stations and found one advertising oldies, and left it there. Amy groaned, but agreed. Fifteen seconds later, Elvis' *Love Me Tender* came on and she remarked how much she liked Elvis and again started singing along.

"Love me, tender,
Love me sweet.
Never let me go.
You have made my life complete,
And I love you so.
Love me tender,
Love me true.
All my dreams fulfilled,
For my darling, I love you
And I always will."

Nick scrunched down in the car seat. It was hopeless, he thought to himself. He was fighting an incoming tide. Amy had planned the whole thing, and the trip would end with her embarrassed and their relationship sour. He was not going to have sex with the boss; there was just no way. Forty-five minutes later, they pulled into the gates of Top Sail Manor and introduced themselves to the concierge, Marie. She greeted them warmly and said that the entire staff was excited about their visit.

"Really? The entire staff is excited about meeting me? I'm not surprised." Amy kicked Nick in the shin, and frowned.

"Ouch!" Marie turned to Nick and asked him if he were OK.

"Oh, sure, I just have a rock in my shoe, that's all."

Amy and Nick followed Marie through the hall, until she stopped at Room 214. Marie opened the door, and Amy followed her across the threshold. Nick stayed in the hallway until Marie turned and looked at him.

"Are you coming in, Chef?" Nick picked up his bag, looked up and down the hallway, and hesitantly walked in and surveyed the suite. In the middle of the suite was a kitchen and living room. On each side was a bedroom with an attached bathroom. Nick emerged from the southern bedroom and looked at Amy. Damn, now he was really disappointed, she had planned this whole thing as some sort of sexual escapade.

"These accommodations OK, Miss Sommers?"

"Perfect, Marie, and please call me Amy." Nick thought he saw Amy wink at him. Amy had already set her bag into the northern room and was listening to Marie as she explained the operation of the refrigerator, the microwave and the coffee pot.

"Any questions?" smiled Marie.

"Nope," Nick replied. Amy again smiled at Nick, who thought that as soon as the door closed, Amy would run across the room and leap into his arms. What a mess this was going to be. He had never felt more awkward in his life. What would happen when he declined her advances, when he told her no. Would he still have a job at Woodmont? Damnit, he wished he had held his ground about this trip and just said no. The first staff meeting after their return will have an awful amount of tension. He could just imagine Jessica reaching under the table and pinching Amy, winking at her as she asked, "Did you and Nick have a good time in

North Carolina?" He really liked Amy as a person and as a leader, and she was certainly attractive. But this was not going to happen. It was way too complicated, and she was not his type.

Marie smiled and excused herself. Nick held the door open for her and thanked her as she left. As Nick was saying goodbye to Marie, he heard another door close. He realized that Amy had just shut her bedroom door. Nick stood there for a minute feeling silly and confused. His Blackberry went off with a text: "gimme 15 then to lobby ;)"

"OK" Nick replied. He walked into his bedroom, unpacked, washed his face, brushed his teeth, and then sent a text to his son letting him know he was at Topsail. Twenty minutes later, they were downstairs in the lobby where they were greeted by Brent Davidson, the Director of Topsail Retirement Community. Brent was maybe 45, tall and lean with a Marine's haircut and a firm handshake.

"Amy, I've heard a lot of great things about you. Your articles on elder care and Alzheimer's care are well known in the community. It's my pleasure to meet you." Amy blushed and introduced Nick.

Brent then turned to Nick. "Hello, Chef; Brent Davidson. What's it like working for a superstar like Amy?"

Nick turned to Amy then looked back at Brent. Was he serious? "Great, it's really great, uh, never a dull moment."

"Well then, if we can get started, how about I give you two a full tour, then we can have lunch. We'll sit with our head of wellness and the health care admin, and Nick, if you want to spend some time with our Chef, he'll be in soon. I think he has a special lunch for you two." Brent walked a few feet in front of them. As they followed him, Nick put his left hand on the small of Amy's back, leaned close and whispered, "Superstar."

Amy shrugged her shoulders and replied, "Some people are easily impressed."

"Amy, I would love to start with our memory care unit first. This facility is only four years old, and has been managed by Creek Side for two years. The original developer incorporated some of your suggestions in the initial design. He was familiar with your ideas from the essays that you published in the AJ about five years ago." Nick turned to Amy, who smiled sheepishly.

"Easily impressed, huh?"

Amy smiled. "I'm a good listener, Nick. When someone tells me what is and isn't working, I make note of it. The health-care community has learned a lot in the past 10, 15 years about how to care for our elders and change from observing, listening them suggesting. In this business, we should never think that we have reached a plateau. There are many different types of dementia, and they have different effects on different people." Amy stopped walking and turned to Nick. "So in an environment of this sort, where we care for dementia patients, it's important to remember that someone with vascular dementia may not respond to the same type of therapy as someone with Parkinson's induced dementia or Alzheimer's. Alzheimer's is also diagnosed post-mortem; the only way to know for sure if someone had Alzheimer's is to perform a brain biopsy. Alzheimer's is the disease, dementia is the symptom. But dementia has many causes, and there are so many facets to dementia and the care of those that suffer from it. The first memory care facility I worked in was so little actual therapy and activity, I was certain that the progression of the disease was promoted by the inactivity. We now know that to be accurate. Alzheimer's is terminal, but that doesn't mean that our patients should be destined to suffering during their journey …"

Amy stopped talking. They stood in a hallway in front of the entrance to the memory care unit. Brent listened intently with his arms folded. The nurse and the CNA standing behind Amy listened as Nick pulled his arms behind his back.

"I'm sorry, I didn't mean to run away with the conversation like that."

"No need to apologize, Amy, none at all." Brent turned to Nick. "See what I mean?" Nick nodded his head, then winked at Amy. Brent opened the door to the memory care unit, waved his arm and asked, "Shall we?"

Five hours later, Amy and Nick sat in the lobby, thanking Brent for his time. "Thank you so much for everything today. I think Nick has made dinner plans for us tonight, and I need to get changed before we go anywhere." Amy took a step closer to Nick and put her left hand on his right elbow. "I'm sure Nick would like a few minutes to himself before we head out as well."

Nick looked at Amy, and dropped his right arm behind his back. Amy pulled her hand back, turned to Brent and extended her right hand as they thanked one another. Brent gave Nick and Amy directions to get to breakfast, and wished them a good night.

Nick was suddenly nervous about going back into the room. "Listen boss, if you don't mind, I'm going to step outside and call Theo, maybe take a walk around the campus, and get a bit of sun before it goes down. I made some reservations for us at this Cuban restaurant off of 43rd street, so we have about 70 minutes to kill. No hurry, OK?"

Amy reached out for Nick's elbow again. "Sure, of course, Nick, I'll be upstairs. I'm going to call my girls."

He turned to the front door and headed outside. He found their walking trail and walked one lap, about three quarters of a mile, before calling Theo. The sun was almost down and it was getting cold, but he wanted to avoid an uncomfortable situation with Amy. He pulled his Blackberry out of his pocket, put in his ear buds, and called his son. "Hey kid, what's up?"

Twenty minutes later, Nick walked back into the room and closed the door. He held onto the doorknob for a few seconds and listened. He heard singing coming from Amy's room. He held still, concentrating on her voice. He heard water. Not running water from a shower, but softly moving bath water. Amy was in the bathtub, singing to herself. He slowly let go of the doorknob. Amy was not singing lyrics. She was softly singing, "La la la." Nick took a deep breath, looked around the room, then quietly walked to his bedroom, slowly closed and locked his door, and took off his coat. He exhaled then looked at the ceiling. He walked into his bathroom, turned on the hot water, took off his shirt and his undershirt, and got out his shaving kit. He looked at himself in the mirror and rubbed his chin. "You know what, dumbass? Has it occurred to you that maybe you're overreacting, maybe she's not interested in you?" He shaved, brushed his teeth, then put on a clean shirt, a black pull-over sweater and the camel hair jacket he brought along. He took a quick look in the mirror then walked out of his room. He heard the hair dryer running in Amy's bedroom, so he sent her a text message – "hey boss I'm in lobby ok?" – then walked downstairs, had a seat in the lobby, and waited.

20

Twenty minutes later, Nick and Amy were driving down Highway 50 on their way to dinner. "Oh wait, Miss Sommers, there's a wine shop. Shall we stop and get a bottle of something to have with dinner. I doubt this place has a decent wine list, would you mind?"

"Oh sure, that's a good idea." Amy turned the car around and pulled into the wine store. Five minutes later, they were back in the car with a bottle of Martinelli Russian River Valley Zinfandel. "I'm glad you picked out a Zinfandel," she said. "I think all the ones I ever had were pink."

"Well sweetheart, just stick with me, and I can teach you all you want to know about wine. Is that a deal?"

"Deal," smiled Amy. "Tell me again where we're going."

"It's called Old Havana's. Their menu looked great, it's small and Chef-owned."

Amy turned to Nick and smiled as she stopped at a red light, then reached for the radio. Van Morrison's *Moon Dance* came on, and Amy started to sing along as she turned up the volume a bit. Nick tried to ignore her. Maybe she doesn't realize what she's doing, he thought. They came to another red light and he looked over at Amy. Maybe she just liked to sing; she certainly had a pretty voice. She looked over at him and winked. Nick turned away while Amy sang. Nick gently shook his head.

"What is it?" asked Amy.

"Oh nothing, I was just wondering if I had the directions correct." Nick looked at what he had jotted down, and realized he had written down turn at 43rd but was that left or right?

"Well, just call them."

He turned down the radio, dialed Old Havana, and put them on the speaker phone.

"Old Havana Cuban, may I help you?" Amy spoke up, saying that they were on Highway 50 headed north, and asked whether they needed to turn left or right on 43rd. A thick Cuban accent responded to turn left on 43rd, go about two miles, and look for "da Chef-rahn, and we behind da Chef-rahn." Amy was puzzled and looked at Nick. "What's a Chefron?" she asked.

"He said Chevron. You know, a gas station."

"Oh, OK, thank you very much. We'll see you in a minute," and she hung up the phone. "I don't know about this; the landmark is a gas station? Lord only knows where you're taking me to eat."

"Well, sweetheart, every once in a while it's good to see the other side of the tracks, wouldn't you agree?" *Sweetheart.* He said it again. Such a corny word, but how wonderful it sounded coming from Nick. Just the two of them in the car, headed to dinner on the beach, the smell of saltwater in the air. For a brief moment, it all felt so special. She envisioned the two of them not on business but pleasure, enjoying one another's company, holding hands and sharing umbrella-crowned drinks, walking on a warm beach, him looking at her longingly and saying:

"Wouldn't you agree, Miss Sommers?"

"What? I'm sorry, I guess I was drifting there for a second. What did you ask me?"

"Not important. Oh hey, it looks like we are coming up on a gas station here on the left, looks like a Chevron." As they slowed down for the turn, Nick took a good look at the Chevron,. It was more of a convenience store, fairly new and well lit. He looked a bit closer and saw a sign that said "Good Cuban Food" in the space next to the convenience store. As he looked closer, sure enough, Old Havana's. He smiled at Amy, who was realizing the same thing. The restaurant was not behind the Chevron, it was *in* the Chevron.

"*Oh my God!*" she fussed. "You're taking me to dinner in a gas station!"

Nick thought this had all the makings of a fabulous evening. A good bottle of wine, a very pretty date, and an ethnic restaurant that pays rent to a gas station. He could barely contain himself as they wheeled into the parking lot. "Sweetheart, I do believe we are about to have a memorable meal." Amy turned to Nick and put her hand on top of his. It had been a long time since a man had looked at her with such a warm smile, and he was happy just to be in her company.

"OK, let's eat then. I'm all yours."

"Ah, music to my ears," he returned. Nick opened the door, and a smiling waiter greeted them. "Welcome to the Old Havana. My name is Julian; do you have a reservation?"

"St. Germaine, party of two."

"Of course, right this way please." Amy followed Julian, and as they moved towards the table, Nick put his hand on the small of her back. She looked over her shoulder at him and smiled, and Nick smiled back at her. Old Havana was small, maybe 36 seats, and as they were seated at the varnished wood table, Nick took in the aromas of lime, a wood burning grill, simmering beef, and aromatic black beans. Yeah, he had made an excellent choice. They shared plates of ham croquettes, fried plantains filled with braised beef, seafood ceviche, conch fritters and black bean soup, all of it delicious. Nick drew conversation out of Amy, and she happily obliged. Her parents were very different people. He was a scientist, she was a nurse and a painter. Her father was the forensic toxicologist for Shelby County in Memphis. Her mother worked in a large hospital as a surgical nurse, and was the type that was always looking for an interesting detour. He was one that always calculated exactly how long a drive across town or the state would take. He would plan their vacations down to the smallest detail, even deciding exactly how long it would take for them to see the State Capitol of Texas. When their time was up, well, time was up and it was on to the next stop.

"Mom and Dad used to get into their best fights when we were on vacation. We would be tooling down the road in our Ford wagon, and Mom would see a sign for an historical marker that was, who knows, five, ten or 20 miles off the road. Well, it didn't matter what it was, it was something new and possibly interesting, and that was enough for her. She would ask him to turn and he would look at this watch and say no, there was not enough time, and she would yell and cry and accuse him of being stubborn. He would call her flighty and reckless, and all the while he was turning around and headed off to see whatever attraction it was that she just couldn't live without seeing." Nick smiled and filled her wine glass.

"So how did you get into this business?" he asked.

"I knew from an early age that I wanted to be a nurse. When I visited Mom at the hospital, it was always so exciting and she was so important. People would constantly call her name and ask her opinion about life-threatening issues. I was smitten at an early age, but when I graduated from high school, I knew that I wanted more than what Mom had. I wanted to rise above and beyond the average nursing career, so I went into psychology first on the advice of a doctor friend. Then I went to nursing school and in my second year, Mom developed early onset Alzheimer's. It was devastating for all of us. We just couldn't accept it, but in a short time she went from not being able to remember phone numbers to getting lost on the way to the grocery store. We had to do something, and we ended up moving her into a memory care facility. We had such a hard time finding the right place. I mean, the places we looked at were awful, but she really needed full-time care. We found a pretty good place in Chattanooga and after I graduated, I realized that I had found my calling. I wanted to make changes in the way our profession cared for elders. My crappy marriage got in the way though, and after Richard and I were separated, I went back to Memphis and started looking for nursing homes that were hiring.

The first nursing home I worked for was in Germantown, and it was awful. Our visiting physician, such a wonderful man, was Joe Bennett. I can remember that when a resident died, he would list the cause of death as boredom or loneliness or maybe a broken heart. I mean, these folks *did not do anything!* They were woken up at seven a.m., medicated, fed, cleaned up, and then put in front of the television or back in their rooms until lunchtime. The same thing happened again at dinnertime. They just wasted away and Dr. Bennett was right; they died of boredom. I tried to introduce programs and activities, but when you're just one person, it's tough to fight the status quo. I had to try. The staff there was dead set against any sort of meaningful change, but I pushed until they relented, and I took a stack of notes to see who would respond to what. I wrote a fairly well-received essay detailing my results, and it was published in the 'Alzheimer's Association Journal.' I moved to a facility in Louisville, was there two years then I got the job offer with the Piedmont Hospital System in Greenville. The administrator asked me to run the memory care unit and he was all gung ho for any sort of change. I thought that the new scenery would also be good for the girls. In a year, I was promoted to health care admin, then to the Director's position. Dad had retired by then and we missed one another, so he decided to move nearby, so we were set."

"What about your Mom, Amy? Did you all move her, too?"

"Mom passed away quickly, Nick. She lasted less than two years in Chattanooga. When death came, it was a blessing. The last few months of her life, she had lost everything that had made her who she was, her personality, her uniqueness, her stories, it was all gone. Towards the end, all she had left was the church hymns she learned as a young girl." Amy pulled a tissue out of her purse and wiped her eyes. "She was on a puree diet and was not responding to much of anything. She didn't even recognize her own little girl. I can remember going to visit her and thinking to myself that today would be the day that she would look at me and smile, call my name, reach out for me, hold me by the hand or hug me. Her last couple of months, she would look right through me. It was if she had become a ghost, a thin, wispy version of herself that held no mass, no memories, nothing. She was gone months before she died." Nick reached out for her hand and held it.

"I'm sorry, Amy, Alzheimer's is such an awful disease. You obviously miss her very much. She must have been very special."

"I do miss her, and when she died, well, she had grandchildren and a husband that had planned for their retirement. They had always talked about the travelling they would do when he retired, they had all these great plans for their grandkids. And then, it was if we were robbed in the middle of the night. Everything that Dad had planned and saved for was gone. He spent a year helping to care for her. He was there for her every day, even when she had no idea who he was."

"Your Dad must be a very special person." Amy pulled her hand back and took a sip of wine.

"He really is Nick, he really is. Thank you for listening."

"You know, there's a guy in our memory care unit, he's in Hawkins, Brubaker is his last name, and he's been there maybe three months."

"Sure, Donald Brubaker, I know him."

"Well, the week he moves in I sat down with him at lunchtime, and he asks me where can he get a replacement key because he lost his. So I reminded him that he doesn't need a key to get in and out of his room, and then he asks me what time is check-out, because his wife will be picking him up in the morning. I was gently trying to remind him of where he was. So then he says, it sure is a pretty day for flying, so I ask him if he flies, and turns out the guy was a commercial pilot with numerous ratings. He tells me he owned several Beech airplanes in his life, starting out with a Bonanza, then a twin-engine Baron. His last airplane was a turbine engine King-Air. He smiles and tells me how wonderful his King-Air was, then goes on to describe its cruising speed and flight characteristics. I mean, one minute the guy is looking for his room key, thinking he is checking out in the morning, and the next we are having this very detailed conversation about the performance characteristics of this very complex turbine-powered airplane. I was stunned. I got my private pilot's license years ago, but I have less than 150 hours. I haven't kept up with it, but I can still hold an intelligent conversation about flight and this guy is telling me all about his airplanes, their maximum range, service ceilings, and how smooth the turbine engines were versus the pistons in his Baron. He even tells me about the time he got a new set of propellers on his King-Air, and how much smoother the airplane was after that. Then five minutes later, he stands up and asks me if I can have his car brought around. What the hell?"

Amy finished her glass of wine. "Nick have you ever seen a photo of a brain from an Alzheimer's patient?"

"Uh, no, why?"

"Alzheimer's literally degrades the brain and creates empty space where before there was gray matter. You have a filing cabinet at home?"

"Sure."

"OK, imagine you have photos stored in that cabinet and those photos are filed according to year. And let's say I was at your house and you wanted to show me a photo of you and your son, and you weren't sure if it was from 2001 or 2002. Eventually, you would find that photo. Maybe you would see another photo from 2002 and you would say, well, this happened right before that, so the photo I want is definitely in the 2002 file. It may take you a while to find that photo, but eventually you will. Your memory works the same way. We keep memories filed away in our brain, and those memories come out when we need or want them. You start your car every day, so memories like that are front and center, things you have learned and repeated over and over. But some memories, say perhaps you made a very special dish about 10 years ago and you haven't made it since ... well, you may need some additional stimuli to help you remember it, say, a photo of that dish or maybe a description gleaned from a phone call to a friend. Then suddenly, it all comes back. You have accessed that recipe in the filing cabinet of your memories. What Alzheimer's does is literally destroy those files. It's as if someone breaks into your house every night and steals your photos, your files, one year at a time. All those memories are gone for good, never to return. That's why Mr. Brubaker can still talk about airplanes, but doesn't remember where he is from day to day. Sadly, one day he will lose the ability to discuss all of those details about flying. Those memories will just disappear and with it, another part of him that makes him unique. Imagine if all your memories of Robin suddenly disappeared, never to return. That's what it would be like."

The interest dropped away from Nick's face.

"Oh, Nick, oh, please forgive me. I didn't mean to say it like that. Please accept my apology?" She reached out to hold his hand, but he pulled away. "Sure, apology accepted. Can we go now, please?" Nick fumed, looked around for their waiter who was nowhere to be seen. Damn these crappy little restaurants with their worthless service, why can't someone sense when a guy wants to get the hell out of here? He glared at Amy, who was obviously disappointed in herself. Good, she should be, and if she reaches for my hand one more time, he thought, I will just *walk* back to the room. Amy put her right hand onto Nick's hand and looked into his eyes.

"Would you like to tell me about Robin?" Nick drew his hand back, then picked up his glass of Zinfandel, drained it then cut his eyes at Amy.

"No. I want Julian to bring our check so we can go."

Nick scanned the dining room, but saw no sign of Julian. He looked across the table at Amy, then looked down as his eyes started to moisten. *Damn this woman!* He wiped his eyes on his shoulders and looked back at Amy. She waited patiently. He looked down at his hands. Two years and two months. Where was his closure? When would he be able to talk about her without breaking down? When would the pain soften? He looked up, halfway hoping that Amy had gotten up and left. She reached out for his hand again, and he pulled away. He leaned back and ran his hands through his hair, then rubbed his face. She wasn't going anywhere. Nick exhaled.

"I was the, uh, sous Chef at, uh, Boulevard Restaurant in Charleston when I met her. We had a booth at the Rhythm and Blues Festival and I was working the grill. Robin was there with her team to compete in the bike races. I had been up since five a.m. and had been cooking for hours, and she comes up and orders a grilled vegetable pita, and she was *so beautiful*. I knew she was a cyclist because her figure gave her away. She was wearing those tight Lycra shorts with a very large men's button down shirt that covered her up until the wind blew the tails up. She smiled at me, even though I was drenched with sweat and soot from the grill. A minute or two later, I had taken a break and stepped behind the booth for some privacy I grabbed a clean shirt and a gallon jug of water to cool down with, took off my shirt and poured the water onto a clean towel, squeezed it out and was cooling down my face and the back of my neck. That's when I saw Robin. She had walked around the back of the booth to eat her sandwich and get a view of the marsh, and I hadn't seen her at first.

" 'This sandwich is every bit as delicious as the view,' she said. Man, did I blush," smiled Nick, as he wiped his eyes. "Robin was sitting down eating this sandwich, off by herself, and I thought I was alone. I certainly wasn't trying to impress anyone; I just cooling off. I put my shirt on and apologized to her, then asked her if she would like some company, and she smiled at me and patted the ground next to her. At those big bike races, the pro men's races are usually on a Saturday afternoon because that's when the crowds are at their best. The ladies usually race on Sunday. The crowds and the purses are thinner, but not much you can do about that. Robin was really into food and was excited about the Charleston race because of all the great restaurants, and I was a cook that was into cycling, so we had a lot to talk about. She was riding for a team out of Asheville, and they only had a regional sponsorship. Racing in Charleston stretched their budget. They couldn't afford to travel much further than that. We chatted for about 20 minutes, and then the guys in the booth needed me and her teammate, Angel, came looking for her, and I told her I would see her later. About 15 minutes after her race started, I left the booth and went down to the start-finish line. The course was almost two miles long, and they would take 20 laps, not quite 40 miles, and it was tough because it was windy that day. The course had a long straight and then it took a sharp left-hand turn. They went up Madeira Street into the wind, slightly uphill to the finish line."

Nick wiped his eyes again and smiled, poured the last of the wine into their glasses. "But here's the kicker; that left-hand turn was a traffic circle, and during the race everyone stayed on the left side of that traffic circle because it was shorter, less distance to travel, see? I was on the start-finish line looking down that street, and with about five or six laps to go, four of them had broken away. They had put some distance on the rest of the group, and of course Robin is in that group of four. Well, Robin wasn't a sprinter, but damn was she smart so on the last lap, knowing she didn't have a chance of out-sprinting this group, she takes to the right side of the traffic circle, a bit more distance to travel, but when she comes out she is carrying more speed. She bends into that corner with a tighter line, and she comes out in front. The other three had to go from the left side of the road to the right side, then set up for the left turn, but Robin moves in the opposite direction, slices inside their line, puts her head down, tucks her elbows close to her hips, and just goes for broke. The other girls are standing up on the pedals, grunting and groaning, but catching too much of that headwind. Robin has made herself as narrow as possible. It was a beautiful move, and she didn't pick her head up until five feet before she crossed the line. When she crossed that finish line, I said to myself, 'It was the sandwich.' Amy smiled and moved her hand towards Nick's, but Nick moved his hands away.

"I caught up to her later and caught her attention and she ran to me, threw her arms around me, and yelled out loud, 'It was the sandwich!'

"We both laughed so hard." Nick peeled the beverage napkin from the bottom of his wine glass and wiped his eyes. "We agreed to meet later that night and exchanged numbers, but I really needed to get back to the restaurant. I was expediting that night, and Boulevard had a Chef's counter that was right in front of the kitchen pass, and well, that night we're busy as we can be. About eight o'clock, I turn around and who's being seated at the Chef's counter but Robin and her teammate, Angel. She just lit up when I turned around. I knew right then and there that I would marry this girl, I just knew it." Nick drained his wine glass. "I hooked them up pretty good, five courses with some matching wines then comped their meal. The entire restaurant staff could see what was going on. The amount of electricity leaping between us could have powered King Street. When I told Robin, 'Dinner's on me,' she jumped up, reached across the counter, grabbed me by my Chef coat and kissed me right on the lips. The cooks and even some of the patrons are all clapping and whistling. I think every hair on my head stood up. She whispered in my ear, 'Take me dancing,' and of course I didn't say no. Wow, could she dance! Next thing I know, it's almost three a.m., and she was not slowing down, but I had been up since oh-dark-30 and was fading, and I guess she could tell. We were at Chelsea's and she pushed me into the corner and kissed me, ran her hands through my hair and pulled me close. She said she is going back to Asheville in the morning, and that I should forget ever meeting her because in all likelihood, we would never see one another again, and she didn't want to fall in love with a guy that lived 300 miles away, and if I followed her to her hotel, she would call the police. I really thought she meant it, I just stood there and watched her walk away. I was devastated, but the next day I knew that I had to see her. I had to hold her and I thought about every word she said while we were together."

Nick wiped his eyes with his shirtsleeves and cleared his throat. "Well, later that week, I made a business proposal to the owner of Boulevard. I proposed to set up an off-premise catering division, and used the festival calendar that also hosted professional bike races that were within a 400-mile radius of Asheville. At the R & B festival, Boulevard had netted almost eight grand over the course of the weekend. It was our first gig like that, so the owner was all for it. So four weeks later, I pull up to the Dogwood Festival in Columbia, and guess who's the first customer at the Boulevard booth? Robin practically leapt over the counter. When I told her how I had convinced the owner to let me cater all of these outdoor festivals, she jumped into my arms and wrapped her feet around me. I never felt so good in my life. I was holding her off the ground, and she had her hands around my neck and was smiling at me. It was such a gorgeous day, and the way her hair sparkled against the blue sky, it was all just so surreal.

" 'You are absolutely insane, Nicholas!' she yelled. 'My very own personal Chef stalker!' "

He was struggling with his words and had to wipe his eyes with his shirt again. Amy had pulled a pack of Kleenex out of her purse, and offered one to Nick. When he reached out for the tissue, Amy held his hand. This time, he didn't pull away. Amy stroked his hand with her thumb and whispered, "You can keep going if you want to."

"God, we had such an amazing weekend. The weather was beautiful, we had time to spend together, and Boulevard made money. The other two guys had already planned on camping out over the weekend, so they pitched their tent right there. Robin's team was staying downtown and when the festival started to shut down, she came and found me. I offered her a beer, but since she was racing the next day, she asked for water. She kept looking into my eyes while she opened and then drank the entire bottle. She wrapped her arms around me, and I asked her if she wanted to go dancing. She pulled me close then whispered, 'Nicholas, will you make love to me tonight?' " Amy smiled and wiped her eyes. Nick looked down at his trembling hands, saw his tear drops fall on the lacquered table.

"She, uh, was, uh, was in her car at a red light, the second in line. Just sitting there waiting for the light to turn green. She was, you know, just going to the damn grocery store, and, uh, this big truck ... he, uh, was, uh ... "

Amy got up from the table and sat next to him, then put her right arm around him and placed her head on his shoulder.

"This truck, a delivery truck, the driver was on the phone and was, uh, had been drinking. It was a Sunday and he took the truck, basically, uh, stole the truck from his employer to help a buddy move, and he, he, uh, cuts his corner way too wide and just plows right into Robin." Amy put her left hand on Nick's shaking hands and held them steady. "The cops told me that she never stood a chance, because there were a couple of cars behind her and that truck was going so fast. But a month later, my cousin Lynn told me that Robin's car was in reverse at the time of the accident. The driver behind her said in the report that Robin actually backed into her trying to get out of the way. That girl had amazing reflexes. She drove an Audi with a five-speed, and with maybe a half-second to react, she had thrown that thing into reverse and floored it. I could never read the accident report, but Lynn did, and she felt that I should know *every damn detail*. Jesus, it took me months to forgive her, she's such a damn attorney. I spent a month consoling myself thinking that Robin never knew what hit her, but damnit Amy, she saw the truck coming and practically backed over the hood of another car trying to get out of the way. She knew exactly what was happening, that she was about to die and she was leaving me and Theo." Nick tried to dry his eyes, but it was no use.

Amy sat up, pulled her American Express card from her purse, and discreetly held it over the edge of the table for the waiter. Julian caught her eyes, then casually walked past the table and without breaking stride, eased the card into his right hand. Amy whispered to Nick, "Come on, let me take you back to the room." They got up from the table. Nick went outside, while Amy settled the bill. When she got outside, she found Nick at the edge of the parking lot looking at the stars. She walked up next him and put her right arm around him.

"The native Americans believed that the stars were the campfires of their deceased ancestors, family members that had passed into another realm. Robin and I were both Christians and believe in redemption and resurrection, but I like that campfire notion. I like to think that Robin often looks down on me, and I can feel her touch, her presence, her spirit. All too often, though, I believe I've disappointed her. I thought I was stronger than this, and I'm certain she did too." Amy moved her hand to Nick's shoulder. "Closure, such a meaningless word. When I was going to counseling, I would hear that word constantly, but I promise you it's a hollow word. The pain of losing Robin is just as acute today as it was two years ago. The bed is just as cold, the house just as lonely, the nights just as long. Some days, it feels like it just happened. I still have nightmares about the police showing up at the house to tell me about the accident. Sometimes, when my alarm goes off in the morning, I think it is the police calling to tell me something has happened to Robin. It takes me a second or two to realize where I am, and how long it's been since she left. Closure, what a goddamn joke. I would give up everything I have, everything I will ever have, just to hold her long enough to tell her goodbye, to tell her what she meant to me, to hear her whisper in my ear one more time, to be able to look into her eyes and see them sparkle, to feel her touch. When she held me close and smiled at me, she still had the same look in her eyes as she did that sunny day in Columbia when she leapt into my arms. You could have all of it, every dime, every possession I have, if you could make that happen. God, how I miss her."

Nick turned to face her and put his hands around her waist. Amy reached up and gently tried to wipe away his tears with a fresh Kleenex, then put her head on his shoulder. The two of them held one another until his tears dried.

"Thank you for asking about her," he whispered.

They drove back in silence, walked into the elevator and when the doors to the elevator closed, Amy reached out for Nick and they hugged one another tightly. She let go as soon as the door opened, and they quietly walked to the room. Before opening the door, she turned to him, put her hands on his shoulders, stood up on her toes and kissed him on the cheek.

"Good night, Nick. Thank you for agreeing to do this." She opened the door, dropped her keys on the counter, walked into her bedroom, and closed the door. Nick closed the room door and looked around. He realized how poorly he had judged Amy. His Blackberry went off. He looked at it and it was a text message from Amy: "goodnight nicholas ☺"

He responded, "goodnight miss sommers".

Nick walked into his bedroom, closed the door and drew a hot bath. He called his son and enjoyed a ten minute conversation with him as the bathtub filled. After he got off the phone, he walked into the bathroom, opened his shaving kit, and pulled out his bottle of prescription sleep aid. He looked at himself in the mirror, became disgusted, and threw the medication back into his kit. He climbed into the tub and thought about what a wonderful day he had had with Amy Sommers, and how much he enjoyed being in her company. When they walked into the restaurant Nick, had put his hand on her back and she had turned and smiled at him. In that moment, he had felt something much stronger than friendship. He saw it in her eyes, and felt it when they touched. Nick thought about all those morning meetings that he sat through. How many times did Amy walk into the room and look for him so she could sit next to him? Had the rest of the team unconsciously left the seat at Nick's right empty so that Amy could sit there? He wondered how long this had been going on. Jessica certainly had been doing this, and maybe Grant, too. He held his nose then slipped under the water. Yes, Amy was very special, but he was a basket case that couldn't go anywhere without breaking down in tears. Why would any woman want *him* in their life? Lynda proved that. He opened his eyes and looked at the ceiling through the bathwater. The recessed light in the ceiling directly over the bathtub glowed and wobbled through the unsteady water. He pinched his nose hard and started counting. Maybe he could reach 60 before he had to come up for air.

21

Nick picked up his Blackberry and called Theo. "Hey kid, I'm back in town, is there anything for supper?"

"Got it covered, Pop. I have a chicken roasting in the oven with some Yukon gold potatoes, Brussels sprouts, Cippolini onions, and I stuffed that dude with plenty of thyme and lemon. It looks like there's a bottle of wine here for you as well, a, uh, Pinot Blanc, oh, and I made us some cornbread."

"Damn, I missed you kid. How was the game last night?"

"We won by 14, Jimmy had a stellar game, he grabbed a boatload of rebounds, and Daniel was solid at the free throw line, plus we nailed a lot of our three-pointers."

"Awesome, sounds great. Listen, Miss Sommers just dropped me off, so I'm in the wagon now. I'll see you in about 15 minutes."

Thirty minutes later, Nick and Theo were enjoying their meal. Nick lifted his wine glass and toasted Theo and his cooking skills. "You're going to make an excellent husband one day, you know that?"

"Thanks Pop. So how was your date?"

"It wasn't a date, Theo, it was a business trip, we've been over this already."

"Anything happen that you want to tell me about?" Nick took a deep breath then took a sip of wine.

"Oh, great" groaned Theo. "Tell me you didn't."

Nick shook his head. "No, I didn't. That's not what I was going to say." Nick looked at his wine, held it up to the light, and swirled it. "Uh, Miss Sommers got me to open up about your mother. I pretty much made a damn fool of myself in a nice restaurant."

"Damn, I'm sorry Pop."

"It just sort of happened, but it, uh, it was good to talk to her, though. It was … I don't know, it was better after, uh, it felt good after my tears dried."

"Sure, Pop, I understand. You two learn anything?"

"Yeah we saw some good stuff, the Chefs I spent time with were all pretty sharp folks, but we have different audiences, different clientele. But it was still good, I took a lot of notes, made some new friends and had some great Cuban food. Miss Sommers is, uh … "

"Is what Pop?"

"A good travelling companion, Theo."

"Uh huh. OK, how about you keep that lukewarm assessment to yourself. I really liked her, Pop, thought she was cool and in case you haven't noticed, she likes you, that's for sure."

"Oh, thanks Theo, I like her too, she's a great boss. Dinner's great. Thank you very much for cooking."

"*Great boss*" mumbled Theo as he shook his head slowly. "You hear about the weather?"

"No, not really."

"We may get some snow in a couple of days. Damn, I wish we could go skiing. We haven't been skiing in three years."

"How much snow?"

"Not sure right now, could be four inches, which for this town is crippling. I really don't want to have any of our games snowed out; we'll end up moving those games to the end of the season."

"Damn, kid, you know what that will mean for me? I'll have to stay on campus. Damn."

"Seriously, Pop?"

"Seriously. The folks in our health-care facility, they can't go anywhere. *We have to get their meals to them*, so myself and Chef Randall, well, we're the only salaried folks in the kitchen, and what if our scheduled cooks don't make it in? We have to get the food delivered, no ifs, ands or buts. Maybe we'll get a cold rain instead. I'll just have to keep my fingers crossed."

The next morning, Theo reached over and swatted his clock radio, sat up and pulled the ear buds out of his ears, and looked at the time, six thirty a.m. He got out of bed, went to the bathroom and washed his face, pulled on a pair of pajama pants, and then walked into the kitchen. The coffee pot was set the night before, so he fixed himself a cup, then walked to the front door and looked out the window. His father's car was still in the driveway. He furrowed his brow, sipped his coffee, then walked to his father's bedroom and opened the door. Nick was still asleep. "Damn" Theo whispered. He tried to pull the door closed, but the cat ran through the door opening and jumped on the bed.

"Get the heck out of here, Butcher. Go on!" Butcher the cat walked up to Nick's face, started purring and rubbed Nick's chin. Nick opened his eyes, petted the cat, looked at Theo, sat up and stretched. "That coffee for me, kid?" Theo looked at the coffee.

"Yeah, Pop, here you go." Nick took a sip and then a deep breath then looked at the clock. "Damn, is it really six forty?"

"It sure is, Pop. You feel OK? You're not getting sick or anything, are you?"

"I feel fine, why?"

"*Why?* Uh, it's like three hours past your normal wake-up time, that's why. Hey, maybe you're in love?" Nick took a big sip of coffee, pulled a pillow from behind his back, and threw it at Theo. Theo caught the pillow and walked out of the room, laughing.

Nick walked into the Armory and said good morning. He was a bit early and most everyone was already there, so they spent a few minutes talking about what he had missed during the last few days. The door opened, and Amy and Cassidy walked in and said good morning. Nick looked for an empty chair. There were two, one on his right and one across the table next to Jessica. Cassidy looked at the two empty seats, and picked the chair next to Jessica. Amy looked at the empty seat next to Nick, so he stood up and held the chair out for her. She was wearing a dark brown, knee-length skirt with a white turtleneck sweater, matching jacket and a set of clock-faced earrings that Nick had bought for her on their second day in North Carolina.

Jessica smiled. "Amy Sommers, don't you look lovely this morning. Are those earrings new?"

Amy reached up with to her right ear and twirled the earring in her fingers. "Yes, they are. They're a present from a dear friend of mine." Nick looked down at his notebook then looked across the room. "OK folks, lots to talk about, the first being the weather forecast. This morning, the weather service is saying that now, we could get up to eight inches of snow, beginning early Sunday morning. And if that's not bad enough, the temperature Sunday night will drop into the high teens, so all that snow will freeze. The high on Monday may not get above 32."

Daniel spoke up. "Miss Sommers, the roads will be a mess until Wednesday afternoon. That's when it looks like the temperature will get into the high 50s."

"Damn, this wouldn't be a big deal in Bethesda," Grant said. "What gives folks?" Nick looked across the room at Grant.

"This county just doesn't have the cold-weather gear, buddy. We don't have all the snow plows and such that states above the Mason-Dixon line do, we don't get snow like this but maybe every 20-plus years, and this is a huge county. Almost 800 square miles, and some of our employees live in rural areas that may not see a snow plow. I'm sure the county will plow the main roads, but we just don't have the cold-weather resources to plow every road every day."

Amy looked across the room. No one looked happy, but when you agreed to work in a facility like this, well, this was something you had to be prepared for. "So by the end of the day, I need a three-day plan from each of you. I want to see schedules, best-case and worst-case scenarios. Nick, you're going to have the biggest challenge. We may have 50 to 70 extra folks on campus, most of them in Overbrook, and we'll have to feed them." Nick took a deep breath. "I may need some volunteers, some of my folks like Xavier live a good 20 miles out. A lot can happen to someone trying to drive into work in heavy snow and ice."

"Grant, by the end of the day, I need a list of empty beds, both in Overbrook and the independent side, and I mean everything. Sleeping bags, air mattresses, guest suites, maybe some of our residents will offer up a spare bed or couch." Amy looked around the Armory at the couch in the far corner. "Hell, we could even put someone over there. Understand? Nick, I want menus for Sunday through Wednesday night. Let's run a small buffet for lunch and dinner each day; that way, we can feed our people as well. Let's keep it simple and hearty, got it?"

Forty minutes later, the meeting broke up. Nick ran upstairs and checked in with Chrissy. Satisfied that she and Juan had everything in place, he started on his snow plan. Four days, Sunday through Wednesday. He wrote lunch and dinner buffet menus based on the menus for Overbrook, and wrote a new schedule putting the same two cooks on Sunday and Monday, and two more on Tuesday and Wednesday. He and Chef Randall would have to stay on campus all four days. Dishwashers, though; how many of his utility folks would show up? He decided to buy enough paper and plastic to get them through, just in case he was short of dishwashers. Next, he took his menus and created a list of items he needed to purchase from Sysco, and then just to be safe, he planned out an emergency menu through Thursday night. Plan for the worst, hope for the best. Maybe he could convince Theo to stay on campus? That would give him an additional pair of hands. Grant was always talking about his wife's cooking skills; maybe he could convince her to help out as well. But Grant had younger kids, so his wife would probably stay home. Jeanine was married and they didn't have any kids; perhaps she could convince her husband to camp out with them. If he had Xavier and Chrissy on campus Sunday and Monday, and Juan and Sleepy on Tuesday and Wednesday, plus himself and Kevin, plus Theo, well, that might do it. They would be humping 14 hours or more a day, but they could get it done. Theo would be his backup plan, and if Jeanine's husband came in, that was backup number two. Nick got up from his desk, grabbed a dozen chocolate chip cookies from the kitchen, and headed to Jeanine's office.

On Sunday morning, Nick and Theo climbed into the BMW. Theo would drop Nick off at work, spend the day by himself, and drive over to Woodmont that night before the roads got too ugly. Jeanine's husband, Paul, was going to come in on Monday. The next three days would be brutal, but so what? He was ready. The snow started to fall about five, lightly at first. As the evening wore on, the flakes became fat and twisted, looking like thick white potato chips. The snow filled in the cracks and crevices of the bushes and shrubs, then soon coated everything it could stick to. By eight p.m., a solid five inches had fallen, with no letup in sight. Nick and Theo stood at the back entrance and watched the snow come down. "Something about falling snow, it absorbs so much sound. We're getting an inch an hour, but it's deathly quiet out here."

"It's damn cold out here, too, Pop. Hey, you ever think of opening another restaurant?"

"Sometimes, but I don't know, it's such a workout. Why?"

"I don't know. Just asking, that's all."

"Well, probably not, kid. I wouldn't want to be tied down to another business, and I certainly don't want to go dumping any of my hard-earned money down the drain. Plus, I don't really have a partner, either."

"You'll find someone, Pop – if you looked in the right place. I know it." Nick zipped up his jacket, folded his arms and looked at his son. "Well, it's not that easy, you know. That's the kind of thing you can't advertise for, a restaurant partner. I would need someone I could trust with my life, and that's not easy to find. We should go skiing again Theo, I'd like that. Maybe during your Christmas break, after the holiday and before you go back to school? Would you want to do that?"

"What I want is something to eat." Nick turned and looked at Theo.

"Are you ever *not* hungry? Come on, I'll fix you something in the kitchen then we have to get to sleep. I'm cooking breakfast in the morning, so I have to get to work about six thirty." Nick walked towards the back door, held it open for Theo, patted him on the back as he walked in, and they trotted up the stairs.

"Well, that means you can sleep until six, right pop?"

"That would be nice kid. I have some left-over prime rib from today's buffet. I'll make us some open-faced sandwiches."

"Now that sounds righteous. So hey, pop, about Christmas, what are your plans? You gonna have to be here, since you were off for Thanksgiving?"

"Yes sir." They reached the top of the stairs, and Nick held the door open. "You want me to get you a reservation? You and Amanda?"

"Thanks, but, uh, her and her family are going to visit her grandparents in Florida.

"Well, you could come over here. Colonel Armstrong would love to have you as a guest."

"OK, that would be cool. Not ideal, but still good."

"Well, what would be ideal, kiddo?" Theo took off his coat and hung it up on the coat rack outside his Dad's office.

"Did you really just ask me that?"

"Yeah, I guess I did. Sorry Theo. How about that sandwich now?"

The next two days were a blur. Nick, Kevin Randall, Tony Torres and Theo shared a vacant apartment with very little furniture. They each had their own air mattress, but shared a television, a bathroom and a kitchen … and that was pretty much it. Nick took the early shift on Monday, Kevin agreed to do it on Tuesday. Since Nick was feeding so many employees, there was a heavy work load for his staff. Theo was pretty good with a knife, but was not covered by the worker's comp insurance, because he was not on staff. Nick had him stick with the safe jobs, such as cleaning potatoes, peeling shrimp, mixing fruit salad, and making green salads, while also helping deliver food to Overbrook. By Tuesday evening, the staff was exhausted, and the roads were still a mess. Monday's high temperature was only 24 degrees, and Tuesday it was 29. Xavier was supposed to go home on Tuesday evening, but with most of the roads still a mess, he opted to stay, even though Nick could not afford any overtime. Amy held two meetings each day, one at ten a.m. and one at four p.m., to make sure nothing was missed. Everyone was stretched thin, but Amy kept everyone focused and positive. There was a steady run of movies in the theatre, plenty of coffee and hot chocolate stations that she asked Tony to set up across the campus, and lots of camaraderie amongst the employees. It may have been ass-busting work, but on Tuesday night, Nick thought to himself that this may have been the best example of large-scale teamwork he had ever seen.

On Wednesday morning, Nick rolled off the air mattress and landed on the carpet. He dragged himself back onto the mattress and reached for his phone, five twenty a.m. At least he wasn't having a nightmare. He closed his eyes and thought how nice it would be to get another hour's worth of sleep, but two minutes later, he decided it wasn't going to happen. Nick was exhausted, but his mind raced with thoughts of what he had to get accomplished today. Breakfast for about 125 folks, lunch and dinner for 175, the thought made his head spin. He quietly dragged himself into the bathroom, hoping that he didn't wake anyone up. Maybe if he could get out of here without waking anyone, they could all get some extra sleep and Nick could crash about lunchtime. Tomorrow was Thursday and the cold temperatures were finally breaking. The high today was supposed to hit 40 degrees, but tomorrow it would climb into the low 50s. He would sleep in his own bed tomorrow night. He washed his face, shaved and brushed his teeth, and then put on a clean uniform. He left the bathroom, picked up his shoes, and walked into the hallway. He sat down in the hallway and put on his shoes. His feet felt like they had expanded by one shoe size, and when he stood up, his shoes felt like they each weighed five pounds. "Come on, Nick, one more 15-hour day, just one more." He rubbed his head then jogged down the hallway towards the familiarity of his kitchen.

Nick walked in and turned on the lights, the hood system and his ovens. Since he was in early, perhaps he could make something special for his team. He went into his office and looked through his cookbooks, and decided on cinnamon rolls. He reached for his King Arthur cookbook. When Xavier and Kevin Randall walked in an hour later, Nick had breakfast for Overbrook ready to deliver, plus two huge pans of warm cinnamon raisin rolls. Nick had made a butter, pecan and cane syrup glaze first, filled his roasting pans with the glaze, then stuffed the pans with the rolls. As the rolls baked, the glaze bubbled up and worked its way through the rolls. When Nick pulled the pans out of the oven, he turned them over onto a large platter, so that the glaze was on top. He had enough rolls for his department, plus about 24 extra. When word got out, there would be plenty of visitors to the kitchen. As soon as he turned the rolls out, he pulled three aside for Amy and her daughters, wrapped them with tin foil, and set them on his office desk. Tony Torres walked in, scratching his head.

"Damn, do I smell cinnamon? Cinnamon rolls! Hell yeah!" Tony poured himself a cup of coffee and grabbed a roll. "Hey, warm cinnamon makes me horny, you know?"

"What doesn't make you horny, Mr. Torres?"

"Sleeping on an air mattress in a room with three other guys during a snowstorm."

"Now that's good news," laughed Nick, as he bit into his roll.

"I think today is our last day here. The low tonight will only be 32, and by late tomorrow morning, it's gonna be 45.

Theo and I will take off after lunch tomorrow. Juan and Chrissy can handle supper, then I'll take Friday off and will be here all weekend."

"Sounds like a plan, Skipper. What are you gonna do with a day off?"

"Honestly? Catch up on paperwork and try to do some Christmas shopping for Theo, and definitely hit the gym."

"Sounds good. OK, Tony has the helm, things to do, places to go, people to see."

"Go get 'em, Mr. Torres."

Hours later Nick sat down in one of the big wing-backed chairs in the Armory. "What time is it?"

"three fifty eight p.m., Nick. You're just in time for the four p.m. meeting that you agreed to come to at nine this morning, remember?"

"Geez, of course. Sorry, Miss Sommers, but I'm beat. I swear I may nod off here." Amy reached out and patted him on the knee and smiled.

"You'll be fine. Just hang in there, OK?"

"Trying to, boss." The rest of the team staggered in.

"Folks, let's make this one quick, please." One by one, the team offered up assessments of their departments. How many employees were on campus? Where was support needed? How many can we expect to show up for the third shift? How many would be sleeping on campus? As Nick listened, the fatigue washed over him, the voices became distant, and he quickly drifted off to sleep.

Stern gave a weather report. The sun would come out early tomorrow morning and the temperature would rise to 45 degrees. The county was making good progress on the roads, so anyone that lived within a ten-mile radius of the facility should be able to get back and forth by tomorrow morning. By Friday morning, there would still be some sloppy roads, but things should be close to normal. As the meeting progressed, the rest of the team kept their voices low out of respect for Nick. Amy heard a service cart rolling down the hallway, and looked up from her notes just as Tony rolled through the doorway with coffee service. Several of the team stood up and quietly clapped as Tony wheeled the coffee into their midst. "Oh, Tony, thank you so much. That is so thoughtful of you."

"No worries, Miss Sommers, glad to help."

"Tony, since sleeping beauty here is out like a light, would you mind giving us a report on the hospitality staff?"

"Well, let's see. Skipper here said we're all good on food, I know he had to change up the health care menus a bit, only two cooks showed up today, though Juan drove into someone's yard and got stuck. So he may show up, but I'm not sure. Flo got here, and that was a relief. Myself and Chef Randall are staying one more night, Theo will try to leave, and then come back tomorrow morning. I think everyone else is planning on going home."

There was a knock on the front door and as Nick walked to the front of his house, he saw a police car in the driveway. What are the cops doing here? His pulse quickened as he reached the door and opened it. A police officer was standing at his front door. "Nicholas St. Germaine?"

"Yes?"

"I'm afraid your wife has been in an automobile accident. She has been transported to the Greenville Memorial Emergency Room. Can I be of further assistance?" Nick's heart rate exploded as panic set in. "What? Where? What happened? How, how, how bad is she? How is she?"

"Mr. St. Germaine, I apologize but that is all the information I have. Can someone get you to the Emergency Room?"

"Robin!"

Nick cried out in a panic, lurched out of his chair and his clipboard fell to the ground and scattered his papers. The entire team was looking at him as his panic took control. His wife was at the emergency room, he had to go now. He looked around the room and for a brief moment, was

unaware of his place in time. Amy reached out for his hand.
\

"Nick, are you OK?" He felt as if he were at the bottom of a swimming pool, struggling for air.

"Hey, buddy, it's all good. You're here with us," said Grant. Nick put his hand to his forehead, felt the bile rise from the pit of his stomach, turned around and rushed out of the room. Amy stood up and looked at Grant.

"Grant, would you please take over."

"Yes ma'am." The team was quiet for a second or two, and Grant hesitantly tried to take up where Amy had left off. Amy trotted down the stairs past the Chicago Room and went to the door leading out to the patio, but saw no sign of Nick.

"Shit." She looked at her phone then dialed the main number for Woodmont. Dawn answered quickly, "Welcome to Woodmont, this is Dawn."

"Dawn, this is Amy. I want you to call up the security cameras, scan only the outside cameras starting with the patio, then the first floor parking lot, then the back door at Overbrook, then the loading dock, and tell me if you see Chef St. Germaine. Do it now, please."

"Yes, ma'am. Is everything OK with Chef?"

"Dawn, do it *right now,* please. Focus on the task."

"Yes, ma'am, give me a second ... one second ... one second ... OK, here we go. Scrolling through the cameras now ... looking, looking, looking, looking, looking, looking, got him! He's behind the maintenance shed near the pond. Oh no! He's ... "

Amy hung up the phone and ran out the back door, but had to remind herself to slow down so she didn't slip on the ice. She trudged through the snow and ice, wishing she had her coat. Damn, it was cold. "Nick!" she called as she approached the shed. "Nick!" She rounded the corner of the maintenance shed, and there he was kneeling down, facing the shed's wall with his hands wrapped behind his head looking as if a prison camp guard was standing over him and pointing a rifle at his head. He was shaking and rocking back and forth on his feet. "Nick! Oh golly, Nick! It's Amy." She bent down and put her hands on his shoulders, but he stood up and grabbed her and held tight as his tears flowed. She held on and whispered, "I'm here, Nick. I got you. I'm here, I'm right here."

"I'm sorry, Amy, I'm trying to be strong."

"I know, Nick, I know you are."

As Amy rushed out, Grant had tried to focus on the meeting agenda, but his concern for Nick got the better of him. He looked at Stern, and asked him if his laptop could access the camera system.

"Good idea," and quickly called up the security camera program. He scanned the outside cameras as Grant, Jessica, Tony, Franklin and Cass stood over him. There was an uncomfortable silence as the entire scene played out in digital black and white, Amy running through the snow to a distraught Nick and him finding comfort in her arms. Woodmont's Director and Chef holding one another tightly, she was talking to him while smoothing his hair. Amy put her left hand on his face and was smiling. She wiped his cheeks with her thumbs and brushed his hair back again, all while Nick had his arms around her waist. Nick was nodding slowly, and they hugged one another again. Amy turned towards the door and held her hand out to him. He took her hand and followed her back into the building. The silence was finally broken by Jessica's sniffles. Cass handed her a tissue, then asked Daniel to close up the laptop.

"It must be tough to have to go through what he did," remarked Grant. "I'm sure he still struggles with it. Listen, why don't we break up our little pow-wow here, and let's just get back to our people." There was a quiet nodding of heads. "And out of respect for Nick, can I ask all of you to please keep this amongst ourselves?" Again, a nodding of heads. Tony spoke up. "Miss Sommers would have done the same for any of us."

Cassidy and Jessica walked upstairs together and when they were halfway up, Cass looked behind her to make sure they were alone. She asked Jessica whether she thought the two of them were in love. Jessica put her hand on Cass' shoulder and lowered her voice. "Let's get to my office, first." Jessica closed her door. "I think so. I think Amy has realized it, but has kept it inside. Nick hasn't expressed it or doesn't realize it yet, but it's there, sure as a sunrise. It's only a matter of time before he accepts it. I think Amy is just waiting on him, plus I think it would be awkward for them. I mean, we all know Nick likes being here, but those two. Well, there is a serious amount of karma going on here, don't you think?"

"You know, Jess, that day back in October when I was watching Nick with Amy's girls, that whole cotton candy thing with Paige, I mean I haven't seen him laugh like that ever. And did you know that was on the second anniversary of his wife's death? He really looked comfortable with them. I told Reggie that night I thought Nick and Amy were growing close. We all knew Nick was seeing that doc, but come on. She was hardly his type and her blowing up in the kitchen at him, well, there you go. Who in their right mind would do that to a guy like Nick?"

"Well, girlfriend, it's obvious that Nick is not quite there yet. But they're close. Oh, they are so close."

"OK, listen Jessica. I have to go. I have some loose ends to tie up, and then I may try to drive home tonight, or maybe Reggie will pick me up. I can't take one more night sleeping on an air mattress, but I may have to. I *really* miss my warm bed and my warmer husband."

"Amen to that."

22

Amy ushered her girls into her Jeep and headed towards Woodmont. "Listen, girls, I know it's Christmas Day and you all want to get home, but I have a lot of people working for me today and I need to spend some time over there, so please, let's have some cooperation, OK? Maybe Chef Nick will have some treats for you, if you behave yourselves, OK?"

"Mommy, I love Chef Nick. I think he's the bestest ever. Do you love Chef Nick, too?"

"Um, well Paige, I think that Chef Nick is a very special person."

"I wish he would come over some morning and cook panjakes for us. Would you like that, Mommy? I'll bet Chef Nick makes the bestest panjakes ever."

Amy looked in the rearview mirror, and caught Rebecca's eye who smiled a knowing smile at her mom.

"Yeah, Mom, wouldn't you like Chef Nick to come over one morning and cook breakfast for us? I'll bet he does make some pretty good pancakes."

"Rebecca, that's quite enough, please. Did I tell you two how wonderful you two look?"

"Mommy, will we see Daddy today?"

"No, Paige, Daddy won't make it today. We will open his cards when we get home, though, and you two can call him."

"Why?" groaned Rebecca.

"Rebecca, he is still your father, and no matter how your father behaves, I expect you to behave with respect towards him. Two wrongs don't make a right." Rebecca looked out the window and grinned, then turned towards her mother.

"Mom, maybe Chef Nick will have a treat for you, too?"

"Rebecca, that's enough, please. Chef St. Germaine and I have a professional relationship, and that's all you need to know."

"Hey Paige, why don't you ask Chef Nick to cook breakfast for us one day?"

"*Rebecca Sommers!*"

"Can I, Mom? Huh, please Mom, can I?"

"Rebecca, you and I will have a serious discussion when we get home."

"*Fine.*" Ten minutes later, Amy pulled her Jeep into Woodmont's driveway, and walked her girls through the front door.

"Hello, Percy. Merry Christmas!"

"Well, Merry Christmas to you all, too. Look at these beautiful Sommers girls. Ho ho ho!"

"Merry Christmas, Mr. Percy!"

"Merry Christmas to you, Paige Sommers. What did Santa bring you today?"

"A new red sweater, some reading books, a new American Girl doll, and a new set of hair brushes, and Chef Nick's gonna make me panjakes for breakfast tomorrow!" Percy's eyes popped wide open. Amy grabbed Paige by the hand.

"Ha, ha! Listen to you, Paige. She's kidding, of course. Kids can say the darndest things, sometimes. We're going to walk through the clubhouse now and say hello. Let's go, girls."

"Merry Christmas, girls. Merry Christmas!"

"Bye Mr. Percy!" Paige shouted. As Amy passed the bathrooms, she asked Rebecca to stay put and walked into the ladies room with Paige. Amy knelt down and put her hands on Paige's shoulders. "Listen, Sweetheart. Let's don't talk about Chef Nick coming over to cook for us, OK? That's not a good idea."

"But Mommy, I really want Chef Nick to cook breakfast for us, and me and Becca like him a lot, and so do you, right, Mommy? And besides, Becca says Chef Nick needs a girl in his life, so that girl can be me Mommy."

"Oh, I know, Sweetheart. Yes, I really like Chef Nick, but little girls should not be asking grown men to come over and cook breakfast. It is just not proper, so Paige, darling, I need you to promise not to talk about that anymore. OK, Sweetie?" Paige twisted her hands behind her back and crossed her fingers.

"Yes, Mommy."

"Mommy loves you very much, Paige."

"I love you, too, Mommy." They hugged one another tightly then walked back into the lobby. Paige was the first one out, and as soon as she opened the door to the lobby, she saw Nick talking to Rebecca, Mr. and Mrs. Hemmers, Doris Peters and Veronica Parker. "Chef Nick!" she screamed. She ran right into him and grabbed Nick around the right leg. Nick let out a mock scream, and started walking with Paige wrapped around his right leg.

"Somebody help me, I have a little Sommer stuck to me in the middle of winter!" Nick was smiling and walking in a circle, the Hemmers were smiling and laughing, and when Nick caught Amy's eye, she was grinning.

"Merry Christmas, Miss Sommers." He reached down and pried Paige off of his leg, held her up and hugged her. "And Merry Christmas to you, too, little Miss Sommers! How much coal did Santa Claus bring you?"

"That's not funny, Chef Nick. Santa brought me real presents and a new American Girl Doll, and Becca got a real cookbook and a real set of knives, and Mommy got a new set of clocks for her ears."

"Your Mommy likes wearing little clocks on her ears doesn't she?" Nick set Paige down on the ground, knelt down in front of her, and told her how beautiful she looked in her Christmas dress. Paige twisted her hands behind her back and said thank you, then looked at her mother, who was talking to the Hemmers. Paige moved a little closer to Nick.

"Chef Nick, I have a secret to tell you," she whispered.

"OK Paige, what is it?" whispered Nick. Paige stood next to Nick and cupped her right hand over his ear and whispered.

"I think you should cook breakfast for us forever and ever, but Mommy thinks- " Amy saw Paige whispering, and quickly whisked her up in the air and into her arms.

"Paige Sommers, aren't you the secretive one?"

"It's OK, she was just telling me about her American Girl doll." Amy set Paige on the ground. Rebecca held out her hand.

"Come on, Paige, let's go into the dining room with Miss Doris and Miss Veronica, and see what Chef Nick made today." Amy called out, "I'll be right there." The girls headed into the dining room with the Hemmers and the other ladies, leaving Nick and Amy in the lobby. They slowly walked towards the dining room.

"You look wonderful in red and green, Miss Sommers, and thank you very much for coming over today. You certainly didn't have to." Amy blushed and looked down, then lifted her eyes to Nick and smiled. She slowly ran her right hand through her hair.

"You look great in white, Nick."

Nick grinned, "well fortunately all of my Chef coats are white."

"Did you all come from Church?"

"Yes we did. Did you get to a service today?"

"Seven a.m., Theo wasn't happy about getting up so early but it was the only way we could go together."

"Did Santa bring you what you wished for, Miss Sommers?" Amy offered him a coy smile.

"No, because you still can't call me Amy."

"I'm working on it."

"What was Paige telling you?"

"Nothing, Miss Sommers. Just silly girl stuff."

"Did she ask you to cook breakfast for us?"

Nick blushed and smiled. "Well, can you blame her? I am a pretty good cook, you know. What little girl wouldn't want a pro like me to cook breakfast for her every morning?" Amy reached out and lightly backhanded Nick on the shoulder.

"I'm sorry, Nick, she didn't mean it." As they slowly walked into the dining room, they were greeted with warm smiles and Christmas wishes from the members.

"Amy?"

"Yes, Nick?"

"Did you get what you wanted for Christmas?"

Amy smiled and turned away, then looked back at Nick. She ran her hand through her hair again.

"Not yet, but I'm working on it." He smiled warmly and looked into the dining room.

"We're going to walk through Overbrook and say hello, then we'll swing through the kitchen on the way back, OK?"

"Of course, Miss Sommers. I need to go check on the guys, anyway." Amy walked through the dining room offering Christmas wishes to the members and staff, while Nick headed back into the kitchen. Amy then gathered up her girls and walked through Overbrook and said hello to all of the nurses, med techs and nurse's assistants. She wished everyone a Merry Christmas and thanked everyone for their hard work and dedication. The residents were just starting their lunch, and Amy was greeted with many warm smiles and Christmas wishes. Many of the staff had brought in boxes of cookies, cake and other sweets to share with one another, and Amy's girls were only too happy to indulge themselves. As they walked into the Hudson neighborhood, she saw Todd Stafford standing at the end of the table.

"Merry Christmas, Mr. Stafford." Todd turned and glared at her. He looked like he had been up all night. His hair was oily and unkempt, he hadn't shaved, and he was wearing a thick hunting jacket, a Willie Nelson t-shirt and dirty boots. He smiled unevenly, and just stood and stared at Amy. "How's your mother, this morning? I understand she had a little bump last night. Hello, Mrs. Stafford. Hello, Chet … Mr. and Mrs. Wilson … Merry Christmas, everyone. Mrs. Wilson, you sure look good in that Clemson Christmas sweater."

Todd steadied himself against the kitchen counter. This damn woman; could she be any more sappy? His temper flared and he pointed his left forefinger at her.

"Listen here, lady! Don't give me any of that fairy tale bullshit. My mother fell this morning, your fat-ass girls here couldn't even be bothered to help her up. You should see the damn bruise on the side of her face." Todd took two steps towards Amy. "How do I know one of your girls didn't rough her up?"

Amy cautiously backed up. "Mr. Stafford, I can assure you that these girls did not harm your mother. I have already read the morning incident report, and when your mother fell, we responded in less than 60 seconds. And please, do not refer to these girls so crudely. They are taking good care of your mother, and do not deserve to be insulted like that." Amy could now smell the alcohol on his breath.

"Mr. Stafford, I believe you have been drinking, and you are being belligerent towards the staff and the residents. I would like you to leave, now." Beverly looked up at her son. Even though her hearing had deteriorated, she could see the look on his face.

"Todd was just leaving, weren't you, Todd?" Todd Stafford spun around and waved his right arm at his mother.

"Do you mind if I finish talking, Mother?"

Paige and Rebecca ran around the corner. Paige was boisterously saying, "Merry Christmas, everyone!" Rebecca stopped in her tracks when she caught Todd's eye. He turned and took another step towards Amy.

"These your little girls?"

"Son, you need to leave. You shouldn't be here in this condition."

Amy turned to Saffron, who was trying to serve lunch. "Listen here, Mr. S, you just needs to hit the road and right now, you hearing me?" Todd cut his eyes at Rebecca.

"How's it gonna feel when your stupid fat bitch of a mother is working for me? She keeps up with this shit, I'm gonna own this fucking dump!"

"You need to leave right now, Mr. Stafford, or I'll call the police."

Beverly clenched her fist and started to cry. "Todd, please leave!"

"Mommy, I'm gonna go get Chef Nick, so he can come down here and make this man stop. *My Mommy is not those things you said, Mister!"* Amy instinctively grabbed Paige by the shoulders and pulled her back.

"Call the police please, Saffron. Right now."

"Yes, ma'am!"

"Well, I was just leaving anyway, lady." He started to walk towards Amy and she tried to give him room, but she backed into the table. She held onto Paige and pushed against the table as much as she could. Paige thought about kicking him in the shin as he went past, but couldn't muster the courage. As he walked past Amy, he moved his right elbow out and brushed against her breasts and smirked. "Cute kids, Miss Sommers." His breath was foul from cigarettes and alcohol, and his eyes were bloodshot. Amy's heart pounded as he walked past, but she looked him in the eye and held on tight to Paige. Rebecca thought about running upstairs and asking Nick to come down here and clobber this guy.

"Rebecca, stay here please."

As Todd headed towards the exit, Amy lurched into the staff's work room, picked up the phone, and called Percy. "Percy, call up the security cameras for the Hudson exit and tell me if Mr. Stafford is leaving. *Do it right now*, please." The bile rose up in Amy's throat, and her heart was pounding. She felt sick to her stomach. She reached for a cup to get some water from the sink, her hand shaking.

"Yes ma'am, Mr. Stafford is in his car and backing up. He's through the parking lot. OK, he is coming up on the front exit, the gate is opening, he's through and gone."

"Percy, *do not* let him back in, OK?"

"Yes ma'am." Amy picked up a tissue and wiped the sweat off of her forehead. "Come on, girls, we need to get going." The brownie Amy had eaten five minutes earlier, combined with the tension made her so sick to her stomach that she was afraid she might vomit. The three of them walked back down the hallway at a brisk pace. Amy could not remember feeling so vulnerable, and kept looking over her shoulder. They got to the staircase at the entrance to the Chicago Room and when she looked up the stairs, she saw

Nick chatting with several members. She kept her eyes on him as she walked up the stairs. The closer she got to him, the safer she felt. Nick looked down the stairs and saw her approach, and he smiled at her. She was suddenly overcome with emotion, and was afraid she was close to tears. As she got to the top of the stairs, Nick sensed something was wrong.

"Wow, you look like you've seen a ghost? Everything OK?"

"Chef Nick, I want you to go clobber that bad man down there!" shouted Paige.

"Amy, what happened?" Amy got to the top of the stairs and put her right hand on her forehead. She was so close to clutching Nick and crying on his shoulder.

"Mr. Stafford, he, uh, he was drunk, I guess, and he, uh."

"He was very, very, ugly, Chef Nick, and he called my Mommy some very bad names, *he needs a punch in the nose!*"

"OK, easy Paige." Rebecca came up the stairs last, and immediately hugged Nick.

"Rebecca, you're shaking. What happened, Amy? What did he say? Is he still here?" Nick felt his heart rate jump and his blood pressure rise. Amy shook her head, and said he had left.

"He was drunk, and he was ugly, and said things I wish the girls had not heard. I almost called the cops, but he left right as Saffron picked up the phone."

"Why didn't you call me?" Amy had her arms wrapped around her own waist. She desperately wanted to be held by Nick, and hear him say that everything was going to be OK.

"I don't need a fight to break out on Christmas morning, Nick."

"I should go down there and make sure he's gone."

"No, Nick, he's gone. Percy watched him leave on the security system."

"He called my pretty mommy fat and stupid, and used *that B word* on her, Chef Nick."

"You should have called me. We can't have that kind of behavior. There are other people to consider here, members, staff, visitors, we need to put a stop to that guy, and quick. Every time he comes back, he'll just get worse. It's inevitable."

"I know, Nick. I need to go write a report right now. Listen, do you think you could take the girls and find them a table to join, so I can have 30 minutes to get that done?"

"Yes ma'am, of course. Come on, you two munchkins, let's get some lunch." Amy turned and walked into her office, while Nick took Paige and Rebecca into the dining room. Before they went into the room he stopped them and asked them to keep this between themselves, then he hugged both of them. Nick walked up to Doris Peters' table and asked her if she and Veronica would like some company.

"Sure, gals, I can tell you two about my Christmas in Tokyo? Would you like that?"

"Sure, Miss Doris," beamed Paige. Nick smiled and thanked Doris, then walked into the kitchen to make sure everything was OK. He took off his apron, washed his hands, and walked up front to Amy's office, lightly knocking on her door. She was pacing back and forth with her head down, and when she turned and saw Nick, she quickly walked over to him and hugged him tightly. Nick held her and whispered.

"I'm right here Amy."

"Oh, Nick, I was so scared. He was looking at the girls and he was just so awful."

"You should have called me." He put his hands on her shoulders and looked in her eyes. "You should have called me, understand?"

"I know, I felt so threatened, so frightened, but I thought he would leave quietly. Mrs. Stafford keeps telling me he's a good person that's just going through a rough time right now." Nick pulled her close and softly rubbed her back. Amy moved her hands up his arms and his shoulders, looked up at Nick and smiled. It felt so good to be in his embrace.

"I'm OK now, Nick. I'll be OK." She released Nick, then took a seat at her desk.

"Do you need me to stay with you?" Her brain screamed out, "*Yes! Yes! Yes!* Please don't ever leave me. Hold me tight and whisper in my ear that you will always be there for me, that you will cook breakfast for me every morning, and dinner every night, that you love me as much as I love you. Please never let me go again!"

"Thank you Nick, I'm fine. Thank you very much."

"OK then, Miss Sommers, I'm going to head back to the kitchen."

"Nick?"

"Yes ma'am?"

"Thank you." Amy watched him walk away, and she momentarily felt flush. She had so many emotions swirling around her. She opened her laptop and told herself to focus on Todd Stafford, then started typing.

23

Nick walked into the kitchen. "Chef Randall, how's our New Year's Eve menu looking?"

"We could use your help, Chef," answered Xavier.

"OK, talk to me. What do we need?" Nick pulled the clipboard with the evening's menu off of the wall, and started rattling off each item. Xavier recited each item's status, and Kevin took notes. "Shrimp Cocktail?"

"Done."

"Chilled Asparagus?"

"Done."

"Beef Tenderloin Station?"

"Uh, tenders are ready to be grilled off, horseradish cream done, red wine sauce done."

"How many tenders you have ready, three or four?"

"Three."

"OK, I'll get another one trimmed and ready."

"Smoked Salmon Martini?"

"Uh, salmon needs to be julienned, capers need to be fried, dill needs ... well, that one's not even close."

"OK, let's get Diego on draining the capers and stemming the dill, and I'll get the rest."

"How about our vegetable crudité?"

"That's done, but the buttermilk dip is not done."

"Butternut Squash Soup is done. We have clean shot glasses ready?"

"Yes, Chef."

"Chocolate Truffles?"

"Done, but we need to get them on platters now."

"OK, will put Tony on that. What about the fruit and cheese display?"

"Did that this morning. I think we need the bread basket and cracker thing done, maybe Tony can have one of his folks knock that out." Nick scanned the kitchen hoping to catch a glimpse of Tony, but no luck, so he headed to the dining room. "Hey, Tony!" he called out.

"Right here, what you need?" Tony had walked up behind him. "Can you spare me one server to make our cracker and bread basket and to platter up the truffles?"

"Sure thing, babe. I'll put Mr. Mallory on it. Anything else?"

"All good." The band had just arrived and was setting up in the middle of the dining room, so Nick and Tony headed that way. Cassidy came up behind Nick and said hello to everyone, then introduced Bill Bennett, who extended his hand to Nick.

"Hey, easy on the grip there, Sampson. I'm a musician, need to keep those fingers in one place."

"Uh, sorry," offered Nick. "And this is Tony Torres, our dining room manager."

"Hey there, Bill Bennett, and this is my brother, Bobby, and our wives. This is Lisa, my Lisa, and that is Sharon, Bobby's Sharon. Cass, I gotta tell you, we love the space and the floor. We're gonna knock 'em dead tonight, baby. We're gonna have them swinging tonight, girl! Oh, and this is Ricky, he's our sax, that's Jerry on drums, of course, Bobby's the clarinet player, John over there is our alto sax, and that's Miller. He's first trombone, and then Joey is second trombone and some alto sax, Reed there plays keyboard and piano, and I'm your trumpet player." Cass spoke up and asked if they remembered their uniforms. "Sure thing, Cassidy, it's all in the bus." Cass had hired the Bill Bennett Orchestra to play a World War II-style USO show.

"Who plays guitar?" asked Kevin. Cass, Tony and Nick turned around when they heard Kevin Randall speak up.

"Oh, hey, Chef, didn't hear you come in. This is Kevin Randall, our sous Chef." The band members all nodded at Kevin as he asked the question again.

"So who plays guitar? Anyone?" Bill spoke up.

"Well, my Lisa here strums, but we generally don't do this show with any strings attached. Hey! No strings attached! Where's my rim shot, Jerry!"

"Work to do, Bill" moaned Jerry.

"You guys want something to eat?" asked Kevin.

"Hell yeah, Chef, what you thinking?" smiled Reed.

"How about some fried chicken sandwiches with bacon, cheddar cheese and chipotle mayonnaise, some steak fries with some of my own spicy ketchup, and a side of apple cider and sweet onion coleslaw?"

"Sweet stuff, Chef!" exclaimed Reed. "Chef here knows how to hook a brother up! Just point me to a sink for some cleanup afterwards, and I'm all yours." Cass, Tony and Nick just stared at one another. This was easily the most conversation they had ever heard from Kevin in a long time. "Sure thing, give me 45 minutes and we're there. In return, I want a sit-in. I've got my Martin Sunburst in the car. Maybe we can do *Sentimental Journey?* " Tony's eyes practically popped out of his head.

"Chef, you asking to play with these guys?" Kevin just stared at Tony.

"Chef, what kind of strings you using?"

"It's strung with Darco nylon, all rosewood with Fishman Aura pickups." Cass leaned over to Nick and whispered.

"What are the chances that Aliens have kidnapped your sous Chef and replaced him with an exact replica, yet one with a personality?" Nick kicked Cassidy in the heel. "Ouch!" Bill turned to the band.

"You guys OK with that?" There was a general nodding of heads, then Reed spoke up. "Seems like we're getting the sweet side of this deal." He walked over to Kevin and high-fived him. "You got some Tabasco sauce, Chef?" Kevin nodded. "Then we have a deal, my friend. *Sentimental Journey,* say in a jazz waltz style, three-quarter time in the second set, about seven forty-five or so? We can even get Jerry here to use his brushes instead of the sticks, maybe give you a softer sound, and the girls here know that one pretty well."

"Well, I'll handle the vocals, too, if they can just give me some background."

"*Chef, you're gonna sing too?* Oh shit, I need a drink," said Tony. Nick spoke up. "OK, Tony, I like this idea. Our folks can see a side of Kevin that they don't get to see. Chef Randall, I'm looking forward to this. Now we get to see what you do in your spare time. OK, let's get back to work, folks." Nick put his hand on Kevin's shoulder, and they walked back into the kitchen.

"Going to my car." Five minutes later, Kevin walked back into the kitchen, carrying his guitar case, and he set it down in the office while Xavier, Chrissy, Diego and Sleepy stared at him as if he were naked.

"Chef Randall, is that your new knife case? Please say yes, because if that was a guitar in there, then that would mean I gotta rethink my entire opinion of the man that is Kevin Randall." Kevin just smiled and walked back to his station, picked up his knife, and started trimming the smoked salmon. Xavier set his knife down and held his hands up in the air. "Now wait just a minute, Chef, you are not gonna get off so easy. Is that a guitar?" Kevin just nodded his head up and down and kept working. "Chef, do you know that we have a band playing in the dining room tonight?" Again Kevin just nodded his head up and down. "Did you just go into the dining room and ask the band if you could sit in with them?" Kevin offered another head nod. "And Chef Randall, do you realize that there will be people out there watching you, and those people may clap, and you may have to say, 'Thank you. Thank you, very much?'" Xavier added his best Elvis imitation for effect.

Kevin set his knife down, and glared at Xavier. Xavier dropped to his knees, folded his hands, and looked up to the heavens. Sleepy closed his eyes, put his right hand over his heart, and held his left hand high up over his head. Chrissy stopped working and folded her hands. Xavier prayed out loud, "'Dear Lord, if you have any goodness left in you tonight, please, please, grant poor Chef Randall here, a mute since birth, please grant him the power of speech just long enough to say, thank you. Please Lord, it is truly and sincerely important."

Chrissy pretended to cry and wiped her eyes with her towel. "That was beautiful, X Man, just beautiful. I think it's gonna work." Kevin turned his back on them and glared at the clock on the wall. Xavier got up off the floor, held his hands up in the air and shouted, *"Brothers and sisters, can I get an Amen?"*

"Amen!" shouted Nick, as he walked into the kitchen. "Now you heard Chef Randall, the clock's ticking. Let's make it happen, people." Three hours later, they were ready to roll. The beef tenderloin, shrimp cocktail, fruit and cheese, bread and cracker baskets, and the vegetable display were all on the buffet by five forty-five. Nick started the passed Hors d'oeuvre with shot glasses of pureed butternut squash soup garnished with truffle oil. Next up were miniature smoked salmon martinis. The bottom of the glass held avocado puree, then a bit of thinly sliced smoked salmon, then a tiny dollop of whipped sour cream, a sprinkle of fried capers, some toasted and buttered bread crumbs, and a sprig of fresh dill. Next came miniature champagne flutes of chilled asparagus spears, with a lemon zest mayonnaise on the bottom of the flutes. Then it was time for the cherry tomato halves, filled with pimento cheese. Nick and his crew worked quietly and efficiently. If a certain hors d'oeuvre only needed two pairs of hands, the idle cooks cleaned up. By seven thirty, most of the food was done and the kitchen was almost clean. The last items to go were the chocolate truffles and the chocolate-dipped strawberries. Five minutes later, Nick was giving Tony a high five. "Another awesome event brother, thank you for all your hard work, Tony, and now I believe it is time for me to dance with some of the eligible ladies."

"OK Chef, don't pull any muscles," grinned Tony. Nick retired to his office to take off his work shoes. Kevin was in a chair tuning his guitar, listening carefully to the note of each string. "OK Chef Randall, I'm going to go dance with some of my rabid female fans. I guess I'll see you out there shortly."

"K," responded Kevin, without looking up. Nick took off his boots and his dirty Chef coat, and changed into his black Egyptian cotton Chef coat that he kept for special moments. He walked into the dining room in his socks, and as he did so, saw several of the ladies raise their hand to him as if to ask for a dance. He had a ten-dollar bill in his pocket and a 5 x 7 note card with three requested songs, which he gave to Bill: *Temptation*, by Artie Shaw; *In the Mood*, and *Don't sit under the Apple Tree*. Bill looked at the note, gave Nick a thumbs up, and turned to the band and said, "*Temptation* anyone? Bobby, you take the lead." Bobby's clarinet hit the opening notes of *Temptation* as Nick reached out for Doris Peter's hand. Doris stood up and smiled.

"What the hell took you so long, Nick? I thought I was gonna fall asleep waiting on my dance partner."

Although Doris was 81, she still had some pretty good moves. The two of them danced for about half the song until Ellen Wright cut in, then the band moved to *In the Mood*, and Nick took turns dancing with the Susan's and Peggy. As the band transitioned to *Don't Sit Under the Apple Tree*, Doris moved back onto the floor and announced.

"This one's all mine!" Three minutes later, Nick and Doris separated and clapped.

"Thank you, Doris." Nick turned around to his left to head back to the kitchen, but not five feet away was Amy Sommers, wearing a white strapless ballerina dress, her favorite diamond pendant and pink heels. She beamed as Nick practically stopped in his tracks. Amy twisted her arms behind her back, smiled, then looked down.

"This next one was a big hit by Harry James and Miss Kitty Kallen in '45." Bill lifted his trumpet and played the introduction to *It's Been a Long, Long Time*.

Nick smiled and held his arms out to Amy. She blushed, then walked the five feet to him, and put her left arm around his waist as Nick took her in his arms. "Fancy meeting you in this joint," he said. Nick pressed his left hand to the small of her back and thought about how many hours it had been since he had shaved or brushed his teeth. He tried not to get too close to Amy, lest he catch her hair on his stubble, but Amy was having none of it. She pulled him close and let him lead her across the dance floor, as Lisa sang:

"Never thought that you would be,
Standing here so close to me.
There's so much I feel that I should say,
But words can wait until some other day.
Kiss me once and kiss me twice,
Then kiss me once again; it's been a long, long time. "

Doris and her girlfriends were watching from their table. "This is not good girls. Look at those two love birds. This is not a good development, not good at all."

"Oh Doris, why are you raining on their parade? You should be happy for them," Susan said. "Don't you know what this means?" rasped Doris. "Nick can't be in love with his boss. Like Marshall Dillon used to say, this town ain't big enough for the two of 'em. Somebody's gonna have to quit, and it sure as hell ain't gonna be Nick. Where's our entertainment gonna come from?" Tony was watching Nick and Amy from a safe distance, when Jackson came up next to him.

"How much longer before Chef realizes the two of them are bound by destiny?"

Tony exhaled deeply. "I don't know, Mr. Mallory." Jackson lightly shook his head and walked away.

Amy moved her right hand up his back and pulled him closer. How good it felt to be in his arms, to have her body pressed against his. She had the left side of her face against his neck, and could feel Nick's pulse through her cheek. She closed her eyes and wished she had tipped the band, so this song would last for five, ten or 15 minutes longer. Amy softly sang along:

"You'll never know how many dreams
I dreamed about you,
Or just how empty they all seemed without you.
So kiss me once,

Then kiss me twice,
Then kiss me once again.
It's been a long, long time."

Veronica spoke up. "You know Doris, if those two are in love, then so be it. Nick deserves a second chance dear, and those sweet little girls of Amy's really need a man in their life." Doris put her head down on the table.

"I need a man too, you know. I can't watch this, I just can't." As the song ended, Amy stepped back a bit, put her hands on Nick's shoulders, looked into his eyes, and whispered, "Thank you."

"Amy?"

"Yes?" Nick hesitated, then turned to the band and clapped as Amy followed suit. She turned back to Nick, smiled, and walked off to say hello to the members. Nick stood there for a second or two and watched her walk away, then turned back to the band. Reed winked at him. Kevin Randall walked up and sat down with the band. He plugged in his guitar as Bill Bennett took the microphone. Nick looked for Amy, hoping she was close by, but she was already on the opposite side of the dining room.

"OK folks, we have a special guest here. Your assistant Chef Kevin Randall is going to join us for *Sentimental Journey.*" Nick walked off the dance floor and stood in the corner. He noticed many of the members had looked up, and several dozen were headed to the dance floor. Kevin closed his eyes, and his guitar came to life as he played the opening chords. Bill Bennett's band slowly joined in behind him, and the girls were humming along. Kevin opened his eyes and looked out at the 100-plus people now listening to him.

"Gonna take a sentimental journey,
Gonna set my heart at ease.
Gonna make a sentimental journey,
To renew old memories."

Nick folded his arms and took in the reaction from the staff and residents as Kevin put his soul into the song. He had a somewhat raspy, distant voice that reminded Nick of a melancholic Bryan Adams. Nick felt a hand on his back, and he turned and smiled warmly as Amy stood next to him. "Did you know Kevin could play like this?" she asked.

"I've known for some time he played a guitar, but never actually heard him play before."

"Got my bags, got my reservations,
Spent each dime I could afford.
Like a child in wild anticipation,
I long to hear that "All aboard!"

"You look fabulous tonight, Amy, you really do. Thank you for being here." Amy ever so gently moved a little closer to him, lifted herself up slightly on her toes to get closer to his ear, moved her left hand up to the middle of his back, and slowly whispered, "Thank you, Nicholas."

"Seven ... that's the time we leave at seven.
I'll be waitin' up at heaven,
Countin' every mile of railroad
track, that takes me back."

Nick let his arms fall to his side and held his hands behind his back. The hair on the back of his neck started to tingle as Amy let her hand drift down his back to his right arm, then her fingers gently glided down the length of his arm, all the way to his hand. When her fingers reached Nick's, they briefly intertwined, and Nick gently caressed her fingers. The electricity leaping between them was palpable. Doris Peters was the only one at her table not watching Kevin; she was watching Amy Sommers. Doris elbowed Veronica.

"Look at that hussy going after our man." Veronica didn't take her eyes off of Kevin, but leaned over to shush Doris.

"Never thought my heart could be so yearny.
Why did I decide to roam?
Gotta take that Sentimental Journey,
Sentimental Journey home.
Sentimental Journey."

Amy and Nick both clapped and cheered. A lot of the members stood up and clapped, and many of them were wiping their eyes. Amy turned and took Nick's hands in hers.

"Goodnight, Miss Sommers. I guess I'll see you Monday morning?" Amy smiled warmly.

"Yes Nick, you will see me Monday morning." She let go of his hands, then walked over to thank Kevin before heading towards the front lobby. Nick watched her glide through the dining room and out of sight.

"Damn." As he watched Amy walk away, Tony passed her and said good night, then came up to Nick and suggested that as soon as the next song was done, the staff would pour champagne for the midnight toast.

"You and Miss Sommers certainly looked good on the dance floor."

"Um, yeah, Tony, she did look good, didn't she?"

"OK folks, Chef Kevin here says he's good for one more song, so how about we all *Jump, Jive and Wail*, so here we go." Kevin stood up out of his chair, stood behind Bill's microphone, and launched into the opening chords, his guitar practically leaping out of his hand.

"Baby Baby it looks like it's gonna hail.
Baby Baby it looks like it's gonna hail.
You better come inside and let me teach how to jive and wail.
You gotta jump jive, then you wail.
You gotta jump jive, then you wail.
You gotta jump jive, then you wail.
You gotta jump jive, then you wail.
Then you wail away."

"*Holy Shit!*" yelled Tony. The kitchen staff, the servers and Dawn, the concierge, were all gathered around the dance floor with various looks of shock and disbelief on their faces. Chrissy couldn't hold back, so she grabbed Xavier and started to dance, the other cooks cheering them on. Doris grabbed Nick and they hit the dance floor again.

"A woman is a woman and a man ain't nothing but a male.
A woman is a woman and a man ain't nothing but a male.
One good thing about him is he knows how to jive and wail."

As Kevin reached the vocal chorus he swung his guitar behind his back and started clapping, hands over his head. Jerry started drumming on the metal rim of his snare to provide a crisp beat.

"Ya gotta jump jive then you wail.
Ya gotta jump jive then you wail.
Ya gotta jump jive then you wail.
Ya gotta jump jive then you wail.
Then you wail away."

Kevin reached back for his guitar as the rest of the Bill Bennett Orchestra tried to keep up. He leaned back and finished the song with a flourish. By then, there was easily 70 people cheering him on. Most of the applause from his co-workers. He grabbed the microphone stand, leaned over with it, then straightened up, tossed his head back, pointed at Xavier, and said an Elvis–style, "Thank you. Thank you, very much!" Ten minutes later, Tony's staff had passed out flutes of champagne, and the band started the countdown with a drum roll from Jerry.
"Happy New Year!" The members drank and toasted, threw their confetti and blew their noisemakers, and drank some more as the band played *Auld Lang Syne*. After about ten minutes, the party was over and the members quickly began filing out. By nine p.m., the dining room was clear and

Tony's staff was cleaning up. Nick's crew was done, so he stayed in the dining room to help out for a bit.

"Bill, Bobby, you guys were wonderful. This was about as perfect as a party as I have ever been to. Thank you so much, and thank you for accommodating my sous."

"Our pleasure, you know the first time I played a New Year's Eve venue like this, we loved it. A crowd of retirees finishes up by eight thirty or nine and we can actually be home by midnight instead of three a.m."

Nick's phone went off with a text message, so he pulled it out of his pocket and took a look. He had three unopened messages: one from his son, one from Amy Sommers, and one from Kelly. All three wished him a happy new year. Amy's was signed with a smiley face icon. He looked at her message for the longest time, trying to decide how he would respond, when Reed passed him carrying a drum.

"Where's your lover, Chef? You two gonna celebrate tonight?" Reed winked at him as he passed.

"Um, she's uh, she's not my lover, she's my boss." Reed laughed out loud and said, "*Yeah right.*"

Nick looked at his phone again and responded to Amy: "happy New Year to you too Miss Sommers", and hit send. "Mr. Torres, I'll see you in a week. Enjoy your time off, sir."

"Thanks, Skipper. If Mr. Mallory needs anything, he's welcome to call, but I may not return his call for seven days."

"Of course!" laughed Nick.

"The cell reception in the Caribbean is terrible, you know."

"Lucky you!"

Tony put his hand on Nick's shoulder and carefully pulled him towards the office. "You know, Nick, Amy is quite a woman, and you two, well, you really looked good together." He patted Nick on the cheek.

"OK, Mr. Torres. I'll see you in a week."

"Yes, sir, see you in a week." Nick walked back to his office, put on his winter coat, locked the door, and headed to his car. Damn, it was cold outside. When he got to his car, he pulled his phone out, climbed in, and turned the ignition.

As the engine warmed up, he looked at his phone. He had three more text messages: one from Tony, one from his cousin Lynn, and one from Candace. All three said, "Happy New Year," and Candace signed hers with a kissy face icon and asked him, "y aren't we celebrating 2gether?" Nick smiled and replied with, "Happy New Year" to all three, then opened Amy's text again. He leaned back and closed his eyes as the engine warmed up and their dance came back to him. He thought about how wonderful it was to have Amy in his arms, the smell of her hair, the warmth of her skin, the tone of her body, and the tenderness in her voice as she sang to him. He gently tapped the throttle and felt the engine soften its subtle vibrations. He sighed, put the transmission in reverse, backed out, and headed home.

24

"Good morning, Jessica, and Happy New Year," chimed Amy as she unlocked her door. "Oh, hey, Amy, and a Happy New Year to you. How was your weekend? Did you stop into the New Year's Eve party Friday night?" Amy set her purse down and turned on her laptop. "Yes, I did." Jessica got up from her desk and walked into Amy's office. "Wow, don't you look great today Jess! Red is your color."

"OK, enough about me, tell me about Friday night. How was the music, the food, the, uh, dancing with Nick?" Jessica sat down in front of Amy, put her elbows on her desk, propped her chin on her hands and smiled at Amy. "I'm waiting," she smirked.

"Well, OK, I did dance with Nick. Just one dance, though, and that was it, that's all. It was just one dance. Satisfied?"

"No."

"Oh gosh, though, what a show they put on. The band was great, they were all dressed in authentic World War II Army uniforms, and their singers had this perfect Andrew Sisters thing going on, and oh my gosh, Kevin Randall sang *Sentimental Journey*, and everyone was in tears!"

"Our Kevin? Sous Chef Randall? He sang? Shy and withdrawn Kevin Randall got in front of a crowd and sang? You're serious?"

"Yes, and it was beautiful, and he played his guitar. Oh, what a voice he has. I can't believe that he hasn't told anyone, or maybe he has. It just didn't get to us, but I tell you what, there wasn't a dry eye in the place."

"Our Kevin Randall sang and played his guitar in front of 100 people. You are kidding me now, right?"

"I know, I know, our Kevin that communicates with note cards. Can you believe it?"

"And then you danced with Nick, right? Did he come and get you, or did you go and get him?"

"Well, he was swing dancing with Doris, the band was playing *Don't Sit under the Apple Tree*, and he and Doris were dancing away. When they were done, the band started playing *It's been a Long, Long Time*. Nick turned around and, well, there we were standing a few feet apart, and so we just sort of. Well, he smiled at me and held his hands out, so we just danced, and that was it." Jessica stood up and pretended to be slow dancing and started to sing:

"Kiss me once then kiss me twice
Then kiss me once again
It's been a long, long time"

"Oh Jessica, stop that, please, it was just one dance. It wasn't a big deal, OK? Now go away; I have work to do, please." Jessica kept dancing with her ghost partner, then gently swayed out of Amy's office singing.

"Work to do, Mrs. Alexander!" Jessica slowly danced herself back to her office.

Amy opened up her Outlook account and watched the emails start to appear. Damn, she hated Monday mornings … 27, 28, 29 and 30 emails dropped into her box. She scanned the subject lines for something really important, and saw one from the concierge labeled, "New year's Eve photos." She looked up from her desk and glanced into the front office. Seeing no one, she opened the email and was greeted with a slide show of 24 photos. A fresh email dropped into her inbox from Jessica labeled, "did you look at the NYE photos yet?"

"Stop, Jessica!" Amy hollered. 'I'm working here. You remember work, right?"

"Yes ma'am, sorry!" Jessica replied. "I will *not* look at these photos right now, but instead will open the emails from the home office."

Amy again glanced towards the front office, and satisfied she wouldn't be interrupted, she returned to the photos. She started the slide show and watched it move through photos of the band, then the servers as they passed around silver trays of hors d'oeuvre, a smiling Tony in his tuxedo, photos of the members, some dancing, all smiling. Then two photos of Nick and Doris dancing, and then a close up of her and Nick slow dancing. Amy paused the slide show and looked at the photo. "Oh no!" she gasped. She had her head on Nick's shoulder, her eyes as well as Nick's were closed, and they looked as happy as a couple of sweethearts at the Senior Prom. Jessica let out a gasp, and a crash came from her office that made Amy think she had fallen out of her chair.

"Amy! Have you seen this?" Damn. Jessica carried her laptop into Amy's office, and sat her laptop down on Amy's desk. Now she had two copies of the photo staring at her. Amy looked up at Jessica from her desk as tears formed in her eyes.

"Oh Amy, why are you so upset?" Amy stood up and Jessica hugged her, then buried her face in Jessica's bosom and cried. Jessica reached back with her right foot and kicked the door shut.

"I know, I know. It's all so complicated," whispered Jessica. Jessica felt Amy's head move up and down. "Have you fallen in love with one of your employees?" Again, Amy's head moved up and down ever so slightly. "Are you torn between the job you're supposed to be doing, and your own emotions right now?" Again, Amy's head moved slightly up and down. "Are you afraid that Nick may not feel the same way as you do?" Amy's head moved up and down a third time. Jessica pushed Amy back so she could look at her, the tears had destroyed her morning make up.

"Oh golly, look at you boss. Come on, let's get you straightened out. Remember, we have a meeting to get to." Amy plopped herself down into her chair and threw her head down on her desk.

"I keep thinking that Nick will come around. I've given him plenty of hints and opportunity. I just know any day now, he's going to see me as something other than the boss. Oh Jessica, what have I gotten myself into? Now I've made a big mess. In 15 minutes, everyone on campus will have seen that photo, and in 30 minutes, Harriett will see it, and Rivers,

Hamilton, the entire company will see it. The whole world will see it, and everyone is going to know. Oh, it's no use, I might as well quit right now. I'm finished. No authority left, no respect left, no nothing. By the end of the day, everyone at the corporate office on down to the part-time housekeepers will have seen this. Everyone that passes me in the hallway will wink at me and say, 'Wow, Miss Sommers, you and Nick sure make a cute couple.' I'm so done. I'll be the laughing stock of the company. I'm ruined, finished."

"Amy Sommers, you better snap out of this right now! As your head of human resources, I can assure you that you are over-reacting, and no one can glean that sort of information from one photo of one dance on one night. So get your butt up and get ready for your meeting. You're over-reacting. Now please snap out of it!" Amy looked up at Jessica, smiled and asked her for a Diet Coke. "OK, but when I come back with your drink I better see some progress here or you're going to wear that soda, understand?" Amy smiled and nodded, then pulled out her purse and started fishing around for some Kleenex and make up.

"That's more like it Amy. I'll be right back with your Diet Coke." Jessica left the office, and Amy's eyes returned to the photo. She leaned back in her chair, closed her eyes and covered her face with her hands. Now what had she done? She was sure that Nick loved working here and the members loved having him here, and now she had jeopardized his position, as well as hers. She had screwed up royally. Harriett was going to have her head. Rivers will be disappointed, her executive team, her staff, what would they think of her? Her computer chimed as a fresh email dropped into her box. She opened her eyes and glanced at Outlook. It was from Cassidy, and the subject line read, "NYE Photos...WOW!!!!"

"Oh no," Amy groaned, "I'm dead." Jessica came back with the soda and found Amy no better. She had her head on her desk and her arms over the back of her head.

"I warned you, now you get the shower!" Amy leapt out of her chair, only to see Jessica standing and smiling. Jessica laughed and Amy started to smile. She finally agreed with Jessica that she was over-reacting. Jessica helped Amy get cleaned up, and they headed out to the nine a.m. meeting. As they passed the copy room, Amy stopped and told Jessica she wanted to grab something out of her mailbox. Jessica stopped to wait, and as Amy was digging through the mail, she heard Amy exclaim, "Shit!"

"*Amy Sommers, watch your mouth, young lady!*" exclaimed Jessica. Amy walked out of the copy room with a letter-size copy of the photo of her and Nick dancing, and handed it to Jessica. Whoever put the photo in her box had drawn a heart around the two of them.

"I'm so dead," she muttered as she walked past Jessica and headed to the meeting. Jessica and Amy walked into the Armory, where most of Amy's team was waiting. Amy scanned the room, but didn't see Nick. "Good morning, and Happy New Year," smiled Amy. "I hope everyone had a wonderful weekend. By my phone, it's already nine so can we please get going? Cassidy, since the New Year's Eve party was such a big hit, would you mind starting off?"

The door to the Armory opened and Nick walked in, said good morning, apologized for being late, and then wished everyone a happy New Year. Amy's heart rate picked up as she watched him walk across the room. As he took his seat, he looked at Amy and said, "My apologies, Miss Sommers." Amy smiled at Nick, blushed and lowered her gaze, before realizing practically everyone in the room was looking at her.

"Uh, OK, continuing on, OK … Uh, thank you, Cassidy. The New Year's Eve party was a very big hit, so thank you for planning it, and, uh, who's next?"

A bewildered Cassidy turned to Amy, "But I haven't said anything yet, Amy." Amy looked over at Cassidy, and realized what she had just done. The room was eerily quiet.

"Amy Sommers, are we going to have to move you into our memory care unit?" teased Jessica. Amy put her left hand over her mouth and laughed, and most of her team laughed as well.

"It's not only Monday, it's the first Monday of the year." said Nick. The laughter took the edge off of Amy's mistake, but she was certain that everyone knew exactly what had happened. The man she loved had walked into the room and had thrown her completely off balance. She looked at Nick, laughed and shook her head.

"OK, Cassidy, now that our esteemed Chef is here, please tell us about the New Year's Eve party!" Cassidy gave a glowing review of the party, and thankfully she didn't mention the fact that Amy had even been there. As Cassidy talked, Amy glanced at Nick, but each time she did, he had his eyes down or was looking elsewhere. As the meeting went on and each member of her team gave their updates on the coming week, Amy struggled to focus. She kept looking at Nick and imagining him walking over to her and asking her to dance. Her Blackberry went off; it was a text from Jessica. She looked over at Jessica then opened it, "focus" was all it said. She smiled at Jessica then looked at Grant.

"OK, Grant's turn, people, and this is pretty serious stuff. We had several incidents with Todd Stafford in the last week, so listen up."

"Thank you, Amy. So Big Todd came in again and exploded at the CNA's and was very ugly, very unruly, and even threatened another family member that happened to be visiting his grandmother. Daniel, after the meeting, I would like to review some security footage with you. Let's isolate his visit, and Amy, after that, can you join us? I have asked for statements from the girls that were in there at the time, and Amy, this may be all we need to get a restraining order against Mr. Stafford." Grant's statement had definitely put a damper on everyone's mood. In the last month or so, Todd Stafford had gone from being a rude pain in the ass to a threat to Woodmont's security. "When Mr. Stafford was here over the weekend, he called Mrs. Campbell's 22-year-old-grandson, excuse my French, please, a fat pussy."

"Oh, for Pete's sake!" groaned Amy.

"There's more. Jacob, the grandson, had baked a cake for Mrs. Campbell, and had come in while Mr. Stafford was seated at the table. The neighborhood had just finished lunch when the grandson shows up with a cake for his grandmother, and he wants the CNA's to have some as well. Mr. Stafford, who was already agitated, tells Jacob that, 'No one wants any of your cake, you big fat pussy, and these two girls here don't need to put on any more weight.' "

"Meaning our CNA's, correct?" asked Jessica. Grant nodded his head. "Jacob was very hurt, and he apparently started to shed a tear or two. Mr. Stafford then laughed at him, at which point Jacob left. So now, by allowing Mr. Stafford to control the neighborhood, we have prevented a visit from a family member. We cannot allow this path to continue. I will not have this guy chasing off other family members and berating our staff. If we do not put a stop to this, what happens next? He already exploded on Amy and her girls, on of all days Christmas. Son or no son, he can't keep doing this."

"Grant, if you don't mind, I want to finish this conversation with the executive team, and in the meantime, please, if Mr. Stafford comes back, please call me immediately, call Grant, call a member of the executive team."

"Hold on, Amy, it gets worse."

"Worse?"

"Yes, ma'am. Nick, the reason this guy had disappeared is because he was in prison in Georgia for almost a year. He beat up a prostitute in Atlanta." The ladies in the room let out a collective gasp. "He was using an alias at the time, he had a fake driver's license, credit cards, the whole bit. Amy, the sooner we get this guy out of our lives, the better for all involved."

"OK, listen. If Mr. Stafford gets unruly and we have to call the police, we want witnesses. Do not approach or attempt to reason with him by yourself. Do so with another team member. Is that clear? At the first sign of unruliness by Mr. Stafford, you are to call the police. Please tell Mr. Stafford that you are calling the police because you feel threatened by him. Everyone understand this?"

Amy looked across the room, and definitely had everyone's attention. Satisfied that her team understood her instructions, she adjourned the meeting. The sales and marketing crew and the nurses excused themselves. Nick, Cassidy, Grant, Daniel and Jessica stayed behind. "OK, Grant, tell us how this process will work. What are our odds of getting a restraining order against Mr. Stafford? "

"Any incident regarding Mr. Stafford needs to be written up and described in detail, and any witness needs to sign that report. I already have a file with a couple of reports. And now, Mrs. Campbell and her family are upset. So the next stop is the State Ombudsman's office, where we will make our case for the order. Amy, you are going to have to sign our request, along with myself and probably Rivers. Our request gets reviewed hopefully in a timely manner, and then perhaps we will get a decision in five business days. In the meantime, I have a photo of Mr. Stafford that I pulled from the newspaper's website that I will post in every venue in Overbrook, along with instructions to call a member of the executive team immediately, should he walk in again. Now, please, this is very important. We need to respond immediately and dispassionately." Grant looked at Nick.

"We cannot get upset, we cannot stare at him. Keep your arms down and your voice low, and once you feel he is threatening you calmly inform him that you are calling the police. But please, none of us can threaten him with any sort of physical action, is that clear? Nick? All clear?"

"Yes, sir."

"Ok guys, everyone understand this?" asked Amy. "Let's have a great day and a happy new year." They got up from the table and headed to the door. Nick held the door open for everyone. As Amy passed, she smiled at Nick and said, "Thank you." Nick returned the smile and winked at her, causing her to walk right into the back of Cassidy, almost knocking both of them over. Nick reached out and grabbed Amy by the right hand and steadied her.

"You OK, Miss Sommers?"

"Oh, um, I'm so sorry, Cass. Yes, thank you, Nick."

"Yes ma'am, my pleasure." Grant was the last one out and Nick let the door close. Grant put a hand on Nick's shoulder and slowed him down.

"Nick, please, we need to get rid of this guy, but if one of us loses his temper in front of Stafford, then that makes it that much harder. If cooler heads can prevail, then we can get our restraining order, and we're all good. Can I count on you, buddy?" Nick looked into Grant's eyes, and momentarily imagined himself throwing Todd Stafford head first off the roof.

"Sure thing, Grant, you can count on me."

"I knew I could, my friend, I knew I could. Have a great day, Chef."

"OK, Grant, you do the same."

Jessica held the front office door open for Amy, and Cassidy came running up behind them and walked into the front office as well. Cassidy quickly closed the door. "Amy Sommers, I just had to tell you how amazing you looked on Friday night!" Amy smiled nervously, and said thank you to Cassidy. "Jessica, have you seen any of the New Year's Eve photos of our stunning Director? Did she ever look like a million bucks!"

"Why no, I haven't, Cassidy," smirked Jessica.

"OK, the two of you can put a stop to this right now. We've all seen the photo of Nick and I dancing. It was just one dance, and that was it. One dance, OK? Now, can we please put this subject to bed?" Jessica and Cassidy burst into laughter as Amy blushed for her third time that morning. *"Damnit!* I can't believe I just said that."

"Girl, you definitely need to put *that* subject to bed." Amy reached out with the papers she was carrying and tried to swat Cassidy, but Cassidy quickly jumped back. "I am not touching that one, no ma'am. Off to work I go boss, have a great day." Cassidy waved goodbye and headed out the door.

"And you, Jessica Alexander, you also have a pile of work to do, bills to generate, December sales reports, and so forth, correct?"

"Yes ma'am, that's correct." \

Amy softened her gaze. "Thank you for saving me in there. I can't believe I did that." Jessica gave her a hug.

"Listen, if you ever need to talk to someone, girl-to-girl, I'm here for you, OK?"

"Thank you Jessica, now please go to work."

"Yes ma'am." Jessica left the office and closed the door. Amy sat down at her desk, flipped open her laptop, and opened up Calendar to get a handle on her day. She made a few quick notes on her daily to-do list, then put her pen down, leaned back in her chair, and closed her eyes and let her mind drift back to New Year's Eve. She remembered Nick's stubble catching on her hair, the tone of his muscles as her hand moved across his back – and she distinctly remembered counting his heartbeat through her cheek. She was certain his pulse had quickened as they danced. She opened her eyes and looked at her door to make sure no one would interrupt her, then opened up the New Year's Eve slide show and scrolled to the photo of them dancing. She clicked Save As, grinned as she labeled it "that subject", and saved it under her "evening close out list". At four thirty every weekday, Amy opened her evening close out list and scrolled through it to make sure she was staying on track. She took one more look at the photo, sighed then looked at her reflection in the framed photo of her daughters. "Now what, Amy Sommers? Now what?" She closed the photo, looked at the time and headed off for a quick walk through Overbrook to check in with the staff.

25

Nick walked through the 1949, where he found Willie Armstrong struggling to get a cup of coffee. "Good morning, Colonel. Can I give you a hand here?" Willie was a bit unsteady this morning, and his walker would not cooperate. Nick took the cup from Willie's hands and poured the coffee for him. "Go ahead and have a seat, Colonel, I'll bring this to you, maybe even grab myself a cup."

"OK then, Nick, if you're going to do that for me, then maybe I'll tell you about the time I put Willie's Wagon down on two wheels."

"Deal, Colonel. You want a muffin, or maybe a Danish?"

"No thanks, just some coffee."

"Have you eaten yet, Colonel? You're not living off of coffee are you?"

"You gonna bring me that cup, or do I have to get it myself?"

"Black with a little sugar, right?"

"Thank you, Nick." Nick brought two cups of coffee and sat down opposite Willie. "So, you put the wagon down on two wheels?"

"Oh, yeah. We had been to Bremen, October of '43, and a 190 had shot us up pretty good on the way out. We had just met up with our escort of '47s."

"Were those C or D model '47s?"

"Razorback Cs from the 8th. The Air Corps didn't start flying the D model until late '43, and the 51s didn't appear until, well, winter of '43. So on those big missions, we didn't have any escort for a good two hours, and of course, that's when we got the hell shot out of us. So anyway, this damn 190 wouldn't let go of us, and on his second pass, he shot us up pretty good. Took out our Number 3 engine and killed little Jim, our tail gunner, and wounded our waist gunner. We were losing altitude fast. Morgan, our ball gunner, well, he was little Jim's best friend, and he knew that little Jim was dead. So he tracked that 190 as he came around for his third pass and he gritted his teeth, chambered his 50s, and his guns started chattering away. Old Morgan was just screaming the whole time. Well, he started putting rounds on this 190, and he got some good hits right on the nose and prop, and that 190 started slowing down. Morgan kept firing, and that 190 just shuddered. Pieces started falling off of it and it's smoking and has about pulled even with us, and then Benny, our left waist, well, that 190 falls into Benny's line of fire and he lets him have it, too. Well, here comes this P-47, and he starts firing at this 190, and damn if Morgan doesn't turn his guns on that '47!"

"Damn, seriously, Colonel?"

"Nick, that fella has just killed Morgan's best friend, and Morgan is going to take that 190 down, and he sure as hell didn't need any help from some Johnny-come-lately '47 jockey. So yeah, he gave that '47 a squirt, and he rolled away. Then Morgan turns back to that 190, and we were certain by then that pilot was dead, because that 190 had slowed to practically our airspeed, and he's burning pretty bad. But Morgan just empties his 50s into it, the fuel tanks ruptured and the left wing collapsed, and that 190 just flopped over and spun away, leaving this black, greasy trail of smoke. Morgan just sat in the ball for the longest time, not saying anything. So by the time we get over the channel, we have lost most of our hydraulic fluid and our right inboard was out. That 190 got some pretty good hits on us. I figured we would set down at the first base we came to, so as the coast came into view, I put the gear down. The 17 had electric-hydraulic controls for the main gear, and damn if we couldn't get but the right side and tail wheel down. So I'm trying to hold on to this airplane for all I'm worth. I was a pretty big fella back then, with hefty forearms 'bout like you, only mine were a little thicker."

Nick smiled and said, "Of course."

"I tell you what Nick, I was just wearing myself out trying to keep that thing from rolling over. I had both feet crushing that rudder, trying to keep her straight. When we lost our Number 3, well, the wagon started pulling to starboard something awful. I had the throttles jammed forward on the three remaining engines, and the guys started dumping everything they could into the Channel ... ammo, guns, spare oxygen tanks, anything they could, and well, the wagon sort of stabilized. Big Jim, well, he and Mack were cranking away on the manual gear release, but that 190 had put a cannon round right into the left gear, and damn, if it just didn't fall right off. I mean, it just went bye-bye, and Morgan was still in our ball turret, and well, he finally spoke up and said, 'There goes our left wheel.' Well, I tell you what, Nick, that airplane was never so quiet. We're all thinking about our landing and how rough that's gonna be. Then Morgan says, 'Whose idea was it to throw out the left wheel, anyway?' Well, we all just had to laugh. We were shot to hell, sunshine and saltwater breezes flowing through that airplane, we had a dead tail gunner and a wounded right waist gunner, three engines turning, and only two wheels down, and damn if were not all laughing away as the English shore comes into view."

"Did you fly over the white cliffs, Colonel?"

"Nick, the cliffs are south near, well, near Dover, and I was stationed at Grafton Underwood, which is 160, 170 miles northwest of Dover. Hell, we were 75 miles north of London. Bremen is in the north of Germany, and this mission didn't take us anywhere near Dover. So we managed to get the wagon back over England, but hell, Grafton was the westernmost base the Eighth Air Force had, so we had a bit of flight left in front of us. We all wanted to get Little Jim back to Grafton and give him a proper burial amongst his friends. So I asked the fellas if they wanted me to try to get her home, and we all agreed, so we limped home at about 100 miles an hour all the way to Grafton. I lined her up for final on 29, and set her down nice and easy on the right wheel. As soon as that wheel touched, I pulled the power back on all three engines and cut the fuel flow and held her up as long as I could, and when that left wing started to dip, well, we all held our breath. That wingtip scraped first, then the outboard propeller caught the concrete, and man, we spun around like a top, the wagon making this awful, scraping noise. Well, we just hung on to anything we could, and we finally stopped spinning and scraping. I guess me and Myers"

"Your co- pilot, right?"

"Yeah, Bob Myers, my co-pilot. Well, we started crawling out and were slapping one another on the back, and then we remembered Little Jim. I tell you, other than burying Mrs. Armstrong, that was about the hardest thing I ever did was to get Little Jim out of the wagon. The fellas had brought him up to the waist gunner's position before we landed. Morgan was pretty upset, hell, we all were." Willie took a long sip of coffee, then set his cup down. He reached out and placed his hand on Nick's, and looked him straight in the eye. "Listen to me ramble on, Nick."

"That's OK, Colonel, I don't mind."

"That was one heck of a New Year's Eve show. Reminded me of the time I saw Glenn Miller. What a show they put on, and those boys the other night were pretty good, too."

"They were good, weren't they?"

"You and Miss Sommers. Well, I was watching the two of you dance the other night. You two sure looked peachy."

"Yes sir, Miss Sommers is a good dancer." Willie leaned back and smiled smugly at Nick.

"Miss Sommers is one fine lady, Nick."

"I know Colonel, I know." Willie folded his arms and furrowed his brow.

"You know, Nick, I was married for 59 years. Me and Mrs. Armstrong built a family and lots of memories together."

"I know you did, Colonel."

"Nick, you're still a young man. You got a lot to offer. I hope you can one day reach a point in your life where you don't blame yourself for losing your wife. I'm one to talk. It took me a few years to stop blaming myself, even though cancer took Mrs. Armstrong from me. I blamed myself, even though I'm not an oncologist, just a dumb pilot. One day, you'll stop blaming yourself and move on. I hope you get to that point soon."

Nick looked at his hands. "I still have nightmares about the police showing up to tell me she was in an accident."

"I'm sure you do, Nick. Eventually you're going to have to convince yourself that it was just that, an accident."

"But I would have cooked dinner for her. She didn't have to go to the store, if she had only listened to me and …" Willie put his hand up, as if to say stop.

"Nick, would you listen to yourself. How much longer can you carry this weight around? You're a strong fella, but you're not that strong." Willie put his hand on Nick's hand and looked him in the eye. "You need to stop carrying that burden, Nick, or it's just going to kill you." Nick looked down and wrung his hands, then looked back up at Willie.

"I'm trying, Colonel, I'm trying."

"Have you ever lied to me, Nick?"

"No, sir."

"You're a good man. Thanks for the joe, I gotta get going. There's a card game in the Armory, and I thought I would wander in and see if I can play a few hands."

"I thought that was a ladies-only game, Colonel?" Willie winkled at Nick as he stood up and steadied himself with his walker. "It is, Nick. It's what a fighter pilot would call a target-rich environment."

"Roger that, Colonel."

"But don't worry, I won't do anything that would embarrass Mrs. Armstrong. She's keeping a close eye on me today, I can feel it." As Willie slowly shuffled off towards the elevator, he sang, "Off we go, into the wild blue yonder." Nick picked up the coffee cups, wiped down the table, and headed back into the kitchen.

26

Nick rolled around in his bed and opened his eyes. There was sunlight coming through his window. "Hey Pop, you gonna sleep the day away or what?" Aromas of orange, cinnamon and warm butter drifted through the bedroom, he pulled himself out of bed then slipped on his pajama pants. Damn, the floor was cold. He put on a pair of slippers and a shirt then walked into the kitchen. "Good morning, kiddo. What we got here?"

"I made us some blueberry orange muffins and poached eggs, plus some fresh OJ." Nick poured himself a big cup of coffee and took a generous sip.

"Dad, you know it's been a while since you had a nightmare. You're practically sleeping normal hours, and I'm kinda worried 'bout you, so I set up an appointment with Doctor Simmons. He had a nine twenty appointment slot open today."

"You're funny, kid. Who's Doctor Simmons anyway?" Theo patted his Dad on the back and looked him in the eye.

"The Love Doctor!" Nick shook his head at Theo.

"These muffins smell great." They sat down at the table. Theo said a prayer asking God to forgive his father for being so hardheaded and having such poor vision, then asked "for this year to be special, full of good news and encouragement for both of us."

"Thanks for breakfast, kid. What are you up to today?"

"I have a game tonight, remember? Why don't you bring a date to the game? Maybe Rebecca Sommers and her Mom will come with you?"

"Alright Theo, that's enough, OK?"

"OK, sorry Pop. Just trying to help here, you know. You *sure* you haven't fallen in love?"

"So what time is your game? Seven, right?"

"Seven p.m., we're home and we're playing J.L. Mann, so it's gonna be packed. Don't be late, OK? And don't bring any food this time. I don't need any of the parents telling me how much they enjoyed my dad's home-made peanut brittle or chocolate-covered pecan bars. My ego is pretty fragile, you know, and if I have another stellar game tonight, I need those moms to tell me how amazing I was, not how amazing my dad's game treats were. You got it, Pop?"

"Sure, Theo, no food. I'll bring a couple of dollars and buy some of that nasty popcorn, OK? Can I bring something for Amanda and her friends though?"

"Oh, come on, Pop, that would be worse!" Nick laughed and winked at Theo.

Nick walked into this office, sat down and opened up his calendar. Tony Torres would return on Monday, no special events today, nothing really going on until next Tuesday, and Theo's game was at seven p.m., so he needed to be done here by five forty five at the latest. He looked at today's schedule: nine a.m. staff meeting, two p.m. dining staff meeting, three p.m. special events meeting. Maybe he could leave after his three p.m. meeting? He looked over his to-do list to see if there was a special project that he owed anyone, then opened up his documents to look over his project list. His eyes were drawn to the "My Photos" folder. He looked outside to see if he would be interrupted, opened the folder and clicked on the photo labeled "NYE dance," the photo of him and Amy dancing. He took a good long look as Theo's words echoed in his mind: "You haven't fallen in love, have you?"

"Yes I have, Theo, yes I have."

Nick was about done for the day when Xavier called out. "Hey, Chef, before you take off, can you deliver these special orders to Overbrook? We have seven plates that have to go, two to memory care, three to Hudson and two to Burgess." He looked at the wall clock: 5:10 p.m.

"Sure thing, X. Chef Randall, you OK?" Kevin nodded. Nick grabbed a pushcart, loaded up the plates and headed for the memory care neighborhood, dropping off the first two plates. He then rolled the cart to the elevator and pushed it in, hit the down button, and then raced down the stairs. He walked up to the elevator door then waited. Candace walked up.

"Nick, are you getting lazy? Why are you taking the elevator?" When the elevator opened, Nick walked in, grabbed his cart, and rolled past Candace. She reached out and pinched him on the bottom as he walked past.

"I'm telling Jessica, first thing in the morning!" Nick quickly made his way to Burgess, telling everyone good evening then rolled the cart to the Hudson neighborhood. He rounded the corner into Hudson and delivered the special orders, waved at everyone, then headed back down the hallway, just as Todd Stafford exited his mother's room.

"Hey Mr. Stafford, how are you?" exclaimed Nick and he extended his hand. Todd offered his hand as well and slowly replied.

"Just fine, Chef."

"Well, that's good to hear. Mom's doing well, too, yes?" Nick's blood began to boil, his pulse quickened, and he desperately tried to keep himself calm. He wanted nothing more than to pick up Todd by the belt loops and toss him headfirst through the nearest window. "Well, come on, I'll walk with you. It looks like you're going my way," and Nick swept his right arm in front of him as if to say, "This way, please." Nick slowed his pace a bit, and cognizant of the security cameras that scanned every inch of this place, put his head down. He took off his cap, ran his hands through his hair, then pulled the cap down tight. When he was a good 12 feet away from the common area of Hudson and without lifting his head or changing his body posture, he asked Todd if he could hear him.

"Sure thing, Chef, loud and clear."

"Good, because this is very important. I swear to God in heaven above, if you *ever* talk to my boss again like you did on Christmas Day, I'll snap you in half like a *fucking twig*. You get

353

that loud and clear?" Nick kept walking and kept his head down, but Todd exploded like Mount Vesuvius.

"I tell you what you little turd, no one talks to Touchdown Todd Stafford like that!" and he moved to block Nick's path while wagging his finger at Nick. Nick kept moving, head down, and went around Todd. He lifted his head up, smiled and politely said, "Excuse me, Mr. Stafford." Todd threw his hands up in the air and hollered, *"What the hell is going on in this place? I swear, I am gonna own this place tomorrow. Bunch of damn morons. Ain't a damn one of ya that knows what the hells' going on around here. You and that stupid fat bitch that thinks she runs this place are all a bunch of morons. I swear, I am gonna own this place tomorrow and every damn one of ya is fired! YA HEAR ME? FIRED!"*

Nick had reached the exit and was holding the door open for Todd. "Mr. Stafford, I believe this is your stop." Todd stuck his finger in Nick's face, and Nick could smell the alcohol on him.

"Hello, Nick? Excuse me, but may I be of some assistance?" Nick turned around and saw Penny walking up behind him. "Hello, Penny. Mr. Stafford here has gotten very upset, however, he was just leaving. He was saying some things he just didn't mean. He is very distraught and in his current state, I believe he is a threat to this facility, so I was making sure he left peacefully."

"Your days are numbered! No one dogs Touchdown Todd like that and gets away with it! You're finished here, you little shit!"

"Yes, sir," smiled Nick, "Good night." The door closed and Todd stormed to his truck, backed out and drove away in a cloud of dust and tire smoke. Nick turned away from the door, smiled at Penny as he rolled the cart past her then made his way back to the kitchen. He walked into his office, shut the door, dropped to the ground and did 50 pushups to try to burn off some of his emotion. He then sat down and emailed a quick report to Amy, copying Grant, Jessica and Rivers that said Todd Stafford went off on him. When he was done, he walked up to the line and said good night.

"Tell your son to hustle, OK?"

"Thank you, X. Good night, Chrissy, Kevin." Nick walked down the stairs then headed to his car wondering if he would have a job on Monday morning. There would be repercussions; Todd would call every number at CSM management he could find. But then what? Nick was certain he showed no emotion, did not rant or wave his arms around, but then what? Well, he was not going to worry about it now. He had a game to get to. If they got rid of him Monday, then so be it. That son of a bitch Stafford had it coming, though. Who in their right mind threatens a woman, talks that way to a woman like he did? He should have *thrown* him out the door.

On Monday morning, after the meeting ended, Amy asked Nick if he could come into her office for a minute. "Yes, ma'am" he replied, be there in a minute.

"What happened between you and Mr. Stafford Friday?"

"He went off on me after I asked him to mind his manners when he's talking to a lady while in the confines of this building. He then threatened to have me fired, he said he would own this place in the morning, he said me and that stupid fat bitch I work for are both done, oh, my apologies. I was, uh, just quoting Mr. Stafford. None of that is coming from me."

"Of course. Are you sure that you did not prompt him, did not bait him in any way?"

"Feel free to look at the security footage, Miss Sommers."

"I have." Nick sat there looking at her.

"Nick, you haven't answered my question."

"I think I have."

"OK, you should know that he has called Rivers, who will probably be here tomorrow morning. Rivers, Mr. Stern and I will conduct an investigation. Do you have any questions for me?"

"No, ma'am."

"Nick, do you understand what's going on here?"

"Yes, I do, Miss Sommers. A broken-down, doped-up scumbag that has a history of violence has threatened you in front of your daughters, threatened me, has insulted and threatened our staff as well as family members of our residents, and *I* am being investigated for being unprofessional. *That* is what is going on, correct?" Amy looked down, then lifted her eyes back to Nick and shook her head.

"We're supposed to be better than that Nick." He stood up and walked to her door.

"Yes, ma'am. Door open or closed?"

"You can leave it open, please." The next day Rivers and Harriett were on campus for the morning meeting. He and Nick exchanged pleasantries and after the meeting was adjourned, Rivers, Stern, Harriett, Grant and Amy headed off to Amy's office to review the security camera footage. They spent 20 minutes scrolling over and over the footage. There was Nick shaking hands, smiling, looking pleasant and walking slowly. And there was Todd Stafford, looking normal one minute, and then ranting, raving and gesturing in a threatening manner to Nick, while Nick kept his composure. Because Nick was wearing his long sleeve Chef's coat and a baseball cap, it was tough to read any sign of emotion in Nick, though. Rivers then suggested looking at the footage of Todd when he threatened Amy and her kids. As they looked at that footage, Todd behaved in much the same manner. One minute he looking almost normal, then in the next, he was pointing his finger at Amy and her kids, yelling and flapping his arms around. Rivers asked Daniel to go back to the footage of Nick and Todd. Rivers was looking for some sign that Nick had instigated the event, but after the third viewing, he was satisfied that Nick had kept his cool.

Rivers spoke up first. "It is obvious that he is a threat to the integrity of our facility, and I'm afraid that if we do not take the next step, then someone is going to get hurt. And from this moment forward, we do everything in our power to keep him off campus, agreed?" Everyone nodded their heads and agreed.

"If you all will excuse me, please, I'm going to make a copy of this and save it, then I'm going to have a word with Nick. After that, does anyone want to join me for lunch in the dining room?" Rivers made a copy of the footage onto a CD, then left Amy's office. "Amy, I'm going to take a walk through the campus and say hello to a few folks, so, if you will excuse me."

Harriett took Amy by the hand. "Amy, can I take you to lunch today? There's that little English Tea Room that I have driven past several times, I would love to try it out." Amy was a bit taken aback, thought about how much work was sitting on her desk.

"That would be lovely, Harriett. Yes, thank you. I'll even drive. Say we meet back here at eleven thirty?"

When Rivers found some privacy, he put the CD in his laptop and carefully looked at the footage a fourth time. He slowed down the playback speed, then zoomed in on Nick's knuckles as he gripped the handle of the cart. He could clearly see the veins popping on his knuckles and wrist as he gripped the handle. Nick was slowly twisting the handle of the cart. Rivers headed into the kitchen and found Nick on the back line, cleaning beef tenderloins. "Nick, do you have a minute for me?"

"Of course. X, you mind taking over this task while I take a spin with the wheel here?"

"Sure thing." Nick removed his latex gloves, washed his hands and grabbed a cup of water, then headed into his office, closed the door and sat down.

"You're looking good, Nick. Looks like you've been keeping up with your workouts."

"Well, when you can't sleep, you might as well do something with your time."

"Nick, uh, you getting along OK with Amy?"

"Yes, sir. I thought we were going to talk about Todd Stafford?"

"We are. Are you sure you did not say anything to instigate Mr. Stafford because you were upset at what he did to Amy in front of her girls?"

"It doesn't take much to set off a mentally unstable person such as Mr. Stafford. He is obviously on cocaine, and the few times I have talked to him, he was drunk or had been drinking. The company should be taking steps to prevent him from coming on campus again, instead of questioning their employees that have tried to prevent him from doing more harm than he already has." Rivers scrutinized Nick. "I agree, Nick. I just want to be sure that our people are acting in our best judgment. I watched the camera footage several times, and it looked like you were going to break the handle off of that cart you were pushing. You were obviously under a lot of stress, correct?"

Nick rubbed his head with both hands. "Rivers, look, that's correct, but I had to take out my aggression on something. Better that cart than that dope Stafford, right?"

"Yes, you're right again. So how you doing? How's Theo?"

"He's great. He's signed a letter of intent with UNC, you know."

"Damn, no, I didn't know. Damn, brother, that is great. UNC, huh? Damn, that is remarkable. Is he planning on going pro?"

"Well, that's his ultimate goal, but honestly, the odds are still against him. We've agreed that he will keep a 3.25 average, or I don't go to any of the games. He needs that education. Anything could happen to him in the next four years. I mean, he could tear his ACL in his last college game and there goes any shot of going pro, and then what? You've wasted four years at a first-class university and you have a degree in basket weaving? Not my kid. He's going to get his degree in mathematics and hopefully go for his master's, if his old man can afford that. Or maybe he can find a suitable employer that will pay for his master's. Pro basketball ... I mean, he's good, but you have to have all the stars properly aligned and at the right time, and then there's still no guarantees."

"Sure, sure, that's great. Good for him." Rivers took a good look at Nick. "Nick, how you doing personally? You sure you're OK?" Nick looked at Rivers and wondered whether he should appease him or tell him the truth?

"I was seeing this doctor. She was wonderful but, uh, things didn't work out so well. I guess it's all part of the process. Work and time in the gym helps. It keeps me out of that empty house."

"OK, I see. I'm sorry things didn't work out for you with your doctor. You getting along with Amy though, correct?" Nick sat back and smiled.

"Amy's a pretty special person, she really is. She's compassionate, honest, hard-working and smart as a whip, plus she's, uh, pretty easy on the eyes, too. It's a shame her little girls don't have a man in their life. She's delightful, yeah we're getting along just fine. Why?" Rivers smiled and nodded his head. Now he was positive that Nick had instigated the encounter with Todd Stafford. He was certain Nick and Amy had developed strong feelings for one another, and like any protective man, Nick had threatened Todd Stafford after Todd had threatened Amy. At least he didn't get physical with Todd, but Rivers was afraid that would be next.

Nick watched as Rivers rapidly rubbed his eyebrow with his left forefinger. Damn, thought Nick, did I just give myself away?

"Listen, how about we grab a beer tonight? Can you meet me at Bailey's tonight at, say, six thirty? Can the guys live without you tonight?"

"You buying, or is CSM buying?"

"Just me, Nick. I'm buying."

"We gonna talk about Todd Stafford?"

"Don't have to."

"Then what will we talk about?"

"Basketball, cars, women, the weather, your future with the company, your call."

"Deal, but how about we go to Northampton instead and have a glass of Nuits St. George, instead of a cheap beer?"

"Because I can afford a cheap beer, that's why," laughed Rivers.

"Oh, so I'm only worth a cheap beer, then?" he teased.

"No, no, Northampton it is. Just give me some directions, OK?"

"Deal. If I text you the address, can you find it?"

"Yeah, of course, I'm not that old. I'll see you there at six thirty." With that, Rivers excused himself and Nick got back to the kitchen.

Two hours later, Amy and Harriett were enjoying their lunch at the Tea Room. Their server set down several small plates of petit sandwiches. "These are cucumber, dill and cream cheese, and this is chicken salad with our homemade crackers. Here we have some Parmesan puffs, some of our mini cheddar cheese biscuits, and two cups of cream of watercress soup. If you ladies need anything, please just ask."

Amy smiled and thanked their server. "It all looks lovely. Harriett, thank you so much for taking me to lunch. Honestly, I rarely get off campus for lunch. This is a treat."

"Oh, you're welcome, Amy." Harriett took a sip of the soup and pronounced it delicious. "Amy, I think you're the best thing that could have happened to Woodmont. You have done such a great job, you really have. I know you earned that bonus and it was significant, but sometimes we just need to hear someone say thank you, don't you agree?"

"Yes ma'am, of course, and thank you for everything you've done for me."

"Um, Amy, on another note, would you mind if we talk about Nick?" Oh boy, here it comes, thought Amy.

"No, of course not. What shall we talk about?" Amy's heart rate picked up and her palms started to sweat.

"Amy, what little I know about Nick, I like. He's done a very good job at Woodmont, and I know he enjoys being a part of your team; he has told me so on several occasions. I guess I would just ask you to practice some discretion."

"What do you mean, Harriett?"

"Aren't you and Nick dating? I saw the photo of you two dancing. You looked so content. I guess I assumed that, uh." Amy looked at her soup then poked at it with her spoon. "Well, that's inaccurate, Harriett. As much as I wish it were true, it's not."

Harriett softly replied, "Oh, my apologies."

"He, uh, well maybe that may change someday, but who knows, I'm, well... "

"I see." Harriett sat up and reached for Amy's hand, and lowered her voice. "Amy, Nick's wife was killed. His wife of what, 12, 14 years? He lost his wife and sold his restaurant because he no longer had his business partner. Amy, he didn't just lose his wife, he lost his *identity*. You and I, well, I'm going to guess and say that the amount of personal trauma that you and I have had to endure in our lives hasn't come close to what Nick went through. If you went through something like that, would you honestly be able to say that you, Amy Sommers, would be ready for another relationship in a given time frame? Would you be ready in 18 months, maybe 24 or 30? When does that much pain ease? How would we know?"

"That's a good point, Harriett."

Harriett released her hand and sat up. "Are you in love with him?" Amy pursed her lips, looked down and nodded her head slightly. "Have you told him?" Amy shook her head no. "And why not?"

"I don't know, Harriett. I think he senses it, but I don't think he believes he's ready. It's just a guess, but it's driving me crazy. He was seeing another woman for a short period of time and the way she treated him was awful. If only."

"Amy, I hired you because you were passionate and driven, not because you were patient. I knew you would do a great job at Woodmont, and that you would challenge your employees to push themselves to be their best. But with this

– and I know you didn't ask me for advice, but I'm going to give it to you – you just need to be patient. Can you?"

Amy stirred her soup, nodded her head slightly, and sighed. "I'll try, Harriett. Thank you."

27

Nick washed his hands, as Xavier patted him on the back. "Thanks for sticking around tonight, Chef. Why don't you take off now."

"OK, X, I'm going to go say hello to some of our folks, then I'm out of here."

"Yes, sir." Nick walked to his office to change into his black Chef jacket, and that's when he heard Ally scream his name. Nick ran towards Ally, she was yelling for a nurse, and Chrissy was already on the phone. Nick grabbed Ally by the shoulders and asked, "What is it?"

"It's Mr. Armstrong," she managed to say.

"*Dial 911 now, please, Chrissy!*" barked Nick, then he bolted into the dining room. Nick ran into the dining room, and found about a dozen members standing in a circle in the far corner. He ran towards them, knocking over a chair.

"OK folks, let me through, please." Willie Armstrong was on the floor clutching his left shoulder. His breathing was raspy, and his eyes were closed. Nick knelt down next to him and held his hand, then asked if anyone had a seat cushion to put under Willie's head. Virginia Rogers was on the other side of Willie, sitting in a chair and taking his pulse. Nick looked around and saw Xavier, and asked him to call a nurse. "Penny is already on the way."

"Go get me the AED right now, please."

"Yes sir!"

"Hey Colonel, can you hear me?" Marsha Hemmers handed Nick a cushion, and he carefully lifted Willie's head and slid the cushion in place. Ginger looked at Nick and mouthed, "Heart," then gently shook her head side to side.

"Nick?" Willie rasped.

"I'm here, Colonel." Xavier knelt down next to Nick and set down the AED, a bright-red artificial defibrillator. He opened the lid, turned on the power and removed the contacts. Nick unbuttoned and removed Willie's shirt, and then asked everyone to back up. Willie's eyes opened, and he grabbed Nick on the arm. He was struggling for breath and was in a lot of pain, but he managed to say, "Let me go, Nick." Nick held Willie's right hand; Ginger had his other hand. Willie was moaning and his muscles were getting uneven electrical impulses from his oxygen-depleted brain, so that his arms and legs moved about as if he were a flimsy scarecrow on a windy day. Willie opened his eyes again and looked at Nick, and managed a thin smile.

"I'm going home, Nick."

"You are home, Colonel. We're all right here." Xavier opened the AED and hit the power switch, and it responded in a flat electronic voice.

"Remove all clothing from patient's chest."

"Place contact pads firmly on patient's bare skin."

Nick took the contact pads from Xavier, and placed them side-by-side on Willie's chest. When the contacts were in place, Nick pushed the "monitor" switch on the AED and it began monitoring Willie's heart, looking for an arrhythmia.

"No one should touch patient right now.'

"I'm going home, Nick," gasped Willie. "I'm going home."

"Pads should not touch one another."

Willie looked like he was trying to get up, but his body was trying to get away from the pain of the heart attack. Willie managed to open his eyes again, looked at Nick, then squeezed his hand so hard the knuckles in Nick's hand cracked.

The AED responded in its flat electronic voice: "Electric shock advised. No one should touch patient right now. Remove all metal from patient's chest."

Nick carefully removed Willie's dog tags, and handed them to Ginger. Willie inhaled a quick gasping breath as a child would right before jumping into the deep end of the swimming pool, whispered, "Natalie" then his body went limp just as Penny arrived and knelt down on Willie's left.

"*All hands off the AED please,*" Penny demanded.

"Electric shock advised. No one should touch the patient right now."

Penny placed her stethoscope to his chest, then wrapped a blood pressure cuff around his right arm and took his pressure. Thirty seconds later, she looked Nick in the eyes, reached out for his hand, and said, "Mr. Armstrong is a DNR, Nick. We need to put that away," and nodded towards the AED.

Nick shook his head and pleaded, *"No, Penny, no, please, he'll be fine. Please let go of him, so I can turn this thing on."* Nick could feel Xavier's heavy hand squeezing his shoulder. He turned to Xavier and asked for his help.

"You need to let him go, Nick. He needs to go home."

"No, Xavier, he is home. Just help me, please. Please help me."

"He's gone, he's gone home," Xavier quietly said.

Nick turned back to Willie's body, wiped his eyes on his shoulder, then caressed Willie's face with his right hand. Several of the members got down on their knees and prayed as Nick's tears flowed. Willie was going home to see the woman that broke his heart 16 years ago, the woman he had loved since elementary school, the woman he had married when he was 21 years old, just before leaving for a war-torn Europe. The woman he talked about every day.

Chrissy leaned close to Xavier and whispered "What's DNR mean X?"

"Do not resuscitate, means if his heart stopped beating he didn't want any medical attention, he just wanted to go."

"Goodbye, Colonel," Nick whispered.

There was a metallic rattle as the paramedics sauntered into the dining room, pushing their stretcher. They rolled up to Willie's lifeless body, and asked to be let through. Xavier pulled Nick aside and put his arm around Nick. Nick wiped his eyes on his sleeve.

"Anything burning on your grill, Xavier?"

"No, sir." The paramedics removed the small AED, and then hooked up their own monitors. In a few minutes, they pronounced Colonel William Armstrong deceased, then, with

Penny's assistance they moved his body back to his room. The funeral home would pick up his body in the morning. Xavier and Nick walked back to the kitchen, and once through the double doors, Nick hugged Xavier tightly. Jackson, Chrissy, Juan, String Bean and Ally all joined in.

"Thank you, all. The Colonel was a very good man." wheezed Nick. Ally reached out and placed her right palm on Nick's face.

"He loved you like his own son, you know that, Chef?"

"Yes, ma'am" Nick sobbed. Nick thanked everyone again, then reminded the staff that they still had people they had to do a job for. "Let's take care of business, please." Nick walked to the hand sink and washed his face with cold water, then dried himself off.

"Listen, Chef, I got it from here."

"OK, thank you, Xavier."

"Yes sir, please take off. Why don't you take your son out to dinner, or something like that?"

"Thank you." Nick looked around the kitchen. His staff had gotten back to work. Some were wiping their eyes, but were doing so as they moved through their business. Nick walked to his office and took off his Chef coat, changed his shoes, and sent a text to his son.

"On way home, anything for supper?" Nick closed his door and slowly walked down the stairway.

Amy looked around the room. Everyone was there, except for Nick. She looked at her phone for a text from Nick, but saw nothing. "OK, folks, by my watch it's time so let's get started. I haven't heard from Nick, I guess he's running a bit late. Grant, would you lead us off, please?"

"Yes, ma'am. For those of you that have not heard, Colonel William Armstrong passed away in the dining room last night. The family is making arrangements right now, and we'll host a memorial for Colonel Armstrong. Cassidy, as soon as the details are finalized, let us know, OK?" Cassidy looked at Grant, and nodded. Grant continued on.

"Everyone knows that Nick was very close to the Colonel, correct? So please be aware of that. I imagine that Nick is going to have a tough couple of days." Grant looked around the Armory; most of the women were nodding their heads and looking down.

Amy Sommers caught Grant's eye. "How close were they, Grant?"

"Miss Sommers, Nick's father passed away when he was nine. It is my guess that Colonel Armstrong was a father figure to Nick, and couple that with the fact that both were widowers. Well, I would say that they were very close." Amy gasped and covered her mouth when she heard Grant mention Nick's father.

"Oh no, I didn't know that. Cassidy, perhaps we can consult Nick regarding Mr. Armstrong's memorial? Perhaps that would help?"

"Yes, ma'am." Amy's Blackberry buzzed with a text. She took a quick look and saw it was from Nick, so she opened it. "will not make meeting apologies"

"Understand, you OK?" she texted back.

"OK Grant, what else do you have for us? How's Beverly Stafford doing and what's the latest on her son?"

When the meeting ended, Amy walked to her office to drop off the stack of information she had collected during the previous hour then told Jessica she was headed to the kitchen to check on Nick. She walked through the double doors, poured herself a cup of water, and looked around. The door to the walk-in cooler opened, and the delivery guy from the produce company walked out pushing an empty hand truck and said, "Thanks Chef." Amy walked to the cooler and found Nick putting away the delivery.

"Good morning, Nick." He had his back to Amy then turned to face her.

"Good morning, Miss Sommers."

"We missed you this morning." Nick turned his back to her and continued moving the sweet potatoes and corn into their proper places. "Yes, ma'am. Can I do something for you?"

"No, thank you, I just wanted to say hello, that's all."

"Thank you, Miss Sommers."

"Nick, if you need something, you know where to find me, OK?"

"Yes, ma'am." Amy let the cooler door close and headed back to her office. When she sat down at her desk, she called Grant. "Grant, I need you to take some time today and pull Nick aside. Make sure we are offering him the support he needs. If he needs time off or anything, please offer it to him, OK?"

"Yes, of course, I'll talk to him before lunch."

"OK, thank you, Grant." An hour later, Amy walked into the copy room and there was Nick, standing over the printer.

"Hey, how you doing?" Nick kept his head down.

"I'm fine, Miss Sommers." She put her right hand on his shoulder. "Nick, would you like to talk about Colonel Armstrong?" He turned to Amy, and his eyes started to moisten. He nodded his head slightly as a tear ran down his right cheek. Amy was overcome, and she opened her arms to him. They hugged one another tightly then she took him by the hand and led him into her office, and the two of them sat down on her couch. Nick reached out for a tissue, wiped his eyes then apologized to her. "Why on earth are you apologizing? Colonel Armstrong was a good man that will be dearly missed. It's OK for you to mourn his passing." Amy reached out and put her right hand on his shoulder.

"Yes ma'am, I know. I suppose that you have more pressing business than to have to deal with me. I'm sorry."

"Oh, Nick, why would you say that? Listen I have been involved in retirement communities and assisted living facilities for many years now, and when you work in places like this, well, you develop bonds with people that are in the twilight of their lives. Our members move here so that they can live in a level of security that their homes no longer provide. They have round-the-clock medical attention, as well as a caring and loving staff. And when they do pass on, they are surrounded by their friends and a surrogate family of caregivers. Nick, Colonel Armstrong did not want to die alone, and that was one of his most important reasons for moving to Woodmont. I read that this morning, when I was going through his papers. Nick, Colonel Armstrong was surrounded by his close friends and his surrogate family, wasn't he?"

Nick wiped his eyes with his shoulder, and Amy handed him the box of tissues. "Yes, ma'am."

"He was also almost 91 and had lived a glorious life and had some amazing experiences. He served his country with distinction. You were very fortunate to get to know the Colonel, to be able to develop a bond with him, and to have him share some of his adventures with you. It was his time to go, Nick. His time was at hand, and we were there for him when he needed us the most. He thought a lot of you and I know you thought the world of him, and who better than you to be there when his time was at hand. I know you are going to miss him, but you need to take solace in the fact that you were there for him when he needed you the most. Can you do that for me?" Nick reached for another tissue and wiped his eyes, nodded his head, then stood up. "Yes, Miss Sommers, I'll try." Amy stood up and put her hand on his right shoulder again.

"And Nick?"

He looked her in the eyes. Amy reached up with her right hand, placed it on Nick's cheek, and wiped away a tear with her thumb. "One of the Colonel's last wishes was that you would call me Amy." He managed a thin smile. "Liar." Amy reached out for him, and they hugged again. Nick whispered, "Thank you, Amy." She held his hand and asked him if he needed to take a day or two off. "No, thank you. I'll be OK, I'll be OK."

"If you change your mind, please let me know." Nick excused himself, retrieved his menus from the printer, and headed back to the kitchen.

Two days later, Woodmont held a memorial for Colonel Armstrong. Cassidy hired a bugler to play taps at the flag pole, and Nick prepared some of the Colonel's favorite foods for the reception in the Chicago room. The Colonel's family had come in and decorated the Chicago with photos that spanned his Air Force career. Most of the photos were taken in towns that Nick had only dreamed of visiting: Anchorage, Rio de Janiero, Paris, London, New Delhi, Honolulu, Tokyo, Prague, Buenos Aires, and even one from Moscow. Most of the residents were able to walk through and meet his family, and Nick met the Colonel's two sons: Jonathan was retired from the Air Force, and Joseph, who was about to retire from the State Department. Their lives and jobs kept them busy, too busy, they confided. Towards the end of the memorial, Jonathan pulled Nick towards Joseph.

"Nick, our father was obviously close to you. We didn't see him nearly enough, but we did talk on the phone quite a lot, and he mentioned you on many occasions. He asked me to make sure that you got this." Jonathan handed Nick a bundle of old books. Nick accepted them, then looked at the one at the top. Jonathan spoke up, "This is his original P-51 training manual, and it's full of his notes. The other is his diary he wrote while he was stationed at Duxford with the 78th."

"No, no, I can't have these. I'm not a pilot, Jonathan. Surely these would be more appropriate for someone that was in the Air Force."

"Nick, our father took many photographs and collected many souvenirs. He loved cameras and honestly, he was, well, somewhat of a pack rat." Joseph laughed heartily. "We have a lot of mementos and he wrote a lot of diaries, and this was his request to us, which we both agreed to. Please enjoy them and who knows, maybe one day you can write a book about him." Nick hesitated, then thanked Joseph and Jonathan.

"I'll take good care of these and will enjoy reading them. Your father was a very good man, and I was very fortunate to have a relationship with him. I'm a better person for knowing him." Nick shook the brothers' hands, then walked out to the parking lot, got in his car and sat in the driver's seat. He carefully opened up the diary and slowly turned the yellowed pages. It looked like the pages had been rubbed with wax for protection. The pages were dated from March of 1944 onward. As he carefully turned the pages, a black and white photo fell out. He turned on the overhead light. It was a photo of a young William and Natalie Armstrong dancing. He was in his Air Force uniform, and she was wearing an evening gown. They were dancing in front of a band. They both had their eyes closed, and Natalie had her mouth slightly open. Was she singing to him? He sighed, then carefully put the photo back in the diary, placed both books on the passenger seat, locked his car, and walked back to the kitchen.

28

Nick opened his eyes, then sat up in bed. He smelled coffee, so he slowly dragged himself out of bed and walked into the kitchen. Theo was making breakfast. "Hey, Pop! Good morning. How about some whole-wheat waffles?"

"Sure thing, kid. Thanks for making the coffee."

"You, uh, gonna go to work today?"

"I don't know. You gonna go to school today?"

"I guess so." Nick took a sip of coffee and walked to the window, then looked outside.

"How cold is it today?" Theo poured some batter into the waffle iron and closed the lid, then turned and looked at his father. He was standing in front of his wedding photo. Theo walked over and stood next to him then put his arm across his shoulder. "I thought you weren't going to do this today, Pop." Nick wiped his eyes.

"Sorry kid, I'm trying, but it's not that easy. It's just not easy."

"I know, Dad, I know, we're trying though." Theo wiped his eyes with his fingers.

"Hey, why don't we both play hooky today and go hiking up Looking Glass? I don't have any tests today, and coach won't mind if I miss one practice." Theo wiped his eyes on his shoulders and walked back into the kitchen. "You can tell me about the wedding once we get to the top of Looking Glass, OK?" Nick sipped his coffee and thought about how many cooks he had today and if there were any special events going on. He took another sip of coffee, turned to Theo, and said, "Sure thing kid. You got a deal."

Twenty minutes later, he called Amy.

"Good morning, Nick. Everything OK?" He cleared his throat.

"Well, honestly Miss Sommers, I'm, uh, I'm calling off today. I've already talked to Tony and Kevin and they agreed, so I'm gonna take the day off, OK?"

"Nick, are you OK? Is there anything I can do?"

"It's, uh, it's my wedding anniversary today, and I'm going to take Theo hiking. I hope you understand."

"Yes, of course, will I see you tomorrow?"

"Yes ma'am and thank you Miss Sommers."

Amy hung up the phone and looked at the email from Harriett that she was about to forward to Nick. "Please send me a dining sales report for Q4, specifically I need alcohol, wine and food broken out. We have a tax issue with the state that needs to be resolved ASAP." She took a deep breath, looked at her own calendar then walked to Jessica's office. "Jess, I need to cancel the eleven a.m. meeting with you and Grant, something's come up. I have to do a project for Harriett."

Jessica nodded and without looking up from her computer replied "OK boss."

The next day, Nick walked in at ten, right after Tony Torres showed up. "How was yesterday, Mr. Torres?"

"All good, Skipper. No worries, and how was your day?"

"Fine. Took Theo hiking up Looking Glass. Damn, was it cold at the top. Cold and windy, but it was good. No phones, no nothing, just the two of us at the top. Everyone here, today?"

"Yes, sir. Oh, and if you see an email from Harriett about a sales report, just ignore it. The boss did it for you."

"What report?"

"Harriett needed a sales report from last quarter detailing wine, liquor and food, something to do with taxes. Maybe we overpaid, not sure, but like I said, Amy did it for you, so just delete it. That gal really likes you, Nick. You know that, right?" Nick nodded his head.

"Yeah, I know that, Tony."

Eight hours later, Nick was getting ready to leave, but he kept thinking about Amy. She deserves something special. Xavier and Juan were cleaning up and most of the kitchen was already tidy. He could confine himself to a small corner, and do what? He leaned against the table, closed his eyes for a second, and thought about Amy. Something chocolate, perhaps, but that's too easy. What girl doesn't like chocolate? What does Amy Sommers enjoy? Doughnuts, of course! Nick opened his eyes and walked into his office, pulled his French Laundry cookbook off the shelf, and turned to the Coffee & Doughnuts recipe. He took off his Chef coat and hung it on the wall hook, pulled a clipboard off of the wall, jotted down the recipe's basics, grabbed a pastry spatula and some measuring spoons from his tool box then walked back into the kitchen nearly bumping into Xavier, who stopped and watched him walk past. Xavier shook his head and put his hands on his hips.

"And what *in the hell* are you about to mess up my clean kitchen for, Chef?"

"Sorry, X. I owe somebody something special. You guys finish up and go, please." Xavier stood his ground. "You're about to bake something, Chef. You have measuring spoons. I really think you need to call it a night and head off to that fancy bar you spend so much time at. They're gonna be wondering where you are. I heard there was a synchronized swimming trivia contest there tonight, anyway, aren't you entered in that?"

"Thanks, X" said Nick as he walked past and headed to the cooler. Nick grabbed the vanilla beans, a flat of eggs, a pound of butter and a gallon of milk, then exited the cooler. Xavier was still in the same spot and as Nick walked past, Xavier grinned and slowly said, "You're making something for Miss Sommers, aren't you?"

"Perhaps." Xavier followed Nick to the stainless steel table. "Listen, X, if you're going to hang out with me, will you grab that sifter, please, thank you." Xavier slowly reached for the sifter and pulled one piece of parchment paper out of the box, placed it on the table, and set the sifter on top of the paper – all while never taking his eyes off of Nick.

"What're you making for her, Chef?" Nick scooped out two and a half cups of flour and dumped them in the sifter, then measured out a half cup of milk into a coffee cup, walked to the front line and placed it in the microwave, then walked back to where Xavier was still standing, and pulled the yeast off of the shelf. He turned to Xavier, smiled then looked him in the eyes.

"Doughnuts."

Xavier slowly nodded his head as his mouth curled into a sly grin. "Miss Sommers likes doughnuts, Chef."

"Yes, she does, Xavier. May I do anything else for you?"

"Miss Sommers is certainly, uh."

"Yes, Xavier?"

"Nothing, Chef, you make your doughnuts." Xavier walked away, returned with the cup of warm milk, set it down, and then told Nick he would be done in about 15 minutes. Nick placed the milk into stand mixer's bowl, stuck his finger in it, and decided it was too hot. He poured in a couple of tablespoons of cold milk and three tablespoons of sugar, whisked everything together, stuck his finger back in the milk, and guessed it was about 95 degrees. He whisked in a tablespoon of yeast, then pulled down his can of malted milk powder, measured out a quarter-cup, and whisked that in. He then pulled four fat vanilla beans from the bag and placed them on the cutting board, split them in half, scooped out the fleshy interior, then scraped that into the bowl with the yeast, and whisked again. He placed the pound of butter on his cutting board and cut off about a quarter of it, placed that in the coffee cup, covered it with plastic wrap, and brought it to the microwave. One minute should do, he thought, as he closed the door.

He then added a quarter-teaspoon of salt to the flour, and sifted the flour over the parchment paper. Next, he separated four eggs and set them aside. Keller's recipe did not call for vanilla beans or malted milk and used only three yolks, but Nick had privately thought to himself that should Amy Sommers ever eat at the French Laundry and order the doughnuts, perhaps she would think that the doughnuts that Nicholas St. Germaine made for her once were somehow just a little bit better. He looked at the yeast mixture in the bowl and found a satisfying frothy top on it. Xavier appeared with the coffee cup of melted butter, and set it down. "Thanks, X." Nick put the yolks into the yeast mixture, placed the bowl onto the mixer, inserted the dough hook, and turned it on its lowest speed. He lifted the parchment paper, and allowed the flour to slowly slide into the bowl. He then poured the melted butter into the dough, turned the speed up one notch, and started cleaning up his mess. When Nick was finished cleaning, he looked at the dough. Since he added a little extra liquid in the form of another egg and possibly some extra butter, he would need a little extra flour. The dough was, as expected, a little on the thin side. Nick scooped up some more flour and sifted it onto his parchment, and carefully added in about another quarter-cup. The dough slowly transformed from a wet and shaggy appearance to smooth, elastic and glistening with fat. Nick stood over the mixer and watched the dough. He picked up a pinch of flour and dropped it in. He was waiting for the dough to form a smooth ball and pull away from the sides of the mixer. It was almost there. The dough was still sticking a bit at the bottom of the mixer, so he added another pinch of flour and waited. Another small pinch of flour, and the dough formed a cohesive ball that rotated around the interior of the bowl. He let the dough orbit around the dough hook for another 60 seconds or so, then turned off the mixer, dusted his hands with a bit of flour, and pulled the dough out of the mixing bowl and placed it in the clean stainless steel bowl.

He wrapped and labeled the dough, placing it on the prep table while he finished cleaning. As he was wiping down his table, Nick thought about a glaze. He placed a pound of confectioner's sugar into a pot, added a quarter cup of coffee, a stick of cinnamon, the leftover vanilla bean pods, and a pinch of salt, and brought it to a boil before putting the mixer away. He brought the remaining whole butter to the bubbling pot of glaze, whisked the glaze a bit, and then grabbed a handful of the whole butter and whisked it in until it had dissolved. He turned off the heat and lifted the glaze to his nose, closed his eyes and took in the aromas of coffee and vanilla, and thought about the smile that would come over Amy Sommer's face as she was met with the most amazing doughnut she would ever have in her life. Nick set the glaze down and ran to his office, grabbed a six-ounce bar of semi-sweet El Rey chocolate from his bookcase, broke it into small pieces, and whisked that into the glaze until it had melted. Using a spoon, he took a small taste of the hot liquid just to make sure it was as amazing as it smelled. He was not disappointed. He covered the glaze, wrapped and labeled it, and placed it on his desk. He set the doughnut dough in the walk-in cooler, locked the coolers, turned off the lights and headed home.

The next morning, he brought his antique doughnut cutter with him. First, he turned on the proof box and set it for 90 degrees, then pulled his handmade rolling pin out of his tool box. He carried the rolling pin, cutter and glaze from the office, and brought them to the prep table. He washed his hands, then brought the dough out of the cooler and un-wrapped it. He dusted the prep table with about a quarter-cup of flour and placed the dough in the center of the flour. Nick then placed a small mound of flour in the corner of the table, and put his hands on the dough. He loved working with egg yolk-rich dough such as this one. The texture was so feminine, so sensual. The dough gave off a very satisfying aroma of butter, vanilla, yeast and sugar. It had leavened overnight and had gone from being fairly dense and putty-like to something almost alive with possibilities. The yeast had worked its magic. Nick heard the click of heels and looked up to see Amy Sommers approaching, and couldn't help but smile. She returned his smile and said, "Good morning." She was wearing a tight, dark blue business suit with a knee-length skirt and a silver linen top, her favorite diamond pendant sparkled between her breasts. Nick's eyes were drawn to the diamond, and this time he let his eyes settle on the rotating beacon for a second or two. Nick had his hands on the dough, and he ever so gently caressed the dough as she approached. "Don't you look lovely this morning, Miss Sommers."

"Thank you, Nick. What're you making?" She stood next to him, and was close enough that their shoulders touched.

"A surprise for my boss." Amy reached across the table and picked up his antique doughnut cutter and excitedly asked.

"Is this what I think it is?"

"Yes, ma'am." Amy broke into a wide grin. She reached out to touch the dough, and Nick asked if she had washed her hands. Amy gave an embarrassed glance to Nick, set the doughnut cutter on the table and walked to the hand sink, while Nick went to get her an apron. When she had dried her hands, he stood behind her and placed the loop of the apron over her head, then put his hands across her waist to tie the apron in the front. She had used a tropical-scented shampoo that morning and her hair gave off a delicious aroma of pineapple, coconut and mango. Nick tried not to touch her, but Amy placed her right hand on his as he was tying the apron knot, then looked over her right shoulder and smiled. Amy reached out for the dough, but Nick slowed her down. "OK, hold on now. We don't have to knead this dough anymore, because we don't want to stretch those proteins out again. You want your doughnuts tender and fluffy, right?"

"Right."

"So all we need is the rolling pin. So take the rolling pin and rub it with a little flour. Just grab a slight handful of flour, and rub the pin with it."

"Where are the handles on this thing?"

"It's a French-style pin, a baton. I had this one made for me by a guy in Asheville."

"Like this?" asked Amy, as she rubbed the flour-coated pin through her hands. "Perfect, Amy. Now, gently roll this dough out until it's about a third-of-an-inch thick." She gripped the pin and pushed down on the dough, making a crease in the center of it and squeezing out a puff of carbon dioxide. Nick asked her to slow down, then stood behind her, reached his arms around her and placed his palms on the end of the rolling pin. "Keep your fingers up, let the pin roll across your palms. Like this Amy," Nick gently rolled the pin across the dough as Amy placed her palms on the pin next to his. Nick whispered, "A delicate dough like this has to be handled gently. If we squeeze too hard, we'll compress the dough, and our doughnuts may not rise properly. If we create uneven dough, then we get uneven doughnuts, and I want them all the same thickness, so they cook at the same time." Amy moved her hands from the rolling pin to the top of Nick's hands, intertwined her fingers in his and ever so slightly backed into Nick, so that her body met his.

"Is this better?" she whispered.

"Oh, that's much better."

Nick put his chin over Amy's right shoulder as he let the rolling pin languidly drift across the top of the dough three more times, until he remembered that Florence was also in the kitchen cooking breakfast. He sighed, then moved to Amy's right side. "Now, pick up the cutter and dip it in that little mound of flour, then tap it on the table to shake off the excess flour." Amy looked at Nick and smiled, and then did as she was asked. Nick placed his hand on top of Amy's as she moved the cutter to the dough. "Now, gently press the cutter down, straight up and down. Don't twist it and don't cover up that little air hole with your thumb. OK, now after the first cut, go back to the flour, tap out the excess and do it again, but try to stay as close as possible to your first cut so that you don't waste any dough." Amy marveled at the sight of the luxurious vanilla bean-flecked dough turning into a familiar shape. The dough was close to room temperature, and the aromas of vanilla, yeast and butter mingled with

Amy's tropical scents. Nick briefly closed his eyes and inhaled, opened his eyes and saw Florence watching them from the corner, smiling. Florence winked, and he returned her wink, lifting his chin slightly as if to say, "Carry on, please, and stop staring." Nick walked to the equipment rack and retrieved a sheet pan, sprayed it with some pan release, and set it down next to Amy. He gently lifted the doughnuts off of the table, placed the holes on one side of the pan and the doughnuts on the other, and looked up at the clock, 8:40 a.m., just enough time for the doughnuts to rise for about fifteen minutes before frying them for the morning meeting. When they finished cutting out the doughnuts, Amy counted them.

"We have 18 doughnuts, Nick. That's enough for me to have eight, and everyone else gets one." Nick smiled, and agreed with her.

"I'll fry these up, and I'll bring plenty of napkins with me. Here, let me get that apron off of you."

She turned to face him, but he looked down at the knot. Amy reached out and held him by the waist. His hands were a bit shaky as he untied the apron. Amy noticed, and asked him if he were OK. He lifted his eyes to hers, and smiled. "I'm fine, Amy. Perhaps I had too much coffee this morning." She gently moved her hands up his waist and, ever so slightly, squeezed.

"Perhaps," she winked. He lifted the apron over her head.

"I'll see you in a few minutes."

Amy walked over to the hand sink, washed her hands and headed for the side door. Just before exiting the kitchen, she looked over her shoulder and caught Nick watching her. She smiled, and kept going. As he cleaned up his mess, Florence walked up next to him. "Hey, stud, if you need to go smoke a cigarette, I can finish cleaning up for you." Nick looked at her and shook his head; Florence offered a hearty laugh then walked away. He placed the doughnuts in the proof box, put the mixer away, and brought the glaze to the front line. He then walked to the bathroom and washed his face with cold water, dried himself off, and took a long look at himself in the mirror. He wiped his face again and returned to his office, sat down, leaned back and closed his eyes. "Much better," he said to himself. He sat and day dreamed, until Jackson walked past his office and fussed, "Wake up, Chef!" He opened his eyes and offered Jackson a thumbs-up, then looked at the clock. 8:52, time to make the doughnuts.

One minute after nine, Nick walked into the Armory carrying a platter of the finest doughnuts he had ever made. Amy had already started the meeting, but as he walked in with the doughnuts, all eyes turned to him.

"I brought a present for Amy, and perhaps she'll share them with us." He set the platter down in front of Amy, and placed a stack of beverage napkins next to them. Amy picked up a doughnut and a napkin then passed the platter to Cassidy, who did the same. Nick took his seat as Amy bit into her doughnut. She closed her eyes and breathlessly announced, "Oh my, Nick, this is just amazing." Amy opened her eyes and looked at Nick, "Delicious," she sighed. As the doughnuts made their way around the room, everyone complimented Nick.

"Well, Miss Sommers helped, so you can thank her as well." Jessica looked at Amy and asked, "Did you really help?"

"Perhaps," she smiled mischievously. Amy turned her gaze to Nick, who caught her eye and winked. Jessica looked at Nick, then at Amy, then back at Nick. The smiles on Nick and Amy's faces said it all. They were in love, and they both knew it. Jessica's phone went off with a text message. She picked it up and saw it was from Cassidy. Jessica looked across the room and Cassidy nodded slightly at her, so she opened it.

"mission accomplished ;)" Jessica set her phone down, and smiled.

Four hours later, Nick was in his office answering several emails, when Chrissy stuck her head in the office. "Hey, Chef, I could use a hand here, please."

"Ten-four, Chrissy. Give me two more minutes in here and I'm all yours, OK?"

"That works. I need some tenderloin trimmed and cut, OK?" Nick's office phone rang, and he glanced at the caller. Damn. It was the Hudson neighborhood kitchen, and they probably were calling with a special order. He let it ring hoping Chrissy or one of the wait-staff would pick it up. When the phone stopped ringing, Nick glanced up from the computer and saw Chrissy on the phone. She quickly turned and looked at him, her eyes suddenly wide open, then ran towards his office. Nick stood up and moved towards the door.

"Chef, there's an emergency in Hudson. Candace is screaming and I hear people crying." Nick leapt from his office and bolted towards the stairway, crashed through the stairwell door and raced down the stairs two at a time. As he got to the bottom of the stairs, he heard his Blackberry ring. The caller ID indicated it was from the Hudson neighborhood. Nick answered it, but all he heard was screaming. He put it back in his pocket, yanked his apron off, exploded through the doors that led to Overbrook and sprinted down the hallway. He ran past two CNA's that were going in the opposite direction. One was crying, while the other was apparently talking to a 911 operator. He heard her say "knife", but she was choking on her words. He passed several employees that were yelling "what's happening?"

Nick picked up the pace. Damn, this place was so spread out. He was breathing hard, and he hoped he didn't run someone over as he took the next corner. He caught and passed Grant, Stanley and Penny, who was carrying her trauma kit. Penny yelled something to Nick, but he didn't understand what she said. He turned the corner and saw one of the wheelchair-bound residents, a red-haired woman that Nick had not met. She was crying and kept saying, "He has a knife. He has a knife." Nick flew through the next corner into Hudson and almost knocked over Candace, who grabbed him by the shoulders and screamed:

"Do not do anything stupid, Nick! The police are on the way!" Her hands were trembling and her tears had streaked her mascara. She wiped her face, sending black smudges across her cheeks. Nick moved her aside, then rounded the corner to the entrance to the Hudson dining room, and stopped. Todd Stafford was in the far corner, his left arm wrapped tight across Amy Sommers waist. He held a thick hunting knife in his right hand, and was pressing it against Amy's throat. Cries and screams came from several of the rooms, a CNA knelt on the floor pleading with Todd to let Amy go, Saffron stood in the corner to Nick's left talking to the 911 operator, Amy Sommers was quietly sobbing, and Todd was yelling at everyone to *"shut the fuck up so I can fucking think!"*

Todd caught Nick's eyes then pointed the knife at him. *"Who's the fucking man, now, huh, you little shit? I'm gonna cut your boss up as soon as the TV cameras get here, so what the fuck do you think about that, huh, you little fucking turd? Then everyone will know what a shit hole this place is."* Nick felt someone grab his hand. It was Chet Bannon.

"Nick, don't let him hurt Amy. You gotta do something fast! Please don't let him hurt her." Nick pulled away from Chet and looked back at Todd. His eyes were wide open and he was waving the knife then moving it back to Amy's throat. He was probably high, which made him unpredictable, but he had the look of a bully and he seemed to be enjoying himself. Todd had everyone scared and crying. If Nick waited for the cops to arrive, Todd might drag Amy into a room and close the door, the thought made Nick's skin crawl. He took a good look at the immediate area around Todd, to make sure there were no overturned chairs or any sort of debris blocking his path. The adrenaline surged through Nick's body, his pulse raced and the bile rose up into his throat. His heart was pounding so hard, it felt like it would crack right through his ribs. Nick took a deep breath then wiped his palms on his pants. Todd didn't want to hurt Amy. He wanted to kill Nick, so why not give him what he wanted? Nick began walking towards Todd, as Amy pleaded with Nick to back up. She had an awful look of panic in her eyes, and was begging Nick to leave Todd alone. Nick heard shouting behind him as Todd pressed the knife flat against Amy's throat and screamed at Nick, *"Did you hear your stupid fucking boss, asshole? She said back the fuck up, because she don't want to get cut!"* Nick was close enough now to smell alcohol on Todd's breath, which gave him some confidence. Maybe I won't get cut after all, he thought. He kept moving forward, eyes focused on Todd, until he was almost within an arm's length. Nick turned slightly and presented his right shoulder to Todd, moved his feet about a shoulder's length apart, took another half step towards him, and opened his hands. Saffron was crying, begging Nick to leave Todd alone. Amy pleaded.

"Nick, please don't, please, Nick, please."

"She said BACK THE FUCK UP!" screamed Todd, and as he did so, he took the knife off of Amy's throat and thrust it into Nick's face – which was exactly what Nick wanted. He quickly extended his right arm out and up, catching Todd on the right wrist, twisted his right hand and gripped Todd's wrist hard then extended his left hand and aimed for Todd's right elbow, finding it with a satisfying crack. He gritted his teeth then pushed as hard as he could on the elbow, sending Todd spinning in a clockwise motion. The centrifugal force threw Amy to the ground, but Todd kept going. After Nick took a step inside Todd's faltering feet, he knew the next stop for Touchdown Todd Stafford was the wall. He collided with the wall with such force that his forehead put a divot in the gypsum, the knife flew out of his hand, and the nearby artwork crashed to the ground. Todd let out a moan of agony. Nick let his left arm drop a bit, then threw Todd into the wall again, and then a third time. Todd was now gasping for air, and blood flowed from his nose and forehead. Nick slammed him a fourth time then applied pressure on the elbow until it snapped like a chilled July carrot. Todd let out

a scream of blinding agony as his radius separated from the humerus and the jagged edge of the bone popped through his skin at the inside of his elbow, showering the wall with blood. Nick released his grip and Todd fell to his knees, his head drooped against the wall. He was gasping for air, his right arm and shoulder were on fire, and he was choking on his own blood. Todd looked up through his bloodied eyes, catching a blurred glimpse of Nick's right fist before it crashed into his facial bone, just to the right of his nose. What little energy left in Todd evaporated, and he collapsed at Nick's feet.

When Nick had first made contact with Todd, Candace had quickly crawled across the floor to get Amy out of the way. By the time she had pulled Amy to safety, Todd was already on the floor in a bloody, gasping heap. Candace picked up Amy's glasses, and held them out for her. Saffron had suddenly stopped talking; the other CNA on the floor was still crying, but not as much. Nick was struggling to catch his breath. He looked down at Todd and prayed he didn't kill him, and was relieved to see his chest still moving in and out. Nick's adrenaline rush give way to a flood of nausea. He breathed deeply, steadied himself against the wall, looked around, and asked Saffron if an ambulance was on the way. Saffron nodded her head. Penny came running across the room with her trauma kit, and knelt down next to Todd.

"*Jesus Christ, Nick.* Did you have to hit him so hard? *A little help here, please*", she yelled, as the blood from Todd's arm began to pool on the floor. Some of the residents came out of their rooms, now that the screaming had stopped. At least a dozen staff showed up, including Franklin, Stanley, Cassidy, Tony and Grant; they tried to make sense of what had just happened. Nick took a few steps towards Amy and Candace, who were both still on the floor. Amy wiped her eyes and put her glasses back on, as Nick extended his right hand to her and wheezed.

"Are you OK, Amy? Are you OK?"

"Help please!" yelled Penny. *"I need some oxygen now, I need to stop this bleeding."* Grant joined Penny then asked Saffron for oxygen. Candace helped Amy off the floor and Nick managed a smile as Amy came within hugging distance, but he was met with a hard, stinging slap across his face.

"You stupid impetuous IDIOT! Look what you've done!" screamed Amy. She turned away from Nick then clutched her hair as she sobbed, *"Oh my God, Nick, what have you done?"* She turned to Candace and asked for a first aid kit, then asked whether an ambulance was on the way. Amy turned her back to Nick, softly crying and rubbing her eyes with her shaking hands. Candace put her arm across her shoulder and was trying to get a look at Amy's neck, but Amy jerked away. She turned and looked at Nick, who was still standing in the same spot, rubbing his sore cheek with a puzzled look on his face. "Oh Nick," she sobbed and ran towards him. Nick wasn't sure if he should hold his arms open or cower in fear of another blow, but she leapt into his arms. Amy wrapped her arms around him, buried her face in his left shoulder and bawled loudly. Through her tears, she choked out, *"I love you."*

"I love you too, Amy."

They held on to one another until Candace interrupted.

"Nick, you're bleeding." Amy released her grip, and saw blood staining the right shoulder of his Chef's coat. *"Oh no! Nick, sit down and let me take a look."* Amy wiped her eyes on her shoulders and made some room for Candace and her first aid kit, then helped Nick out of his Chef's coat. Nick sat down on the nearest chair, and that's when they heard the sirens. Grant looked up at Franklin and Tony and asked them to meet the officers at the front door, and ask them to holster their guns before they came in. Franklin and Tony nodded in agreement then ran to the front, Saffron in tow.

When Todd had hit the wall, his knife had flown out of his hand, giving Nick a five-inch long slice across the top of his shoulder. Candace cleaned his wound, asking Amy to apply pressure to slow the bleeding. "Nick, you'll need to get this stitched up, but I think you're going to be fine."

"I think I'm going to throw up" panted Nick. "Can someone please bring me a trash can." Amy threw her arms around Nick, and the crying started all over. She bawled loudly and squeezed him tight. For a second, Nick was afraid they would fall out of the chair. Her salty tears fell onto his wound and he flinched. He was suddenly flush, his skin clammy, his nausea worsening. Candace pulled Amy off Nick, and asked if she could get a bandage on his shoulder. Amy held his face in her hands then kissed him on the cheek.

"I love you."

"I love you too Amy, but please bring me a garbage can … *Hurry!*" She jumped up and grabbed the tall garbage can from the kitchen and placed it in front of Nick, who gripped the can and promptly emptied the contents of his stomach into it. Candace turned her head as Amy ran into the kitchen, wet a towel with cold water then placed it on the back of Nick's neck. His heaving momentarily increased his blood pressure and his shoulder was now bleeding profusely. He plopped back down in the chair, physically spent. Amy carefully wiped his face and lips, as Candace got back to work on his shoulder. One of the CNAs offered Nick some oxygen, and he gladly accepted. Franklin and Tony came back into the room with two officers, both of whom had their guns drawn. Saffron was following them, trying to describe what had happened. The residents all panicked when they saw the pistols, but when Saffron pointed to Todd Stafford's mangled body and identified him as the culprit, they put away their guns, called their dispatcher with a quick update, and asked about the ambulance's proximity.

"No SWAT team, correct, Sergeant?" asked Grant as the officer kneeled down next to Todd. "Yes sir, no SWAT." The first officer sat down next to Nick and asked, "Chef, you think you can you tell me what happened?"

Nick looked at him through bleary eyes, and slowly moved his head left to right. Saffron was standing behind the cop and fussed.

"I done told you what happened, why don't you believe me?"

Grant heard more sirens outside, and the officer suggested it was probably the ambulance. Grant headed back to the front door and a couple minutes later, returned with three more officers and four EMTs. The first two EMTs went immediately to Todd. The others went to Nick and Amy. Todd was soon loaded up and on his way to the ER, and Nick was placed on the second stretcher. Amy was bruised and shaken up, but was otherwise fine. The EMTs began wheeling Nick towards the front door, with Amy trotting alongside, holding his hand and wiping her eyes. From the stretcher, it looked as if half the staff of Woodmont lined the hallway, many of them reaching out and touching Nick's left hand as he rolled past. Grant helped the EMTs load Nick into the ambulance, Amy climbed in, pointed her right forefinger at Grant and shouted.

"Do not let *anyone* talk to a reporter, do not let *any* TV crews in here, do not let *anyone* leave without counseling and shut down our internet servers *now!* I want you to call Jenkins *right now* and get him here for damage control. He will do all the talking to the press, do you understand me, Grant?"

"Yes, ma'am!" Grant slammed the door then pounded twice on the back of the ambulance. The EMTs had applied a pressure bandage, but the bleeding had not stopped and Nick felt very tired. Amy held his hand and smiled at him, and told him he would be OK. Nick looked up at her, pulled the oxygen mask off his face.

"You know this means one of us can't work here anymore?" Amy put the mask back on his face and looked into his eyes, stroked his face with her right hand, and kept telling him he would be OK. "Call my son, please … my phone … I think it's in my pocket."

"Of course." Amy squeezed his hand. "I love you, Nicholas St. Germaine."

"I love you too, Miss Sommers," he winked, squeezed her hand tight then passed out.

Amy was correct in telling Grant to keep the TV crews out, because once they heard "hostage" on the police scanner, they all raced to Woodmont. However, Dawn didn't let them through the gate, so they just sat out on the access road and filed speculative reports, pieced together from the police radio chatter. Paul Jenkins, the head of communications for Creek Side and a former TV anchor, arrived to provide a calm voice for Woodmont just in time for the six p.m. news. Nick spent a few hours in the ER getting stitched up. Theo showed up in tears, worried sick that he was going to lose his other parent, but by the time he arrived, Nick had stabilized and was feeling better. Theo carefully hugged his father.

"You didn't bring me a toothbrush, did you?"

Theo was standing on the right side of the bed and Amy Sommers was on the left side. Theo noticed Amy and his Dad were holding hands, and Amy kept stroking his hand with her thumb. Theo sat down, "Tell me what happened, and I'll go find one for you."

29

Amy stuck her head in Jessica's office. "Hey Jess, I'm going to take a walk through Overbrook, OK? I'll be back in thirty minutes or so." She made her way through the main lobby, then down to Overbrook, taking the time to wish everyone a happy Thursday, meeting family members, and saying hello to the staff. Candace stopped her in the hallway.

"Miss Sommers, how's my baby doing?"

"He's going to be fine, Candace. I'll tell Nick you asked about him and that you've dyed your hair black again." When Amy arrived at the Hudson neighborhood, she heard Saffron's voice so she stayed just out of sight. Chet Bannon was still at the table; he must have slept in today. He started to back away from the table, but Saffron stopped him. She was training Heather, a new CNA. Amy stayed just out of sight. "Hold on, Mr. Bannon, you can't leave the table looking like that. Saffron carefully wiped his chin then brushed the crumbs off of his shirt. "We can sweep the floor later, besides the floor's supposed to hold crumbs, not your shirt. Now you're looking good, Mister B!"

"Thank you, Saffron. I have a card game I want to get to; I heard the new gal may be there." Amy turned away and finished her walk.

An hour later, Amy was joined by Cassidy, Grant, Jessica and Daniel. "Thank you all for your time. I want to discuss the interview process for our new executive Chef. Jessica has lined up several candidates; we need to coordinate these interviews, because I would like all of us to be involved. Kevin Randall has personally told me that he would like the job, and Xavier James is ready to move up to sous Chef. However, we do need to follow the company's process and interview our people, as well as the other candidates. I would like to see Kevin take the position, as well as Xavier. I know it's close to lunchtime, so I promise I won't keep you long. Rivers has agreed to help, and he will come down as well. Give me a second, and I will get him on the speakerphone."

There was a general nodding of heads, and everyone turned to their laptops and opened up their calendars. When Rivers answered, he repeated Amy's words. "I know it sounds contrived, but we have to post the Executive Chef's position, even though we all know that Kevin Randall will get the job and we will move Mr. James up. We have to go through the process, company policy folks. Jessica is there a day that we can all agree on, so that I can join you all. Would Monday or Tuesday of next week work better?" The team discussed the merits of Tuesday versus Monday, when Amy's Blackberry went off. She picked it up and saw it was a text from Nick, which she quickly opened. "Join me for lunch?" She immediately replied.

"Yes yes yes, when?"

"How about now?" Amy spun around in her chair, and looked out her window. Nick's BMW was in the front, and he was leaning on the passenger door, smiling. She jumped out of her chair and grabbed her purse. *"Meeting adjourned! Thanks for your time, but I gotta go."* She practically tripped over Cassidy's feet as she double-timed it out of the office, past the concierge, and banged her way out of the front door. Jessica, Grant, Cass and Daniel stood up and moved to Amy's window to watch. Stern said, "I can't watch this," and excused himself.

"Hey gang, what's going on? Did Miss Sommers leave?" asked Rivers. "Hello? Hey, you guys still there?" Grant spoke up and told Rivers that Miss Sommers had a family emergency to attend to then winked at Cass and Jessica. The three of them stood at Amy's window. Nick was smiling as Amy approached. She was trotting, but as she got about ten feet away, she broke into a sprint. Nick put his arms out, and she leapt into them. He held her off the ground, and Amy lifted her feet to a 45-degree angle. As she did so, her shoes slipped off her feet. Nick eased her down as Amy reached up and put her hands around his neck. She pulled him close, and they kissed for a long time. Grant whistled in amazement. Amy took her hands off his neck then gingerly touched his right shoulder as she put her left hand over her mouth. They were both talking as Nick took her hands in his, and pulled her close until their foreheads touched. She put her hands around his back, and he put his hands around her waist. They kissed again then Nick walked her to his car, opened the passenger door, held her right hand as she got into his car, then picked up her shoes and handed them to her. He closed the door, walked around to the driver's door, turned to Amy's office window and waved at his audience, then got in his car and closed the door. Jessica offered Cassidy a tissue, and they both wiped their eyes.

"Well, at least someone's eating Chef's good cooking," pined Grant. He backed up from the window and looked at Cassidy and Jessica as they dried their eyes. "Would either of you two lovely ladies care for some Fritos and a Coke? The vending machine was just stocked this morning."

"*Hello*, is anyone there?" asked Rivers. "Grant? Jessica?"

"Sorry boss, it's lunchtime. We'll have to call you back," hollered Grant as he closed the door behind him.

After the lunch rush had died down, Tony Torres headed into his office to catch up on some paperwork. When he walked in, he found a present sitting on his desk. It was about the size of a shoebox, neatly wrapped in red Christmas paper with a sparkling green bow. Tony sat down and picked up the box. There was no card or label attached, so he unwrapped it. He threw the wrapping paper in his garbage can, then took the lid off of the box, looked inside and found a pair of black men's Speedo swim trunks. He also found a greeting card, which he opened. Inside, someone had written, "The pool opens at 7 a.m."

"Murder for Amy"

"A death at a retirement community, hey people die at these places Miss Sommers, you said so yourself."

"Right, I agree detective but all I was saying was that." Detective Christie raised his hand as if to say stop. "Look Miss Sommers if you want to play *Clue* with your little girls when you get home by all means have at it, I'm sorry but I just don't see anything other than a natural death, come on, he was 91. Now if you'll excuse me, I have a serial rapist to track down." As the detective walked past Nick he patted him on the shoulder and said "Chef, I really miss the Tavern. Ya gonna open another place any time soon?"

Nick looked at Amy then turned to Christie and replied "Thanks, I'll think about it." Detective Christie left Amy's office and Nick reached out for Amy and hugged her. "You OK sweetheart?" He asked. "I am now." Amy whispered in Nick's ear, "can you take me to lunch?" The sexual energy leapt through Nick and he shivered. "I thought you had a murder to solve, sweetheart?" Nick and Amy's lips met, they shared a delicious kiss then Nick broke into a smile as Xavier walked into Amy's office.

"Oh come on you two!"

First and foremost I need to thank my family for putting up with my 4:00 a.m. wake up calls in order to write and my beautiful wife Amy for believing in me from beginning to end, she never doubted me. Thank you to the many cooks, servers, dish washers, managers, chefs and bartenders that have been there for me over the years; there are way too many to list them all. To Tom Kleckner for his patient editing and to the many good friends and neighbors, especially our 20:20 group, that supported me unequivocally through this process. Thank you to Sunrise Assisted Living of Metairie, LA, the Woodlands at Furman and the Cascades Verdae for putting up with me. Many thanks to Anne, Val, Karen, Kevin, Mike, Angie, Caryn, Kelly, Beverly, Wayne, Doug, Dave and Kerry for their early guidance. And finally a thank you to the many English teachers and professors that inspired me over the years. Thank you all.

"Like" Doughnuts for Amy on Facebook

Follow @chefjohnmalik on Twitter

www.chefjohnmalik.com

Jump Jive an' Wail
Words and Music by Louis Prima
© 1956 (Renewed 1984) LGL MUSIC Inc.
All Rights Controlled and Administered by EMI APRIL
MUSIC INC
All Rights Reserved International Copyright Secured Used
by Permission
Reprinted by Permission of Hal Leonard Music Corporation

Malted Milk Doughnuts (for Amy)

2 & ½ cups all-purpose flour
¼ cup malted milk powder
¼ teaspoon salt
1/2 cup warm milk (95 to 100 F)
3 tablespoons sugar
1 tablespoon yeast
4 vanilla beans
2 tablespoons whole butter, melted
4 egg yolks
2 quarts frying oil

Glaze
2 Cups powdered Sugar
3 to 4 tablespoons dark coffee
4 tablespoons butter
2 ounces bittersweet chocolate
Pinch of salt

In the bowl of a stand mixer add the yeast, sugar and warm milk. Whisk together.

In a separate bowl sift the flour, salt and malted milk powder. Place the egg yolks in a small bowl. Using a sharp paring knife and a cutting board split the vanilla beans in half lengthwise then carefully scrape the fleshy interior of the beans into the egg yolks.

When the yeast mixture has a frothy top to it (about 10 to 15 minutes) add the egg yolks and vanilla bean, whisk together then add the flour mixture, place the bowl onto the stand mixer, attach the dough hook then turn to low speed and allow the ingredients to mix until they have formed a smooth glossy ball. This should take about four to five minutes. If the dough is sticky and does not form a smooth ball, it may be necessary to add a pinch more flour.

Remove the bowl from the mixer. Cover with plastic then leave the dough at room temperature for at least thirty minutes or ideally allow the dough to sit overnight in the refrigerator.

Lightly dust a clean counter with flour. Place the doughnut dough onto the counter then using a rolling pin, gently roll the dough to about a half inch thickness. Make a small mound of flour, press the doughnut cutter into the mound of flour, tap out the excess then press the cutter into the dough. Place the doughnuts onto a clean sheet pan that has been sprayed with Pam. After all doughnuts and holes are on the sheet pan cover with a clean cloth and allow to proof for about 15 to 20 minutes at room temperature. The doughnuts should be the consistency of a large marshmallow when they are ready for the oil.

Make the glaze. Place coffee, butter and a pinch of salt in a sauce pan over high heat and whisk while bringing to a boil. Whisk in the powdered sugar and continue whisking until a smooth paste has formed. Remove from heat, add chocolate and continue whisking until a smooth glaze has formed. Add vanilla bean pods and if you like cinnamon, a dash of cinnamon. Place glaze in a wide bowl and set aside.

Heat the oil to 325 degrees Fahrenheit. If the oil is much hotter the sugar in the dough will burn before the doughnuts actually cook so use a candy or high heat thermometer to monitor the temperature of the oil. *Carefully* place the doughnuts into the hot oil, only cook about three or four at a time. Too many at one time will drop the temperature of the oil. After about two minutes in the hot oil turn the doughnuts over, continue cooking for another sixty seconds until golden brown. Remove from oil and place on a baker's rack. Allow doughnuts to cool for only a minute or so before dipping in the glaze. Enjoy!

Note: Doughnut cutters come in many sizes. Sometimes I use a small biscuit or cookie cutter, other times I use a traditional round cutter so the amount of doughnuts will vary on the size of your cutter. The scraps of dough can be cut into small pieces and fried as well. Cinnamon Sugar or Powdered Sugar can be used in lieu of the chocolate topping, just place sugar into a Ziploc bag, add donuts and shake.

Roasted Zucchini with Red Pepper Sauce & Comte Cheese

2 each fresh zucchini
2 tablespoons olive oil
2 shallots, peeled
2 cloves garlic, whole
1 onion, peeled and rough chopped
2 Red Peppers, roasted, peeled and seeded
2 tablespoons Olive Oil
Juice of 1 lemon
Salt & Pepper to taste
Chopped Fresh Chives

Wash the zucchini then cut into thick bias slices. Splash with Olive oil then lightly season with salt & pepper. Grill or Roast at high temperature for about 10 minutes. Toss the onion, garlic and shallot in a small amount of olive oil. Place in a baking dish and roast in a 350 degree oven for about 20 minutes or when the edges of the onion are light brown and the vegetables are translucent. Place the peppers and other vegetables in a bar blender then puree. Add the lemon juice then taste and season. Strain if a very fine sauce is desired.

Shave the Comte cheese over the zucchini, decorate with the red pepper sauce, garnish with chives and more olive oil then season with salt & pepper.

Duck Breast

2 Duck Breast
Salt & fresh ground pepper

Trim off any excess fat. Using a very sharp knife score the fat side of the duck breast, as if you were about to play tic-tac-toe on the fat. This will allow some of the interior fat to melt away and will make the finished product crisper. Season with salt & fresh pepper. Sear the breast in a hot skillet (cast iron works best) over medium high heat, fat side first. The breast should cook about five or six minutes, if the pan smokes, turn the heat down a bit. After five minutes flip the breast over, turn heat to very low and let the breast cook for about three or four more minutes. Remove the breast from skillet, the set aside. The breast should sit for about five minutes before slicing. When ready to slice be sure and slice against the grain, long thin bias slices work best.

Cherry & Pinot Noir Sauce

2 shallots, minced
2 cloves garlic, minced
1 onion, diced
1 teaspoon duck fat
1 cup Pinot Noir
1 cup veal or duck stock
1 Lemon
1/2 teaspoon fresh Thyme, washed leaves only
12 cherries (Fresh or Dried), pitted
Salt & Pepper to taste
1 tablespoon butter

In a small stockpot over medium heat add the duck fat then shallots, garlic and onion. Saute until translucent. Add the pinot noir wine. Allow the wine to reduce by 75% then add the stock. Allow this to reduce 75%. Strain the sauce, place back into the stock pot then add the cherries and allow the sauce to simmer for about two minutes. When the sauce has the consistency of thin honey and coats the back of a spoon swirl in the butter. Season the sauce with salt & pepper then taste. Pour the sauce over the duck breast then garnish with the fresh thyme.

Whipped Sweet Potatoes

2 each Sweet Potato or Yams
Pinch of Salt
2 Tablespoons fresh butter
1 Tablespoon honey
1 vanilla Bean
Fresh Pepper

Wash the sweet potatoes carefully. Roast in a 350 degree oven for about 75 minutes or until the skin of the potatoes has shriveled and they are noticeably bubbling. Remove from oven, allow the potatoes to cool for about 5 minutes then peel. Place potato pulp in a large bowl, add salt, honey and butter then push through a food mill, a strainer or whip with a fork or whisk. Scrape half of the vanilla bean and place in the bowl, stir in, taste and enjoy.